THE
EXTINCTION
AGENDA

THE
EXTINCTION
AGENDA

MICHAEL
LAURENCE

ST. MARTIN'S PRESS
NEW YORK

First published in the United States by St. Martin's Press, an imprint of St. Martin's Publishing Group

THE EXTINCTION AGENDA. Copyright © 2019 Michael Laurence McBride. All rights reserved. Printed in Canada. For information, address St. Martin's Publishing Group, 120 Broadway, New York, NY 10271.

www.stmartins.com

Designed by Omar Chapa

The Library of Congress Cataloging-in-Publication Data is available upon request.

ISBN 978-1-250-15848-2 (hardcover)
ISBN 978-1-250-15850-5 (ebook)

Our books may be purchased in bulk for promotional, educational, or business use. Please contact your local bookseller or the Macmillan Corporate and Premium Sales Department at 1-800-221-7945, extension 5442, or by email at MacmillanSpecialMarkets@macmillan.com.

First Edition: August 2019

10 9 8 7 6 5 4 3 2 1

For Alex Slater and Pete Wolverton

Free men of every generation must combat renewed efforts of organized force and greed to destroy liberty. Every generation must wage war for freedom against new forces that seek through new devices to enslave mankind.

—Robert Marion "Fighting Bob" LaFollette Sr.,
Platform of the Conference for Progressive Political Action (1924)

ONE YEAR AGO

1

JULY 24

There are no shadows in the valley of death.

The sun blazes with such ferocity that anything resembling shade evaporates, like every last drop of water in this godforsaken desert—with the exception of the sweat that started soaking through the navy blue windbreakers of the FBI agents the moment they stepped out of the green- and-white Border Patrol Explorer, of course. It wasn't even seven in the morning yet and already it had to be over a hundred degrees. Wavering ribbons of heat rose from the brick-red sands, making the creosotes and chollas and ocotillos appear to burn with invisible flames. A diamondback's rattle buzzed from somewhere behind a snarled mass of flowering prickly pears.

Crazy to think that this desolate and essentially uninhabitable cor- ridor was one of the most hotly contested regions on the planet.

Special Agent James Mason paused in the sparse shade of a saguaro cactus, lifted his ball cap, and wiped the sweat from his brow with his forearm. His close-cropped blond hair was already soaked. He reseated his hat, tugged down the brim to shield his eyes, and scrutinized the cloudless sky over the rocky crest uphill for the first sign of what was in store for them in the canyon on the other side. Supervisory Agent Javier

Velasquez, the Border Patrol agent who'd driven them out here from Ajo Station, stood silhouetted against the rising sun. One of his best trackers was waiting for them at the site of the discovery he'd called in just over two hours ago.

By the time Mason reached the top, Velasquez was already picking his way down the eastern slope through a maze of cacti and paloverdes toward a dry wash lined with ironwoods and hackberry trees on this side and a stratified red escarpment on the other. They were roughly twenty miles north of the Arizona-Mexico border, twenty-five in every direction from anything that could pass for civilization, and deep in the Ajo Mountains.

Mason caught a glimpse of a dark hunched shape in the streambed as he glanced through the branches of an ironwood, the emerald leaves of which shimmered like a viper's scales. He raised his hand to block out the sun and again scanned the cloudless sky.

"Where are all the carrion birds?"

Special Agent Spencer Kane clapped him on the shoulder as he passed.

"You figure out in a hurry that any exertion costs you hydration, and once you start losing fluids, there's just about no way of getting them back." He was tall and had the kind of physique that made it impossible to determine his age. His Nordic blue eyes were framed by crow's-feet and his hair had faded from blond to silver, but he carried himself with the air of a man in his prime. "First lesson you need to learn out here. Don't waste your energy. Even the buzzards know that."

Mason followed Kane to the edge of the trees, where the branches still shook from Velasquez's passage. They'd only been partners for a few years, but they went way back. Kane had personally recruited Mason at a time when the latter desperately needed to find his direction in life, then served as something of a long-distance mentor through the FBI Academy in Quantico and Mason's first posting in the Twin Cities. He'd been instrumental not only in bringing Mason back home to the Denver Field Office, but in securing his assignment to this high-profile strike force, which would be a nice feather in his protégé's professional cap.

"Remember that human-trafficking ring we shut down a while back?" Mason asked.

"Bastards knew they were about to get caught, so they killed those poor girls and buried them out in the corn rows."

"We spent three months tracking them and still might never have found the farm where they were holed up if it hadn't been for all the crows in the fields."

"You think we're wasting our time here?"

"I sure as hell hope so."

They pressed through the thorny branches and hopped down from the bank onto the coarse gravel and silt. Mason hadn't noticed there'd been a gentle breeze until it was gone. The air was heavy and oppressive. A horrible stench hit him squarely in the face. He covered his mouth and nose, but the damage was already done. The smell of decomposition was already lodged in his sinuses.

Velasquez stood with his back to them, conferring with his subordinate, who glanced up at them with an expression of apprehension, if not outright suspicion. He had Hispanic dark skin and eyes and wore the standard forest green paramilitary uniform all USBP enforcers wore in the field, with a Heckler & Koch P2000 .40-caliber semiautomatic on one hip and a telescoping steel baton on the other. He acknowledged them with a nod.

The dirt crunched underfoot as they approached. Mason stopped short when he saw the reason they'd been summoned all the way out here and whistled appreciatively.

"Now that's what I call a taxidermist's wet dream," Kane said. "Now . . . just for the sake of argument, let's pretend I'm not a taxidermist. How about instead I'll be a federal agent who was unceremoniously awakened from a dream costarring the lovely Sofía Vergara and has yet to have his first cup of coffee."

"Lead Border Patrol Agent Rafael Silva," Velasquez said by way of introduction. "These men represent the FBI on the Bradley Strike Force. Special Agents Kane and . . ."

"Mason," he said, and shook Silva's dirty hand. "Special Agent James Mason."

"Wonderful," Kane said with a clap. "Now that we're all old friends, why don't you tell me, Lead Agent Silva, what in the name of God does any of this have to do with me?"

Silva glanced at his boss, who gestured for him to proceed.

"I was cutting sign down off the Destruya Drag—"

"That means he was searching for tracks or any other indication that undocumented aliens had recently passed through," explained Velasquez, interrupting.

"Right. We'd just busted up a route the smugglers had been using for a while, so we knew word would get back to the coyotes and they'd be forced to adapt on the fly. Branch off their usual path somewhere south of here. I picked up sign about three miles down the wash and followed the tracks until I caught a whiff of this stench."

Mason scrutinized the trail leading in their direction from the south. There was a riot of footprints, one set trampled on top of another. Staggering gaits. Uneven treads. At least six distinct sets of tracks. There were disturbances in the dirt, where it looked as though one of them had fallen and struggled to rise again.

"What kind of time frame are we looking at?" he asked.

"Just over twenty-four hours. Night before last. Maybe a couple hours before sunrise."

There were dark splotches all over the ground. The fluid had congealed into the dirt as it dried. Mason used a twig to excavate one patch and rolled it over. Blood. No doubt about it.

"And you're basing that deduction on what? The tracks?"

"I could read this sign in my sleep. These people weren't trying to be sneaky. They were in big trouble and they knew it."

At the heart of the pattern of droplets was an impression in the dirt shaped like a man, had he fallen diagonally forward and landed on his shoulder and face. The upper half of the imprint was smoothed into a shallow trench. Someone or something had come along and dragged the body upstream and around the bend, obliterating its own tracks in the process.

"Figure they were mules?" Kane asked. "Maybe one of the rival cartels—"

"No." Mason studied the clumps of dried blood. The smell. It was more than just death. There was something wrong with the smell. He covered his mouth and nose with his sleeve. "They were sick."

"Well, that would explain all of the birds."

Mason had to step over and around the avian carcasses, decomposing where they'd fallen, as he walked to the north. They littered the streambed for as far as he could see. Massive turkey vultures and crested caracaras and crows, which seemed tiny by comparison. Crusted blood on their beaks. Feathers disheveled and lusterless. Eyes sunken. Positively crawling with black flies.

They say the meek shall inherit the earth, but he was convinced it would be the flies.

"So, then, where are the bodies of the people who came through here?"

Mason stared to the east. He was pretty sure he could see flares leaping from the sun, which seemed to be getting closer as it ascended. They'd be lucky if the mercury didn't top 115.

If the corpses were still out here, he had a hunch that after a full day in this heat they wouldn't be incredibly hard to find.

2

Six sets of footprints turned to five, then five to four.

It was easy to tell where the bodies had fallen. They'd left contorted impressions in the dirt, droplets of congealed blood, and the drag marks that highlighted their posthumous northern migration. That, and the concentration of dead carrion birds clustered around the imprints.

"We should be wearing biohazard suits," Velasquez said for the hundredth time. "These birds are probably breeding disease and we're breathing the germs right now!"

"Then we're already dead," Kane said. He didn't appear worried in the slightest.

Mason wished he shared his partner's confidence. He had a new bride waiting for him back home in Colorado, who'd undoubtedly prefer it if he didn't return with some nasty pathogen. Or in a box.

He counted forty-three dead birds over roughly a two-mile stretch. Apart from the flies, nothing had attempted to scavenge them.

Four sets of tracks became three. Two of those remaining collapsed next to each other. Silva said the lone remaining walker had pulled on their arms in an effort to get them to stand again, before kicking sand everywhere in frustration and continuing onward to the north.

They intermittently lost the sole set of tracks, thanks to the drag marks from the others. No effort had been made to brush them away. It was a contradiction that the bodies had been used to erase the prints of those dragging them, and yet the trail they had left in the process might as well have been illuminated with running lights. It was almost as though—

Mason glanced over at Silva. He'd stopped off to the left and crouched over the drag marks. He fingered the edge. The expression on his face betrayed his recognition a heartbeat before his hand found the butt of his pistol. He'd come to the very same conclusion.

The birds and the trail hadn't been deliberately left behind. Whoever had made them simply hadn't had the opportunity to erase them yet.

Mason drew his Glock 23 FG&R and sighted down the streambed ahead, where it bent back to the east around the sandstone outcropping. The ironwoods lining the bend were so dense, he could barely see the ridge behind them.

It was the perfect place for an ambush.

"What's going on?" Velasquez said.

"Shh!"

Kane's eyes locked onto Mason's. He had a two-handed grip on his own sidearm, which he directed down at the sand between his feet.

A high-pitched buzzing sound erupted from the valley ahead of them.

"ATV," Silva whispered.

Kane took off at a sprint as the whine of another engine joined the first. Then another still.

"Call for tactical support!" Mason shouted back over his shoulder. "I want ground teams converging on our location! And get a bird in the air! Now!"

He took off after Kane, who rounded the bend without bothering to clear it. He heard Velasquez barking orders into his transceiver behind him as he went low around the stone embankment.

The buzzing sound grew more distant by the second.

The ravine wound to the east before opening into a straightaway. Kane was a good ten strides ahead of Mason, but he was closing the gap fast. He could hardly hear the motors over his heavy tread and even heavier breathing. His body was already overheating.

By the time they found the ATV tracks, the sound was a memory. He doubled over to catch his breath and watched the sweat dripping from his face onto the sand. Kane paced with his hands on his hips, sucking wind, until the others caught up.

"We have vehicles en route from both directions on Highway Eighty-six," Velasquez said. "Maybe five minutes out."

"It's already too late." Kane snatched the two-way out of the Border Patrol agent's hand. "They're long gone."

Mason could barely see the single set of footprints they'd been following beneath all of the new prints, which had been made by large men wearing heavy-duty work boots. There were so many that he hesitated to even wager a guess as to how many men had arrived on what appeared to have been four-wheel all-terrain vehicles.

The faint thupping sound of chopper blades materialized from the west and he saw the dark shape of an ICE—Immigration and Customs Enforcement—Black Hawk streak across the sky.

"They found the last one over there." Silva pointed to a small swatch of shade behind a boulder. "No sign of a struggle."

"Any indication of what they might have been smuggling?"

"All I can tell you is that if they were moving anything, it couldn't have been in any kind of quantity. Their footprints are too shallow and the distance between them is too long. They couldn't have been carrying anything much heavier than the clothes on their backs."

"Then what the hell happened here?"

"They couldn't have gotten four ATVs onto anything smaller than a tractor trailer!" Kane shouted into the two-way. "I want roadblocks set up on Eighty-six east of Why and west of Tucson! Search every semi and horse trailer and get me another goddamn Black Hawk!"

He thrust the transceiver into Velasquez's chest, turned, and bellowed at the top of his lungs. A startled flock of doves took flight from a thicket of paloverdes as his voice echoed away into oblivion.

"Come on," he said. "We've got a long walk ahead of us."

3

The Douglas P. Bradley OCDETF Strike Force was named in honor of the U.S. Immigration and Customs Enforcement special agent in charge who, along with his wife and teenage son, had been killed in a home invasion six months ago. The Sinaloa Cartel hadn't publicly taken credit for the murders, but chopping the bodies into dozens of pieces and keeping the decapitated heads fit their modus operandi. The strike force itself was an offshoot of the Organized Crime Drug Enforcement Task Force, and, as such, fell under the auspices of the United States Attorney's Office and the special agents in charge of the Phoenix branches of the various federal law-enforcement agencies involved. It brought together the assets and strengths of a veritable alphabet soup of acronyms like the DEA, ATF, FBI, ICE, and IRS, along with the local police and correctional departments. A veteran DEA agent and administrator, Rand Marchment, coordinated the strike force's activities from Washington, D.C., and answered directly to the secretary of the U.S. Department of Homeland Security, which meant they had pretty much free rein to do whatever they needed to do under the all-encompassing umbrella of the Patriot Act.

The strike force met in a small windowless room at Ajo Station, twenty-seven miles north of the Lukeville port of entry and situated at the western edge of the Tohono O'odham Reservation. The station itself was responsible for patrolling and policing seven thousand square miles of desert and sixty-four of the most violent and inaccessible miles of the international border.

The sprawling complex was a hotbed of activity twenty-four hours a day. Explorers rocketed in and out of the enormous lot behind the main building, depositing full loads of undocumented aliens rescued from the heat and confiscated drugs to be entered into the evidence storage warehouses. It was a turnstile operation. Illegals were booked, fingerprinted, caged in holding cells, and then transported by bus to the detention center in Eloy, where they were loaded onto another bus and dropped back off on the other side of the border to try their luck again.

The shouting and banging from the other side of the wall were ceaseless, and yet somehow they always sounded exactly the same, as though both the agents and the immigrants had learned their roles by rote and were merely performing their parts. Those inside the room, however, were dealing with something they'd never seen before.

A rectangular table dominated the small room. As they had been the last to arrive, Kane took a seat at the foot, while Mason leaned against the back wall, by the door. They'd only just received the formal findings from the crime-scene response team—CSRT—and Mason had barely had time to organize them into something reminiscent of an actual briefing on the drive over, with his laptop bouncing on his thighs.

The ICE representative was a small, dark agent named Ray Mondragon, although everyone called him "Razor" because of the long, thin scar that bisected his right brow and cheek. He was seated on the right side of the table in his customary forest green cargo pants and T-shirt with his agency's shield on the breast. He'd split his childhood between living on the O'odham Reservation and in a Tucson barrio, which meant that not only did he know this area better than anyone, he had the kind of relationship with the police departments, both on and off the reservation, to seal it off at a moment's notice. He served as liaison with the Border Patrol, which brought to the table a veritable army of agents, air and land vehicles, and a SWAT team with specialized desert-combat training, known as BORTAC.

Agent Travis Becker of the ATF sat across from Mondragon, his heels on the table and his omnipresent cap pulled so low on his forehead that none of them had ever seen his eyes. His team had its finger on the pulse of the smuggling arteries through the vast desert and a network of informants both stateside and in Mexico.

DEA Special Agent James Templeton, who'd been hand-selected for this operation after a successful run in Miami through the cocaine-crazed eighties, assumed a position at the head of the table. As the senior officer, he served as de facto leader and dealt directly with Marchment back in Washington. He struck an imposing presence and reminded most people of the guy from the Allstate commercials, especially when he spoke. He looked pointedly at Kane, who nodded for him to proceed, and got right down to business.

"This should go without saying, but since Marchment has both the DHS and the U.S. Attorney's Office crawling up his ass, he insisted that I stress the importance of the fact that none of the information discussed in here leaves this room." Templeton looked from one agent to the next, soliciting the requisite nod or grunt. "I trust you've all familiarized yourselves with case file number oscar alpha sierra zero seven two four dash zero five, provided this morning at approximately eleven hundred hours, so I propose we don't waste any time and go straight into the briefing Kane and Mason have prepared. I understand the CSRT has *finally* released its findings?"

Kane nodded.

Everyone opened their laptops or brought their tablets to life in order to view the briefing Mason had sent to each of them maybe fifteen minutes ago. Mason reached past Becker to attach his laptop to the projector and focused the image on the creased screen affixed to the wall. Once Kane reached the head of the table and Templeton had taken a seat, he killed the overhead lights.

Kane leaned forward and braced both hands on the edge of the table. Tiny dead vultures spotted his chest, while his massive shadow reared up behind him on the screen.

"Our worst fears have just been realized. We have to act immediately and decisively before this thing gets out."

4

"All they'll say is that it's 'genetically similar' to HPAI H1N1—highly pathogenic avian influenza A," Mason said. "They won't commit to anything beyond that until the results of the PCR testing come back. They're doing their best to buy us some time before they call in the CDC and the veil of silence falls."

"How contagious are we talking?" Becker asked.

"Extremely. Especially by airborne and droplet transmission. Coughing, spitting, the transfer of bodily fluids by making contact with an exposed surface and then rubbing your eyes or nose. The level of contagion is largely dependent upon physical proximity. In theory, the virus can't survive for very long outside of a living host, though. H1N1 remains viable on environmental surfaces for anywhere from two to eight hours, a fraction of that time in this heat, but we're not taking any chances. Kane and I got lucky. From here on out, everyone is expected to carry gloves and a respirator mask in the field."

"Are we still working under the assumption that the humans infected the birds and not vice versa?" Templeton asked.

"Internal body temperature, postmortem lividity, and the level of insect activity place the time of death for the birds between sixteen and twenty-four hours prior to our arrival. The Border Patrol officer who made the initial discovery is convinced that occurred after the victims passed through, which fits with the rest of the physical evidence."

He clicked quickly through the technical data in the CSRT's report.

"Our working theory is that seven people entered the valley, and over a stretch spanning roughly three miles, six died and the seventh was collected, along with the remains of the decedents, by a team we speculate numbered between four and six. They were subsequently transported to the north by ATV and to a rendezvous point east of mile marker twenty-nine on Highway Eighty-six. The vehicles were driven onto what we believe to be a semitrailer, based on the lone set of tracks we were able to glean from the shoulder. While it was moving. Whatever their ultimate goal, these men were well trained, and had we not stumbled upon the scene when we did, we undoubtedly never would have known they'd been there."

"Do we have any idea where the victims originated?" Razor asked.

"At this point, it matters more where they are now than where they started," Kane said. "Right now, kids, we're wasting time we don't have. Somewhere out there, an unidentified group has gained access to potentially inexhaustible reservoirs of a virus similar to the bird flu, which is, by all appearances, one hundred percent and seemingly immediately fatal to birds and at least eighty-five percent fatal to humans. This isn't someone's science fair project we're dealing with here. There's no doubt in my mind that the end goal is weaponization of the virus."

"What do we have to go on?" Templeton asked. "If they didn't have time to cover their tracks, then they had to have left some kind of evidence we can use."

"Which brings me to the forensics report," Mason said, and hit the clicker. A graph that looked like an EKG strip with dozens of large, irregular spikes appeared. "Forensics collected samples of the dirt and gravel found in the tread of the footprints, the ATV tracks, and those of the semi where it briefly rode up onto the shoulder, then ran them through a gas chromatograph–mass spectrometer. What you see here are the trace compounds transferred from the bottoms of the shoes and the tires, which presumably contacted the same floor at some common location. And that's exactly what the results bear out. As you would expect, there's the standard array of hydrocarbons associated with fossil fuels and motor oils you'd find on any garage floor. Now here's where things get interesting. . . ."

He clicked the remote again to change the slide. This one demonstrated three more spiked lines set against axes labeled "Abundance" on the left and "Time" across the bottom.

"All three samples demonstrated spikes in acetoin, 3-methyl-1-butanol, heptanol, and hexanol, which are metabolites found in spoiled meat. In addition, the GC–MS detected the presence of VOCs—volatile organic compounds—specifically esters, aldehydes, ketones, carboxylic acids, and sulfur compounds. Again, these compounds are prevalent in spoiled meat."

"So we're looking for some sort of slaughterhouse or meat-processing plant," Templeton said.

"Not necessarily."

"I've seen something like this before," Becker said from beneath his cap. "When we were following a lead on an arms racket. VOCs in concentrations that high could also mean we're looking for someplace with a lot of blood on the floor. When we found where these guys were storing their weapons, the Zetas had already been there. Body parts had been stacked in pyramids in the middle of the room."

"That's right," Kane said. "Mason said *meat*, not *beef*."

The room fell silent.

"Surely whatever trace evidence sticks to the tread of a tire wears off after a while," Razor said. "There has to be a finite amount, right? And if the trace transfers to whatever it contacts, then at some point all of the trace leaves the tire and is replaced by different kinds of trace it picks up from whatever it drives over."

"Leave it to ICE to state the obvious," Becker said.

"*¡No seas, güey!* Isn't there a moonshine ring in Kentucky you should be busting up?"

Templeton stifled a chuckle.

"I see where he's going with this," Mason said. "For there to have been trace on the wheels of the semi, it couldn't have been driven very far."

"And considering we have Eighty-six locked down and we cleared all of the semis passing through the roadblocks . . ." Templeton said.

"They couldn't have had more than a fifteen-minute head start before we had a bird in the air."

"No way they made it to Tucson."

"They never left the reservation," Becker said.

"Razor . . . You know this place," Templeton said. "What's out there within a fifteen-mile radius, accessible by road, and large enough to hide a semitruck?"

Mason scrolled through his saved images until he found the detailed satellite imaging of the reservation. It took several seconds to triangulate the location where they'd found the tracks, then the point to the north where the ravine intersected the highway. He centered on it and scaled the zoom to a rectangle roughly thirty miles wide. Aside from Highway 86, there were no paved roads and it was nearly impossible to distinguish the dry creek beds from the few winding north-south gravel roads. The east-west Border Patrol–enforced drags were easy to pick out to either side of the Ajo Mountains. Had any vehicles crossed them, they would have set off one of the Oscars—the radio beacons that alerted dispatch when their motion sensors were triggered.

They had to have gone north into the mountains along one of the narrow roads that adhered to the rugged topography.

Mason tapped the map on the screen with his finger at a point where the valley narrowed and the mountains on the eastern side appeared to have been artificially straightened.

"What's this here?"

All eyes turned to Razor.

"There's a quarry up there, but it's been closed since before I was born. And even then it was in such bad shape that it would have fallen apart if you looked at it hard enough."

"Can you get a drone with infrared and thermal-imaging capabilities over that area?"

"Way ahead of you."

Kane hit the lights and Mason stepped aside to make room for Templeton.

"Get that drone airborne, Ray. The rest of you . . . full night tactical gear. Rebreather masks. I want you on-com and ready to roll in ten minutes." He looked around the table. "What are you waiting for? We can't let that virus get off the reservation."

5

The night was as dark as any Mason could remember. The moon, if there was one, must have been hiding behind the storm clouds boiling from the western horizon. The wind whipped sand sideways across the valley. It sounded like sleet pattering against his windbreaker and the side of the decrepit wooden structure, the majority of which had already fallen down the hillside. Broken planks stood from the sand like bleached bones. Cacti grew on and around them. What little remained of the framework of the chutes led down the hillside to a thicket of ironwoods and a stream maybe a foot and a half wide.

He could barely hear the others whispering through the comlink in his ear over the sound of his own breathing through the respirator, which covered his mouth and nose. Even though he knew where they were, their black fatigues and the fortuitous sandstorm made them impossible to see.

Thermal imaging from the predator drone confirmed the presence of eight distinct sources of heat in the warehouse on the opposite side of the mill from him, just shy of where the red rock had been mined into steppes ascending the mountain. There had been a flurry of activity inside. They all knew what that meant. The men inside were in the process of enacting their hurried exit strategy.

It was now or never.

The BORTAC SWAT team had been trained for precisely this scenario and served as the tip of the spear. They had four men positioned at each of the two doors—one on the north and the other on the south, which was situated beside the narrow gravel road that wended downhill from beneath the cranelike conveyor chute. Mason covered the northern team from the rear, while Kane guarded the south. Once the SWAT team penetrated the structure, he and Mason would advance and assume containment position in the doorways. Becker and a sniper were positioned on the ridgeline above the structure, from which they had unobstructed views of both exits through the scopes of their rifles. Razor was currently streaking across the desert in their direction on an MH-60L Direct Action Penetrator Black Hawk piloted by the Border Patrol's best air interdiction agent. Templeton was in a mobile command station parked approximately eight miles to the south, where he and his team coordinated the operation, utilizing satellite and drone imagery.

They were on Templeton's mark. When he gave the signal, they were going in hard and fast.

This was why Mason had chosen to become a field officer.

This moment right here.

He heard the *thupp-thupp-thupp* of the chopper blades, streaking toward them from the west. The chatter in his ear ceased, only to be replaced by the hollow rushing sound of his pulse. The order would be given any second now.

Any second.

Mason adjusted his grip on the .223-caliber M4 carbine, set to fire three-round bursts, and readied himself to press the button that would activate the laser sight.

Time stood still.

His mechanical respirations slowed.

And then Templeton's voice was in his ear and the world erupted into frantic life.

The red laser streaked from his assault rifle and struck the door a heartbeat before the SWAT guys emerged from the shadows, a battering ram readied between the two in the lead. They swung it and struck the door. The cracking sound of the wood splitting echoed across the valley, in stereo, as the same thing happened on the other side of the building. They shouted and charged—

A blinding light.

A wall of superheated air struck Mason, lifted him from the ground, and tossed him onto his back. The deafening roar of the twin explosions rolled through the valley like thunder. Flames burst from the demolished doorway. Burning men and debris rained down on the shrubs and gravel and struck the wooden ruins all around him. Flaming silhouettes streaked across his peripheral vision, hurled outward over the nothingness to plummet down upon the treetops below.

Black smoke billowed out through the side of the building and his eyes filled with tears.

Mason struggled to his feet and swung his rifle from left to right, cutting his way through the smoke with the red laser. Flames lapped at his feet from burning wood and body parts. He tried to make sense of the situation. The doors had been rigged. The SWAT guys were dead. Given how hard he'd been thrown backward by the explosion, there was no way of knowing whether or not Kane had survived on his side. He couldn't see Becker or the sniper uphill through the smoke, which swirled at the behest of the Black Hawk overhead. Something about the sound of its blades was wrong, like a heart missing every fourth beat. He caught just a glimpse of it as it banked steeply off to the west.

Templeton was shouting in his ear, but he couldn't make out the words. The explosion had thrown off his equilibrium, and a hollow sound resonated somewhere inside his head.

His instincts and training kicked in and he advanced toward the burning doorway, moving low and fast. Even with the respirator mask, he still tasted smoke. His eyes burned so badly, he could hardly keep them open.

Smoke swirled and eddied past him and through the gaps in the burning roof. The floor was bare earth covered with a lifetime of accumulated gravel and grit. The wall to his left had been boarded over where the conveyors that brought the stones from the structure next door had once passed. Rusted equipment lorded over the room.

Mason nearly tripped over the first body, which lay facedown on the dirt, arms folded under it. The telltale triangular butt of a Steyr AUG assault rifle protruded from beneath it. Utility boots. Tall. Broad shoulders. Thick legs. Male. There were two holes in the back of his black neoprene balaclava—.22 by the size of them. Two shots to the base of the cranium, execution-style.

He didn't have to roll the dead man over to know that he wasn't one of theirs.

Mason's laser sight diffused into the smoke, which alternately concealed and revealed sections of the room around him. The flow of air through the burning building made everything seem to come to life with movement.

Static in his earpiece. The crackle of encroaching flames.

There was another body partially hidden behind the heap of scraps from the ruined conveyor. Same black balaclava, matching entry wounds through the back of it. Twin Steyr AUG.

He crouched and, without taking his eyes from his sight line, slid his left hand beneath the neckline of the man's mask. No pulse, obviously, but it hadn't been long at all since he'd had one.

What in the name of God was going on here?

Mason stood and pressed on. He glimpsed another body off to his right, behind what looked like a rusted mine cart. And then the smoke swallowed it again.

Three men positioned exactly where he would have posted them were he preparing to defend the northern entry into the structure. Not only had these men known they were coming, someone had seized the opportunity to tidy up his own mess.

Movement ahead of him, toward the rear of the structure.

He ducked behind the nearest cover. A plastic sheet flagged on the other side of the broken conveyor leading up through the roof. The flames reflected from it even as they started to consume it.

A shadow passed behind the plastic.

Mason crouched back down. Blew out his breath slowly. Killed the laser sight. Rolled to his left and lunged to his feet, rifle seated against his shoulder. Heart pounding in his ears, making the edges of his vision throb. He saw the shadow through the smoke, aligned his barrel with it. The sheet rippled as it melted upward toward the ceiling. It was thick and opaque, like the kind painters used as drop cloths.

He paused and watched the shadow for any indication that his presence had been detected. The figure appeared to be reaching up for something, lowering it, and then reaching back up for something else.

The sheet brushed against Mason's shoulders as he ducked under the flames and dripping plastic.

The man's posture stiffened. He reached for a silenced pistol on the shelf in front of him.

"Don't do it," Mason said.

The man made the grab and whirled to face him.

Mason saw the man's eyes widen through the holes in his mask before the first bullet in the burst destroyed his respirator. The second took a bite out of the right side of his forehead, and the third struck the wall beside his ear. Given how fast it had happened, it looked as though his head had simply vanished.

His pistol clattered to the ground beside the large steel briefcase he'd been hurriedly stuffing with computer components. The wall behind him held an enormous shelving unit overflowing with servers and hard drives and monitors—all of them now spattered with his blood.

Mason turned around. On the far side of where the impromptu entrance had already melted clear up to the ceiling was a bank of portable generators. The existing decrepit wooden wall to his right, between the slats of which he could see the reflections of flames on plastic, was already smoldering.

The smoke washed over him from behind as he approached the lone exit, an uneven doorway that had been sealed with a double layer of plastic sheeting. He pushed one side to the left and the other to the right and stepped into a room mercifully free of smoke. To his left were steel drums with pumps on the top and long nozzles, like industrial-size weed sprayers. The floor was sealed concrete. There was a drain set into the middle. He could see through the plastic covering the back wall of the structure where it abutted the hillside. To his right was another plastic-sheet wall formed around what looked like the framework of a greenhouse that ran nearly the length of the building.

He paused at the second double-flap doorway and watched for movement inside.

A loud crashing sound to his right. The front half of the old structure came down. Flames leaped up over his head and raced across the roof.

Mason fired a triple burst through the drop cloth, lowered his shoulder, and dove through. The moment he hit the ground, he rolled until he got his feet under him and then stood facing into the greenhouse. No return fire. Which was a stroke of luck, considering he was so distracted by everything around him that he would have made an easy target.

He tried to breathe. Couldn't. All he could do was look from one side of the room to the other. Stalls had been erected on either side of a central aisle. Nailed to the wall above each were handwritten signs with seemingly random assortments of numbers and letters. Bodies had been hung beneath them by chains connected to the overhead framework. Long chains with hooks that looped through the upper ribs at the junction of the thorax and the neck, and beneath the lower ribs above the waist. Through both shoulder girdles. The corpses were entirely naked and in various stages of decomposition. Their chins hung to their chests and their lips had curled back from their bared teeth. The woman closest to him had little hearts painted on her toenails. There had to be at least a dozen of them hanging on either side. All dark-haired and dark-skinned. And positively crawling with flies.

A man appeared in the aisle about twenty feet ahead of him, as though he'd simply materialized from the first plumes of smoke that drifted between them.

"Hands behind your head!" Mason shouted.

The man cocked his head first one way and then the other in a manner reminiscent of a predatory bird. He wore a full respirator mask over his face and a wide-brimmed Panama hat. The hint of a tie and a black suit coat were visible above the top of a gray butcher's apron smeared with bloody handprints. His black leather shoes shined with the advancing flames.

"Down on your knees! Hands behind your head!"

The man tipped up his chin as though to better appraise Mason. His irises were a startling shade of blue outside of nature's traditional palette. He had no brows and the skin around his eyes and on his forehead was pink and welted. Or maybe that was just the reflection on his face shield of the flames eating through the plastic walls.

Mason sighted the dot from his laser right between the man's eyes.

As a kid, he could have parted the fur on a deer's back at three hundred yards; Quantico had refined his innate ability and trained him to hit the ticks. There was no way he was missing from this distance.

The man with the blue eyes wagged his index finger at Mason and then pointed at the stall to his right. Kane stepped out from behind the wall, the slender barrel of a Steyr pressed into the soft spot behind his jaw and under his ear. Mason could barely see the crown of his captor's head over Kane's left shoulder. Kane shrugged, as though to let him know that things might not have been going as planned but that he still had everything under control.

Mason kept his laser pinned to the man's forehead, below the brim of his hat.

More smoke drifted between them, momentarily concealing him. When he appeared again, there was a cell phone in his hand.

His eyes narrowed. At first it looked like he was wincing, but then it hit Mason. He was smiling beneath his mask.

"Shoot him," Kane said through the comlink in Mason's ear.

"You do and we're all dead!" a deep voice shouted from behind his partner.

Mason could easily neutralize the man in the mask at this range, but even he might not be fast enough to get off another shot before the second man put a bullet through Kane's head. If he took care of the more immediate threat to his partner, the man with the blue eyes would still be standing out in the open, with nowhere to hide.

"Shoot him, Mason."

"This whole place is wired!"

"Take the shot, damn it!"

Mason swung his rifle toward the man trying to use Kane as a human shield. Pulled the trigger. Watched the top of the man's head vanish as he looked over his partner's shoulder.

Kane stumbled forward and the Steyr fell away from his head.

Mason's laser sight sliced through the smoke like a scythe. He was already firing before it reached the man with the blue eyes, who stumbled backward when the first bullet took him high in the shoulder. A ribbon of blood unspooled behind him. He pressed his thumb to the screen of his cell phone.

Mason saw his eyes.

His ultramarine eyes.

The reflection of a ball of fire blossomed inside them.

Then the world became light.

And pain.

6

Mason awoke with a groan and tried to sit up. Something sharp prodded the inside of his elbow. He tried to pull it out, but someone held his hand.

"Shh," a soft voice whispered. "Try not to move."

He glanced around the room. A large window, through which he saw only sky. A cord tethering him to an IV bag. A bedside monitor displaying his racing heart rate. Walls the same color of yellow as the blanket covering him. A television mounted near the ceiling. Laminate cabinets and a bathroom.

His eyes finally settled on his wife, who was seated beside his bed in a faux-leather chair. She was smiling despite the tears on her cheeks.

"Hey, Angie."

She placed her hand on his cheek and buried her face into his neck.

"Don't you ever do this to me again," she said. "You hear me?"

He tried to wrap his arm around her back, but even thinking about moving ignited the pain that spread throughout his body. It felt like he'd been kicked squarely in the chest by a horse, and his face . . . he could see stitches from the corner of his eye, feel the warmth of superficial burns on his forehead. He kissed the top of her head and regretted even that minuscule movement.

"Kane?" he asked.

She raised her face, and he read the truth in her expression. Her lips quivered and fresh tears shimmered in her emerald eyes.

"He didn't make it."

Mason let his head fall back onto the pillow and stared up at the ceiling.

It was his fault Kane was dead. Had he listened to his partner and killed the man with the blue eyes, he would have prevented the explosion and maybe even still been fast enough to hit the second man. Or maybe shooting the man in the hat would have provided enough of a distraction for Kane to take care of his captor himself. Or perhaps after witnessing his partner's death, the second man would have been willing to trade Kane's life for his freedom. None of those possibilities had registered in Mason's mind at the time, though. His sole focus had been on saving his partner, whose blood was now on his hands.

The door opened and a lanky man with chest hair blooming from the V-neck of his scrub top entered. He wore a white lab coat, and a stethoscope was bundled into a pocket stitched with red letters. Dr. Alan O'Ryan. A man in a black suit followed him into the room.

"Mrs. Mason . . ." the man said.

"He just woke up," Angie said. "There's no way in hell I'm leaving him."

Mason sized up the man with a single glance. He positively reeked of power. Tailored suit. Expensive watch. Polished leather shoes. Silver hair. Dark, alert eyes that dismissed everything around him except for Mason.

"It's okay, Angie," Mason said. "Agent Marchment and I only need a few minutes."

His wife's eyes sought his. She recognized the name, either from him or through the course of her own work, and understood the gravity of the situation. Mason nodded subtly to assure her that everything was under control. She brought his hand to her lips, kissed his knuckles, and gently placed his arm beside his leg.

"I'll be right outside if you need me."

"This won't take long," Marchment said.

Angie brushed past him without a word. She opened the door, looked back, and closed it gently behind her.

"I think that's the first time she's left your side since she got here last night," Dr. O'Ryan said. He smiled, removed Mason's chart from the bracket on the bed, and set about making notations.

Marchment sat in the chair Angie had vacated, slid a folder out from beneath his jacket, and removed a report. Mason already had a pretty good idea what it said. The ranking DEA agent and bureaucrat ostensibly in charge of the Bradley Strike Force waited for the doctor to check Mason's vitals, examine his EKG strip, perform a cursory physical examination, and test his pupils before clearing his throat. The doctor took the hint. He returned the chart to its holder and disappeared into the hallway.

"The secretary of the United States Department of Homeland Security wanted me to personally congratulate you on the success of your mission," Marchment said. "Thanks to our strike force, whatever contagion was inside that quarry never left the reservation. No one outside of this room may ever know it, but the country's a safer place because of you."

"The men in the building," Mason said. "They knew we were coming. They could have easily smuggled the virus out through the open desert."

"We have every reason to believe the threat was contained."

"Until people start dying," Mason said.

Marchment smiled patiently and straightened the stack of papers on his thighs. Whatever Mason might have thought, his superior obviously wasn't going to hear it, not when he'd already taken credit for the victory.

"You've been through a lot these past few days. You both have. What do you say we run through this debriefing so you can get back to your wife?"

Mason took a deep breath, steeled himself, and listened as March-ment detailed the fate of his colleagues.

Of the eighteen law-enforcement officers who had launched the assault on the stone quarry, only five had survived. Becker had maintained his position up the mountainside; the sniper who'd watched the first explosion tear through his teammates had not. Had the ATF agent not shown that kind of discipline, he might not have survived to drag Mason out of the rubble. The pilot of the crippled Black Hawk had managed to land it on the opposite ridge. *Land* being a subjective term, anyway. He'd sustained significant intracranial hemorrhaging, but Razor had gotten the worst of it. The doctors were optimistic that he'd at least regain partial use of his legs. Templeton, who'd been miles away from the disaster, escaped largely unscathed. At least physically. He wouldn't soon be able to forget the images he'd witnessed via satellite relay or the accompanying sounds of his colleagues being slaughtered.

Forensics teams were still sifting through the wreckage and anticipated they'd be doing so until roughly the end of time. As it was, they were going to have to get exceptionally lucky to make any positive identifications of the victims Mason had seen hanging from chains, especially after the second explosion incinerated their bodies and dropped the rear half of the building and countless tons of rock onto what little remained. If their theory about the victims having been undocumented aliens was right, no one would ever know to come looking for them, let alone in storage boxes at the Pima County morgue. Grim as it was, at least there'd been enough left of them to confirm that the virus hadn't survived the blast, a fact corroborated by the CDC's Epidemic Intelligence Service, which claimed it dealt with emerging infections like this one on a daily basis and seemed genuinely disappointed to be leaving with little more than a sack of dead birds.

Most of those who died in the siege were shipped back home to their loved ones. In most cases, their next of kin had to content themselves with ashes and not be too picky about whose they might actually be.

Mason signed himself out of the hospital AMA so he could ride back to Denver with Kane's coffin. There was nothing inside it, but that wasn't the point. His widow deserved to have a polished box with a flag draped over it unloaded from the cargo hold of a plane. She deserved a proper funeral with a motorcade. And she deserved the courtesy of her husband's partner looking her in the eye when he told her that her husband had died with valor in the service of his country. That he had died a hero.

As he stood over Kane's grave, leaning on his crutches and staring at the empty coffin, he thought about what he could have done differently. Truth be told, he'd thought of nothing else since awakening in the hospital. The fact that everything had transpired too quickly was no excuse. He'd been in a position to save his partner's life and he'd failed. He remembered Kane's final words in his earpiece, the expression on his partner's face when he took the shot over his shoulder, and the pair of inhumanly blue eyes beneath the brim of a Panama hat as the world became fire. There were a dozen different choices he could have made, any one of which could have led to Kane standing beside him rather than his widow, whom Mason hadn't even known existed until he was informed she would be receiving the coffin at the airport.

Kane had always preached the importance of separating the personal from the professional. Of all the things his partner had taught him, that was the one thing Mason wished would have stuck.

"Spencer never told you about me, did he?" she said.

Mason shook his head and continued to stare down at the empty casket.

"That's my Spencer, all right." She smiled and tipped her face to the sky. The tears on her cheeks glistened. Her name was Christina and she was beautiful in a way Mason attributed to class and wealth. Her dark hair was pulled back with enough force to draw lines of strain from the corners of her brown eyes to her temples. "He talked about you, though. You should know that."

Mason glanced at her from the corner of his eye.

"He saw a lot of himself in you. Or maybe he just saw a younger version of himself." She sighed. "You were with him when he died."

It was a statement, not a question. Mason had known he would eventually have to address the issue, but he had trouble recalling the words he'd rehearsed thousands of times in anticipation.

"He died a brave man in the service of a country that will never be able to repay the debt—"

She cut him off with a laugh. There was no humor in it.

When he looked up, she was trying to wipe away her tears without smearing her mascara.

"You all tell the same stories, which is to say you speak without actually saying anything. I know my husband is—was . . . a brave man. I know he cared deeply about his country. Probably more than anything else. I know things about him that I will never share with anyone. Because they're mine. Mine in a way that maybe someday you'll understand." She gave up the battle and smeared her makeup across her cheeks. "Tell me his last words."

Mason looked downhill toward where Angie waited in the car, her face hidden behind the reflection of the sun on the tinted window. He prayed his wife would never be in this woman's position.

"He said, 'Take the shot, damn it.'"

Christina was quiet for a long moment. When he looked up, she wore an expression he couldn't quite interpret.

"I figured it would be something like that." She sniffed. "I was hoping he made his peace with God at the end."

He debated about trying to tell her what she needed to hear, but he realized she'd see right through him.

"Spencer always said we Catholics have a 'good gig,'" she said. "That we can do whatever we want in life as long as we ask for absolution at the end. So that was how he lived, with the belief that with his dying breath he could weasel his way through the gates of heaven and meet me there."

Mason didn't want to tell her that the room in which her husband died—a room filled with the decomposing remains of anonymous immigrants hanging from the ceiling by meat hooks—was obviously beyond even God's sight.

"Tell me . . ." She took Mason's hand and turned him so that she could look into his eyes. He was self-conscious of his lack of eyebrows. Not to mention the C-shaped scar around his left eye. They were further reminders that he had lived, while others, including her husband, had died. "Could you have saved him?"

He met her gaze for the first time.

"Yes."

Mason left her at the graveside, staring in the opposite direction across the green field, toward where swans floated on a clear pond shaded by elms. In that moment, as he walked downhill toward his waiting car, he experienced complete clarity of thought.

He might have failed to save Kane, but he'd be damned if he wasn't going to avenge him.

PART I

Freedom is never more than one generation away from extinction.

—Ronald Reagan, address to the annual meeting of the
Phoenix Chamber of Commerce (1961)

TODAY

7

Denver, Colorado

OCTOBER 27

A lot of things had changed since Mason left Arizona. He'd changed. He no longer cared about his professional cap, let alone how many feathers it had. He could effectively do his job in the shadow of the Rockies, and there was no denying that he needed to spend more time with his wife. Or at least make more of an effort to do so. Besides, his wasn't the only career to consider. He had to break down doors and shout at the top of his lungs to strike fear into the hearts of his adversaries. His wife could do so with a mere phone call. She represented the arm of the government whose reach crossed state lines and international borders, a three-letter entity that elicited terror in criminals and law-abiding citizens alike, an agency that served the principal and non-partisan interests of the United States of America.

His wife was an IRS agent, and a damn good one at that. Agent Angela Thornton Mason specialized in corporate fraud criminal investigations. She liked to say she could find a single dollar bill filtered through a dozen shell companies and offshore accounts in less time than it took to do her hair. Mason had no reason to doubt her. He'd witnessed her following paper trails so creative and circuitous that he doubted even the team of accountants who hid the money knew where it was anymore.

He'd also spent roughly a quarter of his adult life waiting for her to do her hair.

Unfortunately, there was one thing she could do that he simply couldn't. She'd figured out a way to leave her work at the door.

Mason, on the other hand, was unable to turn his mind off. No matter which line of thought he followed, it always led back to the nightmare in Arizona. Were it one of those things he could simply switch off like the ignition in his car when he pulled into the garage, he would have done so in a heartbeat. Without hesitation. A guy should only have to relive the deaths of his friends and colleagues so many times.

He wasn't so out of touch with the world around him that he couldn't see what he was doing to Angie. She reached out, and he pulled away. She wanted to help him, to break down the walls he'd erected around himself. He understood that on a conscious level. The problem, however, was that the only way to bridge the growing chasm between them was to tell her what had happened at the quarry. Not the sanitized story that had garnered commendations for those who had survived. The truth. And even he wasn't entirely sure what that was anymore. All he knew with any kind of certainty was that he was directly responsible for Kane's death, that his split-second decision had cost his partner his life, that it was his fault there hadn't even been enough of him left to bury.

Maybe a part of him believed that needing her help was a sign of weakness. More likely, he subconsciously recognized the enormity of his failure and realized that it was only a matter of time before he failed her, too. He told himself that he was somehow insulating her from the knowledge that there were monsters out there smuggling horrible diseases into the country, sociopaths like the men in the quarry who didn't spare a thought for their victims. He didn't know what their endgame might have been, but every fiber of his being screamed that whatever it was, it wasn't over.

Not by a long shot.

But while Mason was chasing ghosts, he lost sight of the living. It wasn't until one morning, while he and Angie sat across a table set with their untouched breakfasts, that he noticed her staring into her lap and unconsciously twisting her wedding ring. A ring wasn't a complicated piece of equipment. It was like a light switch in that sense. It was either on or it was off. Twisting implied a measure of uncertainty, and since the ring was on her finger at the time, it didn't take a genius to figure out the alternative she was contemplating. He knew right then and there that either he changed something in a big hurry or he was going to lose her.

If he hadn't already.

"Remember the day we met?" Mason asked.

She continued to look down, but he saw the hint of a smile on her lips. The way the sunlight passing through the window of the eating nook fell on her auburn hair made it appear to glow. She was every bit as beautiful as she'd been the first time he saw her.

"You were sitting in the bleachers, two rows back from the bench. We were down by one at the end of the second period. The buzzer had just gone off. I was heading toward the locker room when I looked up and there you were. Red sweater. Black snow cap. And the most amazing emerald eyes I'd ever seen."

She looked up, and he realized how long it had been since he'd actually made eye contact with his wife. Her hands ceased their restless movement.

"You remember what I said?" he asked.

"Of course I do. You were the most arrogant man I'd ever met."

"I want to hear you say it."

She shook her head and allowed herself to smile.

"You said, 'I'm going to win this game and then I'm going to take you out.'"

"So I came out in the third period—"

"And got checked so hard, you were barely able to make it off the ice."

"But I did exactly what I said I was going to do."

"You did nothing of the kind. You lost by three."

"Yet you were still waiting for me outside in the snow."

She smiled and reached across the table. He took her hand in his and felt her ring press into his palm.

"I'm still waiting for you."

She squeezed his hand one last time and then rose and started clearing the dishes. He would have done anything for her. Anything except for the one thing she needed him to do.

He was halfway up the stairs when she spoke in a voice so small, he couldn't be entirely certain he'd heard it.

"But I can't wait forever."

8

They lived in a two-bedroom turn-of-the-century bungalow in a trendy neighborhood, south of downtown. The house had been gutted and retrofitted with central heating and air, despite the fact that the massive Siberian elms and ponderosa pines kept the house shaded year-round. They'd left the original plaster walls alone, at Angie's insistence. The only real concession Mason had sought was a satellite dish. No man should have to live like a savage in this day and age.

The main floor consisted of a tiny living room with a massive bay window and a well-appointed and functional kitchen. It kind of had to be, considering how tiny it was. There was a dining room and a mudroom and a skinny staircase with a maple banister that led to the second floor and both bedrooms. The master was large enough for a king-size bed, but little else, and the bathroom still smelled faintly of the old people who'd lived there before them. Mason had commandeered the spare bedroom and converted it into a home office. He'd covered the walls with maps of Southern California, Arizona, New Mexico, Colorado, and western Texas and riddled them with color-coded thumbtacks connected by lengths of yarn. Any even tangential reference to trafficking along the Mexican border was marked. By the time he added pictures and newspaper clippings and various notes, Angie had started calling it his "den."

He told her it was for his current assignment with the Metro Trafficking Task Force. And while that might have been true from a certain perspective, she understood that it was only peripherally related. That this room was where he kept the demons he'd brought back with him from the desert.

There were eight different colors, each of which corresponded to one of the major Mexican drug-trafficking organizations: the Sinaloa Federation, the Cártel del Golfo, the Knights Templar, La Familia Michoacana, the Cártel Jalisco Nueva Generación, Los Mazatlecos, the Beltrán-Leyva Organization, and the various splinter groups of Los Zetas. The cartels functioned just like any other multibillion-dollar corporations. They branded themselves in a way that their rivals wouldn't be able to miss. They each tended toward a main trafficking focus and a signature way of dealing with their competition. The Sinaloans controlled the lion's share of the cocaine trafficking and had a penchant for beheading their rivals, mutilating their remains, and displaying them in public. The Zetas counted among their ranks a large number of former elite commandos from the Mexican Army whose skills allowed the organization to expand from drugs into extortion, kidnapping, and the protection racket. The New Generation Cartel of Jalisco favored indiscriminate slaughter and overt demonstrations of brutality. And on and on. It was depressing to see all the violence plotted out like this, visualizing the systematic conquest of the American Southwest by merciless merchants of death whose *familia* made the Sicilians look like Shriners.

Rainbow colors radiated upward from the southern border, through towns like Tijuana and Monterrey, but the vast majority formed lightning bolts that shot into the interior of Arizona from Sonoyta, Sasabe, Agua Prieta, Naco, and Nogales, open sections of the desert where there were no fences, no deterrents, and an entire Native American reservation that served as a big red carpet. Apparently, the border strategy was to funnel all the trafficking into one narrow shipping lane, one that could potentially diminish the number of invaders by heat attrition, but otherwise was left largely untended, while U.S. Customs and Border Patrol stations filmed TV shows and showcased their taxpayer-funded armadas for the media. It was as though the policy makers had simply decided to leave the back door open for a lover to sneak in during the night while publicly decrying infidelity at the tops of their lungs.

As though there were some things that the powers that be *wanted* to pass through the net.

By weeding out the events he could conclusively attribute to known cartels, he was able to hone in on the reports that fell in the gray areas. The majority were merely crimes of opportunity, individuals or unaffiliated groups attempting to get a leg up, most of which culminated in arrests, deportation, or bloodshed. And then there were others that seemingly went unnoticed, events that he believed would lead him to those he was certain had eluded them at the quarry, the men responsible for smuggling the deadly virus into the country, not to mention the death of his partner.

And a staggeringly high number of them involved fire.

Mason discovered the first instance by accident. In a file related to the seizure of a large quantity of methamphetamines in the town of Eagar, northeast of Tucson, one of the responding officers noted that he'd been summoned to the scene while on his way to investigate a fire in a remote barn with suspected casualties. On a whim, Mason tracked down the report of the actual fire investigation, which consisted of about three formal sentences and a succinct summary involving presumed immigrants being trapped inside by a fire of their own accidental creation. He called the investigator—Sgt. Judd Morton with the Eagar PD—who informed him that such incidents weren't as uncommon as he might think. These illegals exhausted themselves in the desert, broke into some rancher's barn or shed, and crashed in the hay with a cigarette hanging from their mouths.

And so it had been on his own dime that he traveled back to Arizona forty-eight hours later and stood before the charred rubble. He took pictures from every conceivable angle. Nothing remained. Not a single wall stood. The majority of the debris had been cleared and loaded onto a fleet of trucks that belonged to the deep treads positively littering the site, which was at the bottom of an arroyo, invisible from just about every vantage point. There were already fresh stacks of lumber and building materials waiting to give rise to a new structure. Were it not for the faint yellowish discoloration of the soot on the branches of the surrounding trees, he probably would have been able to let it go, but he'd learned a little about chemical accelerants after nearly being incinerated on his last visit and knew that benzene was a volatile and explosive aromatic hydrocarbon that burned with an almost dirty yellow chemical flame. A subsequent call to the Pima County Medical Examiner's Office confirmed that the victims' bodies had been converted to little more than ashes and hopelessly unidentifiable chunks of bone.

The pictures he took that day were the first he tacked up on his wall. Others followed, the majority of which he copied from the investigative files or clipped from small-town newspapers. Some incidents lacked photos, so he simply pinned up the paragraph-long mentions he found hidden toward the back of the local sections.

A surprising number of the fire-related immigrant deaths were accidental, as Sergeant Morton had said, but there were still a good number that had been ruled as such that Mason simply didn't buy. In most cases, the victims were discovered to have various degrees of burns over their bodies. Some weren't even burned at all; they had merely succumbed to the smoke. It was the incidents in which no physical remains had been salvageable that he discreetly looked into in his spare time. He plotted them on his maps with red thumbtacks and connected them with red yarn. Six incidents in all. Hardly enough to form a readily identifiable pattern by anyone's standards, but the nature of the coincidental elements they shared was impossible to ignore. That, and the fact that the line connecting all six incidents shot straight upward like an arrow from the quarry where his team had been ambushed on the Tohono O'odham Reservation into Saguache, Colorado, southeast of Pueblo.

He had discovered an unidentified ninth organization operating under the radar on an interstate route that led directly into the heart of Colorado.

The Metro Trafficking Task Force was organized by the Department of Justice, specifically the United States Attorney's Office, and combined the resources of the DEA, FBI, ICE, Colorado State Patrol, and local police and sheriff's departments. Its stated mission expanded upon the basic pursuit and apprehension of individuals responsible for the import and distribution of narcotics to encompass all the various forms of trafficking—from human beings to weapons—along the Front Range of the Rocky Mountains. While the task force was primarily staffed and funded at the state and local levels, the various federal agencies assisted with operational and tactical support when needed and interceded when investigations crossed state lines.

Mason had volunteered to serve as the FBI's liaison to the task force so he could gain access to inside information and keep himself close to any investigation even peripherally related to what had happened in Arizona and his newly identified ninth trafficking organization. The flaw was that he had to sit through these weekly meetings in the conference room at the Denver Federal Center, which tended to last anywhere between forever and eternity, but they beat filling out paperwork, which was why he was running late this morning.

He slipped in through the rear door, to find the conference room dark, save for the screen at the front of the room, beside which stood a woman he immediately recognized, even in the dim light. He rarely crossed paths with his wife in a professional capacity, but she never failed to impress him. When Angie was in her element, she commanded the room, just as she did now. She wore a gray skirt suit with a cream blouse, and her wavy red hair was pulled back in a ponytail. The light from the projector reflected from reading glasses he didn't know she wore.

Mason leaned against the back wall while his eyes adjusted to the darkness.

"We're basically at the mercy of the banks." Angie clicked through slides featuring account numbers and dollar amounts. "We have no choice but to rely on them to voluntarily report suspicious financial activity. If they don't, it's nearly impossible for us to track interest paid to foreign account holders, since the funds aren't subject to federal income tax."

"You're suggesting the banks are complicit?" an officer asked from a table near the front of the room.

There were eight rectangular tables, each large enough to accommodate a dozen people, yet only a few, clustered together by affiliation, sat at each. Most handled undercover operatives and confidential informants or supervised those who did. The remainder were advisers or bureaucrats representing the various oversight committees. Mason recognized the federal contingent at the table farthest from the stage and took the open seat beside his partner.

"What I'm telling you is that banks are in the business of making money. There's a reason that U.S. banks are the preferred choice for laundering cartel profits." Angie clicked her remote and the screen changed to a world map with arrows radiating outward from Mexico, the largest of which struck America right in the heartland. "During the last fifty years, more than one hundred billion dollars in illegal money has flowed out of Mexico and into the international financial system. Now, you have to understand that a commercial bank makes roughly eighteen percent profit on the money it takes in, so its sole mission is to get as much money through the door as humanly possibly. An investment bank earns close to a quarter on every dollar it brings in. This is a huge industry that's threatened by anyone who tries to cut off the flow of cash, especially task forces like this one."

"I'll never be able to figure out how you landed someone like her," Mason's partner whispered.

Special Agent Jared Trapp looked like a windstorm followed him wherever he went. His hair was a mess, his clothes disheveled, and somehow he'd already grown a week's worth of stubble in the last few hours, all of which combined to make people instinctively underestimate him. He and Mason had been partners for nearly eight months now and had pretty much hit it off right away, undoubtedly because Trapp had worked with Kane during the investigation into the collapse of World Trade Center Building 7 on 9/11. Mason figured that gave him the kind of motivation he needed in a partner if they were going to track down those responsible for their mutual friend's death.

It also didn't hurt that he was a genuinely nice guy who believed in the job he was doing.

"You and me both," Mason said.

Angie wasn't telling these officers anything they didn't already know, but Mason could tell by the way the right corner of her mouth rose ever so slightly that she was about to.

"Which is where regulation TD9584 comes into play. While it was originally enacted to complement the Foreign Account Tax Compliance

Act to help us pursue tax evaders, it allows us to identify anyone hiding money in another country for any reason. Assuming we have specific target information, like the account numbers provided by your CI working for the Sinaloans. We traced them to a bank in Matamoros containing close to two million dollars and registered to this man. . . ." She clicked to a picture of a plump Hispanic male with a light complexion and gray hair. He wore a plain blue suit and spectacles. "Meet Fernando Trejo, who—thanks to his construction company—was able to launder more than fifty million dollars for any number of untraceable entities by simply wiring it across the border into accounts he set up for dummy land-development companies in Texas and Arizona."

"So what's his connection?" an officer from the Lakewood PD asked.

"I'll field that question," Blaine Martin said.

The special prosecutor for the Justice Department emerged from the shadows at the side of the stage and turned on the lights. He looked more like an actor playing the role than an actual attorney, which told Mason everything he needed to know. Martin had designs on politics. He guided Angie from center stage with his hand on her lower back.

Mason sat up a little straighter in his chair.

Martin leaned against the lectern in a practiced, easy way that must have played well with juries.

"Of that fifty million," he said, "we've traced twenty-six million in what we believe to be bribes from the Sinaloa cartel to government officials in Tamaulipas and Nuevo León, five million to Trejo's personal holdings, and another four million to accounts scattered throughout the American Southwest. The remaining fifteen million was dispersed over the course of the past twelve months in amounts of less than two grand to hundreds of accounts, from all of which that money was then transferred into a total of ten accounts right here in Colorado. Bogus accounts established for shell companies. Thanks to Angela's relentlessness, we learned that they were all cleaned out and closed within the past ten days." Not Agent Mason. Angela. "That means we potentially have fifteen million dollars out there on the streets right now and our only option is to treat it as though it's actively in play."

"What's our working assumption?" someone asked from up front.

Angie stepped forward.

"We're cultivating a source who claims to have information about a human-trafficking organization with that kind of resources."

"Here in Denver?" Trapp asked.

"Possibly," Martin said, and glanced at Angie. "Assuming the information checks out."

"Not at that price tag," Mason said. "Fifteen million's too much money, even for the skin trade. At five to ten grand a head, you're talking about literally thousands of people being sold like cattle. There'd be a line of buses on the highway from here to Wyoming."

Angie glared at him.

"We can't be dealing with a simple buy, either," one of the DEA agents said. "No one could move that quantity of drugs up the I-Twenty-five corridor without us knowing."

"My sources would have heard if there were going to be any major shipments of heroin or meth," another officer said.

"Weapons?" a Denver PD officer suggested.

"That would have to be either a huge cache or one really big bang," Trapp said.

"And that's precisely why we can't afford to rule anything out," Martin said. "For all we know, that money could be halfway around the world by now, but we have to do our due diligence on this one."

Angie caught Martin's eye, tapped her watch, and gathered her belongings. He nodded and started to wrap up the meeting while she slipped out the side door.

Mason excused himself and exited through the rear door. He caught up with his wife in the hallway.

"I didn't know you were going to be here today."

"Despite my telling you ten times?"

"Look, Angie, I'm sorry—"

"You shouldn't have called me out in front of everyone like that."

"I didn't call you out."

"Did you consider the possibility that maybe I know something that you don't?"

"Of course, but I know how traffickers work."

"And I know how they *think*."

"Angie . . ."

The fire faded from her eyes, but her cheeks remained flushed.

"Consider how much planning went into this," she said. "How much patience you'd need to transfer that much money over such a long period of time and in such small amounts. How deep your pockets would have to be not to miss fifteen million dollars. These aren't your average traffickers. I'm convinced there's more to this than either of us—"

The side door burst open, filling the hallway with the clatter of chairs and a riot of voices. Martin emerged with his briefcase, checked his watch, and headed straight toward them.

"We really need to talk," Angie said. "Make time for me tonight, okay?"

She straightened her jacket, turned toward Martin, and flashed her professional smile.

"Yeah," Mason said, although with the way she'd said it, he wasn't entirely sure he wanted to have that conversation.

Martin offered him a curt nod and swept his wife away down the hallway, again with his hand on her lower back. He leaned closer and spoke directly into her ear the moment they were out of range. The men exiting the meeting shoved past Mason to either side. Still, he stood there, watching his wife and Martin until they rounded the corner and vanished from sight.

Maybe none of the officers on the task force had any idea what was potentially being smuggled into the state, but now that he really thought about it, he just might know someone who did.

10

In that fleeting moment in the quarry before his world had erupted into flames, Mason witnessed the true depths of humanity's capacity for evil, depths he had previously been unable to fathom. He searched for it in the eyes of the people he passed on the street, listened for its presence in their words, but each and every one of them looked and sounded just like him.

Well, not *every* one of them.

The man sitting in the purple vinyl booth with the window over-looking the club at his back had no pretentions that he was like every-one else. He existed on the fringes of society, in the shadows all people cast, servicing the baser needs everyone has, but would rather no one knew about. As such, the man with the jet-black hair slicked back from his long face and the ash-colored suit, which undoubtedly cost more than Mason's car, considered himself in the business of discretion.

His name was Ramses Donovan and he'd been one of Mason's best friends since he was twelve years old.

As far as criminals went, Ramses followed a civilized code reminis-cent of the early mafiosi, courtesy of his father's influence. He was merely a purveyor of vices, a middleman of sorts who connected individuals of questionable taste with their interests of a more discerning nature.

As such, no one moved anything along the Front Range without trig-gering the peripheral alarm system of Ramses the Great, whose idea of legitimacy didn't quite mesh with Mason's. He had a conscience, seem-ingly arbitrary though it was, and took exception to anyone doing any-thing that might bring unwanted attention to some of the more unsavory aspects of his legitimacy. He and Mason would never agree about the distinction between an escort and a prostitute or the definition of a recre-ational drug, but when it came right down to it, his morals more closely resembled Mason's than those of most of the agents with whom he worked. Ramses also knew that a certain measure of give-and-take was necessary to maintain a working relationship with the various authorities.

"Something's going down tonight," he said. "In an abandoned build-ing out near the old airport. Back behind the runways. Based on how little anyone seems to know, it has to be something pretty big. That's all I've got, though. Any of this comes back on me and I'm taking it out of your ass."

Mason had called Ramses the moment he left the Federal Building. He knew his old friend wouldn't say anything over the phone, regardless of whether or not he had any information, but that wasn't the point. That Mason was even asking him in such a manner conveyed the direness of his request, one that was rewarded with an invitation to join Ramses at his newest club later that evening, which, presumably, would give him time to look into the matter.

"Don't you trust me anymore?" Mason asked. "That really hurts."

"You think that badge of yours is going to keep me from hurting more than your feelings? I'm serious, Mace. You know that I'm a legitimate businessman and have a reputation to uphold."

Even he couldn't say it with a straight face.

Ramses had always been able to make Mason smile.

"You know I can't protect you if this goes south."

"Please," Ramses said. "Who do you think you're talking to here? When have I ever needed anyone's protection?"

"All I'm saying is that if these are the guys I'm looking for, there's definitely the potential for blowback."

"Then you'd better not screw up."

"Words to live by," Mason said. "Say hi to your old man for me."

"Tell him yourself. I've got a pathological aversion to going to prison."

"Better keep your head down, then, Ramses."

"I could say the same."

Mason smirked and headed for the door.

"You know I wouldn't have done this for anyone else," Ramses said to his back.

"And you know I wouldn't have asked if it weren't important."

"Just try not to get yourself killed, okay?"

Mason left him in his private suite and felt the bass pound against his chest the moment he opened the door. The lights strobed and the music blared. Generic *oomph-oomph* techno music. He descended the stairs and pressed through a sea of writhing bodies. Go-go dancers in long boots and short skirts were suspended above the throngs in cages that fit the general motif. Club Five had once been a slaughterhouse, one of the building's many incarnations, and Ramses had gone to great lengths not to spend a dime on its renovation. He deserved a little credit for the name, though. Not only was it his fifth club, but also a subtle nod to the Vonnegut classic.

Trapp was waiting in the emergency exit alcove beneath the staircase on the opposite side of the dance floor, looking like he'd rather be just about anywhere else.

"It's happening tonight," Mason said. "In an abandoned building out by Stapleton."

His partner nodded and shouldered through the door into the alley. The flashing lights from the club washed across the mud and wet asphalt, highlighting the parabolic dimples on the puddles. The cold sleet drenched his head and shoulders. The door closed once more and darkness descended.

Mason's Grand Cherokee was parked on the far side, behind a Dumpster, so it wasn't visible from the main road. Mason got in the car and called in the location Ramses had given him. He was rewarded with a rendezvous point and confirmation that a tactical team would be waiting when he arrived. His partner hesitated outside the passenger door until Mason revved the engine and gestured for him to hurry up.

Trapp didn't say a word as they weaved through the congested downtown streets. Mason waited until they hit the highway before calling him out.

"Do you have something to say to me?"

"You trust this guy?"

"Ramses?"

"He's running escorts out of all his joints and probably owns half of the marijuana dispensaries in town."

"He's never claimed he doesn't."

"Donovan doesn't get a pass, Mason. One of these days we're going to have to run him down and not even you will be able to stop it."

Mason hoped it wouldn't come to that, but if it did, he'd make sure he handled it himself.

He exited I-70 several miles from where the runways of the old airport used to cross over the highway, then wended his way through a maze of deserted streets between industrial buildings until he reached his destination. He turned through the open gate and followed a blind gravel drive behind a shipping warehouse that looked like it hadn't been used in decades. The Metro Denver SWAT vehicle was waiting in the parking lot. The Lenco BearCat—Ballistic Engineered Armored Response Counter Attack Truck—was painted black and looked like a Humvee on steroids.

Mason parked, killed the lights, and ran to the BearCat. The rear doors opened and he and Trapp bounded up into the rectangular cargo hold. Benches lined the reinforced walls on either side beneath narrow windows that served as embrasures. The overhead fixtures had been fitted with red bulbs that cast little of anything resembling actual light. He closed the doors behind them and barely sat down before the driver took off.

There were six men in the back with them, three on either side. They wore black uniforms and helmets with night-vision apparatuses standing from their foreheads. Their black face paint made their eyes appear disembodied. Mason sat directly across from Trapp, whose expression had become unreadable.

"Traffic cameras recorded a total of four vehicles passing through the gate to the decommissioned zone less than an hour ago," one of the officers said. Mason recognized him from the task force meetings. Rivers. The team commander thrust a helmet with built-in two-way communications, a half-face respirator, and a Kevlar vest into Mason's chest. "Two came out."

"That could mean anything," Mason said. "The vehicles that left could be completely unrelated or the buy could have already gone down."

"Which is why we need to get there before the other two cars come out."

"A company called Regal Properties bought all the remaining administrative and cargo buildings when the airport closed," the officer beside Trapp said. He read from a tactical tablet, which was receiving data as fast as it could be gathered. "Regal planned to convert them into luxury apartments and upscale residential homes, but was forced to file Chapter Eleven when it was determined there were unacceptable levels of jet fuel in the soil and groundwater, and remediation buried it in debt. Renovations were halted in unknown stages of completion. The bank now owns everything out there and doesn't appear to be in a hurry to do anything with it."

"How many buildings are there?" Mason asked.

"Six."

"Do we know which one they're in?"

"Satellite imaging shows the two vehicles—a nondescript sedan and a large SUV, most likely a Chevy Suburban—parked outside the building closest to the outer perimeter. The administration building."

"Neither of those cars is large enough to carry fifteen million dollars' worth of anything," Trapp said.

"Even if this is a buy," another officer said, "that doesn't necessarily mean the actual exchange will go down here."

"Can we access the building's layout?" Mason asked.

"There are three floors, although we don't know the extent of the construction," the officer with the tablet said. "Based on the original blueprints, each level looks the same, with a square hallway lined with offices on both sides. There are stairwells in each of the four corners."

Rivers turned on his own tablet and leaned closer so Mason could see.

"We'll park right here, behind this building." Rivers tapped the screen. "It'll conceal our approach from the west until we're about fifty yards from our target. Rojas and Telford, you'll take up cover position along this fence line. Willis and I will head around the back and enter from the east. You and your partner stick with Porter and Rasmussen, who'll penetrate the building from the west. We'll clear each level from the four corners—watch your sight lines—and continue upward as a unit. Standard rules of engagement. Anderson?"

"Sir," the driver said through the speaker in the partition that separated the cab from the hold.

"You and Rodriguez stay with the truck. If things get ugly, we're going to need you to get us out of there." The officer swept his gaze across each of them in turn. "Any questions, now's the time to ask them."

Mason slipped the bulletproof vest over his head, donned the helmet, and switched on the com. He drew his Glock and chambered a round. Took a deep breath and blew it out slowly. When he looked up, Trapp was staring right at him from beneath the brim of his helmet.

"Are you certain Donovan isn't setting us up?"

"He trusts his intel. And I trust him. So, yeah . . . I'd wager my life on it."

"You'd better be right, because once we go out those doors, that's exactly what we're doing."

11

The BearCat slowed and the driver extinguished its lights. Mason couldn't see a blasted thing inside the truck, let alone through the slit windows. He fitted his mask over his mouth and nose and lowered his night-vision apparatus. The others reappeared in shades of green and gray, the triangular stocks of their AR-15s to their shoulders, their barrels directed at the ground between their feet.

The smooth buzz of pavement gave way to the grumble of gravel. The truck shook crossing the uneven ground.

Mason readjusted his grip on the Glock in his right hand and reached for the handle on the door with his left.

The BearCat shuddered to a halt.

Trapp and Mason each threw open a side and bounded out into the night. They covered the other men as they piled out and jogged around the side of the old cargo warehouse. Two men—Rojas and Telford—sprinted to either side and disappeared into the tall weeds, from the anonymity of which their sight lines would be clear all the way to the administration building.

A skeletal structure rose from the dark horizon, tattered plastic drop cloths flapping over the gaps where entire sections of the external walls had been removed. The building was dark, save for a weak glow emanating from the top level. The sedan and Suburban sat silent and lifeless in the overgrown parking lot to the south of what had once been the main entrance.

Despite the tumbleweeds snarled in the chain-link fence, Mason identified a loose section and lifted it for the others to crawl under. He followed them into a mud lot spotted with heaps of construction materials covered with tarps. They split up as planned. He caught a glimpse of the officers—Rivers and Willis—streaking around either side of the building as he ducked beneath a plastic tarp and entered the main level, with Porter on his heels. Trapp and Rasmussen fanned out to his right.

Despite their best attempts at stealth, their wet soles squelched and echoed all around them. Water plinked into puddles on the concrete. The plastic drop cloths snapped in the gusting wind, which pattered them with raindrops that sounded like buckshot. Sporadic flashes of lightning limned concrete support posts, bare girders, and dangling cables with an ethereal blue glow. There were stacks of lumber and drywall near the exposed iron staircase to Mason's left, which Porter ascended, his rifle raised toward the landing. He couldn't see Trapp or Rasmussen climbing the matching staircase to his right, but he heard the hollow *ting* of one of their boots hitting the bottom stair a second after his did.

Mason held his Glock in a two-handed grip and pointed it upward as he climbed. He passed Porter on the landing and continued upward. Crouched beside the doorway to the second level. Waited for Porter to assume position on the other side.

The second level still had the majority of its framework, although giant holes had been punched through the plaster where thieves had stolen all of the copper. He detected movement in the shadows at the far end of the hallway. Even with the night vision, he could barely see Rivers peering out from the stairwell at the far end of the hall.

No sign of movement.

Mason gave the signal and they headed up the stairs again. As before, Porter cleared the first landing and Mason made sure no surprises awaited them at the top, where the stairs terminated at a concrete landing. They pressed their backs to the walls at either side of the doorway.

Time slowed to a crawl.

Mason tuned out the rushing of his pulse in his ears and concentrated on regulating his breathing. Listened for any sound to betray the presence of his prey. It had taken him a year to find anything resembling a lead on the men who had massacred the strike force in Arizona. A single mistake and he might never find them again. He couldn't let that happen. He needed to end this.

Right here and now.

He eased the trigger into the sweet spot and stepped out into the open. The whole upper level had been scoured to the bare girders, save for the webs of electrical work woven between them. The wind had torn the plastic sheeting attached to the southern wall, making it snap and flare inward. Rainwater dribbled through the roof. Entire sections of the floor were missing. He could see down into rooms filled with scraps of wood and Sheetrock that had been tossed down from this level.

A small chamber had been erected in the center of the open area. A room roughly the size of an office cubicle. Each of the four walls consisted of opaque plastic sheeting stretched tightly from the floor to the ceiling. A faint glow radiated through it.

Mason felt more than saw Trapp and Rasmussen exit the darkened stairwell to his right as he advanced, sighting the dimly lit chamber down the barrel of his pistol. Rivers and Willis emerged from the stairwells on the opposite side of the building. Together, they converged on the plastic square.

Something wasn't right.

Mason raised his night-vision apparatus. The light was messing with its optics. He glanced from the corner of his eye at Trapp, who advanced in a shooter's stance, focused solely on the taut drop cloths.

He couldn't put his finger on it. All he knew was that his instincts were screaming for him to pay attention to a message he couldn't consciously decipher.

Trapp hung back. He must have sensed the same thing.

Porter and Rasmussen passed them and approached the makeshift chamber at the same pace as their teammates.

Again, dim light. No movement.

The plastic couldn't have been drawn any tighter. All straight lines and corners. No entrance. No exit. There was something wrong with it, too. Fluid beaded on the inside.

Perspiration.

The four officers reached the cubicle.

"We're too late," Rivers said through speakers in their helmets.

Mason stopped and watched one of the droplets of condensation swell and then dribble down the plastic. He followed it with his eyes all the way to where it ran into a dark shape near the ground, leaning against the drop cloth. It almost looked like a body—

Porter grabbed the plastic and pulled it away.

The dim light flickered.

"No!" Mason shouted.

He whirled and sprinted in the opposite direction. Watched Trapp drop out of sight.

The floor opened up beneath Mason and he plummeted toward a heap of rubble. A wall of heat struck him from behind and sent him cartwheeling a heartbeat before the air filled with flames.

12

Mason climbed out of the back of the ambulance. He felt like he'd been hit by a train, but he knew better than to complain. A dozen stitches on his forearm and thigh, some bruises that looked a lot worse than they felt, and a mild concussion were vastly preferable to being wheeled from the building in a body bag and loaded into the back of the medical examiner's van like the four officers who'd entered the administration building with them. Trapp had survived with little more than bumps and bruises and was already on his way to the Denver Field Office to be debriefed.

Mason thanked the paramedic and made his way across the muddy lot. The sedan and the Suburban had been rented with fake driver's licenses and neither of the two cars that passed through their net had license plates or any identifiable features. He hoped the physical evidence would be a little more helpful.

A uniformed officer controlled access to the building with a digital clipboard. Mason signed in and followed the passage the CSRT had outlined where people could walk without contaminating the crime scene. There were only a few evidence specialists in their white jumpsuits on the first floor. He found more activity on the second floor, where the hallway was now awash with light. Looking through one of the massive holes in the wall, he saw a crew of criminalists photographing, videotaping, and collecting trace evidence from what had once served as an office. The walls were scored black. He smelled a petrochemical accelerant. Maybe a hint of something almost sweet. An iron ladder led upward into a black-rimmed hole in the ceiling, through which an intense light shined.

The nature of the trap finally struck him. This office was directly beneath the room made of plastic sheeting on the top floor.

There were even more people working on the third level. A scorched starburst covered the ground, at the center of which was what was left of the framework of the ruined structure. He saw the hole in the floor that had saved his life. Had he run in any other direction, he'd have been on his way to the morgue, too.

There was another smell up here, almost hidden beneath the scents of burned wood, consumed carbon, and chemicals. One he knew all too well. One that still haunted his dreams.

From where Mason stood, he could see five distinct bodies. Or at least what was left of them. They were skeletal and black, their arms curled to their chests like a dead bird's feet. Their mouths were wide open, as though screaming into the abyss that had opened before them. Whoever they were, he owed them a debt of gratitude. Had he not watched that droplet of condensation roll down the plastic to where one of them had fallen against the drop cloth, he might have been a step too slow.

A white-garbed investigator broke away from the others and walked toward him from across the room. The glare of the intense bulbs made his face shield appear to glow. He was mere feet away when Mason finally saw his face.

Todd Locker wore his greasy hair long, and small glasses were perched on the tip of his nose. It was the kind of eccentric look you'd expect from someone in his forties, but Mason couldn't imagine that Locker was even as old as he was. He was thin and effeminate, but had a deep, melodic voice that made even the description of the butchered remains in a quadruple homicide sound almost as though the victims had simply drifted off into a peaceful sleep. As the assistant director of the Rocky Mountain Forensics Laboratory, it was his job to coordinate the efforts of the evidence-collection teams with the various law-enforcement agencies on-site. When it came to the meticulous investigation of a crime scene, there was no one better than Locker. Unfortunately, talking to him was often an exercise in frustration. You never knew where he was going to start or end up. He tended to jump right into the middle of the conversation at a seemingly random point only he knew.

"Contractures," he said. Mason stared expectantly at him for several seconds before he finally proceeded. "The victims were dead before the fire consumed them."

"So you figure this was somebody attempting to kill two birds with one stone? Clean up his mess and take us out in the process?"

"You aren't listening. The dead guys have contractures. That means every muscle in their bodies tightened to such a degree that they essentially folded in upon themselves. Imagine every joint capable of bending doing so up to and then beyond its physical limits, like the way an insect shrivels under a magnifying glass."

"I know what contractures are, but I'm not sure I understand the implications."

"We have five bodies. Each of these five bodies has premortem contractures. That's not the kind of thing that happens when you get stabbed or shot or beaten to death. It's a specific physiological response elicited in five distinct individuals. A specific *autonomic* response, meaning some external stimulus acted upon their central nervous systems. That's not the kind of thing that can happen without some sort of pathological impetus."

"A biological agent," Mason said.

Something clenched inside him.

"There's absolutely no trace of whatever agent might have been used. We found the melted remains of what we believe to be some sort of aerial dispersion mechanism, but that's about it. And you smell that syrupy scent? My working hypothesis is that they spread the agent on some kind of atomically stable yet combustible liquid aromatic hydrocarbon. The GC–MS ought to be able to determine which one, but based on the way they sealed the chamber and maintained static airflow around the flame you described, I'm guessing the violent reaction to oxygen was designed to both consume and obliterate whatever traces might have otherwise existed. Contrary to outward appearances, this was a very sophisticated self-cleansing gas chamber. Considering this agent incapacitated the men inside before they could even rip through a single sheet of plastic, there's no way it had sufficient time to metabolize."

"What are you saying?"

"Look at the condition of the remains. Whatever killed them was undoubtedly incinerated with the outermost layers of tissue."

"So why would someone make sure we followed their trail only to have it end here?"

"Best of luck with that."

Locker offered a bashful grin and headed back into the destruction zone.

Mason was going to need a lot more than luck. He knew all about biological agents, hydrocarbons, and cooked meat. It had taken him all this time to even come this close to finding the people he suspected were ultimately behind the massacre at the stone quarry. Whether they had intended to kill him or merely send a message, their plan had achieved the opposite effect. He was more determined than ever to track them down.

13

"They knew I was getting close, Chris. They had that trap ready and waiting because they could feel me right on their tail. But they made one big mistake."

"What's that?"

"They missed."

Mason had known Special Agent in Charge Gabriel Christensen for almost three years, but he still hadn't quite figured out how to read him. Chris wasn't your typical government bureaucrat. He'd learned how to walk the fine line between taking care of his agents and playing the game of politics. That was to say he bowed to no one and was fair to a fault. Often brutally so. As they stood outside the back door of Club Five, bathed in the glow of the pulsing red and blue police lights, Mason could see the toll the job had taken on him. His silver hair was thinning on top and the lines around his eyes and mouth had deepened enough to fill with shadows. He still cut a formidable presence in his dark suit, despite the burden he bore on their behalf.

"I thought you were going to say their big mistake was killing four police officers." He didn't look at Mason when he spoke. He didn't have to. "How's the wife, Mason?"

The change of subject was so sudden, he couldn't formulate a reply.

"Don't think for a second that I don't know what this job can do to you," he said. "It gets under your skin, like an itch you can't scratch. It becomes all you can think about. Day and night. Until one morning you wake up and you've become someone even you don't recognize anymore. That's no way to live."

"You weren't there, Chris. You didn't have to watch Kane die. You don't know what it's like to see your partner consumed by flames every time you close your eyes."

"I've seen more good men killed than anyone should have to, but that doesn't mean I carry their weight lightly. You have to leave the job at the door or else you'll drive away your reasons for doing it in the first place. And then you're no use to anyone."

Christensen turned away from the crime scene and made his way through the police cordon. Mason lost him behind the throng of bystanders trying to get a peek past the uniformed officers who'd used their vehicles to seal off the alley. The club had cleared out the moment he and Trapp entered with an entourage of policemen. Now that the party people knew the drama wasn't for them, they'd regained their curiosity.

Christensen's words had more than stung; they'd been a warning on both a personal and a professional level. Mason had become his job. He lived it and breathed it and allowed it to consume him. Every waking moment was spent in the pursuit of the traffickers who thought they could flood this country with drugs, weapons, and even human beings.

America had galvanized behind the tragedy of 9/11 and launched a war against an entire nation for the actions of its extremist minority. All while civilians were butchered and beheaded in border towns, drugs flooded into the nation's school systems, and young people and innocents and law-enforcement personnel were killed by the tens of thousands every year. Why did the media turn one into a televised event and refuse to cover the other when narco-insurgents racked up body counts on American soil that rivaled any Al-Qaeda nutjob's wet dreams? The answer was both simple and infuriating.

Money.

It was more lucrative to wage a war than to win it.

But Mason had discovered there were worse things than drugs crossing the Mexican border. Far worse things. He couldn't simply stand by and let it happen. The consequences of doing so would be catastrophic. It terrified him to imagine what people like the man with the blue eyes and the Panama hat intended to do with the kind of biological agent he'd been experimenting with in the abandoned stone quarry. He wasn't so blind to the inner workings of his mind that he failed to recognize that he'd thrown himself into the war in the hopes of destroying one ghost and avenging another.

The thumping beat struck him from behind. His shadow stretched away from him across the muddy puddles on a mat of colored lights. And then the closing door sealed off the club once more. He turned to face Ramses, whose hands were cuffed behind his back. Trapp shoved him toward the alley by the back of his jacket.

"I take it things didn't go quite as planned?"

"Four officers were killed, Ramses."

"The glass is always half empty with you, isn't it? You should be thankful that the rest of you survived."

"Tell that to them," Mason said, and inclined his chin toward the gathering of uniformed officers just outside the police cordon.

"They don't look like they'd be overly receptive to my particular brand of positivity. I've got a hunch my dance card's going to be full for the rest of the night."

Mason stepped around Ramses and spoke so that only Trapp could hear him.

"I need you to take him in. Personally. Make sure he arrives in one piece."

"I told you, Mason. Donovan doesn't get a pass. I say we turn him over to the nearest uniform and wash our hands of him."

"You and I both know we were set up tonight. Just like my strike force last year in Arizona. If the two events are connected, as I suspect, Ramses is just about the only one who can help us connect the dots. We need him alive and in working order if we're going to get to the bottom of this."

"The DPD wants blood. I can't make any guarantees."

Mason glanced toward the officers, whose eyes bored straight through him and into Ramses. Rojas and Telford were among them, the black face paint smeared from their eyes and cheeks by tears. He could positively feel the rage radiating from them. Not that he blamed them. He would have felt the very same way in their position, but if he allowed them to take Ramses in, his old friend would never make it to the precinct.

"Do this for me, okay?" Mason looked his partner in the eyes until Trapp grudgingly nodded. "Thank you."

"Don't thank me. If you're wrong about Donovan, I'll feed him to those sharks myself."

Mason nodded and approached Ramses.

"I know you stuck your neck out for me," he said.

"Remind me not to do it again." Ramses was surprisingly calm for someone about to be subjected to what promised to be a brutal interrogation. "Look, Mace. My attorney's waiting for me at the station. What do you say we get this show on the road so I can be home before sunrise?"

"This isn't going to be fun for you."

"I've survived worse." The way Ramses said it made Mason wonder what could have been traumatic enough to scar his old friend like that, but he realized he was probably better off not knowing. "Just do me a solid, okay? Don't take me in like this. I have my reputation to think about."

"What do you mean?" Mason asked.

"I can't have anyone thinking I'm getting cozy with the feds."

"Are you sure?"

Ramses nodded and visibly prepared himself.

Mason punched him squarely in the jaw.

Cheers erupted from the gathering of policemen.

Ramses dropped to one knee and let his head hang. He spat blood onto the concrete, then wiped his chin on his shoulder and stood up again.

"Anyone ever tell you that you hit like a girl?"

Trapp shoved him past Mason, toward where another agent was waiting to manhandle him into the rear seat of an unmarked FBI Crown Victoria. Mason glanced back at the sound of the closing car door and caught one last glimpse of Ramses' face before he vanished in a blur of lights and sirens.

14

Mason went straight up to his den the moment he got home. As he placed a red thumbtack where the old airport had once been and connected it to the others with yarn, his frustration finally caught up with him. He wanted to tear everything from the walls, to lash out at something, anything. To feel, even momentarily, as though he actually had control over something in his life.

Instead, he simply stood in the middle of the room and let the light of the moon wash over him through the gap between the curtains.

"I didn't hear you come in," Angie said from the doorway behind him.

"I was trying not to wake you."

"I waited up as long as I could. You should have called."

Mason couldn't bring himself to look at her. He didn't want her to see him like this.

"There's something I need to talk to you about. Something important."

"Can it wait until the morning, Angie? It's been a rough night."

She drew a breath, as though she were about to speak. He prepared for the onslaught to commence. Instead, all he heard was the sound of her footsteps heading back down the hallway to their bedroom, which was a thousand times worse. She closed the door behind her with a soft click, and for the first time in his life, he felt utterly alone.

15

Mason woke up on the floor with a red line of sunlight bisecting his face. Angie was already gone. She'd left a note for him at his place at the table, beside an empty bowl and a box of cereal. He pretended not to see it. The message was clear, though. *We need to talk tonight. Please.* There was nothing he wanted to do less, but it was going to happen at some point, whether he liked it or not. Everything that was wrong between them was his fault and he knew it. He loved his wife and would do anything in the world for her, except for the one thing she would undoubtedly ask him to do.

He called his voice mail on his way to work. There were four messages. The first was from his father and it had been left two days ago. Had it really been that long since he'd last checked? He simply wasn't in the mood for drama this morning, so he skipped it without listening. The second was from his wife at seven last night. All she said was that she hoped he was coming home soon, because she really needed to talk to him. He deleted it and moved on. The next call had come from his home number at just after ten, but the message consisted of nothing more than the click of the phone disconnecting. He didn't recognize the number of the fourth caller. The message had come in just under an hour ago, presumably while he was in the shower. At first he heard nothing and almost deleted it. Then came the sound of clicking heels. And a voice he would have recognized anywhere.

"I need a room."

The ground fell out from beneath him.

Mason pulled to the side of the road and pressed his hand over his opposite ear to better concentrate on the message. His pulse was thundering so loudly that he couldn't decipher the reply of a deep voice he hadn't heard before.

"Just one night."

Another mumbled reply.

"Cash."

There was a clunking sound and a metallic clatter. A lockbox opening.

A muffled crumpling sound as the caller adjusted his grip on the cell phone.

A dark finger of black smoke rose into the sky over the tops of the elm trees across the street. He watched it diffuse into the slate gray sky over the mountains as he strained to hear.

A scraping sound. A wooden stool on tile? Scooting closer. He could hear the deep voice humming.

The skittering sound of a key sliding across a countertop.

"Room's around back. Corner suite. Park right in front of the door and no one will be able to see your car from the road."

Another scraping sound as Angie snatched the key. He imagined her long nails, possibly the diamond of her engagement ring, raking the counter.

"No interruptions," his wife said.

"You got it, Miss . . ." The clatter of a clipboard. ". . . Smith."

The clacking of heels.

"Excuse me." Angie's voice was louder, closer to the microphone.

Another crumpling sound.

Then a click.

Mason felt like he'd been kicked in the stomach. His pale face reflected from the inside of the driver's side window against a sky now roiling with smoke.

"If you would like to replay this message," a digitized female voice said, "please press . . ."

He didn't know what to do. Where to go. His only thought was to drive. He pulled into traffic and heard the squeal of brakes. A silver sedan flashed across his rearview mirror. He didn't even slow down.

16

By the time Mason drove into the lot of the field office—a modern four-story building composed of a checkerboard pattern of mismatched bomb- and bulletproof glass panels—he'd at least recovered a small measure of functionality. He redialed the number that had left the message, only to be redirected to a recording that the subscriber was either out of range or had turned off his or her phone. He debated calling his wife, but the last thing he wanted was the image his mind conjured with the thought of Angie answering her phone and talking to him while another man gripped her by the hips.

There's something I need to talk to you about. Something important.

He turned on his scanner and dialed in a police band to call in a reverse listing on the phone number, only to find the channel buzzing with activity. Officers and ambulances responding to the fire that was now a dirty black smear over the Rockies. He was just about to turn to a different frequency when he heard two words that cut through the clutter in his brain.

". . . room nine . . ."

He tried to focus on the voices.

". . . responding. We got flames pouring out the roof of the whole west wing. . . ."

". . . can't tell how many people are in there. . . ."

". . . see through all the smoke!"

". . . Code Three to four eight one six Federal. That's the Peak View. . . ."

"Oh God."

Mason sped out of the parking lot and across town as fast as he could, all the while watching the smoky horizon drawing closer by the second. He drove on instinct alone. His mind couldn't rationalize the flood of thoughts, let alone latch onto any one in particular. All he knew was he needed to get there.

And that he was already too late.

I need a room.

He hit I-70 and rocketed toward the mountains, weaving through traffic to the tune of blaring horns and screeching brakes.

Just one night.

Took the Federal off-ramp so fast he nearly rolled his Grand Cherokee. Turned south and knifed through oncoming traffic.

Cash.

A steep hill rose ahead of him, at the bottom of which a thin stream flowed through a wide gravel bed littered with trash. He blew across it and ascended into the smoke. On the left, a whitewashed motel advertising hourly rates on a flickering neon sign, an adult bookstore with a live peep show, and trailer homes scattered uphill through the deciduous trees. On the right, fireworks warehouses that catered to out-of-state clientele, a Mexican market with bars on the windows. And set off behind them, beneath a tall sign with a stylized silhouette of a mountain range, was the source of the ink-black smoke and the flames flickering through the branches of the cottonwoods.

An officer had pulled his cruiser sideways across the entrance to the motel lot to bar access and stood beside it directing traffic. Mason drove straight up over the curb, crossed the parking lot of the market, and sped down the cracked asphalt drive into the trees.

No interruptions.

Two more cruisers blocked the road. He was out of his car and running before he even knew he was going to. He charged through a mist of ash and water. A crowd had gathered near the office of the adobe motel. It was an L-shaped unit that stretched westward and away from him, toward where the fire trucks were parked. The hillside fell away sharply on the other side of the building, where the trees grew in one impenetrable snarl all the way down to the invisible stream. Uniformed officers simultaneously questioned potential witnesses and tried to maintain something resembling a perimeter.

Mason shoved through the gathering and nearly bowled over an officer as he sprinted past the office door, through the breezeway, and rounded the back side. A concrete stairway led down to a dry pool set into the hillside. The doors to his left started with number sixteen and diminished as he ran. There were two ambulances in the lot west of the pool, on the other side of a Dumpster that looked like it hadn't been emptied in months, their twirling lights staining the smoke. He saw the shapes of two other vehicles behind them, little more than shadows through the smoke. He was coughing so hard, he had to pull his shirt up over his mouth and nose. The streams from the fire hoses positively turned the sky to water above him. Smoke boiled through the roof of room number eleven; flames flickered behind the brown curtains. The front wall of unit ten was black. The door opened upon a room churning with smoke and fire. Flames had expanded the doorway to room number nine. Its half-consumed door was ten feet away on the short staircase leading down to the parking lot. The shattered glass from the window glittered on the ground, where it swirled with the black soot in the foamy water.

Mason stopped before what was left of the front wall of the room, water pouring down on him, and stared at his soaked feet for a long moment before he finally summoned the courage to look inside.

The world slowed around him.

He heard shouting, as though from a great distance.

Smoke gusted across the room on sheets of water propelled by the high-pressure hoses. Through the tempest he saw a dresser turned to charcoal, an old TV with a shattered tube, the blackened door to the bathroom. And to the right, in the center of the room, what was left of a king-size bed. All that remained of the painting hanging on the scorched wall above it was a single tattered corner where roses still bloomed. And beneath the bloodred flowers, tangled on top of the bed, were two blackened corpses, their flesh cooked to their bones. Everything that could burn was already gone. Two human beings reduced to black shapes with their mouths wide open, lying on top of each other in a position that left little room for interpretation.

Someone grabbed him from behind. The next thing he knew, he was pinned under a man's weight while his arms were twisted behind his back. He drew in a breath that came with a mouthful of filthy water. Gagged. The man shouted down at him, but Mason was oblivious to the words. All of his attention was focused on the Lexus CT 200h hybrid in the parking lot. Matador red mica. It was covered with soot and ash, but there was no mistaking it. He parked his car beside it in his garage every night.

Something broke inside of him and he shouted in anguish.

He prayed for the water to rise over his face and usher him into the darkness.

17

The last time Mason had seen Blaine Martin—alive, anyway—he was guiding Angie down the hallway with his hand on her lower back and his lips to her ear. Had he stepped up right then and there, his wife would still be alive. He hadn't recognized the threat, or maybe he'd simply chosen not to. He'd just been so certain that he and Angie would be able to work out their problems. Never once had he so much as considered the idea of her straying, but he had to accept his own culpability. He found it easy to hate the special prosecutor, even easier to hate himself. After all, Martin was the monster of his own creation.

He was one of those guys who radiated confidence from his veneers to his just-so tan to his every-hair-in-place style. In so many ways, he was both like Mason and not. He was the Mason of a different time line, one in which he finished law school instead of dropping out to join the FBI. The Mason who opted for the BMW over the Grand Cherokee. The Mason who wore Brooks Brothers suits rather than jeans and a T-shirt. And apparently the Mason his wife had wished he could have been. And for the life of him, he couldn't fault her for it. He brought nothing but grief to those who loved him, and over the past few years he had spent nearly as much time graveside as Death himself.

He watched Martin's funeral from a distance, concealed behind the branches of a weeping willow. He recognized a handful of people, most of whom he'd met through his wife, and watched without feeling anything as Martin's parents and a woman in her mid-thirties openly grieved. Had anyone asked him why he was there, he wouldn't have been able to come up with a single reason. Maybe a part of him wanted to see the kind of world into which his wife had been lured, a world in which she would ultimately have been safe from the demons that walked in his shadow.

By the time Martin's parents said their good-byes and the woman Mason assumed was his wife had fallen to her knees beside the hole, he felt like a voyeur.

His wife's funeral was a different story. He'd felt the weight of every single pair of eyes of those in attendance boring through him. No one knew what to say to him, which was fine, considering he wouldn't have known how to respond. Everyone was well aware of how she'd died. Despite his alibi, he could see in their eyes that they weren't entirely convinced he hadn't been party to her death. After all, were their roles reversed, each and every one of them knew they'd at least contemplate the notion of exacting a measure of revenge. What it all came down to was that he had turned into an object of pity in their eyes, a man who hadn't been husband enough for his wife or good enough at his job to keep her out of harm's reach. To keep her alive. He was a failure on every level. And it was human nature to treat failure like a disease.

Angie's mother, who'd moved to an estate in Palm Springs several years prior as something of a trial separation, had made an effort to be cordial, but her father hadn't even been able to look at him. He'd simply stared at the closed casket and then at her grave with an almost impassive expression on his face, as though his inner being had checked out and left only his physical vessel in attendance. The one time Mason met his stare, it was as though his father-in-law didn't even see him, which he considered a blessing. He was sorry the man had lost his daughter, but he wasn't sure if he could convey that without allowing a hint of anger to enter his voice. It wasn't like they'd ever been especially close, anyway.

Paul Thornton wasn't the kind of man who went out of his way to welcome a guy into the fold. He was the patriarch of the Thornton family empire and still managed the day-to-day operations and the corporate assets, despite rapidly approaching the age when men of his stature started looking forward to honing their golf swings and, in his case, to Angie's older brother Victor taking the reins. Paul's grandfather, Wesley Thornton, had grown the business from the chief supplier of beef in the state to one of the three largest meat producers in the country, mainly by ruining the competition, seizing their land, and paying the right people to be looking the other way while he did so.

His son and Angie's grandfather, Francis "Frank" Thornton, had diversified into corn, wheat, and various grains and turned a multimillion-dollar cattle ranch into a billion-dollar agricultural empire. While Frank still dabbled in the business from the comfort of his motorized wheelchair, Paul had been CEO of AgrAmerica and the public figurehead since long before Mason even met him. Considering the levels of success his predecessors had achieved, there seemed to be little more he could do than maintain the status quo, but Paul wasn't the kind to just sit on his inheritance. He gambled—and gambled in a huge way—on genetically engineered crops and led the charge in pioneering the use of hormones and steroids in livestock.

A part of him had always thought that Angie would eventually bring her financial acumen back to the family business. More than that, though, he was proud of his daughter for going her own way and not simply accepting the crown. Probably the only reason he'd allowed Mason to marry his daughter, at least in his own mind, was because Mason came from enough money that Paul could be confident he wasn't after his. Plus, Mason's relationship with Angie could potentially be used to curry favor with his father, a United States senator, who sat on any number of agricultural committees and chaired the U.S. Senate Committee on Commerce, Science, and Transportation.

Before Paul headed back to his waiting limousine, he'd shaken Mason's hand, opened his mouth as though about to say something, then simply nodded and walked away.

Mason's own father, the esteemed J. R. Mason, had stood beside him through the whole process. He'd taken care all the arrangements for him. Or, more likely, had one of his staffers do so for him. Either way, Mason appreciated it. His old man had even returned from Washington for the entire week, which might not have sounded like much, but for his father, it was a grand gesture of support. He wasn't one of those touchy-feely guys who did things like express his emotions, participate in any kind of physical displays of affection, or acknowledge the existence of anyone or anything outside himself, for that matter, but he'd been there when Mason needed him and allowed him plenty of space when he didn't, for which he was grateful.

All he'd really needed was his father's presence beside him. In the pew at the church, at the graveside, and in the limo on the way home. They both knew what his father thought about the choices he'd made in life. The great and mighty J. R. Mason made no secret of his disappointment in the path his son had chosen, a different path from the one he and his father—and even his before that—had walked. A different path from the one he had plotted out for Mason.

18

Mason's father stopped by his house on the way to the airport. Mason had been sitting on the front porch with a beer in his hand, staring blankly across the street at the park, when the sleek black Town Car passed across his field of vision. The dark sky had opened and released a torrent that beat a timpani on the overhang above him and flooded the gutters. The rain would probably turn to snow before the storm was through.

The driver climbed out, opened an umbrella and then the door for his father, and walked him up to the porch, where he left him without a word and returned to the car.

The senator sat down beside him and opened one of the beers from the six-pack behind him. They sat without speaking for the longest time, listening to the thunder and watching the lightning crackle though the clouds.

"Do you remember when your mother died?" he finally asked.

"Not the kind of thing a kid is likely to forget."

"You know what I mean."

Mason set aside his beer. Talking about his mother with a bottle in his hand didn't seem right.

"I thought the sun would never rise again," his father said. "For a long time, it didn't. Not that I could see anyway. I was thirty-eight years old and had a twelve-year-old son. My job didn't have the same meaning anymore. Nothing in my life did, for that matter. I reached a point where I needed to make a choice. I could either wallow in self-pity or grab life by the reins and take charge of my destiny."

"I'm not you, Dad."

"Doesn't change the fact that you're a Mason. Yours was never meant to be a common destiny, son."

Mason shook his head. Classic J. R. Mason pep talk. From the man whose grand destiny consisted of driving his wife to drink herself into the grave and shipping his son off to private school so he could embark upon a quest to rule the country.

Before he entered the political arena and orchestrated his meteoric rise to prominence in the Senate, he was the kind of lawyer who approached every case as though he were going into battle. Defeat was an unacceptable outcome. Even winning, it seemed, was often not enough. He needed to crush his opponent, to grind him beneath his heel.

As far as prosecutors went, he'd been in a class all his own. His record pretty much guaranteed him the district attorney's office. It also didn't hurt that he was the son of James Richmond Mason Jr., whose seat on the U.S. Supreme Court had never really been contested and who had served as chief justice nearly since the moment he first sat behind the bench. As his father, the first James Richmond Mason, had before him.

Mason's father used to say that you could learn more about human nature during a single day in a courtroom than from any number of textbooks. He said people only lie when they're talking, but always tell the truth when they shut their mouths. So Mason had taken it upon himself from an early age to learn how to read their tells.

Funny, he used those skills every day in his profession—and he was exceptionally good at utilizing them—but he'd been blind to what was going on with his own wife.

"Thanks for being here, Dad."

His father nodded and clapped him on the knee. The expression on his old man's face was impossible to read, as usual. He stood and stared out through the rain toward the distant lake. He looked both regal and old in a way Mason never imagined he would be able to. His father's silver hair was impeccable, his eyebrows tweezed to perfection, and his profile was the kind that would one day look good on a coin or a bill, if he had his way. And Mason had no reason to doubt that he would.

"What are you going to do from here?"

His father spoke with his back to him, as though he either already knew the answer or it was of no real consequence.

"I'm going to grieve for my wife."

He signaled to his driver, who scurried back up the walk with the umbrella and guided him back to the Lincoln.

19

According to the Kübler-Ross stages of grief, Mason was stuck in denial. Not the denial of his wife's death—he'd seen incontrovertible proof of that with his own eyes—but of her infidelity. Granted, one could make a strong case that he'd seen incontrovertible proof of that, as well, but he felt as though he would have known if she had reached the point of seeking physical consolation in the arms of someone else. Maybe *known* was the wrong word. Sensed. He should have felt it, something intangible, something in her voice or her mannerisms.

But he hadn't.

Lord knows he'd pushed her away, but Angie had never been one to hide from her problems. Neither of them was especially good at communicating their feelings. They'd both been raised in homes where the outward expression of emotions was viewed as an exploitable sign of weakness, or, at best, an indulgence granted to children of a certain age. Surely she would have told him when she reached the point of cheating. Whatever might have transpired between them, she was his wife, and he believed in his heart that they would have overcome their problems if they'd been given more time.

He tried to think of the last words she had said to him. Instead, all he heard was the determination in her voice when she'd said, "No interruptions."

At least he could count on his partner. Trapp not only took a huge risk slipping him files related to the fire at the motel, but also offered to back him up during a meeting he'd called with Christensen, who'd expressly prohibited him from participating in any portion of the investigation, even though the nature of the murders fell squarely in line with the MO of the perpetrators he'd been tracking. Call it a gut instinct or even wishful thinking, but the pieces fit. The monsters who had killed Kane and deliberately infected the immigrants he'd seen hanging from chains had an affinity for fire and knew how to cover their tracks, as they'd demonstrated time and time again, most recently in the building by the old airport.

The problem was, he was the only one approaching the deaths of his wife and her presumed lover as murders. Of course, he was also the only one who'd heard the message on his voice mail. Nothing good could come from releasing it, though, especially considering it supported the official narrative. He needed to find whoever had recorded the conversation and figure out why. And to do so, he needed his special agent in charge's blessing to formally work the investigation.

Unfortunately, Chris had a pretty good idea why he'd called the meeting and was ready and waiting the moment he and Trapp walked through his office door.

"You stay away from it," he said. "Anything you do will only compromise the investigation."

"What investigation?" Mason asked. "As far as I can tell, no one's doing a damn thing."

"How would you know?"

Mason realized his mistake too late.

Chris tugged his fingers through his hair and glared at Trapp for several seconds before sitting in the chair behind his desk. He gestured for them to take seats across from him. Mason plopped down into the proffered chair and watched a flock of geese cut across the gray sky over his boss's shoulder.

"Look, Chris, I—" Trapp began.

"You and I will talk later," Chris said, and turned to Mason. "I won't pretend to know what you're going through. I don't even want to imagine it."

"If you're trying to make me feel better, you're not doing a very good job."

"It's not my job to make you feel anything. My job is to give you a kick in the ass when you need it. And right now it's taking what little patience I have left not to do just that."

"You know as well as I do that something's not right here."

"Know? What I *know* is that I have a stack of reports written by everyone from the ME to the fire inspector to half a dozen different officers at the DPD that tell a different story."

Mason knew exactly what they all said. He'd been relegated to reading reports written by others, reports that he shouldn't even have. The police interviews had been brief and superficial and riddled with innuendo. The manager of the Peak View Inn had remembered Angie, but he'd claimed not to have seen anyone else enter her room. None of the witnesses questioned had noticed anything out of the ordinary, at least not until they heard the explosion, which the fire inspector had ruled to be accidental, a consequence of faulty wiring and a pinhole leak in the radiator. The combination had blown out the front wall and dropped the flaming roof onto the foot of the bed.

Locker had even gone out of his way to personally deliver the news that the medical examiner had formally filed the cause of death as asphyxiation, which meant that Angie had been alive when the room filled with smoke. Mason had asked if that precluded some other form of incapacitation. The expression on Locker's face had been one of sympathy as he awkwardly took his leave. It was at that moment Mason realized the people in his life were merely humoring a man they believed was trying to absolve himself of the guilt of sending his wife to her grave.

"They're wrong," Mason said.

"I'll let you be the one to tell our experts they don't know what they're doing."

"Not their observations. Their conclusions. They're missing the bigger picture."

"And what is that?"

"That this case is related to both what happened out by the old airport and down in Arizona last year."

"So show me your proof and I'll lead the investigation myself."

"In all three instances, an explosion was used to erase the physical evidence."

"Did they use the same explosive devices? The same detonators?"

"No, but—"

"What about the crimes themselves? What's the relationship between them?"

"I'm still working on—"

"So what you have is a theory uncorroborated by anything resembling actual evidence."

Mason stood and planted his hands squarely on Christensen's desk. "Damn it, Chris! They killed my wife!"

Christensen raised his eyebrows and cocked his head.

Mason closed his eyes, blew out a long, deflating breath, and slumped back into his chair.

"Give us the room," Chris said.

Trapp glanced at Mason from the corner of his eye. They both knew how badly he'd screwed up. Christensen had baited him and he'd stuck his head right into the snare. Trapp rose without a word and disappeared with the soft click of the door closing behind him.

Chris sighed, swiveled his chair, and looked out the window. When he turned around again, his expression had softened.

"Now's an emotional time for you. I get that. Every day I have to focus all my energy on distancing myself from the realities of this job, but that doesn't mean I don't have sympathy for what you're going through."

"I know how I must sound—believe me—but you know me. You know how I work. Tell me you have another agent with better instincts."

"That's not the point."

"That's precisely the point. Right now every fiber of my being is telling me that the same people who killed Kane and the SWAT guys out at the old airport are responsible for my wife's murder."

Christensen looked Mason squarely in the eyes. His lips writhed over his teeth.

"I want you to go home," Chris said.

"Chris—"

He held up his hand to silence any dissent.

"Take some time to grieve. Come back Monday morning. We'll sit down and talk. See if things still look the same after you've had time to process everything."

"And if they do?"

"Monday, Mason. Until then—like I said—leave this alone."

Chris abruptly returned to his work and Mason recognized the conversation was over. While it hadn't gone as well as he'd hoped, it hadn't gone as poorly as it could have, either. He didn't look forward to going back home, but maybe if he stared at the maps in his den long enough, he might be able to find the proof he needed to convince his SAC that there was a connection between the events in Arizona, at the airport administration building, and at the motel, which resulted in the death of his wife. And he couldn't shake the feeling that he was running out of time to do so.

The drive home passed in a blur. He was already mentally examining every facet of his proposed ninth trafficking organization when he pulled into his driveway, killed the engine, and bounded up to the porch.

He threw open the front door and stepped into the foyer.

Caught a flash of yellow in his peripheral vision, streaking toward his right foot.

It was a piece of paper, a single sheet torn from the Yellow Pages of a phone book. Folded, as though it had been wedged into the crack of his front door. He picked it up and opened it.

Nine words had been written on it in pen with an unsteady hand.

Big, bold words scribbled across columns of names and advertisements, from Hospital Equipment and Supplies through Housecleaning Services.

IT WAS NOT AN ACCIDENT.
I NEED YOUR HELP.

PART II

And what the dead had no speech for, when living,
They can tell you, being dead: the communication
Of the dead is tongued with fire beyond the language
  of the living.

—T. S. Eliot, "Little Gidding" (1942)

20

Denver, Colorado

NOVEMBER 12

Mason called in a favor to get the letter fingerprinted and run through the NGI—Next Generation Identification—system, a national database that contained biometrics, including fingerprints and facial recognition, for more than 100 million people. He was disappointed, but not entirely surprised, when no match was found. All it meant was that he was going to have to dig deeper into his bag of investigative tricks.

The failure to find a match wasn't the end of the world, either. The database included every civil and government employee, all military personnel, and every person who'd ever been arrested. Much of the investigative process involved the elimination of potential suspects, and in one fell swoop, he'd cleared a full third of the population. That left a mere 200 million, which was a much more manageable number.

The problem now was that unless he got lucky and stumbled into whoever had left the note, he was going to have to wait for further communication. And waiting was something he was not prepared to do. He needed to maintain what little momentum he had going, which meant that, despite the glaring lack of evidence, he needed to revisit the case files.

Any crime essentially boiled down to three critical factors: means, motive, and opportunity. Means could vary and opportunities could be manufactured. Motive was the key. And motivation was a constant. The way he saw it, everything came back to whoever was attempting to smuggle the virus into the country and their ultimate goal, which he had to believe was weaponization. Homeland might have been convinced that the threat had been eliminated, but if he was right, the motive behind the ambush in Arizona was also the same as it was in the airport administration building and, later, at the motel where his wife was killed. He had to consider himself coincidental to the first case, and probably even the second, but he couldn't rule out the personal nature of the third.

It was a distinct possibility that he'd gotten too close and his adversaries had lashed out at him by hitting him where he was most vulnerable. That logic had a gaping hole right in the middle of it, though. If they could find his wife, then they could easily locate his house, and most nights he was inside, fast asleep and unprepared to defend himself. And why call to let him hear his wife registering for a hotel room? Whoever had left that message wanted him to believe that his wife had gone to that motel with only one intention, and one that could be corroborated by the physical evidence after the fire. So why go to that extreme unless the person wanted to leave no doubt about the story he or she was selling? As far as he could see, that was the weakest link in the chain and the one he most needed to exploit.

Mason used a reverse phone number lookup site to find out the cell phone's service carrier. This, in turn, provided him with its registered serial number, which could be traced through the manufacturer to a Radio Shack in Santa Fe, New Mexico. Store records confirmed that it had been paid for in cash and not activated until three months later. Video surveillance was limited and the digital files were purged every other week. The SIM card had been removed and undoubtedly destroyed immediately after the call was placed.

The way he saw it, that left two potential approaches: the direct and the circuitous routes. The direct meant that he was going to need to return to the motel in order to actually investigate the scene. If that turned up nothing, then the circuitous meant he was either going to have to sell a judge on a subpoena there was no way in hell he'd grant, or get in touch with an old friend he hadn't seen in years.

Whatever the case, at least he had something vaguely resembling a plan.

The Peak View Inn still looked a lot like it had the last time he was there, only not actively burning. Although that might have been an improvement. The parking lot was still discolored and the building itself had taken on an ash gray cast. The weeds and bushes overgrowing the sidewalk were brown and wilted. There were only two cars in the lot, one of which presumably belonged to whoever was working the desk. According to the police report, the man who had registered his wife was the thirty-six-year-old manager, Terrence Everett.

Mason parked and stared to the west. Scaffolding had been erected around the end of the wing. Sections where the walls had been removed were covered with plastic sheeting. Construction scraps littered the walkway, which was pretty much covered with cement dust. Considering it was a Sunday, he wasn't surprised to see construction had come to a standstill.

He walked through the breezeway beside the office and glanced around the side and past the empty pool toward the rear parking lot. Always best to make sure you weren't going to get an unexpected surprise when you were dealing with people who dealt in indiscretion. A mess of broken CDs glittered on the ground around the overflowing Dumpster, beyond which he saw a single car, an older-model sedan. It was plastered with soot and ash, clotted and streaked by the recent rain, to such a degree that he wasn't entirely sure what make, model, or color it was. It was parked in the same spot where his wife's Lexus had been.

The hinges squealed when he opened the front door and entered the office for the first time. He took a quick mental snapshot. To his right, a rack brimming with brochures for local attractions, the top quarter of each dusty and sun-bleached. Past them, a unisex bathroom with a thin wooden door that didn't fit quite right in the frame. To his left, a bulletin board covered with thumbtacks and photocopies, most of which offered services running the gamut from private dancing and massage to outright prostitution. The registration desk directly ahead of him spanned the entire width of the office. A section to the right was hinged to swing outward. He guessed it was bolted from the inside. There was a clipboard beneath a handwritten sign that read DON'T STEAL THE PEN. He rang the bell beside it.

A man emerged from the door behind the desk. He was stumpy and bald and had prison green tattoos slithering up over his jawline from his fat neck. Glancing over his shoulder, Mason could see a hazy room with nicotine yellow cinder-block walls and a sofa bed. The man had tiny, alert eyes that quickly assessed him and sought the only exit, which was behind Mason. His thoughts played out on his face. He was willing to play the odds that he could get past Mason if he had absolutely no other choice. Without a doubt, this was a man who'd spent much of his life in a cage.

"You got to sign in if you want a room." He spoke with a slight lisp, as his teeth had rotted to brown nubs.

"There's no pen."

"Damn it."

He grumbled something under his breath and ducked back into the rear room.

Mason figured his wife had walked directly to the counter, just as he had. The person who had left the message on his voice mail had been standing with his back to her, perusing the brochures. Or maybe the bulletin board. Mason glanced up to his left and then to his right, then back to eye level when the man returned and tossed onto the counter a ten-cent Bic he'd taped to a plastic spoon. Mason read through the list of names scrawled on the ledger. He didn't imagine any of them were real.

"You signing in or what?"

"What happened to the cameras?"

"What cameras? I don't know what the hell—"

"The one that was mounted right up there." Mason pointed at the ceiling above him and to his right, where one would have been positioned to view the safe he assumed was under the counter by the man's knees and the registrants, if they were close enough to the counter. He turned and gestured toward a spot diagonally across the room, above the entrance. "And the other one that was over there."

There were circular holes in the water-stained acoustic tiles, through which the cords had once passed, and a triangular discoloration where the bases of the cameras had been mounted with three small screws.

"Look, man. I don't need no trouble."

"Then tell me where they are and show me where you keep the footage."

"I don't know about no cameras. My old lady's cousin owns this place. He needed someone to hang out back here and check people in from time to time. That's all. He pays me cash and I hardly got to lift a finger."

"You didn't answer my question."

"What do you want from me, man? There wasn't no cameras when I got here."

"And when was that?"

"Week ago Monday."

"What happened to the guy who was here before you?"

"I don't know. Probably flaked after the fire. I mean, he was here when them people got kilt." He looked both ways, then leaned across the counter and whispered, "You can still smell it back there."

He stepped back and nodded sagely. Mason felt his face fill with blood. The man backed up and raised his hands to his sides.

"Listen. I don't got nothing to hide. You want to come back here and check it out, you go right ahead. My PO don't got to know nothing about this, does he?"

"You let anyone who walks in off the street back in the office?"

"You kidding me? Half the people come in here I don't even want to be in the same room with. I don't got no beef with no cops, neither. I've been in enough trouble to last ten lifetimes."

"You think I'm a cop?"

"Don't no one come into a place like this who isn't looking to either get some action or bust someone for doing so."

He must have sensed he'd misspoken. He opened the hatch without a word, led Mason into the back, and left him alone in the room. It smelled of body odor, sour cigarette smoke, and alcohol. He found where the cords had been run down through the ceiling from the other side of the wall and the empty shelf where the recorder had been. There were no tapes or DVDs or digital storage devices of any kind.

Mason found the desk guy smoking out front as he came out. He left him with his card and instructions to call should he hear anything about where Everett might have gone. Looking in his rearview mirror, he saw the man watching him all the way out of the parking lot.

Maybe that hadn't been as productive as Mason had hoped, but he'd learned one very important detail: Terrence Everett hadn't run off on his own. Whatever those cameras recorded had been worth killing him to collect.

21

The cadaver dogs sniffed out Everett's body beneath the freshly poured foundation in the room where Angie died. By the time the CSRT chiseled away the concrete far enough to get a good look at his body, the sun had already set. Lights on tripods ringed the oblong hole, at the bottom of which lay what could only loosely be considered a human being. The flesh had pretty well begun to decompose, however slowly, thanks to the lack of oxygen, and sagged from the bony framework. Everett's thick beard and long hair made him look almost simian. There was a sharply demarcated ligature line across his neck. No secondary indications of a struggle. It had been a professional job—quick, decisive, and perfectly executed. Someone had simply come up behind him, wrapped a wire cord around his neck, and strangled him in the most dispassionate manner possible. The level of putrefaction and the lack of anterior hypostasis—the settling of blood after the heart stops beating— suggested he'd been thrown down there and covered with concrete immediately after his death. If the new desk guy, a relatively harmless ex-con named Vince Cobb, who'd served time for grand theft auto and welfare fraud, was right about the date Everett had abandoned his job, that meant they were looking at sometime between Saturday night and midmorning Sunday, at the latest. The conspicuous gap in the registration log all but confirmed it.

Mason stared down at what was left of Everett under the harsh glare, listening to the plastic drop cloth snap on the wind. His rap sheet was unimpressive as far as both criminals and sleazy motel managers went. He'd done a couple of stints in Cañon City for possession with intent to distribute and aggravated assault, but the rest of the offenses were small potatoes—petty larceny, criminal menacing—and there'd been nothing within the last three years. That meant he was smarter than your average recidivist. Mason hoped prison had taught him a lesson or two about paranoia, as well.

He shoved through the plastic and walked out into the night. I-70 was a long white line of streetlights through the swaying branches. Beyond it, the night had just begun to come to life on Federal. Neon Day-Glo colors lit up the facades of the strip clubs, where the parking lots around back were always full, even on a Sunday night.

Mason had called his partner as soon as he left the motel to let him know where he was and what he was doing. As he was expressly forbidden from working on this case, he needed someone else—someone he trusted—to take charge. He'd put Trapp in an awkward position and they both knew it. And if he caught the kind of flack Mason anticipated, he wasn't inclined to think his partner would be doing him any other favors for the foreseeable future. In fact, Trapp had been doing his best to be anywhere Mason wasn't since the CSRT arrived.

The signs had all been there. He just hadn't recognized them until he saw the holes where the security cameras had been mounted. The rapid response of the insurance company and the speed with which they'd gotten a construction crew on-site should have tipped him off from the start. And there was no reason at all for the cement dust, since they shouldn't have needed to replace any portion of the foundation. The ash and soot on the car in the back lot meant it had to have been there during the fire, but it sure as hell hadn't been parked in that spot. He hoped the mess of broken DVDs and jewel cases in and around the Dumpster meant what he thought it did. It was too sloppy for the rest of the cover-up. He was banking on Everett's having figured out the implications of the security recording and quickly trying to make it look as though there was no surveillance by removing the system and throwing away the other recordings. He was also counting on Everett to have learned enough from his prison experience to have made a copy of the original disc and stashed it somewhere as a bargaining chip.

Unfortunately for him, there had been no bargaining.

The owner of the motel's name was Ralph Schaub, and he was

waiting in the office when Mason walked through the door. He was a large man in a custom-tailored suit, the kind that shimmered under the light when he moved. He wore large gold rings and had a pencil-thin mustache that looked like it'd been drawn onto his upper lip. His black hair was slicked back from a forehead that bloomed with perspiration.

Schaub looked up, and Mason read the truth in his expression.

"Where's your studio, Ralph?"

His eyes widened, his mouth parted, and Mason knew he had him dead to rights. He'd done his homework while the CSRT had been jack-hammering. In addition to the Peak View Inn and the Riverside Inn down the street, Schaub also owned an adult bookstore, a strip club called Derriere's, and a production company named Voyeur Videos, which distributed hack-job DVDs and ran a subscription-based website with live cams. The majority of his titles fell in the amateur category, and his site featured sporadic and unannounced live feeds. You didn't have to be a brain surgeon to guess where they'd been filmed.

"I'm sorry?" Schaub swallowed hard. Whatever was in there seemed to get stuck where the collar of his shirt bit into his gelatinous neck. "I'm not entirely sure what you mean by . . ."

He lost his train of thought when he saw the expression on Mason's face.

"Anyone we use in a film or live broadcast has to sign a release waiver and gets paid a flat fee."

"And those who don't know they're being filmed?"

He opened his mouth, then closed it again.

"Your motel receipts gross what? A couple hundred bucks on a busy night?" Mason reached over the counter, unlocked the hinged door, and joined Schaub. The enormous man sat awkwardly on the stool, which hadn't been designed to accommodate his weight. "That's a mighty impressive safe if all you're protecting is a small stack of bills. Solid steel. Digital keypad and keyed lock tandem. Grounded electrical adapters and data safe storage. I guess you never can be too careful, can you? And you *are* a careful man, aren't you, Ralph? Never been arrested. I should say, never been *convicted* of any crime. I wonder if that has anything to do with the large cash withdrawals you pull from your various accounts on a rolling basis every other month."

Schaub tried to swallow again, to no avail.

"You see, Ralph, my wife was an investigator for the IRS. A damn good one, too. You can't live with a woman like that without a little of her skill rubbing off on you."

He made a garbled noise Mason couldn't quite interpret.

"You'll have to speak up, Ralph."

He cleared his throat and tried again. It still came out as little more than an indecipherable grunt.

"I want you to open the safe for me, Ralph."

Schaub's eyes darted for the door. They both knew his chances of getting to it first. Mason slid his right hand under his jacket for good measure.

The front door squealed as Trapp entered. He didn't appear too happy that Mason was behind the counter with the owner.

"Special Agent Trapp," Mason said. "This is Mr. Ralph Schaub, the owner of this fine establishment. Mr. Schaub was just offering to open his safe for us."

Had his partner not walked in when he did, Mason would undoubtedly have put him in an even more untenable position. To his credit, Trapp maintained a studiously neutral expression, joined them behind the counter, and gestured for Schaub to proceed.

Schaub hiked his pants, knelt on the floor, and set to work with fingers that were remarkably dexterous for their size. When he opened the steel door and sat back, Mason saw pretty much exactly what he'd expected. There was a digital relay panel with numbers from one to sixteen and two more, which read O1 and O2. Beside each number was a button that would light up when pressed. A small dented cash box sat next to it.

"So the manager serves as the casting director," Mason said. "He makes sure the guests sign in, and if they're attractive enough, he pushes the button to turn on the hidden cameras in the corresponding room when he puts their money in the safe. One quick motion for both. And considering most people pay in cash and don't use their real names, you must have a pretty hard time tracking them down to sign the waivers and pay them, I'd imagine. Most of the registrants probably aren't the kind who want their exploits known, so you don't need to worry about them coming back looking for their paychecks, either. In fact, I'll bet some of them are probably more than willing to pay *you* to make the proof of their little indiscretions go away, aren't they, Ralph?"

"Most of the girls are paid well." The sweat was positively running down his face. "They know what they're doing, and their partners are only too happy to participate."

"Was there a camera setup in room nine?"

Schaub again glanced at the door, and Mason had his answer.

"The old security cameras in here? They were just for show, weren't they? So people wouldn't think you'd stepped into the digital age. So they wouldn't suspect anything. Hell, they weren't even functional, were they? But Everett panicked. He tore out that old system when he realized the fire hadn't been an accident, hoping that he'd fool whoever did it if they came back for him."

"Which they did." Trapp recognized the direction Mason was trying to steer the interview. "The ligature they used to strangle him nearly took his head clean off his shoulders."

"Everett destroyed the DVDs in the foolish hope that no one would see through his deception, but he wasn't entirely stupid, was he? He had a backup copy somewhere, didn't he?"

"We have off-site digital storage," Schaub said.

"You're not going to make us go to all the trouble of getting a warrant, are you?" Trapp said.

Again, Schaub swallowed hard and had to jerk at his collar to make room for his pride to go down.

"No, sir," he finally said. "I'm happy to be of assistance in any way ·I can."

22

Schaub's studio took up the entire back half of the second level of Derriere's, above the open dressing room, where the dancers changed, and the small bedrooms, where he claimed they napped between sets. It *was* exhausting work, after all.

The studio had been soundproofed and the equipment inside was probably worth more than the entire building around it. Mason didn't know a thing about soundboards, but this one appeared to be state-of-the-art. Again, he was surprised by Schaub's dexterity as he manipulated several different functions at once to make the images on each of the four monitors above the central console come to life. Trapp and Mason sat on either side of him, while a pair of computer evidence specialists from the Rocky Mountain Forensics Laboratory watched him to ensure that he didn't try to erase the data and waited for their turn to swoop in and confiscate the recordings.

Schaub was obviously hoping that his helpfulness would buy him a little leniency when it came to the eventual investigation into his side venture. Mason really didn't care one way or the other. Schaub catered to an element of the population whose seed was more beneficial to the greater good of society in a tube sock than in the gene pool. He was perfectly content letting them have each other.

"So we have footage from both the office and the room on the day in question," Schaub said. "Which one do you want to see first?"

"The room," Trapp said.

Mason closed his eyes. When he opened them again, he was staring at a row of black screens. The first and third had date and time stamps, the second and fourth running time and blank rectangles for image capture. The numbers scrolled past, but the darkness remained the same.

"There's nothing there." A note of panic crept into Schaub's voice. "Not even sound."

The numbers scrolled faster and the monitors flickered, yet the unmarred blackness remained. Somehow, Schaub managed to sweat even more, producing the unmistakable scent of fear. His fingers flew across the console.

"Someone must have deleted it," Trapp said, and cast Mason a sideways glance.

"No." Schaub hadn't made a fortune in this arena without highly developed survival instincts. He knew the consequences of bringing them to his inner sanctum and not giving them what they wanted. "This is the actual recording. The camera's been disabled."

"You really expect us to believe that this one recording just mysteriously doesn't work?"

Trapp nodded to one of the computer specialists, who stepped forward and hovered over Schaub until he vacated his seat.

From where Mason sat, it looked like the new set of hands was doing the very same thing as the older, sweatier ones.

"I'm telling you, the system recorded exactly what you see. No image. No sound. Either the cord was cut or the camera itself was disabled," Schaub said.

"Then shouldn't we have seen someone disable it?"

"Not if the camera wasn't recording at the time. It only goes live when someone pushes the button on the control panel in the safe."

"So you're telling me—"

"He's right," the agent said. In addition to having some of the best physical evidence specialists in the country, the RMFL boasted the cream of the crop when it came to the science of computer forensics. "The feed was disrupted at the source."

"There's no way of retrieving any footage or sound?" Mason said.

"There never was any to retrieve."

"Were the other rooms functional on that same day?"

Mason rarely worked this type of investigation, so he'd never dealt with either of these agents. The man at the console looked more like a buzz-cut marine than your stereotypical computer whiz. His partner fit the computer geek mold, though. All he was missing was a bow tie and a pocket protector. Or maybe Mason was too quick to judge him. The bulge beneath his jacket didn't quite mesh with that profile. The agent caught him looking, smiled, and showed off his holstered SIG Sauer P229 Equinox .40 S&W.

The screen filled with an image of a woman with a dragon tattoo on her lower back sitting astride a man. She leaned back and gripped him by the knees. She wore a black-and-white sequined Mardi Gras mask with peacock feather fringes over the upper half of her face and a pout meant for the camera. The noises she made were obviously for the viewer's benefit. The man beneath her kneaded her thighs and grunted. The overall image quality was startlingly good, even in the low light conditions.

"It looks like the cameras in the other rooms were working just fine," the evidence tech at the computer said.

"They weren't the only thing working," Trapp said.

"The time and date stamp are within an hour of the other recording."

"How does the manager determine which room he assigns to a guest?" Mason asked.

"The, um, regulars get the rooms along the front." Schaub cleared his throat. "One through eight. They have the best, uh, lighting. The parking places are also clearly visible from Federal. The rooms around back are reserved for guests who require more . . . discretion. The parking slots are set down the hill behind the trees, so they're invisible from every direction. Room nine is the farthest from the office, which adds an extra dimension of privacy."

"Or at least the perception of it," Trapp said.

"So Everett would have made that determination on the spot?" Mason asked.

"As long as there wasn't another guest in there. In which case, he would have assigned them to number eleven, two rooms down. Again, privacy."

Every time Schaub said the word *privacy,* Mason had to fight the urge to lunge from the chair and squeeze him around his fat neck. He stared at him long and hard, watched even more sweat bloom from the sleazebag's forehead and upper lip.

"What aren't you telling me, Ralph?"

"Nothing. I mean, nothing that really makes any kind of difference one way or the other."

"Ralph."

"The guy who died. I recognized his picture from the paper. I've seen him around, if you know what I'm saying."

"You knew who he was and what he did and you were building a file you could use to blackmail him."

His head turned as red as a tomato and the collar of his shirt visibly darkened with sweat.

"Look, I . . . we—"

"The woman whose picture was in the paper with his. The woman who died in room nine. Had you ever seen her before? Were you building a file on her, too?"

"Mason," Trapp said. He felt his partner's hand on his shoulder. He didn't realize he'd jumped up out of his seat. Schaub had both hands in front of his face in anticipation of the blow, which, fortunately for both of them, never came. "Take a walk, okay? Go get some air."

"We have video from the office," the tech said.

Mason shrugged off Trapp's hand and turned to face the monitor. There were two different angles, as he'd anticipated, only from opposite corners than he had been led to believe by the nonfunctional decoys Everett had pulled down.

The two cameras were pointed at each other, but also downward at roughly a forty-five-degree angle. The monitors on the left displayed the feed from the camera behind the front desk. They were date- and time-stamped Thursday, October 29, 11:19:36 A.M. and featured a solid view of the safe at the bottom right, the hinged door, and a portion of the rack filled with brochures at the top left, above the counter upon which the sign-in sheet was situated. The names were clearly legible. The registrant would have to have been right up against the counter for his or her face to be visible, though.

There was a man standing near the brochures. Only his polished black shoes, slacks, and the bottom of his long overcoat were on the screen. He was facing the rack. In his left hand was a small black rectangle that could easily have been a cell phone.

The images on the right featured the same date and time stamp. One had real time, the other elapsed time. Both showed the front desk from the vantage point of the camera mounted beside the front door, directly above the rack of brochures, although only the far end of it was visible in the bottom right corner. The primary focus was on the counter where the guests registered. The man standing by the brochures was outside the camera's range. His shadow stretched across the floor and up the front of the desk. He wore some sort of broad-brimmed hat. Angie's auburn hair was a frozen blur of motion near the bottom as she entered through the front door.

"You sure you want to see this?" Trapp whispered.

Mason could only nod. He already knew the transcript by heart. How much worse could the visual accompaniment hurt?

The tech let the feed roll, and Mason watched his wife walk away from one camera and appear on the next with the same clicking of heels he would never be able to forget. From behind, she looked calm and composed. He was glad not to be able to see her face. She'd worn a tight black skirt that accentuated her curves and a button-down blouse that revealed just a hint of the lace on her bra. A man with long, greasy brown hair stepped out of the doorway from the back room on the left screen and in front of the camera on the right. Terrence Everett, live and in the flesh.

"What can I do you for?"

He dragged the stool forward and plopped down on it.

"I need a room."

The lower legs of the man holding the cell phone turned subtly toward Angie in the upper corner of the screen on the left. On the right, his shadow stretched up the backs of her calves.

"How, um, long you think you might be needing it?"

"Just one night."

Everett gestured toward the clipboard and Angie signed it while he leaned beneath the counter and plucked the key from its slot.

"How you want to pay for that?"

"Cash."

She set a bill on the counter. Everett opened the safe, dropped the fifty into the cash box without offering to make change, and pressed the button for room nine.

The legs behind Angie and to her right stepped closer to the rack. The man removed one of the brochures with a gloved hand.

Everett scooted forward and started to hum an off-key rendition of "Strangers in the Night." He slid the key across the counter and leaned onto his elbows in what appeared to be an effort to get a peek down Angie's blouse.

"Room's around back. Corner suite. Park right in front of the door and no one will be able to see your car from the road."

She snatched the key from the counter in one quick motion and turned to leave. Mason had a clear view of her face on the right monitor when she said, "No interruptions."

The thundering of his heartbeat ceased. He tried to read her expression. To glean the truth from it. To detect the lie. To gain any sort of insight into what had been going through her mind, but her expression betrayed nothing and her eyes were hidden behind sunglasses.

"You got it, Miss . . ." Everett spun the clipboard around and grinned. ". . . Smith."

Angie strode toward the door.

The lower legs turned and the man stepped into her path. Just his shoes were visible on the left. On the right, the shoulder of his charcoal overcoat, the brim of his hat.

She glanced up at him.

"Excuse me."

He tipped his hat as she brushed past him. Mason caught a glimpse of the man's gloved thumb pass over his cell phone.

And then Angie was gone.

"Something I can do for you, bud?" Everett said. "They got movies and a live show across the street."

The man glanced in Everett's direction on the right monitor and the desk clerk nearly toppled backward from the stool.

Without a word, the man in the overcoat and hat turned and headed for the door. When he passed across the camera's view, Mason saw just his heels on the left and the wide brim of a crisp fedora that matched the overcoat on the right. The man held the brochure he had plucked from the rack in front of his face for good measure, and then he, too, was gone.

"Rewind until you find where the man in the overcoat enters," Mason said.

"What are you looking for specifically?" the tech asked.

"A clear shot of his face."

Angie walked backward into the office, spun to look at the desk clerk, who bounced around for a moment before retreating into the back room. Angie slapped the bell and then walked in reverse out the door. The man's feet vibrated as he shifted his weight from side to side for a good length of time before he finally whirled and walked backward out the door.

"Slow it down," Mason said.

The tech reset the feed and slowed the playback speed. The man entered the office with his head down, his face shielded by the brim of his hat, his collar turned up around his neck. With the gloves on, it was impossible even to distinguish his skin color, let alone any identifiable traits.

"Damn it."

"Hang on," the tech said. "I've still got one idea I think might work."

Mason stepped closer and watched the monitors as the tech forwarded the footage to the point where his wife finished her transaction and turned to leave.

"What kind of magnification is this beastie equipped with?" the tech asked.

Schaub had been slowly inching his way toward the door behind them.

"More than I ever had any use for."

The tech played the recording forward in slow motion. One step. Two. Angie was away from the counter. The man's feet moved on the left screen and his shoulder appeared in the bottom corner of the monitor on the right. Angie raised her eyes to meet his. As her lips parted to speak, the tech paused the feed. He zoomed in on her face, readjusted his central focus, and then zoomed in even tighter on the lens of her sunglasses over her left eye until it filled the screen. The image was distorted and out of focus. A series of filters passed over the image. With each pass, the picture gained resolution and contrast. By the time the tech leaned back and laced his fingers behind his head, Mason was pretty certain his heart had stopped beating.

Despite the distortion caused by the contour of the reflective lens, he had no problem making out the details. The man had tipped his hat with his right hand, which obscured a good portion of his face. The skin on his left cheek was mottled and sinewy, as if it had been badly burned. No eyebrows grew from his scarred forehead. The raised collar of his coat concealed his mouth and nose, but what little Mason could see was more than enough.

The ground dropped out from beneath him as he stared at the man's eye.

It was a shade of blue unique in all of nature.

In fact, he'd only seen irises that color on one person.

And until that moment, Mason had been certain he was dead.

23

By the time Mason got home again, darkness and exhaustion reigned. The thought of climbing into a scalding shower to scrub off the taint of Schaub's world sounded incredible, but he couldn't bring himself to cross the front threshold. He just stood on the porch, staring through the open doorway at a house that was no longer his. The part of him that lived inside had died with his wife.

It struck him that they would never bring a child home to this house. He would never throw a ball with him in the yard or swing with her in his lap. He would never walk through this door to the sound of laughter or the smell of his wife's spaghetti. He would never hear her breathing in his ear or feel her hands on the muscles in his back.

He stared at the furniture in the living room and the paintings on the walls, and at the dinette in the kitchen, where his investigative files were spread around his wife's final communication to him. *We need to talk tonight. Please.* There was nothing he wanted to do more and yet it was the one thing he would never be able to do again.

This was a stranger's house. Or maybe he had become a stranger to it. The thought of spending another night in it was more than he could bear, but when it came right down to it, he had nowhere else to go.

He was at a crossroads and the time had come to decide which direction his life would take. The decision itself was so monumental that he had to break it down into a series of smaller, less significant decisions. He wasn't accomplishing anything just standing there, so he made the decision to enter the house and close the door behind him.

Heading upstairs for a change of clothes was an easy decision. Easier still was the decision to get in the shower. The hot water worked its magic and he emerged looking and smelling like a new man. Or at least a clean man. It also helped him formulate his thoughts. He had brought all of this pain upon himself. He had brought evil back with him from Arizona and tracked it through his home. He was responsible for his wife's death. He had failed to kill the monster who murdered his partner and then his wife. That one moment had changed everything. That one decision.

Take the shot, damn it!

Had he shot the man with the blue eyes first, his partner might still be dead, but his wife would be alive. A split second to think it through. Not even that. He had acted on instinct and made the wrong decision. He needed the next one he made to be the right one, for the answer to the question he was about to pose to himself would set the course of the rest of his life.

What should I do now?

The answer was so simple that even he couldn't screw it up.

He was going to track down the man who had murdered Angie and Kane. He was going to find the man with the blue eyes. And he was going to kill him.

He changed into clean clothes, holstered his Glock under his left arm, and looked around the bedroom that was no longer his. Angie was in everything he saw. Her scent haunted the room. She was no longer here, though, and she would never be coming back.

Neither would Mason.

He loaded Angie's personal laptop into its case, took it by the handle, and went down the stairs. He stopped dead in his tracks on the landing. A yellow triangle protruded from the seam around the door. He opened it and a folded piece of paper fell to the floor.

Another page torn from a phone book, covered with scores of fingerprints, none of which would lead him to the person who had left the message. It consisted of only four words this time.

WILL YOU HELP ME?

He took one of his business cards from his wallet, stepped out onto the porch, and wedged it in the door behind him. When whoever left the notes was done playing games, he could pick up a phone and call Mason. He didn't have any more time to waste. If the man with the blue eyes was still alive, then there was a chance he'd brought the virus with him.

Mason was already formulating a plan when he climbed behind the wheel of his Cherokee. He needed to consider everything he knew about the man with the blue eyes, who obviously knew his identity, which meant he had to assume that the man knew everything there was to know about him. He couldn't afford not to. Unfortunately, that meant the man with the blue eyes also knew about his father, which opened up a whole new can of worms, but he had to consider every possibility.

What did he know for sure?

The man with the blue eyes favored fire as his means of erasing any sign of his presence, assuming he was also responsible for the string of fatal blazes leading northwest from the Arizona-Mexico border. Perhaps his flair for pyrotechnics stemmed from having been severely burned; maybe his facial disfigurement was as a result of it. If so, there was likely a record of it somewhere.

He was part of a group trafficking pathogens into the country, and Mason's gut told him the end goal was weaponization, which fit with the fact that even Ramses couldn't find out what was being sold on the third floor of the building by the old airport. The same group was responsible for the deaths of thirteen law-enforcement agents at the stone quarry, and he fully believed they had known the strike force was coming because someone had tipped them off. Someone within their own ranks.

He'd been shot in the shoulder. Mason had seen that with his own eyes. Maybe the man with the blue eyes wanted to exact his revenge, but if that was all, why not come directly at him?

It wasn't much, but Mason had worked with less.

The problem was, there was only one person who could potentially lead him to the man with the blue eyes, and he had a hunch that help would come at a fairly painful price.

24

Mason called Club Five while he was driving. Assuming he heard correctly over the deafening music, Ramses hadn't come in yet, but they expected to see him at some point. Mason hadn't talked to his old friend since watching him being driven away in the back of his partner's Crown

Victoria. While he knew Ramses wouldn't hold him personally accountable for the treatment he'd undoubtedly received at the hands of the police, he would demand a measure of recompense. The scales always had to remain balanced with him, which was simultaneously one of his more damning qualities and one of his most redeeming ones. He inherited that trait from his father, who'd earned an advanced degree from the eye-for-an-eye school of thought. Mason pitied the guy who put Ramses' old man in prison when he finally saw the light of day.

Horace Donovan had been raised in the Bronx, cut his teeth in South Boston, and launched his career in Vegas at a time when the town sat on the brink of becoming an amusement park for sinners. He helped clubs find dancers and dancers find shows. He connected out-of-town guests with ladies in need of a little supplemental income. He lured developers into the heart of the desert and convinced them that they never wanted to leave. "King of the Eternal Sands," he called himself. A modern-day pharaoh. And it was only fitting that his first wife should bear him a son and that he should name that son after the most powerful ruler the Egyptian Empire had ever known, Ramses II.

And then everything started to change. Vegas decided to incorporate and make itself over as the Disneyland of the Desert, ushering in a new world of white tigers and dancers with their tops on. Everything was fake, from the pyramids to the smiles to breasts stuffed so full of silicone they didn't even bounce anymore. And then there was the new wife twenty years his junior, who was little more than a kid herself and wanted nothing to do with his.

So Ramses was shipped off to the John C. Fremont Academy of the Rockies in Colorado, where he ended up sharing a room with Mason. The son of a career criminal and the son of a prominent prosecutor turned politician. One could argue about the moral shades of gray between the two professions, but as long as the checks cleared, the school would issue a navy blazer to just about anyone.

Considering everything they'd been through together, Mason knew Ramses wouldn't have deliberately sent him into a trap. His old friend was nothing if not meticulous. He would have verified the veracity of the intelligence before passing it on, especially knowing that one of these days he would step far enough across the line that Mason would have no choice but to take him in. When that day arrived, there would be no hard feelings. If Mason showed up on his doorstep with a warrant for his arrest, he would offer his wrists without argument. That was why Mason regretted the way things had gone down the night the officers died in the explosion. Ramses had taken a risk to get him the information and had surely been rewarded with a beating on both a personal and a professional level.

Ramses lived on the top two floors of a black glass building that looked like an obsidian spike driven into the heart of lower downtown, or LoDo. He'd stripped them bare and turned them into his own private playland of sorts. Every room had a wall of windows that looked out upon his private domain, the world he had conquered. There was even a swimming pool on the roof with a glass bottom that cast strange shifting shadows across his living room, day and night.

Only one of the six elevators in the lobby went all the way up to his suite, and he'd replaced the button with a key slot, which meant that Mason had to stand facing the nearly invisible security camera above the panel of buttons, hit the hidden call button, and talk through the speaker.

"Well, well, well," Ramses said. "I have a hunch you didn't come all this way because you were concerned about my well-being, so I'm thinking either you're here with a bouquet of flowers and an apology or you need something from me. Again. And considering I don't see any flowers . . ."

"I'm sorry," Mason said. "Now would you bring me up already?"

"I'm not really feeling the sincerity."

Mason stared directly into the camera so his old friend could see his eyes when he spoke.

"Ramses. They killed my wife."

The elevator doors closed. They were stainless steel and polished to such a degree that he found himself surrounded by dozens of imperfect copies of himself, all of them staring at the digital readout as the car climbed to the 24th floor.

The elevator opened upon a dark, cavernous space with deep blue ambient lighting. This was the room where Ramses brought and entertained his guests. There were overstuffed black leather chairs and couches everywhere, silhouetted against the night sky and the skyscrapers.

The doors closed behind Mason, sealing off the light. He waited for his eyes to adjust to the dimness before advancing into the room.

"Do you have any idea how badly you inconvenienced me the other night? I was barely out of lockup in time to catch breakfast."

"Four officers died, Ramses. You're lucky they aren't still working you over in an interrogation room."

"I do a favor for a friend and end up in cuffs. I'm not sure you and I share the same definition of luck."

Ramses was sitting in a deep leather chair maybe five feet away, his right ankle propped on his left knee, his hands gripping the armrests. He cocked his head first one way, then the other. The darkness concealed his expression.

"I need your help," Mason said.

Ramses' white teeth glowed blue when he smiled.

"But uh, now you come to me and you say, 'Don Corleone, give me justice.'" It was a serviceable Brando. "But you don't ask with respect. You don't offer friendship. You don't even think to call me 'Godfather.' Instead, you come into my house on the day my daughter is to be married—"

"Damn it, Ramses. Are you going to help me or not?"

The lights snapped on with a thud, illuminating the entire level. Massive glass terrariums filled with tropical plants, flowers, waterfalls, and all kinds of reptiles were staggered around the room like pillars. The blue lights provided heat and artificial moonlight. Were Ramses not such a good criminal, he would have made an amazing zoologist.

Mason cringed when he saw Ramses' face. There were stitches on his right cheekbone and his eyes were ringed with faded yellow bruises. The cut on the bridge of his nose was going to leave a nasty scar. But it was the fire in his eyes that concerned Mason the most.

"Pretty freaking sweet, right?" Ramses stood and gestured to his face. "Compliments of the DPD. Just what I always wanted. A disfigurement. I remember waking up that day and thinking to myself, 'Man, if only there were a way of adding a little character to my face, something that would not only make me look like Frankenstein, but would hurt like a motherfucker, too.'"

"You done? I liked the opening bit, but the rest was fairly contrived."

Mason heard the crack and tasted blood in his mouth before he even saw it coming. He landed squarely on his rear end and sat there for a long moment, opening and closing his jaw to make sure it still worked.

"I owed you that one," Ramses said.

"The hell you did." Mason dabbed his lip with the back of his hand. "You asked me to punch you as a favor."

"And now I've returned that favor. See how well the system works? Surely you, of all people, didn't think for a second I wouldn't repay the debt, did you?" He smirked, grabbed Mason's hand, and pulled him to his feet. "You weren't the only one who was set up that night, you know, and I don't take kindly to being used. So I've been making some discreet inquiries on my own."

Mason followed him across the main room to a wide spiral staircase that wound upward into an anteroom with sheets of water trickling down chiseled marble on three sides and a single stainless-steel door set into the fourth. Ramses tapped a series of numbers into the digital combination pad and the door slid back into the wall.

"And . . . ?"

They entered a wide tiled foyer with potted trees that reached all the way up to the twenty-foot ceiling, where the diffused moonlight cast wavering shadows across the pool on the roof. There were bedrooms to either side, tucked back around the other side of the waterfall room. Ahead, three stairs led up to an elevated living area with a massive flat-screen television, the most comfortable furniture ever made, and the kind of computer setup Bill Gates probably had in his own house. All of it surrounded by windows that gave onto open sky.

"Beer?"

"Ramses."

"All I know is that no one knows anything."

"You're deliberately trying to piss me off now, aren't you?"

"That's your answer. None of the usual players are involved. The guys moving drugs are worried that someone might be horning in on their territory. The weapons guys feel the same way. All anybody knows is that someone's doing something, but no one has any idea who they are or what they're selling. They're working on the fringes, keeping to themselves, not forcing any confrontations. They might as well be ghosts. So what does that tell you?"

"I would know if we were dealing with government operatives."

"All I'm saying is if it looks like a duck . . ."

"These people are responsible for the deaths of nearly twenty federal and local law-enforcement officers. There's no way the government—"

"I know one person you could ask straight up."

"My father liked Angie a lot more than he's ever liked me. I guarantee you that if he knew anything about what happened to her, he'd have already done something about it."

"So what do you have to go on?"

"That's why I came to you. I'm looking for someone. The kind of guy that anyone who's ever seen him won't be likely to forget."

"I can ask around. But if he's as connected as I suspect, even asking questions is going to stir the hornet's nest. Are you prepared to handle the whole swarm?"

"This is the man who killed my wife, Ramses."

Ramses stared him directly in the eyes for several seconds, his jaw muscles clenching and unclenching.

"Whatever you need."

Mason handed him one of the printouts he'd made of the man with the blue eyes on the lens of his wife's sunglasses. Ramses glanced at it briefly, nodded, and then tucked it inside his suit jacket.

"I'll see what I can do, but I'm going to need a little time."

"Time's a luxury I don't have. When I last saw this guy, he was dealing with some really scary stuff."

"How scary?"

"Biological."

"Christ. I'll see what I can dig up. What are you going to do in the meantime?"

"Considering that picture is all I have to go on, my only option is to try to draw him out."

"I guess you're just going to have to start beating the bushes."

Ramses smirked and led Mason down the hallway to the left, past a bedroom with what looked like a jungle gym built above the bed and a bathroom with an enormous Jacuzzi spa and sauna, and to the end of the corridor, where it simply terminated against a full-height window, through which they could barely see the distant lights of Colorado Springs, sixty-some miles to the south. He didn't recognize the false opening in the wall to the left until Ramses walked through it and guided him into a room he undoubtedly never would have seen under any other circumstances.

"What the hell is this?"

"Think of this as my toolshed. This is where I keep my bush beaters."

25

Mason had to admit that there was something empowering about driving through downtown Denver in the middle of the night with a Thunderstorm bullpup assault rifle in a padded case behind his rear seat. The OTs-14 Groza was originally designed for postcollapse Russian special forces and came equipped with an under-barrel grenade launcher that could be swapped for a suppressor, interchangeable barrels with different lengths to suit his various tactical needs, and a range of optics from full-day to night vision. He had a dozen clips filled with 7.62×39 mm cartridges that could be fired at a rate of 750 rounds per minute and five grenades he figured would open a lot of doors for him. And all of that in a sleek futuristic design that weighed less than seven pounds. It was a beautiful weapon that had become a casualty of financial circumstances and somehow had found its way into the hands of a sin merchant like Ramses and God only knows what other criminal element.

Ramses had always been vigilant. In his business, it paid to be prepared for every possible contingency. It was a long fall from the tightrope he'd chosen to walk, but that "toolshed" of his appeared to have been designed to withstand a siege.

His life's goal hadn't always been to follow in his father's footsteps; in fact, quite the opposite. He'd actually attended West Point—thanks in large measure to a glowing letter of recommendation from a congressman who owed Mason's father a favor—where he'd majored in information systems engineering before becoming completely disillusioned with the entire military complex. He never told anyone about the events leading to his discharge, and Mason knew better than to force the issue.

Truthfully, Mason was surprised Ramses had lasted as long as he had. He'd had good money on him washing out in under a week. Ramses wasn't the kind of guy who got along well with people in positions of authority. He'd just been so determined not to end up like his father that he'd put himself in the only situation where even he couldn't succeed.

While Ramses' time in the army might have exposed him to some facets of the government Mason probably didn't want to know about, he couldn't fathom how any federal agency could be involved in this situation. He understood that an unknown entity moving stealthily around the fringes fit the mold, but he just couldn't see the motive. Why would anyone in a position of power need to import a virus when there was a readily accessible storehouse at the CDC in Atlanta? From what he understood, it wasn't incredibly difficult to requisition any of their diseases through normal channels—with the right qualifications, anyway. Why massacre its own strike force?

Mason didn't buy it.

He pulled to the side of the road, scrolled through the memory on his phone, and dialed a number he hoped an old friend hadn't changed since last they spoke. If anyone could figure out which bushes to beat, it was this guy. There was no message, only a beep.

"It's Mace," he said. "Call me back."

He looked around and realized he didn't know exactly where he was or how he had gotten here. He'd been driving without a destination, hoping continuous motion might stimulate inspiration. A ceaseless string of lights crossed the elevated section of I-25 in his rearview mirror. He was in an industrial corridor where all the buildings cringed away from the road behind chain-link fences. Half of them were abandoned; the other half looked as though they should be. There was even one that reminded him of a fortress. It had concrete walls, barred windows, a three-bay garage, and backed to the South Platte River. Compared to the neighboring buildings, it was practically free of graffiti. A faded FOR SALE sign hung from the fence, and undoubtedly had for a long time.

A forlorn train horn echoed in the distance.

It wasn't until that moment that he realized just how quiet and deserted this area was, when once it must have been the artery through which the lifeblood of the city's economy flowed.

Mason had just started to drive again when his phone rang.

"That was quick," he said.

"Is this James Mason?" It was a woman's voice, deep and resonant, almost as though it created an echo of itself. "Agent James Mason of the FBI?"

"Yes." The word came out like gravel. He cleared his throat and tried again. "This is Special Agent James Mason. With whom am I speaking?"

"Will you help me?"

"I have some questions for you."

"Will you help me?"

"Yes."

She covered the phone and made a noise that sounded almost like a sob.

"There is a park near Forty-fourth and Sheridan. Across the street from the old amusement park. Do you know it?"

"Yes."

"There is a playground on the east side of the lake. In this playground is a jungle gym. Be there in twenty minutes."

Click.

He looked at the number on his caller ID, committed it to memory, and dialed a number he knew by heart. He was already talking when the operator answered the phone.

"I need a reverse listing on a phone number. Area code three zero three, four two six, one nine one six." He had to fight with gravity to keep the Cherokee from rolling as he swung through the red light on Santa Fe and sped toward the highway. "Tell me you've got something for me."

"Sir, I need your identification—"

"SA James Richmond Mason. Badge number victor tango alpha zero one one two nine six three two three."

"Yes, sir. The number corresponds to a pay phone at the Seven-

Eleven on the corner of Sheridan and Twenty-sixth. Can I be of any further assistance?"

Mason terminated the call and pinned the gas pedal to the floor. From his experience, people who gave you short notice to be somewhere at a fixed time either intended not to wait beyond the allocated time or planned to be gone by the time you got there.

He hit the off-ramp onto Sheridan at the fourteen-minute mark, blew through the light, and sped to the south. The skeleton of a roller coaster reared up to his right from behind age-old maple trees. As soon as he saw the trademark hacienda entrance to the Lakeside Amusement Park, he cranked the wheel to the left and shot past the western edge of the park. The lake reflected the moon like a black mirror behind the cattails. He took the first entrance and parked in the lot. Leaped out of his car. Hurdled the gate. Sprinted into the darkness. The path leading to the playground was lined with mature blue spruces that minimized visibility. There were trees everywhere, in fact. It was the perfect place to set up an ambush, and this was definitely the kind of neighborhood where you could count on no one to have seen anything. But he had to take the chance.

The evergreens peeled back from a playground that had seen better days. He slid his right hand under his jacket and gripped his Glock. Took in everything around him at a glance.

There was no one here.

Elapsed time: seventeen minutes.

Mason turned slowly in a circle, scrutinizing every shadow behind every branch, sifting through every sound. He couldn't hear anything over the cars racing past on the highway and the wind rattling through the cattails.

The park was a five-minute drive from the pay phone where the woman had made the call, which meant she could have been here in time to set up in an invisible surveillance position or to have already come and gone. On foot, the walk from the 7-Eleven would have taken twice the given amount of time. No, this was how she had intended the rendezvous to play out, so what was he missing?

The pea-size pebbles crunched underfoot as he stepped from the path and walked into the playground itself. Bare metal showed through on the swing set and jungle gym. He read the graffiti in case there was a message for him. Looked for anything that didn't belong. The problem was, he didn't know what he was looking for. Nothing on any of the ladders or bridges or crow's nests or slides. Nothing taped to the undersides of the swings. It wasn't until he crawled through one of the holes and stood under the dome of monkey bars that he saw what he'd been summoned here to see.

A dozen dandelions had been tied together to form a ring roughly six inches in diameter. It had been left in the dead center of the area beneath the dome. The pebbles within the ring were still damp and discolored from being recently turned over. He knelt and excavated them slowly, cautiously. Glanced over his shoulder every few seconds. Another six inches down he encountered a plastic Ziploc bag, which he carefully removed by the corner, between his thumb and forefinger, so as to leave as few prints as possible.

He needn't have bothered. He smelled the alcohol she had used to wipe off any potential latents the moment he had it all the way out of the ground. Inside was a small stack of pictures—not actual photographs, but digital images printed on plain paper, the kind you could find anywhere and everywhere. The top picture was grainy and discolored, as though the printer had been in dire need of a new ink cartridge, and yet he still recognized the Peak View Inn and the outline of a figure wearing a long overcoat and a wide-brimmed fedora silhouetted in the breezeway. He didn't need to see the shadow's face to identify the man with the blue eyes.

Mason opened the bag and again caught a whiff of alcohol. She hadn't used film that could be traced to a developer, nor had she printed the images at a Kinko's or some other location he could potentially run down. She'd used her own printer and cut down the images herself so as not to leave any prints. Whoever she was, she was positively terrified of someone.

He dumped the remainder of the images from the plastic bag and used the sleeve of his jacket to spread them out before him. There were six in all, each of them taken from a different vantage point behind the motel, down the hill and behind the pool, and from the dense cover of the pines and scrub oaks. There was one of Blaine Martin looking over his shoulder as he opened the door to room number nine. Another of him climbing out of a silver Audi in the parking lot. Great care had been taken to capture both him and his license plate at the same time.

Mason viewed the remaining pictures through a prism of tears. His wife looking back in the direction of the camera from in front of an open door, through the gap of which he saw Martin's face. Angie getting out of her Lexus, matador red mica, plate number LBN-230. Ascending the stairs from the parking lot, briefcase in hand, glancing behind her. She'd been worried someone might see her, which was not an uncommon trait among adulterers. What was, however, was taking a briefcase to a tryst.

The photographs proved what he'd known in his heart all along. His wife hadn't been cheating on him. With that revelation came a measure of absolution. He hadn't driven Angie into the arms of another man, but he also hadn't been there for her when she needed him most. He would never be able to forgive himself for that, no matter how long he lived, but he'd be damned if he wasn't going to make those responsible pay for what they'd done.

His phone rang in his pocket.

Mason glanced at his watch. Right on the twenty-five-minute mark.

He didn't recognize the number on the caller ID. Must have been another pay phone. He mentally filed it away so he could determine the location. Answered without taking his eyes off the pictures.

"Did you find what I left for you?" the caller asked.

"I'm looking at the pictures now. Did you take them?"

"Will you still help me?"

"Yes."

"Can I trust you?"

"Of course, I'm a federal agent—"

"That means nothing. Your wife said she was going ask you to help us. Did she?"

"She said we needed to talk. . . ." Mason's words trailed off into silence. "How did you know where I lived?"

"I met with Angela once. Before. I followed her home."

"Why didn't you just talk to me there? We should meet in person and get—"

"Not until I know I can trust you. You do not know what the people looking for me are willing to do."

"How do you propose—?"

"I assume the briefcase your wife took to the motel was destroyed in the fire. Inside of it was the tax audit of a company called Fairacre Ranch Surplus and Auction. I will call you again in exactly eighteen hours."

Click.

Mason looked at his watch: 2:00 A.M. on the nose. That gave him until 8:00 P.M. tomorrow—today, technically—to figure out the relationship between the unknown trafficking organization, his wife's murder, and the financial audit of a seemingly inconsequential agricultural company.

This development also introduced a variable he hadn't considered. He wasn't the only investigative agent in the house, and he certainly wasn't the best. Angie had been far more dangerous than he was, especially to a certain faction, a faction that controlled an enormous amount of wealth and, with it, all the trappings of power and influence. He'd never stopped to think that it could have been her investigation that drew the man with the blue eyes from the shadows and forced him to risk revealing himself when she started getting too close. And since he'd obviously made it out of the quarry alive, Mason had to assume he'd taken the virus with him, which meant he'd had a full year to weaponize it and prepare it for release.

The tumblers finally started to fall into place.

He was up against a powerful entity with fifteen million dollars in cash and the willingness to murder federal investigators, massacre an entire SWAT team, and expose five men to an unknown biological agent to get what it wanted. And if what it wanted was the virus, then suddenly the stakes were even higher than he imagined. Worse, the elements of escalation and acceleration could mean only one thing.

He was running out of time.

Mason gathered the evidence and carefully returned it to the plastic bag. He was nearly to his car when his phone rang again. This time he recognized the number. He couldn't help but smirk when he answered.

"What took you so long?"

26

Gunnar Backstrom claimed to be on a private plane over the Maluku Islands in the Pacific Ring of Fire when he returned Mason's call, although since he said it over an unencrypted connection, that likely wasn't where he really was. Lying had always been second nature to Gunnar, which served him well in his chosen profession. It came from being the scholarship kid at a private school full of children whose paths had already been paved for them with fortune and success. These were the offspring of corporate presidents and CEOs, prominent bankers and lawyers and surgeons, and people who had the kind of money to offer their children the best of all worlds. How could someone whose care packages included gently used shoes and homemade scarves contend with classmates like that?

He lied. He lied a lot.

It got to the point where only he could keep up with the stories coming out of his mouth. He lived them and breathed them and rehearsed them until there were no holes that could be exploited, but he quickly learned that in order to actually compete, he needed more than stories. He needed to change the battlefield. He was at the Fremont Academy for one reason and one reason only. He was brilliant. That was his advantage. Everyone else was there because their families could foot the bill. He was there because the school had sent recruiters to his grandparents' farm in Middle of Nowhere, Wisconsin, to offer him a scholarship, which, considering what they charged for board and tuition meant they must have *really* wanted him.

Mason had assumed that working in the cafeteria after meals was a condition of that scholarship until he discovered Gunnar had been sending everything he made back to his grandparents, who needed every little bit of help they could get to hang on to their farm. So when it came to long weekends and holidays, he couldn't afford to go home like most of the others and ended up staying in the dormitory with the kids whose parents wanted them to have every opportunity in life, as long as that life was led somewhere else. People like Ramses, whose new stepmother would sooner welcome a pack of rats into her home than her husband's only child, and Mason, whose father had embarked upon a quest to rule the world, or at least the country.

He never actually said what had happened to his parents that led to his living with his grandparents. During the early years, he'd told a dozen different stories, but by sophomore year, he'd stopped talking about them altogether. His only link to his former life was a single photograph of his grandparents, which he tacked to the wall beside his bunk. They were old and frail and dressed in clothes they'd obviously made themselves. And they were off-limits to anyone attempting to tease him. He had to hack into the school's computer system and destroy a few GPAs before his tormentors finally took the hint.

By the time he graduated, though, Gunnar had given up on trying to impress his classmates. He recognized the value of his intellect and embraced a future beyond the reach of even the wealthiest among them. His free ride carried him through six years at Harvard, where he graduated summa cum laude, with twin doctorates in business economics and strategy, and the boy who'd grown up fabricating stories in an effort to fit in utilized those skills in conjunction with his education to enter the lucrative world of corporate espionage.

He'd called himself a corporate terrorist for hire before 9/11 made the usage of the word *terrorist* light up every satellite listening station around the world. Now he merely billed himself as a financial securities and acquisitions consultant. He was hired to find out where an organization was the weakest, discover the best way to exploit it, and determine the right time to strike. His fingerprints were all over hostile takeovers and billion-dollar mergers. From time to time, he also found himself in the employ of the federal government, although that was the only detail his confidentiality agreements allowed him to disclose. Needless to say, his office was his plane and no one found him if he didn't want them to.

He could also do things that Mason couldn't, at least not without going through channels he had neither the time nor the patience to pursue.

"This isn't a social call," Mason said. "I need your help. It's about Angie."

"You have my condolences," Gunnar said. "I watched her funeral, you know."

"I didn't see you there."

"Eye in the sky, my friend."

"You tasked a satellite to watch my wife's funeral?"

"There was already one overhead."

"What are the odds that a satellite just happened to be in the right place at the right time to view my wife's funeral?"

"Slim, but not entirely outside the realm of possibility."

"So what's your theory?"

"As you know, I have to keep my finger on the financial pulse of the key players, and it's been erratic for a while now. I'm talking about extended periods of relative calm followed by big bursts of activity. Massive, over-the-top transactions that seem to be designed to attract attention and grab some headlines, while a ton of smaller transactions are firing off in every direction at once. These smaller transactions? They're all going through shells and subsidiaries, only to end up converging in some deep pockets. It feels like the powers on Wall Street are consolidating their holdings, like they did before 9/11, only on a much larger scale. There's a lot of subtle manipulation going on right now and that has me thinking that something big is building on the horizon."

"What does that have to do with my wife's funeral?"

"Think about how many people important to those key players were in attendance. It makes sense that someone would be keeping a close eye on them, especially if my theory is correct. Look at your immediate family alone. Angie's father is head of one of the largest agricultural conglomerates in the world and yours is a prominent senator who most feel will make a run at the presidency sooner than later. Throw in dozens of influential businessmen, policy makers, and high-ranking federal officials and you're looking at a lot of power consolidated in one small space. And, unless I'm mistaken, there were a few people mixed into the crowd who didn't belong."

"CIA?"

"Not on the ground. That's not their style. I don't know, and that's what concerns me."

"Why didn't you tell me any of this until now?"

"You'd just lost your wife, Mace. You didn't need me burdening you with speculations while you were trying to grieve, especially when there was a chance the positioning of the satellite was entirely coincidental."

"Angie was murdered, Gunnar."

He was quiet for so long that Mason thought he'd lost the connection.

"Gunnar?"

"You're certain?"

"Without a doubt. I'm convinced she got too close to something through the course of her work and she was killed because of it."

"That changes the dynamics of the situation, doesn't it?"

"You don't sound overly surprised."

"Let's just say I had a healthy amount of skepticism about the circumstances surrounding her death."

"Why?"

"Because the explanation I heard for why she was in that motel room didn't sit right with me."

"You should have said something."

"How long has it been since last we spoke? A lot could have changed between the two of you since then. Besides, you know me, Mace. I see conspiracies everywhere I look."

"And you're generally right, I'd imagine."

"More often than not."

"So what do you see here?"

"I've been hearing whispers about Angie's old man making a move to topple one of his main competitors in the global market, which would weaken it enough domestically to make its acquisition a foregone conclusion. Interestingly, I've also heard the Thorntons have been creeping their way into the pharmaceuticals game. Word has it your father-in-law's a solid minority shareholder in two of the three largest overseas conglomerates. You know who has an honorary seat on the board of those two companies, as well? Here's a hint: He also chairs the Senate Subcommittee on Bioengineering."

"There isn't a board or committee my father doesn't sit on."

"I'm sure you're right."

"What are you trying to tell me?"

"Some people who are generally content to sit back and watch things unfold are now actively making a whole lot of subtle moves. These guys are the kind who never do anything unless the risk is great and the reward even greater. The kind who don't ordinarily pop up on my radar unless they're influencing global events."

"Who are we talking about?"

"Powerful people who hide so well behind corporate smoke screens that even I don't know for sure."

"You must be losing your touch."

"Trust me. I will figure this out." Mason heard the scream of wind shear in the background. "But that's not why you called, is it? What can I do for you?"

"Three things, actually, and I don't have a lot of time. There's more at stake here than you know, Gunnar. Someone out there has a deadly virus that could already be weaponized—"

"Not over an unsecured line."

"You know something, don't you?"

"A few pieces might have just clicked together. Tell me what you need."

"What do you know about a company called Fairacre Ranch Surplus and Auction?"

"Never heard of it. Sounds like something well below my pay grade."

"It's important, though. Can you check into it?"

"No problem. Next?"

"I've got a picture of a man and I need to put a name to the face."

"If it's within my power, consider it done."

"One more thing," Mason said. "If I gave you pay phone numbers and times, would you be able to get me imagery?"

"Without breaking a sweat. Are you flying under the radar on this one?"

"For now. I want to follow this lead and see where it takes me before I call in the cavalry."

"Send me the numbers and I'll email you what I find. You can use the same email address. If you still have it, that is."

"Funny." Mason typed the phone numbers and times into the body of the message, attached the picture of the man with the blue eyes, and sent it off into cyberspace. "You haven't been making my phone ring off the hook, either."

He heard the roar of engines and the hiss of pressurized air. And beneath it all, the sound of typing.

"You know how much I appreciate this, right?" Mason said.

"Just keep your eyes open, Mace. If you're in as deep as it sounds, you're going to need to tread very lightly."

"You're making me paranoid."

"Good. Paranoia is highly underrated. It's an attribute you generally only hear people ascribe to the living."

"You'll get back to me?"

"Check your email. Let me see what else I can dig up on my end and I'll call you back. In the meantime, like I said, be careful. I can feel the pressure building; it's only a matter of time before the storm breaks." There was a loud whine that sounded like landing gear being lowered. "Follow the money, Mace. It's always about the money."

Gunnar terminated the call.

Mason leaned back in the driver's seat of his Grand Cherokee and watched the headlights of the cars speeding down the highway flicker through the branches of the trees. Exhaustion was setting in once more. He needed to reestablish forward momentum, so he sat up straight and opened his in-box. As promised, Gunnar had sent him an email with attachments.

The first was in black and white and focused primarily on a street. He could read the license plate number on the fender of an older-model Camry. The picture had obviously been taken by a traffic cam mounted above an intersection. On the right side of the image was the telltale facade of a 7-Eleven. There were three pay phones at the end of the brick wall. The woman stood with her back to the camera, as deep into the shadows as she could get. She wore a baseball cap with either long hair tucked up into it or short hair concealed by it, and a jacket that disguised her figure. Were it not for her slender legs and the fact that he'd heard her voice, he might have mistaken her silhouette for a man's. He could see just the headlights and bumper of a car idling on the other side of the Dumpster.

The second picture was from the viewpoint of an indoor ATM. Its reflection was on the plate-glass window behind a skinny Hispanic kid, who wore the expression of someone who was nervous about something. Maybe the mere thought of walking out the door with a wad of cash in that neighborhood. Mason didn't care. It was what he saw over the kid's left shoulder—across the street—that caught his attention. The storefront was dark, but he was able to make out a portion of the hand-painted sign. *FLORISTERÍA*. The front windows were painted with blooming vines and tropical fish. He'd seen that building before. A combination flower and pet store. Low rent. Bad area. There was a pay phone around the side. The same silhouette stood beside it, one hand pressed to the person's ear. The car parked beside the figure faced the camera, its headlights washing out the license plate number and any other potentially useful details.

It was truly frightening how quickly Gunnar—a private citizen, as far as Mason knew—had accessed this kind of information. Scarier still that he'd been able to zoom in on just the figure, clean up the noise, enhance and sharpen the resolution, and send those images to him, as well, while carrying on a conversation.

Mason still wouldn't be able to pick the woman out of a crowd, but at least now he had something to go on. She was somewhere between five four and five six, at the most. Maybe 110 pounds soaking wet.

Try as he might, though, he couldn't figure out where she fit in. He was dealing with a young Hispanic woman in her twenties, early thirties at the most, presumably an immigrant. She'd been here long enough, however, that she'd been able to learn the English language, if not such intricacies as contractions. Her fingerprints weren't in the NGI. She'd been at the motel the day his wife died, or at least wanted him to think so. She was scared of someone she feared could find her anywhere she went, and she claimed to need Mason's help. His help, specifically, because of his relationship to Angie. Or because of hers?

He needed to find out who she was and, more important, what she knew about his wife's death, and apparently Fairacre Ranch Surplus and Auction was the key.

27

Mason spent the remainder of the night going through the files on Angie's laptop. It was perhaps the only time in his life that he wished she'd brought more of her work home with her. The IRS had already terminated her remote access, so he wasn't able to get into her case files. The only saved files even remotely related to finances were their own, which Mason had been more than willing to let her handle.

All her contacts were of a personal nature, and he knew each and every one of the names. There was nothing out of the ordinary in her email in-box, sent files, or list of deleted items. The files in her word processor program were innocuous. Mostly letters. A novel he had no idea she'd started to write. Her Facebook and Instagram accounts were easy enough to crack, but there was nothing that struck him as even remotely out of the ordinary.

He went through her folder of photographs with tears on his cheeks and the kind of soul-deep sorrow that he equated with physical pain. There was their vacation in Maui. Their trip to Disney World. Their wedding and reception. Their first Thanksgiving. Their first Christmas. So many firsts. So many lasts. So many memories they would never have the opportunity to make together. She was so beautiful, so full of happiness and life. And he could see toward the end how his actions had begun to wear on her.

The rising sun bled the sky red to the east. It reflected from his rearview mirror in stark contrast to the darkness that still lurked over the Rockies. He'd seen pictures of Denver from the turn of the last century, from back when its population was a mere 100,000 or so and there were fewer than two billion people on the planet. There was a part of him that wished he could go back to that simpler time, when bad guys wore black and carried their weapons out in the open. And even then, shooting—actually taking someone else's life—was considered the last resort. He supposed it was inevitable that as the world population soared to eight billion, any one life became devalued.

The only thing resembling an actual clue was buried in Angie's browsing history, and even that was a far cry from the kind of monumental lead that was going to bring everything into focus. Hidden among the sites she frequented—the bookstores and blogs and social-networking sites—nearly lost in the banks of her Google history, was a search for a single item he didn't recognize. An address. One lone address he didn't recognize in an area of town that neither he nor his wife would ever have had any reason to go.

He followed the link to the search, zoomed in on the map as far as he could go, and then clicked to enlarge the street-level view. The ranch-style house at 6900 Market Street had red bricks, a green roof, and a concrete porch with weeds growing from the cracked steps. The lawn was patchy and yellow. A juniper hedge obscured the only window on the front of the house. It was an anonymous and invisible house in an anonymous and invisible neighborhood.

There was no telling whether the picture had been uploaded yesterday or five years ago. All he knew was that if it somehow pertained to her work, Angie wouldn't have even thought about it at home unless her curiosity had gotten the better of her.

And if he wanted to figure out why she'd searched for it, there was only one way to do so.

28

Commerce City was an industrial sprawl north of downtown Denver. It squatted at the intersection all the major interstate shipping lanes, from border to border, coast to coast, and everything in between. There were FedEx and UPS hubs and trucking companies of all shapes and sizes. Semis rumbled through, day and night. There wasn't a single point where you were more than a five-minute walk from the kind of truck stop you could see from space.

While it might have been a suburb in the most literal sense, few locals viewed it as such. It was a commercial district that lingered beneath an omnipresent cloud of industrial fumes and exhaust, and alternately smelled of burned rubber, flatus, or animal by-products, depending upon which way the wind decided to blow.

In recent years, however, superstores and factory outlets had crept in among the warehouses and wholesalers, bringing with them restaurants and hotels and affordable housing developments. And lost in the thick of it all, or perhaps deliberately forgotten, were the older homes that long ago had been built for the factory workers who kept the industrial lifeblood pumping. They were solid houses built during the post–World War II glory years, when men returned home to find job opportunities galore and launched the baby boom that led to a doubling of the world's population during the span of half a century. Where once opportunity blossomed, it now slunk off to die. Most of the houses had fallen into disrepair. Some had boarded windows. The majority had sunburned lawns and skeletal shrubs, tar-paper roofs and peeling paint. Some homeowners had erected fifteen-foot chain-link fences around their properties, and yet their front doors were still covered with graffiti.

Mason found the street for which his wife had searched a couple of blocks behind a Flying J truck stop and so close to the convergence of highways that he could hear the constant buzz of traffic even with his windows rolled up. He could just see the distant crown of skyscrapers in his rearview mirror as he drove down the street, watching the house numbers steadily increase. The people on their porches scrutinized his car with open hostility. As it turned out, he didn't even need to see the address to the pick out the right house.

A few green tufts had grown from the scorched black lawn, but the house itself wasn't putting forth the same kind of effort. The bricks appeared to be the only things holding the framework together. The bush from the picture was gone, as was the majority of the roof, over which the soot-coated chimney lorded like a tombstone. The front door had been eaten by flames, but not fully consumed, and somehow it managed to remain closed behind a long string of yellow police tape that fluttered on the breeze.

He pulled to the curb in front of the house and stared at the charcoaled ruins for a few minutes before he finally parked and got out. The neighbors made a show of going back into their houses as he walked across the lawn and ascended the steps to the porch. He nudged the door open with his shoe and covered his mouth and nose to avoid the ash and soot that billowed out. While he didn't know a whole lot about the nature of fire damage, it was obvious that this hadn't happened within the last few days. Either the owner or the insurance company had written it off as a lost cause. Maybe both. No effort at all had been invested in its renovation or even in cleaning up the mess. There were standing puddles of water on floors that had been burned to the bare concrete and floorboards in spots. The interior walls merely provided a framework upon which the remaining roof could decompose. There was no furniture, at least none that had survived the blaze. Only what looked like the charred remnants of a small desk. That was all. No entertainment center. No bookcases. No dining room table. There wasn't a single appliance in the kitchen. Just the one desk, if that was even what it had once been.

Mason stood in the center of the living room and turned in a circle. He was missing something, but for the life of him, he couldn't figure out what. Everything had been cleared out either prior to the fire or sometime afterward, which didn't make any sense, considering the house itself had been left to rot. Burned wood crunched underfoot. He heard the sound of water dripping somewhere below him. A quick stomp on the floor produced a hollow *thump*.

The doorway to the basement was off the kitchen. He clicked on the mini LED Maglite he kept on his key chain and stared down into the darkness. There was little left of the stairs, most of which formed a charred heap directly beneath the abrupt ledge. He smelled the faintest hint of a petrochemical accelerant beneath the overpowering stench of what he guessed to be a stew of mildew and sewer water.

The fire had been started down there, but why?

It was a good ten feet straight down. He knelt, swung his legs over the edge, and lowered himself until he was barely above the rubble, then let go.

Mason shined his light around the basement to get his bearings. The walls were bare concrete and stained with rust and water. Pipes ran up and down them and crossed beneath the floorboards overhead. There were two windows, both of them caked with soot and barely large enough to slither through on his belly, if he were even able to jump high enough. The standing water all around him had to be a good foot deep. Droplets dripped from above with a metronomic plinking sound.

He stepped down into the frigid water and waded away from the stairs. It was black and soaked his pants all the way up to his knees. His flashlight beam couldn't even break the surface. He had to shuffle his feet to keep from tripping on debris or slipping on the film that had settled onto the concrete floor. He was quickly losing the feeling in his toes, but not fast enough to prevent him from experiencing what felt like the outside three toes on his right foot snapping when he stumbled into something unforgiving. It was long and straight. He ran his shoe along its edge. Some kind of metal. He stepped over the rim and encountered more metal. Thinner, intersecting pieces in a gridlike pattern.

Mason marked the spot, sloshed back to the stairs, and returned with a broken length of wood. He wedged the thinner end of the board under the object and levered it upward. It was remarkably heavy, but it progressively became lighter as the water drained through its bottom surface. Once he had it high enough that he could get a grip on it, he dropped the wood and raised it with both hands. It stood several feet taller than he was when he finally had it upright and balanced. The metal was covered with a grungy paste and had begun to rust. He wiped away some of the crud and revealed a small hinged door. An ornate brass placard had been affixed to it. It read simply SUITE 304. He smeared away more of the muck. There were dozens of doors, all of them labeled by suite number. Each of them opened onto a deep slot that would have met with the wall if the unit were pushed up against it. He knew exactly what he was looking at, but it was so out of context in this flooded basement that he couldn't fathom why it was here.

And then it hit him.

The interior of each individual partition was carbon-scored and corroded, as were both the inside and the outside of the doors. This large unit had been dragged down here and its contents used to ignite the blaze, which had gutted the entire house. Perhaps whoever set the fire expected the upper portion of the house to collapse onto the basement, but the fire department had arrived too quickly. Or maybe, with the surfaces purged of fingerprints, they simply didn't care. After all, how many people would actually recognize the implications of what they were seeing?

The whole scenario had the unmistakable feel of a rush job. Whoever had dragged all the units down here to set them ablaze had definitely sensed he was about to be caught. The edges of even more units and their open doors broke the surface of the water around the corner. There had to be at least ten of them, maybe more.

Mason needed to verify what he'd found. If he was right, then he might finally have something he could actually work with.

He climbed up onto the remains of the stairs, jumped to catch the lip of the step above him, and hauled himself up. There had to be a section of the plaster that hadn't burned. One small patch was all he needed. He found it on the southern wall in the living room. A mere swatch maybe two feet square, but it was enough. He could see the gridlike pattern of discoloration where the unit had been mounted against the wall for an extended period of time. He imagined every wall in the living room and the kitchen and the bedroom, from floor to ceiling, covered with those units. Rows and rows of post office boxes that served as physical suites for the businesses registered to them. Stacks of mail inside each, waiting to be bundled and shipped to the owners, wherever they lived. He imagined a woman sitting at the desk he'd first seen upon entering with a computer in front of her, a hands-free microphone near her mouth, and the telephone ringing nonstop. Pictured her answering every incoming line, pretending to be the secretary for each of the different businesses corresponding to the various suites, taking messages and routing calls all around the world. That was why Angie had been looking into this house, why she had broken her own rule about even thinking about work at home. It was a one-stop shop for criminal enterprises looking to acquire the appearance of legitimacy.

Suddenly, everything made sense. He knew exactly how this burned house connected his wife to the woman who'd called him on the phone last night.

He ran out the front door, cleared the steps, and jumped into his car. Grabbed his laptop. Searched for Fairacre Ranch Surplus and Auction. He already knew what he would find. It was in the small print at the bottom of a home page that looked exactly how he would have expected a ranch auction site to look.

Commerce City had relaxed its regulations on corporations in hopes of luring out-of-state businesses and creating jobs, not to mention revenue. After all, corporations needed more than mere tax breaks, especially in this economic climate. They needed incentives. In addition to state and income taxes on a sliding scale and exemptions that afforded a large measure of bookkeeping creativity, the city had incentivized the act of incorporation itself. And what was a corporation if not an entity capable of serving as an imaginary storefront, behind which personal assets could be hidden? They could be owned by anyone, managed completely anonymously, and used to discreetly shuffle funds between accounts, just like those Angie had used to track the fifteen million dollars laundered south of the border.

Fairacre Ranch Surplus and Auction, LLC, listed the burned house beside him—6900 Market Street—as its corporate headquarters. Suite 416, in fact. The implication being that it was on the fourth floor of an office building in a city whose name alone validated its professionalism, when it was really nothing more than a PO box inside a decrepit house with hundreds of others.

All the suites belonged to shell companies.

Hidden not in the Cayman Islands, but inside an anonymous house in their own backyard, were hundreds of seemingly legitimate turnkey corporations that could be used to create the appearance of legitimacy for financial transactions, hide assets from lawyers and governments, and limit personal liability for the owner, all while concealing his true identity.

Angie had done precisely what Gunnar had just told Mason to do. She'd followed the money and made the connection between the missing fifteen million dollars, the woman who'd given him the tip about Fairacre, and the unidentified ninth trafficking organization he'd been hunting for the last year.

She'd found the people responsible for testing the virus on the undocumented aliens. For the slaughter of the SWAT team in the administration building and the strike force in Arizona. For the murder of his partner, Spencer Kane. And, in doing so, she'd forced them to step out of the shadows and placed herself on a collision course with the man with the blue eyes.

And now she was dead.

PART III

I see in the near future a crisis approaching that unnerves me and causes me to tremble for the safety of my country. As a result of the war, corporations have been enthroned and an era of corruption in high places will follow, and the money power of the country will endeavor to prolong its reign by working upon the prejudices of the people until all wealth is aggregated in a few hands, and the Republic is destroyed. I feel at this moment more anxiety for the safety of my country than ever before, even in the midst of war.

—Abraham Lincoln, letter to Col. William F. Elkins (1864)

29

Denver, Colorado

NOVEMBER 13

Mason's great-grandfather, the first James Richmond Mason, was larger than life. At least from a historical perspective. He died before Mason was born, but not without first placing his indelible stamp on a nation in transition. He started his career as an attorney, no better or worse than any other. He earned his law degree from the New York Law School and began his professional life as a defense counselor before sidestepping into corporate law, where he handled famous clients like William Henry Vanderbilt, Thomas Elliot Richter, Henry Clay Frick, William Waldorf Astor, and R. J. Mueller, whose combined fortunes represented nearly half of the world's wealth around the turn of the twentieth century.

He could have lived a long and comfortable life on those retainers alone. Instead, he decided to utilize his station for the public good. He maintained his legal status as special counselor to his existing clients and helped establish the Mueller Endowment and the Richter Foundation, all while hurling himself into the political arena, the War Department specifically. He helped expand the scope of the existing branches of the military and organize schools of advanced study for the special forces, for which he was rewarded with a position in Teddy Roosevelt's cabinet.

None of his ideas was implemented a moment too soon, it turned out. It wasn't long before the country found itself embroiled in World War I, during which he served as special envoy to Great Britain and France on behalf of then president Woodrow Wilson. All the while, he worked toward peace through international cooperation by helping to found the League of Nations and the International Congruity Alliance. He even managed to find the time to marry Mason's great-grandmother, Isabella Touring Mason, and produce an heir. When he finally "retired," he served as chief justice of the U.S. Supreme Court and director of the Richter Foundation, a position he used to endow the Society for Lasting International Peace.

Mason remembered hearing those stories as a kid and thinking that was just what old people did in those days. As if there was nothing extraordinary about his great-grandfather's achievements. It wasn't until he read about him—the first James Richmond Mason, whose name he bore—in his freshman U.S. history class that he recognized the significance of what his great-grandfather had accomplished as a single human being in a sea of billions.

He'd felt small and insignificant in a way he never had before. Until that moment, he'd cultivated the same worldview as every other teenager: The sun and the moon revolved around him and there was no life on the planet more important than his own. The feeling that no matter what he did he would never fulfill the expectations set forth for him and live up to his family name had been almost crippling. He was a fourteen-year-old kid whose greatest personal achievement consisted of being able to run a spaghetti noodle in through his nose and out of his mouth, and suddenly he was burdened by the expectation that he would fulfill some magnificent destiny for which he had no blueprint.

Now here he was, shoving his way through the crowded corridors in the Federal Building, water squelching from his ruined shoes, smelling like he'd just crawled through a sewer. He'd spent the night in his car and couldn't remember the last time he'd gotten anything even remotely resembling a good night's sleep. He couldn't have been any further from living up to the Grand Mason Destiny if he tried.

His only lead was the house at 6900 Market Street. It was registered to a man named Herman Jacobsen, who, coincidentally, was CEO of more than thirty corporations, president of another twenty, and sat on the board of directors for nearly two hundred others. The fact that Mr. Jacobson had died in 1997 seemed to be doing little to impede his goal of world financial domination. The actual business being run at that physical location—Colorado Corporate Trust, or CCT—was registered and incorporated in Cheyenne, Wyoming. Only as Mason read through its corporate filings on the computer in his office did he truly realize the scope of its reach.

CCT didn't merely provide incorporation services; it provided entire companies. Complete corporate entities with CEOs, like Mr. Jacobsen, and board members and practicing lawyers on retainer, who could instantly invoke the attorney-client privilege. Real histories that could be tracked and investigated and proved to be perfectly legitimate. On paper, anyway. CCT offered something better than a shell company in the booming industry of financial deceit; it sold what's known in the financial sector as "shelf" companies.

These were dummy businesses that had been launched years before, incorporated under fictitious names, registered to provide nonexistent products or services, and then set up on a shelf to age like wine. The longer they aged, the more they cost. Some sold for high six-figure sums, while the majority changed hands in the upper five-figure range.

CCT offered a full-service plan. It provided a receptionist who fielded calls for all the different businesses, relayed the messages to the appropriate contact addresses, and managed the various websites. All in addition to forwarding the mail that found its way into each of the corporate "suites" he'd discovered in the flooded basement.

It was a scam of monumental proportions, the kind of con that made a whole lot of very rich people even richer by allowing them to hide assets in unrelated companies where no one would think to look, duck regulations that applied only to certain industries, and funnel profits into accounts the IRS couldn't find, let alone reach. This was the kind of completely legal, yet entirely unethical, financial deceit the government purportedly wanted to make transparent, and yet not one of the six hundred companies housed at 6900 Market Street had ever been subjected to more than a superficial financial audit.

At the moment, Mason only cared about one of those six hundred. Fairacre Ranch Surplus and Auction was incorporated in August 1998, with the stated mission of providing consignment and auction services for everything from used equipment to seeds and grain. The corporation owned a single plot of land roughly in the middle of nowhere on the plains east of Brush, Colorado. Herman Jacobsen was listed as the sole proprietor of the limited-liability corporation and had posted gross revenue of less than fifteen thousand dollars annually ever since. The website featured pictures of what looked like pieces of junk and the seemingly absurd prices at which bidding would begin. There were even testimonials from satisfied customers on both sides of the dealings.

It had to be one of the most perfectly orchestrated frauds he'd ever seen.

He understood how auditing their financials wouldn't be in the company's best interests, especially if a routine tax audit had been passed up the chain to a bulldog like Angie, but what could it possibly have to do with the woman who would be calling him in roughly ten hours? He needed to find out who actually owned the corporate entity and what they were trying to hide. And without his wife's records, he could think of only one place to start.

30

Mason had just rounded the corner from his office when he ran into SAC Christensen, who was on his way in.

"I thought you were going to come see me first thing this morning."

He was unable to interpret the expression on his boss's face until he crinkled his nose and looked down at Mason's filthy pants. There was no mistaking that one.

"Sorry, Chris. I was running down a lead and it totally slipped my mind."

"A lead? For which case?"

Mason opened his mouth, then realized anything he might say would only make the situation worse. He closed it again and averted his stare.

Christensen nodded, as if confirming some inner suspicion. The vein in his forehead bulged and his lips writhed. When he finally spoke, it was through clenched teeth.

"My office. Now."

Mason followed him down the hallway. Everyone they passed sensed Chris's mood and cleared the way. Even his secretary tried to look busy when he passed her desk and opened the glass door to his office. Mason knew he was in big trouble when he saw his partner sitting in the chair facing the special agent in charge's desk. Trapp stiffened when they entered, but didn't turn to face him.

A part of Mason had always known this was how it would play out. Were the shoe on the other foot, he might have done the same thing. He would have talked to his partner before ratting him out, though. Then again, he hadn't given Trapp any warning that he was going to put him in this position in the first place. Mason couldn't blame him for covering his ass.

"Sit."

Christensen eased into the high-backed leather chair behind his desk and stared holes through Mason. There were no pictures of his family. No homemade cards or pictures drawn in crayon. He only knew Christensen had a wife because he'd seen her once at an awards banquet years ago, and guessed he had a son because there was a rising star in Behavioral at Quantico with the same last name. This office belonged solely to the special agent in charge.

Mason sat and glanced over at Trapp. As usual, he looked like the wind had blown him in. He acknowledged Mason from the corner of his eye.

"Was I in some way unclear about my expectations when I told you to be in my office first thing this morning?" Christensen asked.

"No, sir."

Mason looked his boss in the eyes and saw the fire that was about to consume him.

"And when I forbade you from participating in the investigation of your wife's death, did my choice of words confuse you?"

"Is 'forbade' really—?"

"Damn it, Mason!"

"No, sir."

"Then why in God's name are we sitting here right now?"

He stood abruptly and turned to face the window. On a clear day, you could see all the way across the city to where the mountains met the sky. Today, a dirty haze of smog clung jealously to the skyscrapers.

"Sir. Special Agent Trapp had no knowledge—"

"You don't think I already know that? Who the hell do you think that is sitting next to you looking like he just sold out his mother for a back-alley hand job?"

Trapp finally looked at Mason, who made a gesture he hoped his partner would interpret as an apology. Then he turned back to Christensen, steadied himself, and took it squarely on the chin.

The whole meeting was a blur, for as Christensen was verbally undressing Mason, he experienced a moment of mental clarity that had thus far eluded him and was actually able to plot a course that would get him moving in the right direction. Granted, the logical part of him recognized that he was a man standing naked in his front yard, cackling wildly as he hurled torches onto the thatch roof of his own house, but it was a liberating feeling. As Christensen had shed his personal skin in favor of the professional when he entered his office, Mason was shedding his professional skin, which had suddenly become far too constrictive. He was unencumbered by any ties that bound him to his former life, save for one.

And right now, that was the only thing that mattered.

Mason watched himself hand over his badge and Glock as though from a distance. He heard the word *suspension*, but was too lost in thought to notice the length of time that preceded it.

He left the building unescorted, which he supposed said something about the severity of his predicament, and sat in his car with zero security clearance and just about as many personal possessions.

That was about to change, though.

He might not have had an eidetic memory, but recalling seven numbers he'd seen the night before wasn't beyond his abilities. Neither was throwing down a quarter of a million dollars with a simple transaction he could make from his cell phone. After all, he'd inherited his wife's trust fund, despite his father-in-law's lawyer's best efforts to block it. He didn't imagine Angie would mind if he used a small portion of it to help him catch her murderer. He could have drawn from his own trust fund, but he wasn't in the mood to field an angry call from his father.

The listing agent had been more than happy to part with the property and undoubtedly would have negotiated the price. Mason didn't care about the money, though. He wanted expediency and was willing to pay for it.

And he was in a hurry to get out of town.

He wasn't about to let anything as inconsequential as the loss of his badge keep him from doing his job.

31

Mason made one quick stop before he hit the highway. He bought a thermal long-sleeve shirt and jeans, a pair of Wolverine work boots, and a winter jacket, and left his reeking clothes in the Dumpster behind the store. It was roughly ninety miles from Denver to Brush. He made the drive in just over an hour.

The town itself reminded him of every other small town in Colorado. There was a main street and side streets with businesses that suffered for not being on the main street. It was probably just a prejudice of his, but everything looked dusty. Then again, considering the wind leaped up from the flat plains without warning and blew the loose dirt sideways from the sugar-beet fields, everything probably *was* actually covered with a layer of dust.

The whole small-town lifestyle seemed foreign to him, as though not only had he descended in altitude, but had traveled back in time. There was a part of him that wished life could really be this simple. And then he saw how full the parking lot was at the Drink King Bar and realized that it wasn't.

He blew through the town in less time than it took to program the address for Fairacre Ranch Surplus and Auction into his GPS. The computerized voice guided him off the highway and onto a poorly marked off-ramp. He headed southeast from there, across a seemingly interminable stretch of beet and winter-wheat fields and feral acreages that appeared to be cultivating tumbleweeds.

The slate gray horizon promised snow.

The silver arches of massive sprinkler systems with airplane tires flew past. None of them looked like they'd been moved in quite some time. Occasionally, a small house materialized from the fields in the distance, followed in short measure by the arrow-straight dirt driveway that serviced it. The bubblegum pink asphalt gave way to gravel, which pinged from the undercarriage and wheel wells. A rooster tail of dust rose behind the Grand Cherokee.

He had a hunch he was nearing his destination even before the computer voice finally piped up and let him know that his turn was coming. The barbed-wire fence to his right had fallen in sections. Several seasons' worth of tumbleweeds were inextricably tangled with the wires. Half of the weathered gray posts were broken or absent altogether. Whatever had once grown in the fields had died long ago. Wild grasses and weeds ran rampant among the desiccated carcasses of sunflowers. A rickety cross stood testament to the passing of a scarecrow. The crows had made themselves at home in its absence. They lined the telephone wires and flapped to stay balanced on top of weeds that couldn't accommodate their weight. He could feel them following him with their eyes.

Mason pulled off the road onto a driveway that was nearly overgrown with dead weeds and stared through the skein of dust on his windshield toward the wooden structure barely visible at the farthest extent of his vision, then got out and dragged the aluminum gate off into the weeds.

He drove slowly, taking in everything around him.

The homestead rose ahead of him, simultaneously growing from the flatlands and decomposing before his very eyes as he neared. It was situated just this side of a ravine. Judging by the skeletal cottonwoods, no water had flowed through there for a long time. The branches were spotted with crows.

The road widened into a turnaround, in the center of which was a hump of bare dirt where he guessed flowers had once grown around the rusted wagon wheel standing from it. The house was a stereotypical ranch, the whitewash sandblasted to the bare gray wood. Behind it was another, larger wooden outbuilding, or at least what was left of it. The charred remains of a cattle chute led into it from the rear. A series of interconnected corrals formed a veritable timber maze in the field to the north.

He parked and let the dust settle before he climbed out. Everything was still. No wind rattled through the dry fields. Nothing moved behind any of the windows. Even the crows perched along the roofline seemed to be frozen in time as they watched him walk around to the back of his car and open the trunk, where he kept his own personal Smith & Wesson Sigma series model SW9VE in the cutout beneath the false floor. It was a beautiful American-made handgun that seemed to have been designed to fit his palm specifically. It held sixteen 9 mm rounds in the magazine and one in the breech. With the custom chrome slide, two-tone black polymer finish, and laser sight, it looked positively futuristic. He pulled it out, checked the clip, and shoved it into the recently vacated holster beneath his left arm.

The sound of the closing trunk echoed across the prairie.

Gravel crunched underfoot as he approached the front door of the house. He gave it a solid rap and felt the wood shudder. There wasn't so much as a single tire track on the windswept turnaround. He tried the knob. It didn't work. He stepped back and tried his foot. It worked like a charm.

The door rebounded from the wall behind it and he stopped it with his shoulder. Pistol drawn, he advanced into the main room. The only real sound was the creaking of floorboards beneath his weight. There was an old couch and an even older rocking chair. Both of them had been shoved against the wall to hold the dusty curtains in place. A wood-burning stove sat cold and dark on the opposite side of the room. There were no pictures on the walls, only the discolorations where they had once hung. The floor was bare wood that had shrunken just enough that he could see the dirt underneath it in spots. The lines of wear were readily apparent. He followed the main path into the kitchen, where he found avocado-colored appliances that didn't look like they'd been used in a decade.

The bedroom had seen use somewhat more recently. The mattress rested on the floor next to the box spring, both of which were stained and dirty. A cracked mirror hung on the wall beside a closet door that opened upon empty space. He could barely see his reflection through the dust.

The lone bathroom featured a claw-foot tub with a ring of rust and a toilet that he supposed was more appealing than the public stalls in a bus station, but just barely.

It didn't look like anyone had been in here for quite some time, but with the rate the dust accumulated on him as he walked, it could have been only a few hours.

Mason exited the way he'd entered, without bothering to close the door behind him.

The crows scrabbled to keep him in sight as he rounded the side of the house and cut a path through waist-high weeds toward the out-building.

Only the charred framework and the northeastern corner of the structure remained to support what little of the roof survived. The walls along the front side—or at least what he assumed to be the front side—were completely absent, as were those on the western side and the majority of the northern. It was as though someone had arrived to put out the fire too late to salvage more than a portion of it, or per-haps the wind had merely shifted and blown the flames in a different direction.

He entered where he estimated the front door had once been. The ground inside was overgrown with weeds and wild grasses. He couldn't see any hint of soot or ash on the soil. This place hadn't burned anytime recently.

Snowflakes fell through the large gaps in the roof and twirled down around him like glitter.

The main room was roughly 40 feet deep and 150 feet wide. What looked like the blackened carcass of a platform or a stage protruded from the weeds to his left. Support posts stood every twenty feet. The majority were now black stumps, at least in the western half. Those in the eastern half were burned nearly all the way through, yet they somehow managed to hold a large chunk of the scorched roof aloft.

The knee-high vegetation made hissing sounds against his jeans.

Tumbleweeds had collected against the rubble of what he suspected had once been an interior wall. He closed his eyes and pictured this place in better times. An auctioneer on a small wooden stage, a ramp to either side of him and a steer behind him. Farmers shouting out bids from the open area, where their wives fanned themselves and their rambunctious children climbed on bales of hay. The interior wall would have separated the auction floor from the holding pens, where the animals awaiting their turn had been led up the chute from the corrals to the north of the building.

He kicked through the weeds and broken wood toward what remained of the northern wall. All that was left of the stalls that ran the entire width of the building were square black nubs under the tangles of brown grass.

The smell of manure lingered. Faint. Smoke and ash. Burned wood. The merest hint of some kind of fuel. Old smells.

He caught something hard with the toe of his boot. It made a clanking sound. He knelt, swept aside the weeds, and extricated a length of rusted chain. The remainder was stuck solidly in the dirt. He looked up into the rafters, where the rusted metal wheel of a pulley still hung. There were more chains, rusted and broken, coiled on themselves in what was left of the adjacent stalls. They had hooks on the ends of them, too.

The sections of the wood-plank wall that still stood in the northeast corner were charcoaled and seemingly held together by the rusted hatch of the cattle chute, which had broken from its chain assembly and leaned in the doorway designed to admit livestock. There was a gap perhaps just wide enough to squeeze through between the fallen door and the frame. He could see the wooden ramp leading up to it from the maze of aged timber on the other side.

The walls formed a dead end in the corner. Feces and bones marked where some animal or other had once made a den. He brushed at the carbon scoring on the wood and exposed deep parallel scratches. They aligned just about perfectly with his fingertips.

The similarities to the quarry in Arizona were undeniable. The stalls with the chains dangling from the ceiling. The abandoned nature of the building. He tried not to envision the bodies of naked men and women hanging from the rafters as they decomposed. Tried not to hear the buzz of flies. The evil of this place radiated from the ground beneath his feet, where it had soaked into the soil on the blood of innocents.

Mason prayed it hadn't been as bad as he imagined for the victims, that a merciful God had taken pity on them and spared them this misery, but there was no doubt in his mind that this was a place outside of His reach. And he knew full well that no matter how horrible he imagined it must have been, in the flesh it would have been infinitely worse.

He stepped back out of the corner, to find a cold wind had risen from the east. It rippled through the weeds and assaulted him with snowflakes.

Dark clouds spread outward across the sky.

Mason thought about his wife, who, for whatever reason, had sought out this place specifically, her relationship to the woman who had called him last night, and the reason why they would have been meeting with a federal prosecutor in a sleazy motel.

He'd seen what he'd come here to find, but he didn't feel vindication, only sickness in the pit of his stomach. The sooner he was away from this wretched place, the better. He was only too happy to watch the burned barn fade back into the fields in his rearview mirror as he drove away.

32

Fairacre was the key. If Mason was right about the stalls in the auction house having been used to test the virus on human subjects—like he'd seen firsthand at the quarry in Arizona—then he'd finally found the lead he needed. Angie had obviously recognized there was something important about it, too. The woman who would be calling him later tonight had said that his wife had been carrying the audit of Fairacre with her when they were supposed to meet at the motel, the same day the man with the blue eyes miraculously returned from the dead and murdered her, just as he had Mason's partner, Spencer Kane. He could positively feel the connections starting to line up.

Whoever had purchased the Fairacre shelf corporation was out there somewhere at this very moment. Mason was looking for someone with money, someone who, whether intentionally or not, had stepped out of the fringes and into an industry where there were no strangers. Whether the farmers on these plains grew produce, harvested grains, or ranched cattle, it was a small-enough community that everyone knew one another. More important, they had to keep tabs on the competition if they were going to survive in the cutthroat agricultural world. An unknown entity purchasing an old cattle auction house wouldn't have gone unnoticed, even one that didn't subsequently burn to the ground. Someone had to know something, especially someone who made it his business to learn everything there was to know, if only to use that information to ruin anyone who stood in his way. And since Mason was already all the way out here . . .

The AgrAmerica corporate headquarters were north of the city of Greeley, which began in the same fashion as many other frontier towns, as a stagecoach station. Following the Civil War, a newspaperman by the name of Nathan C. Meeker arrived and founded the Union Temperance Colony, a religious utopia that pioneered irrigation techniques that turned the small private enterprise into an agricultural juggernaut seemingly overnight. Co-ops developed and money flowed, but where there was wealth, there was always someone who wanted a larger cut of it. Chief among them was Angie's great-grandfather, Wesley Harrison Thornton, who had seized the reins of the cattle industry the moment the colony's founder and moral backbone left for the White River Indian Agency, where he later died in infamy.

As it grew, Greeley became something of a big city crammed into a small town's body. It had a disproportionately large immigrant population, thanks to Angie's grandfather Frank, who pioneered the use of cheap, mostly illegal labor. He brought them in by the truckload and set them to work in the meat-processing plants, where the loss of fingers or a hand, or even a full arm, was considered a small price to pay for employment. Town officials ignored such minor incidents and the authorities always seemed to be looking the other way. Especially when it came to anything that happened out near the AgrAmerica feed lots, processing plants, packing facilities, or corporate HQ, which was why Mason was surprised to see a pair of uniformed policemen bolstering the security presence at the front gates.

The AgrAmerica campus was more reminiscent of a military base than the home of the soon-to-be second-largest agricultural conglomerate in the world. The five-hundred-acre administrative complex was surrounded by a twenty-foot chain-link fence capped with concertina wire and a ditch with reeds and stagnant water he was certain his father-in-law thought of as a moat. There was one entrance and access was controlled by a guard shack staffed by a private security firm. There were never fewer than a dozen guards on duty at any given time, two of whom paced circles around incoming vehicles, using long poles with mirrors on the end to search underneath them. Another used a German shepherd—which shed like nobody's business, as Mason well knew—to search inside every car, as it had been trained to smell any sort of contaminated biological matter by the metabolic wastes the organisms produced. All while the main guard checked credentials and eventually raised the gate.

The inadvertent admittance of a single pathogenic organism could potentially compromise any number of sensitive research projects and set the scientists back years. Of course, the company was less worried about the biological matter coming in than going out. Genetically modified seeds and organisms were worth fortunes on the open market and could potentially make one company and break another, which was one of the main reasons why the scientists on the more delicate projects were actually required to live on-site through the duration of their contracts.

He passed through security with only a cursory inspection—by their standards, anyway. After all, he'd married into the family and been here a dozen times before. That didn't mean he could come and go as he pleased, though. His father-in-law's personal assistant had been notified of his arrival and instructed the guard to send him directly back to Building Seed, where his father-in-law would meet him when he finished whatever megaimportant thing he was doing.

Mason dreaded talking to him. Maybe Paul didn't blame him for Angie's death, but if that were the case, he'd be the only one in the room who didn't. Mason wasn't prepared to share the fact that he believed she'd been murdered because of a case she was investigating, though, so he needed to tap-dance around discussing it at all. Not that he could pretend it hadn't happened. They would always have that between them and Mason would forever be a reminder of what Paul had lost.

Building A had once encompassed the entirety of the corporate empire. It was a single-story structure that looked like an elementary school and housed a visitor's center and the offices of lower-level management. Building B rose across the field behind it, which featured a man-made pond with a spectacular water display surrounded by a ring of flags. The building itself was far less impressive. It was a great gray monolith—that kind of looked like a dormitory—with smoked-glass windows and balconies off the offices of department heads. There was a helipad on the roof, and the top three floors served as temporary living quarters for visiting VIPs.

Building Seed functioned as something of a cross between R&D and a giant trophy case. Technically, it was actually two separate buildings, C and D, thus the übercreative nickname—CD: Seed. He doubted he was the only one to roll his eyes at the explanation, just the only one who'd done so in front of the CEO while sleeping with his daughter.

Mason had been inside just twice. The last time had been years ago, before Arizona, but it wasn't the kind of place a guy could easily forget. The two buildings were bridged by an elaborate glass structure reminiscent of the Louvre. It was an architectural marvel, which, while stunning, paled in comparison to what was housed inside. Crops grew in every conceivable way: from soil, from sponges, from indoor ponds, from vertical surfaces, from where the roots adhered to glass balls suspended in midair. It was like walking into an M. C. Escher drawing, the way the bioengineers overcame the constraints of space and gravity. There were fruits and vegetables of all shapes and sizes, pollinated by bees the color of the setting sun and butterflies with wings nearly as big as a grown man's hands. They called it "the Bridge to the Future," or simply the "Futures," and it was a sealed environment. In addition to showcasing the company's featured long-term visions, it housed the pet projects of the various engineers, who were given carte blanche to follow their hearts as long as they performed their contracted jobs to Paul's satis-faction.

Visitor parking was behind the main entrance to Building C. Ma-son was really in no hurry to talk to Paul, so he sat in his car for a few minutes to collect his thoughts and formulate the best approach. He watched cranes raising what looked like HVAC equipment onto the roof of a monolithic structure across the acreage behind him in his rearview mirror. Whatever Paul was building back there was flat-out enormous. It looked almost like a shopping center or an airport. Trust the Thorntons not to do anything half-assed.

He closed his eyes, let out a long sigh, and climbed out of the car. The temperature felt as though it had fallen a good ten degrees already. The snowflakes were only marginally larger, but that was about to change. The storm clouds darkened as they gathered over the distant mountains in the reflection on the glass facade as he strode toward the door, which opened onto the main lobby. The floors were polished marble, the deep chairs leather, and the potted plants imported from some tropical paradise or other. He was greeted by a woman who made no introduction. She simply ushered him through the access-controlled door beside the reception desk and into the hallway on the other side.

"Mr. Thornton will meet you in the Futures momentarily." The security badge clipped to the lapel of her cream-colored blouse identified her as Ava Dietrich, but didn't list her title. Mason could barely hear her over the clacking of her stiletto heels and the resulting echo. She was tall and thin, but had the musculature of an athlete. Her calves bulged with each step and her triceps formed inverted Vs as she swung her arms. She wore her platinum blond hair longer in the front than in the back. "I should advise you that Mr. Thornton has a very busy schedule today and can't afford to spare more than a few minutes of his time."

Mason figured he was supposed to say something that would make him sound grateful, but he just nodded and watched the closed doorways pass on either side. She took the first right and used her badge, which contained a security microchip, to activate the stainless-steel door. It slid back into the wall only long enough for them to pass through, then closed behind them. There was another door in front of them, identical to the last. He knew from previous visits that these doors could not be opened at the same time. Considering the nature of the experimental species inside, it was a necessary precaution. Any one of these engineered crops or animals could potentially decimate its natural counterparts and have ruinous effects on the entire ecosystem.

It was more than mere paranoia, though. Any number of anti-GMO organizations and lobbies were ready and waiting to sink their teeth into such a juicy morsel.

The blond woman opened the interior door without a word and showed him into the vast greenhouse. She glanced back at him over her shoulder. He caught the briefest glimpse of eyes a cold shade of blue, like the frozen heart of a glacier, and then she was gone with the clatter of heels.

Mason wasn't easily impressed, but he had to admit this place could do it every time. He probably should have been concerned on some level about this kind of thing being an abomination of nature, but if you could develop crops that would grow in arid regions where children were starving to death every single day, why the hell would anyone object? Of course, these were also regions where the average female produced more than four offspring. Were all of them to survive, the population boom would be loud enough to hear around the globe. He just wasn't the kind of guy who enjoyed knowing that somewhere children were dying while the civilized world waged endless moral debates about the merits of feeding them.

He wasn't about to share that thought with Paul, who'd learned more about dying children than any father should have to. He'd been so still that Mason hadn't even noticed he was there. Just sitting on the other side of a garden planted with tall golden grains, leaning back on a bench, staring up at the sky through the slanted glass wall overhead. Mason sat down beside him, laced his fingers over his belly, and followed his father-in-law's gaze.

The leading edge of the storm scudded past. He couldn't remember ever seeing clouds move so fast.

"Ever wonder why we don't make clouds?" Mason could tell by the tone of Paul's voice that it was a rhetorical question. He didn't care what Mason thought, anyway. He had something to say and, as usual, would say it in his own way. "We can make fake snow and ice. Why not clouds?

They could bring rain to regions where nothing will grow and help forestall the effects of climate change while we figure out a long-term solution. Really . . . how hard could it be?"

A butterfly settled on Mason's knee. He watched it open and close its powder blue wings several times before again taking flight.

"I'll tell you why. It's because the people who live in those godforsaken deserts choose to do so. Even though they're dying off in droves. They just sit there and wait for someone to save them. To send them food and medicine. To send them magic seeds that will grow in their barren soil. To make their clouds for them."

"So why do you do it?"

A wistful smile traced Paul's lips, and then it was gone. He didn't need to reply; they both knew the answer. It was for no other reason than he could.

"Did you know that in just over a decade the world's population will reach eight billion? That's more than even optimistic estimates suggest the planet can sustain. We'll run out of water. Food. Every resource we depend upon will be depleted. And why? Because we're keeping entire peoples alive with our medical and scientific advances, when a hundred years ago they would have died off. Back then, we would have shrugged and chalked it up to natural selection."

"I figure that's probably good for your business, though. Don't you?"

Paul sat up abruptly and looked at him with eyes that reminded him of his wife's. He'd aged a lifetime since Mason had really looked at him last. The lines on his face were more pronounced, the silver hair at his temples had overtaken his entire head, and it was readily apparent just how tired he was.

"I've spent my entire life taking care of everyone else at the cost of the few people who truly matter to me. How is that even remotely fair?"

"I've asked myself the same question."

Paul looked at him with a curious expression on his face, then leaned back in his seat again and returned his attention to the clouds.

"It was a nice service. As far as such things go. Angela would have approved."

Mason closed his eyes and focused on not letting his breathing betray him.

"I saw you there. With Frank."

"Victor was there, too."

"I didn't see him. I guess I just assumed he was still in Germany."

"Switzerland. And why on earth would you think for a second that he'd miss his sister's funeral?"

"He never showed much interest in her life up to that point."

Paul's hand clenched into a fist. Mason had pushed that button harder than he'd meant to, but he wasn't particularly concerned about his father-in-law's feelings. Strange, though, that Paul seemed to be sparing his. While his anger was evident, he almost appeared resigned. Everyone grieved in different ways, he supposed.

"Why are you here, James?"

"I wanted to talk to you about something."

"Anything to do with pulling a quarter of a million dollars out of my daughter's trust fund to buy a run-down warehouse?" He looked at Mason from the corner of his eye. "Didn't want to dip into your own? Worried the good senator might not approve?"

"It has to do with a case I'm working."

"A man doesn't find himself in a position like mine by accident, son. Think of me as a big old spider in an even bigger web. Nothing happens without plucking on one of those threads. You're off the reservation on whatever it is you're doing, and some seem to think you're on the verge of losing more than your badge."

"Are you threatening me, Paul?"

"You aren't listening. If you and I were going to lock horns, you'd see me coming from a mile off. Games are for children, and I . . ." He paused when he realized what he'd said. "I'm too old for games. So are you, James."

"You're just looking out for me, then, right? I didn't know we had that kind of relationship."

"I have a busy schedule to keep."

"I can see that."

"You don't want me as an enemy, son."

Mason leaned forward and shook his head. He hoped the movement would make Paul turn to face him. He was only going to get one shot at this, so he needed to make it count. When the bench creaked, he turned and looked Paul squarely in the eye.

"What do you know about a company called Fairacre?"

"Nothing," Paul said. He stood and tucked his tie back into his jacket. "I trust we're through here, then?"

Apparently, they were.

"Always a pleasure to see you, James. Pass along my best to your father. Despite the circumstances, I do hope you and I can maintain a friendly relationship. My daughter was everything to me. Maybe one day you'll help me see the world through the eyes of the woman she'd become. Assuming you knew."

Mason had been prepared for worse.

"I can see myself out," he said, but Paul didn't hear him. He was already walking away, as though by physically turning his back on Mason, he'd made him disappear.

It didn't matter. Mason had what he needed now. He just wasn't quite sure what he was supposed to do with it.

He'd recognized the expression on Paul's face when he asked about Fairacre. He'd seen it before, when they first met. Angie had brought him to this very building, what felt like a lifetime ago, to meet her father.

"Daddy, there's someone I want you to meet," she'd said.

Paul had turned to Mason expectantly, as though he'd better not be wasting his time.

"This is my boyfriend. James Mason."

Paul had stepped toward him, wiped his palm on his thigh in a practiced motion meant to show he was just a regular guy, and extended his hand. The expression on his face when he spoke had been the same one he just exhibited.

"Pleased to meet you, James."

Even then Mason had known he was lying.

33

Mason couldn't seem to wrap his mind around the implications of Paul's knowledge of Fairacre. If he only recognized the name, why wouldn't he just say so? Of course, having heard of it didn't necessarily mean that he had any idea of the horrors that had potentially transpired inside the auction house. But why else would he feel the need to lie? To get the answers Mason needed, he had to find out who had purchased the Fairacre shelf corporation. Until then, he was just going to have to trust his instincts, and right now they were telling him to follow the dirt road to the west of Building Seed toward where all of the action was.

He drove into a makeshift lot where a construction trailer had been set on a dusty skirt and surrounded with heavy machinery. There were earthmovers and cement mixers and trucks of all shapes and sizes—pickups, flatbeds, Caterpillars. Industrial Dumpsters overflowed with waste, and construction scraps were heaped in seemingly arbitrary piles. The road was deeply rutted from the enormous tires of the earthmovers. He parked in the flattened weeds, amid a random assortment of cars he assumed belonged to the workmen. One car stood apart from the others: a sleek black Cadillac SUV that didn't have a single speck of dust on it.

Mason's phone rang. He surveyed the scene in front of him, looking for the man he knew was out there somewhere, and answered without taking his eyes off of the building.

"It's about time, Gunnar. Tell me you have something for me."

There was no immediate reply. He was just about to see if he'd dropped the call, when the person on the other end spoke and made him wish he'd checked the caller ID.

"James . . . What on God's green earth are you doing?"

It was his father.

"Right now? Just sitting in my car, watching the world pass by."

"Can you imagine my surprise when I received a phone call informing me that my son had been suspended?"

"Kind of caught me off guard, too. Look, Dad, I—"

"Do you know the lengths to which I had to go to convince the director of the entire Federal Bureau of Investigation to even consider overriding your special agent in charge's disciplinary action?"

"This has nothing to do with you, Dad. Believe it or not, I can handle this on my own."

Mason spotted a tall man in a dark suit standing in the middle of a circle of men wearing flannel shirts, jeans, and dirty work boots and gesturing toward the structure towering over them.

"Nothing to do with me? My son's decided to flush his career down the toilet and it has nothing to do with me? I refuse to stand by and watch you self-destruct. Regardless of what you might think, you are my son and it's my duty as your father to intercede when I see you making the kind of decisions that will have lasting consequences."

"I appreciate your concern, but everything's under control. Really."

The man in the suit broke away from the others. Mason wanted to catch him before he found out he was here. He needed the man's first reaction to be unguarded.

"I loved her, too, you know. Angie was like a daughter to me. And don't think for a second that I don't know exactly what you're dealing with. I lived it. I survived it. I triumphed over it. You need to focus on something else. Find a project. A goal. Something at which you can direct all of your energies."

"Way ahead of you, Dad."

He ended the call and climbed out of the car. The door was barely closed when the phone started ringing again. His father wasn't the kind to give up easily, but he was also a patient man who recognized that the key to winning any battle was in the timing. That was one of the few lessons he had taught Mason that actually stuck.

He intercepted Victor when he reached for the handle of his car door.

"Sorry I didn't see you at the funeral," Mason said.

Victor stiffened at the sound of his voice. He saw his brother-in-law's eyes widen in the reflection on his window. He was composed when he turned to face Mason. He and Angie had never been especially close. She was five years younger and the product of Paul's second marriage.

Mason had never met Victor's mother, but it wouldn't have surprised him to learn that he didn't actually have one and that Paul had instead figured out a way to clone himself. Victor was simply a younger version, with the same mannerisms and expressions and laugh. Only he was about three inches taller. He was being groomed to one day take the reins of AgrAmerica. That was, if he could pry them from Paul's cold, dead grasp.

Victor proffered his hand and Mason shook it.

"Jim, I didn't expect to see you. Always a pleasant surprise, of course. What brings you all the way out here into cattle country?"

"I was up this way, so I figured I'd swing by and talk to your old man. I didn't know you were in town."

"I haven't been back for very long. I was in Switzerland, getting the Bern branch off the ground."

"Why Bern?"

"It's a beautiful city, for one. For another, we're looking to establish an Eastern European presence, but aren't quite ready to jump in with both feet. The area isn't as politically stable as we would like. At least not yet. Besides, the Swiss are a little more forward-thinking when it comes to the direction our company has chosen."

"You mean their regulations are more relaxed."

"I prefer the term *progressive,* but there is something to be said for a government that understands its relationship to industry. That's not why you drove all the way out here, though. Where are my manners?" He draped his arm over Mason's shoulders, guided him away from his car, and made a grand sweeping gesture toward the construction. "Allow me to present the future world headquarters of Global Allied Biotechnology and Pharmaceuticals."

"No more AgrAmerica?"

"The name itself implies a limited reach. If we want to compete in the international market, we need to begin thinking and acting with a much broader set of parameters."

"So I take it you won't be calling it Building E?"

"Please. A and B are old and outdated. They look like they were built by Neanderthals. And my father can have his little glass lab. What we need is a building that says we are a leader in the market, a leader in the business world as a whole. It needs to be a building that people will recognize, no matter where they live. A grand structure that fits the vision of the corporate brand. It needs to scream confidence and power."

"It's going to have to scream pretty loud if you actually want people to know it's here. You can barely see it from the other buildings, let alone from the road."

Victor's laugh was the kind they taught in classes for the rich and condescending.

"You kill me, Jim. Tell you what, come back when she's finished and I'll give you the personal tour. *Then* you'll see what I'm talking about." He casually turned Mason once more and ushered him toward his car. "I'd love to catch up, but I'm already running late for a meeting I'm not at liberty to discuss, with people who aren't accustomed to being made to wait. I only budgeted enough time to make my presence known. For what we're paying these guys, it's important they understand that they have to keep this project on schedule. Starting after eight or knocking off a minute before five won't be tolerated."

"Have you tried giving the foreman a whip?"

Victor laughed.

"It's too bad we never really got a chance to get to know each other, but I hope you realize that you'll always be part of the Thornton clan, Jim." He cupped his hand over the side of his mouth as though to impart a secret. "Lord only knows we could use someone on the right side of the law in this family."

Again, the laugh, the handshake, the clap on the shoulder. And then he was in his car, preparing to back up. Mason stepped closer and signaled for him to roll down his window.

"I almost forgot. I was just talking to your dad about a property east of here that came up in an investigation I'm working. He thought you might know about it. Fairacre Ranch Surplus and Auction? You know anything about it?"

"What on earth would make you think that I know anything about ranching?"

Victor laughed at the old family joke they all told, then rolled up his window and drove away in a cloud of dust that made the snowflakes that had settled on the ground rise once more. Mason had seen it, though.

The brief whitening of his brother-in-law's knuckles as he squeezed the wheel just a little tighter. The slight bulge of his jaw muscles. The prominence of the vein in his temple. The way his eyes darted quickly to his right before he spoke.

Like his father, he knew something about the Fairacre property.

And lied about it.

34

Mason watched Victor's car drive all the way across the field before climbing into his own. All of this about GABP was new to him. Surely Angie would have mentioned it had she known, especially considering the size of the building and how much money they must have been spending. It was easily twice the size of all of the other buildings combined, but as far as he could see, there wasn't a single window. He couldn't imagine something that impressive being built just to create more office space, even executive suites.

The flakes on the windshield cleared with a single pass of the wipers. There were two messages on his phone. He figured one of them was his father calling him back to get in the last word. He checked the incoming call log. In addition to his father's cell number, there was another he immediately recognized. He called it back without listening to the message.

"Tell me you have something I can use," Mason said as soon as Gunnar answered.

"I take it you didn't listen to my message."

"I saw the number. Figured I'd rather hear it straight from the horse's mouth. What've you got?"

"Remember that picture you sent me? The one with the guy with the hat and half a face?"

Mason sat up straight. Gunnar had his undivided attention. They were talking about the man who had killed his wife and his partner, Angie and Kane.

"Did I lose you, Mace? You still there?"

"Tell me you know where I can find him."

"*When,* you mean. I can't tell you where he is now, but I can tell you where he *was*."

"What the hell is that supposed to mean?"

"That's just it. I don't know. I cleaned up his image, which ended up erasing a lot of the scarring, and fed it through a dozen different facial-recognition databases, including your own Next Generation Identification system. All that got me was a whole lot of nothing. So, on a whim, I ran it through a little program of my own design that also searches an enormous database of periodicals, newspapers, and other printed documents in both public and private collections. Anything that at some point or other has been scanned or uploaded to the Net. That's where I found six separate incidences of his face in photographs."

"So give me what you've got and I'll figure out how to make sense of it."

"Yeah. Good luck with that, Mace."

"What aren't you telling me?"

"The first instance I found of his face was in a black-and-white photograph from a newspaper."

"Good. That ought to help establish the link I'm—"

"Slow down, man. Listen to what I'm saying. The first instance was in a German newspaper called *Der Stürmer* from March fourteenth—*get this*—1939."

"There's no way. That would make him, like, a hundred years old. The man I saw couldn't even have been fifty. Your program screwed up."

"Not a chance. It might match fewer points on the face than the NGI system does, but it's no less accurate. I'm telling you, Mace. That's him. That's the same man. At least according to the program."

"I guess you're going to have to spell it out for me."

"I'll speak slowly so even you can understand. In 1939, your guy was photographed in Cairo, Egypt, and the picture was printed in a German paper."

"What else have you got?"

"Seriously? We're just going to gloss right over that?"

"I need something useful, Gunnar. You said six pictures, right? What about the others?"

"Guizhou, China, 1956. Hong Kong, 1968. Zaire, 1976. The Congo, 1981. India, 1994. This guy's been all over the place, but not once has he been identified in any of the captions. None of them is especially clear. All you can see in any of them is part of his face in the background of photographs where he, I assume, was captured on film without his knowledge."

"That doesn't make any sense, Gunnar."

"You're telling me." Mason heard a voice other than Gunnar's, but couldn't make out the words. "Look, Mace, I've got to handle something I'm actually being paid to take care of. So I'll send you these pictures and you can figure out what to make of them."

"Anything about the woman from the pay phone?"

"I doubt she knew the cameras were there or, even if she did, that we would have access to technology that allowed us to see the images. This is a woman who is accustomed to making sure that no one gets a good look at her. For my money, there's something distinct about her that would make her readily identifiable and she's used to going to such great lengths to hide it that the act itself has become second nature to her."

"So, that's a no?"

"You need to work on expressing your gratitude." He sighed. "Correct. That's a no."

"And Fairacre?"

"Whoever did the work on that one knew what he was doing. I've tracked it back through half a dozen different shell companies all over the world, but I've yet to come to the end of the paper trail. Trust me, though, I will. This is the kind of thing I do for a living and I earn a fortune doing it. Make no mistake, I will find out who owns it."

"What if I gave you a theoretical ending point? Would you be able to work backward?"

"It's my turn to ask what you aren't telling me."

"I'm playing a hunch."

"Okay. Yeah. I can do that. Hit me."

"Try Global Allied Biotechnology and Pharmaceuticals. Or maybe GABP."

"Not a name I'm familiar with, Mace, and I know them all."

"Then maybe it's about time we learned a little more about them."

35

Mason wanted nothing more than to pull to the side of the road and look at the pictures Gunnar had emailed to him, but the storm was getting worse by the second and he couldn't risk being stuck out here if they closed the highway back into Denver. His eight o'clock deadline with the woman who'd sent him in search of Fairacre was rapidly approaching and there was no way on this planet he was going to miss it.

The accumulation encroached from the shoulders to the edge of the lanes, erasing the yellow lines. The interstate truckers he passed had their lights on and heaps of snow on their roofs.

By the time he reached the city proper, he'd driven out of the worst of it. The snow was hardly falling at his new home when he arrived, but he could see in his rearview mirror that it wasn't far behind.

He pulled up to the gate and got out of his car. This was the most impulsive decision he'd ever made. Just looking at it now—this decrepit building surrounded by weeds and shrubs and cottonwoods that threatened to pull the roof right off of the garage, illegible graffiti on the facade, and a thick layer of dust on the insides of the windows—he had to laugh.

Mason realized just how tired he was as he stood on the desolate street with the sound of his laughter echoing across the industrial wasteland. When the echo finally died, he spoke to himself out loud. "What have I done?"

He unlocked the padlock with the combination the Realtor had given him, swung open the gate with a deafening squeal, and drove inside. He left the car running as he locked the gate behind him and then drove down the gravel driveway to the building itself. As arranged, the Realtor had left the middle garage door unlocked. He raised it and pulled his Grand Cherokee inside. It reeked like someone had used a ton of dust to soak up an oil spill, and hadn't bothered to pick up the rodent carcasses rotting somewhere out of sight. He hoped the inside smelled a whole lot better.

The keys and the paperwork were sitting on the concrete stairs leading up to the interior door. Considering the money was already sitting in an escrow account, the agent wasn't overly concerned about the title paperwork. Mason could fill it out at his leisure and mail it back in the envelope provided. With the state of the economy, the length of time the building had been on the market, and the fact that he'd offered a whole lot more than the Realtor had been prepared to accept, he'd been more than accommodating when it came to honoring Mason's unusual requests. His goal had been to get into this place without putting forth any effort, to simply walk away from his old life and into a new one. Unfortunately, the moment he stepped through the door he realized that had been a pipe dream.

The interior looked like it had been ransacked by dust bunnies, the kind that breed in the absence of humanity and thrive without airflow. He stood there for a long moment, trying to figure out if it was physically possible to kick his own butt, then retrieved both of the laptops from his car and walked into his new home.

The Realtor had assured him that the interior was in good condition, and it probably had been the last time he was in here. Judging by the cobwebs and the sheer volume of dust that had accumulated on the drop cloths covering what Mason hoped might be furniture, he hadn't been in here since approximately 1982. At least he'd been true to his word when he said he'd restore the water and electricity.

While his laptop was booting up, Mason searched for the bathroom, which was functional, but just barely. He immediately regretted yanking the drop cloth off of what turned out to be a desk. It took the dust forever to settle and even longer for him to stop coughing. He centered his computer on the table in front of him, opened his email program, and brought up Gunnar's pictures, which just about knocked the wind out of him.

The first picture was the one Gunnar had described over the phone. The dateline clearly indicated the photograph had been scanned from the issue of *Der Stürmer* dated March 14, 1939. It was possible that whoever'd scanned it had made a mistake. Judging by the clothing the primary subjects were wearing, however, the date couldn't have been very far off. The caption was in German. Mason picked out the names SS Sturmbannführer Walter Bollmann and Wehrmacht

Generalleutnant Wilhelm Fahrmbacher and the words *Cairo* and *Egypt*.
The man front and center was dressed in a gray uniform with a black
collar and his visor cap was pulled down low over his forehead. He stood
before an Opel Admiral Cabriolet with the canvas top down. A man
dressed in a leather trench coat and a peaked cap with an eagle insignia over the black visor sat in the backseat. A dozen other men surrounded the vehicle, smiling at the camera from beneath their pith
helmets. They all wore beige uniforms that bore no insignia. Summer
utilities. Only one man was not facing the camera. He was captured
while turning his face away from the photographer, but Mason would
have recognized him anywhere, even in faded black and white and with
his features shadowed by the brim of his helmet. He'd stared into the
man's eyes as he'd incinerated Kane and seen his reflection on the lens of
Angie's sunglasses mere minutes before her death.

Mason now understood what Gunnar meant. There was no doubt
in his mind that this was the man for whom he was searching. Only it
couldn't possibly be the same man, because he had been in his twenties
when this picture was taken and that was roughly eighty years ago.

He opened the second picture and located the same man immediately. The name of the paper and the date had been translated into
English: *Hung Chung She Po (Chinese Times)*, February 27, 1956. There
were three men in the front, wading in a rice paddy. They wore nondescript civilian clothes with broad-brimmed hats draped with mosquito
netting. One seemed to be scooping something out of the water with a
net while another provided a receptacle into which to deposit whatever
the first man was catching. The third was the focus of the image. He held
up a small discolored test tube to the sky, as though evaluating what was
inside. The man in the back—the man with the blue eyes—was again
captured in profile. His legs were blurred by motion as he shoved through
the reeds toward the shore under a netted veil.

The third instance was from the British newspaper *The Times*. It
was dated July 13, 1968, and Mason recognized Hong Kong even without the caption. A group of men in dated isolation suits and gas masks
loaded bodies into the back of a panel truck. Right there on the street.
People wearing paper masks over their mouths and noses watched from
beneath the awning of some sort of market. The man with the blue eyes

stood in the crowd. Only a portion of his face was visible behind the plastic visor of his gas mask, but that was more than enough.

Der Spiegel. A German weekly magazine. September 1, 1976. The picture had been taken in a jungle of some kind. Gunnar had said Zaire; Mason had no reason to doubt him. The men wore black outfits, helmets, and, once again, gas masks. The man in the forefront knelt in the mud with some kind of field case full of eyedroppers and bottles. Another held back the broad, leathery leaves of a shrub. The man with the blue eyes was standing beside the trunk of a tree in the background, staring at something outside of the camera's range, his face beneath his helmet devoid of expression.

May 20, 1981. *The New York Times.* "Searching for clues in the Congo," the caption read. Two men who could have passed for astronauts in their white isolation suits and helmets were wrestling a screaming monkey into a burlap sack. The man with the blue eyes was barely visible over the left shoulder of the man holding the bag. He was wearing a jungle hat, a khaki vest, and a respirator. He appeared to be talking to another man, whose face was largely obscured by the man battling with the simian.

September 22, 1994. AP News Services. "USAMRIID scientists evaluate water quality of new aquifer in Surat, India." There were two men standing in the water flowing though a ditch lined with wild grasses. One leaned on a staff while the other collected samples in a series of test tubes. The man with the blue eyes stood up on the bank with a group of men whose faces were cropped by the top of the image. He looked older, though. His belly had grown large and he held what might have been a cane, or maybe just a stick he'd found on the ground.

Mason leaned back in the chair and stared up into the cobwebs. This was an earth-shattering revelation, and yet none if it made the slightest bit of sense. There was something here, though, crying out for him to recognize it, but for the life of him, he couldn't figure out what. The only thing he knew with any certainty was that these pictures were the key to blowing this thing wide open.

The man he'd seen in Arizona before the world turned to light hadn't been as old as the man in the final picture. At least not that he could tell. The lower half of his face had been concealed by a respirator and his skin had been burned to the consistency of wax, but his eyes hadn't been those of an old man. And the man photographed in silhouette in the breezeway at the Peak View Inn had by no means been fat or elderly.

He opened the image capture from the lens of his wife's sunglasses and stared at the man's face. Even with his visage distorted by the curvature of her lens and his features remodeled by fire, Mason could tell he wasn't as old as he appeared in 1994. At a guess, he would have said the man was in his late twenties in the first picture, the one from 1939, which would have made him in his eighties when he was photographed in India. There was no way the man he'd seen in person was more than a hundred years old.

Mason scrolled back through the images and watched the man with the blue eyes age from one decade to the next. The changes were subtle at first, but they were more exaggerated in the picture from the Congo and unmistakable in the one from Surat.

His laptop chimed to let him know a new email had been delivered to his in-box. When he saw it was from Gunnar, he clicked the subject line and opened the message. It contained three sentences: *I expanded the database to include libraries, museums, and pop culture magazines, which I generally filter out, since the people I usually research aren't historical, for one, or foolish enough to allow the paparazzi to capture them on film. The same pictures came up again, plus three more. Prepare to have your mind blown.*

Mason enlarged the message and scrolled down to the first picture. It was black and white and so old that it had begun to crack around the edges. There were two women with heavy, old-fashioned white nurse's uniforms and hats. They wore white cloth masks tied over their mouths and noses. Spread out before them was an array of cots draped with thin men under horse blankets, their faces sunken and their eyes closed. IVs in glass bottles hung over their beds. A man with a smock and cap was administering something through a syringe into the emaciated arm of one of the patients. Only the upper half of his head was visible above his cloth mask. That was enough, though. More than enough. The caption beneath the picture read: "Library of Congress; National Photo Company. Richter Foundation physicians treat members of the First Division, Cantigny, France, 1918."

He looked more closely at the man in the picture. At his eyes. It wasn't possible. It simply *was not possible*. Judging by his wrinkles and the slight recession of his hairline, he had to be in his forties or fifties. By now even his headstone would look older than the man he'd seen in the flesh.

The second picture had been taken eighty-four years later and half a world away. It was from November 2002. *Newsweek*. "Soldiers inspect poultry as farmers arrive at an outdoor market in Shunde, Foshan." Men in camouflaged fatigues, respirators, and shoulder-length gloves dug through a cart brimming with what looked like the featherless carcasses of ducks. Several soldiers with assault rifles held a crowd at bay, toward the right side of which was a man wearing a wide-brimmed Panama hat and a suit that looked like the kind English bankers wore in the thirties. The camera caught him turning. His eyes were a startling shade of blue, but his face was unscarred.

The final picture was from a Mexican shock rag called *¡El Nuevo Alarma!* dated March 15, 2009. Heavily armed *federales* guarded a macabre display that would never have been printed in an American tabloid. Dozens of hogs had been strung up by their rear hooves and their throats slit. Their filthy bodies were covered with flies. Behind them, against the backdrop of a lush tropical forest, the man with the blue eyes gestured to several soldiers, who obediently turned to look. This was the man who had smiled at Mason as he brought the quarry down on his head and at his wife moments before he killed her.

A century's worth of photographic evidence of an immortal man who cropped up all around the world, seemingly sticking his head out once every decade or so. Never drawing attention to himself. Only being captured on film in a handful of cases, even though he appeared to be in a position of authority in each scene. And not once was he identified in any of the pictures.

Mason's cell phone rang. He glanced at his watch. Eight o'clock on the nose.

It was time.

His pulse made a rushing sound in his ears.

He slowly blew out his breath, closed his eyes, and answered in a voice he hoped made him sound a whole lot more confident than he felt.

36

The woman had given Mason an address and then immediately disconnected. Finding it online had been a piece of cake. Getting there, on the other hand, took some doing. He'd gotten off of Highway 287 south onto Highway 285 west and then taken the first exit to the north. It struck him immediately that she'd chosen a location with two major thoroughfares within a hundred yards of an isolated point that required a circuitous approach to reach by vehicle.

The residential neighborhood was dark, the houses run-down. This was the kind of neighborhood that attracted the deaf and the blind, the people upon whom you could always count not to have seen or heard anything.

He rounded a bend and descended into a shallow valley, at the bottom of which flowed the same river that ran behind his new home. Turning to the south, he came upon a vast stretch of flat land surrounded by a tall ramshackle fence and even taller evergreens. It wasn't until he saw what remained of the movie screen that he realized where he was.

This old drive-in theater was the perfect location for a clandestine meeting, especially on short notice. There was only one way to reach it by car, and his headlights would have been visible moving through the dark neighborhood uphill. She could have a car waiting for her off either of the intersecting highways, he realized. All she would have to do is hop the fence—which had already fallen in sections—run down the hill and across the river to the east or charge through the woods to the south and she'd be miles away before he ever got his car out of the neighborhood.

He passed the ticket booth and the concession stand. Every window had been boarded over and covered with graffiti. The chain had been cut and the gate dragged back into the weeds. The ground rose and fell in front of him. The peaks were crowned with weeds that had to be at least three feet tall and nearly buried under the heavy snow. He could barely see the tops of the metal posts that had been stripped of their speakers. His only option was to take the circuitous route around so as not to tear out his undercarriage on anything lurking beneath the weeds or crumple his hood around one of the poles.

The woman could have been hiding in any number of places. There were several exceptional vantage points from which to view his approach from afar, all of them densely forested by design so as not to allow anyone a clear view of the screen without paying admission. Had he been in her position, he would have chosen a location to the south, somewhere behind the screen. He'd have his car waiting by the eastbound ramp on 285. Sprint downhill, under the westbound lanes, and she'd have access to any number of major north-south corridors.

Mason rolled to a stop and glanced at the clock: 8:18 P.M.

The falling snowflakes glittered in his headlights. There were no other tracks. Given how fast the snow was accumulating, though, his own would be invisible soon enough. It was a location as dark as any within twenty miles. The only illumination came from the headlights that winked through the trees from the highways.

His phone rang, and he picked it up immediately.

"Drive in front of the screen," the woman said. "Back up to it, so you are facing the direction you came from. Get out of your vehicle, but leave the door open. Drop your keys on the seat. Stand ten feet in front of your car, facing the screen."

She disconnected without waiting for acknowledgment.

Mason did as she asked. He drove around the front row until the remains of the screen towered over him, then backed right up against it. He knew exactly what she was doing, since he would have done it the same way. Only he would have made the other person strip to his boxers so he couldn't hide a weapon anywhere he would be able to get to it in a hurry.

He killed the engine, climbed out, and tossed his keys onto the seat, as instructed. He left the door open so the light would make the interior clearly visible and show her that he had come alone. Then he walked around the front of his car, stood in the wash of the headlights, and turned so that he was staring right into them. The lights blinded him, so he wouldn't see her coming from behind the screen until she was around the hood, and even then he wouldn't be able to discern any details, only her silhouette against the glare.

Mason held his open palms out to his sides and waited, his breath blowing in clouds back over his shoulder.

"Hands behind your head," she said from directly behind him.

"Very clever." He did as she asked and laced his fingers. "You knew I wouldn't drive straight through the lot since I couldn't see the poles through all of the weeds."

She reached under his jacket and took his Sigma.

"Take off your clothes," she said.

"If it's all the same to you, I'd really rather—"

"Take off your clothes!"

The fear in her voice was palpable. She was wired and terrified, not the ideal combination for someone holding a gun on him. He'd heard something else, though—an accent that up until now she'd done an amazing job of hiding. Like the rest of her precautions, he'd imagine speaking unaccented English was another survival technique she utilized every day.

"Chiappas?" he said.

"Pants, too."

"No, Oaxaca. Am I right?"

"You can leave those on."

Mason stood in only his boxers and socks, hands again behind his head, shivering against the brutal wind. He'd given her every opportunity to kill him. The fact that she hadn't told him she needed him as much as he needed her.

"What did you learn about Fairacre?" she asked.

"It's a shelf company. A nonexistent corporate entity that owned a lone property on the eastern plains."

"Did you go there?"

"Yes."

"Tell me what you saw."

"A house that hadn't been occupied for a long time and a burned outbuilding where . . ."

"Where what?"

"Where I believe people were tortured and killed."

"What kind of people?"

"The kind who were used to smuggle a deadly virus into the country. Couriers who were sent out across the open desert to bypass Border Patrol checkpoints. Test subjects whose lives meant less than nothing to the men who infected them."

She cried softly behind him.

He took a chance and started to turn around.

"¡Parada! ¡Cambia!"

He turned back to face his headlights. It was getting colder by the second and he was already shivering harder than he ever had in his life.

"Who owns it?" she asked.

"I don't know."

"Lie to me again and I will shoot you in the back of your knee."

"Really. I don't know. Yet. How about you answer a question for me? How did you know my wife?"

"She was helping me. I only met her once. Martin brought her in. The week before . . . before they died."

"Martin needed my wife because he couldn't follow the money trail on his own, could he? He needed someone good, but also someone he knew could do the job without drawing a lot of attention. And it's because of that—because of you—that she's dead."

The woman remained silent.

"The first time you met her," Mason said. "It was an interview of sorts, wasn't it? You were testing her to make sure she wasn't involved."

"No. Martin checked her out before he even contacted her. He needed to figure out if we could trust her. I was against bringing anyone else in from the start, but he said we needed someone who could get into places that we could not reach on our own."

"So what is the Justice Department doing about it now? If they knew what he was investigating, then they should have just picked right up where—"

"You do not understand the kind of people who are involved. If he said a word to anyone, they would have found out. I made sure he was not going to talk to anyone else before I even approached him about it."

It clicked into place. Mason remembered what Ralph Schaub, the owner of the Peak View Inn, had said.

I've seen him around, if you know what I'm saying.

"You knew who Martin was and you devised a plan to blackmail him."

"There was no other way. If I had gone to the police, the people who are after me would have known right away."

"You trusted Martin?"

"Trusted *him*? No, but I trusted him to save his own skin. As long as I had the pictures, I could count on his cooperation. And if I even sensed he was going to turn on me, I would have put them in his wife's hands myself before I disappeared."

"But if you were afraid of going to the police, what made you think the Justice Department would be willing to help you? They would have had to instigate a formal investigation, which would definitely have involved the police and the FBI. Without gathering enough evidence, there's no way in hell they would ever have considered prosecuting—"

"Prosecute? None of this would have made it into a courtroom. These people have too much power. I was using Martin to help me find out exactly who was involved and where they were. And then I was going to kill them myself."

"How did you know about Fairacre?" Mason asked, but the answer struck him before the words were all the way out of his mouth.

"How do you think?"

"Jesus. How did you—?"

"I am asking the questions!"

Her voice echoed across the field and down the hillside. He heard the buzz of tires on the wet highway and her heavy breathing as she tried to regain control of herself and the situation.

"Fairacre wasn't the first." Mason spoke in a voice barely louder than the sound of the settling snowflakes. "There were others before it. I've been hunting these people for the last year. And it's cost me *everything*."

"Do you know what they do to you there?" Her breathing accelerated and the accent crept back into her voice. She was physically behind him, but he could tell she had vanished into another place and time she rarely chose to visit. "Do you have any idea what they intend to do to all of us?"

"They took everything from me. All I have left is anger. Pain. I *will* find them. I *will* track down everyone responsible for this and I *will* stop them, but I need whatever you know in order to do so."

"And what will you do to them when you find them?"

Mason thought of the bodies in the quarry, hanging from hooks and crawling with flies. The expression on Kane's face before he was enveloped in fire. Angie's body, incinerated on what was left of the bed. Her smile and her voice and the sensation of her touch. He thought about the man with the blue eyes and all the suffering he'd caused. And he thought of what he'd seen behind those eyes.

This man was evil.

The world would be a better place without him in it.

"Whatever it takes."

"How do I know I can trust you?"

"You don't. How do I know you're not setting me up?"

"I have not shot you."

"I guess that's about the best I could hope for. And my clothes. Do you mind?"

"Not just yet."

"You're going to have to trust me sooner or later."

"Trust must be earned."

"Then now's as good a time to start as any." Mason was tired of letting her run the show. He deserved some answers, too. "What do you know about the man with the blue eyes?"

A sharp intake of breath behind him.

"You know who I'm talking about, don't you?" He turned around to face her and focused immediately on the barrel of her pistol, which was steady in her grasp. It was an older-model Walther P22 semiauto, the kind you could pick up at just about any sporting goods store or pawnshop. Didn't mean it wouldn't turn his brain into spaghetti, though. His Sigma was a bulge in the left front pocket of her coat. "Tell me what you know."

She wore a baggy black down jacket and a pair of jeans covered with mud from kneeling in the bushes. The hood of the sweatshirt she wore underneath the coat made it impossible to see more than her chin.

"Talk to me. At least tell me your name. You have to—"

Mason advanced a step and she shot the ground at his feet in one quick motion. An explosion of dirt and snow struck his bare thighs and chest.

"For Christ's sake! Just tell me what you want me to do!"

He raised his hands and took another step back.

"I want you to pick up your clothes."

He did as she asked.

"Now what?"

"Carry them across the lot to the west and throw them over the fence."

"This isn't necessary."

"Start walking or I will shoot you."

"You won't shoot—"

A thunderous crack and Mason was on his back in the snow, clutching his clothes to his chest. The bullet passed so close to his head that had he been any slower to react, he wouldn't have had to worry about shopping for a surround sound system for his new place.

"Okay. Okay. Damn it. I'm going."

"I will be aiming at your back, between your shoulder blades. If you so much as think about looking back, you will spend the rest of your life in a wheelchair."

He walked along the line of weeds, which limited the amount of accumulation directly beside them. Not that it really mattered. His feet were so cold that each step felt as if he were walking on broken glass. It was maybe fifty feet to the fence, but it felt like he'd walked a mile by the time he reached it.

The moment he heaved his clothes into the air, he heard the engine of his car roar. He whirled and sprinted back toward where his taillights glowed red against the far fence and the trees behind it. His Grand Cherokee rounded the bend and rocketed past the rows of weeds, the concession stand and the ticket booth, and blew through the front gate.

He slowed to a walk and bellowed in frustration.

37

By the time Mason found his car, it was nearly ten-thirty and he was shivering so hard he could barely walk. The woman had parked it to the west of the neighborhood, in the parking lot of what looked like it had once been a restaurant of some kind, the Cherokee's hazards flashing to alert him to its location. He could only assume this was where she'd had her own car parked and waiting. She'd locked the doors and left the keys packed in a snowball on top of the front tire.

He just sat in the driver's seat with the heater blowing full blast into his face and closed his eyes for several long minutes before he finally picked up the note she had left folded on the passenger seat. Another half sheet torn from the Yellow Pages. An address written right in the center of a slew of car detail shops. And beneath it, a time.

5325 WEDGEWOOD CIRCLE #9.

7:00 A.M.

His Sigma was underneath his seat. He made a resolution never to relinquish it again under any circumstances. That was when he'd lost control of the situation. The woman had planned and executed the meeting to perfection, and he'd been so eager to do whatever it took to get the information he needed that he could have easily gotten himself killed.

The roads were slick, the going was slow, and by the time he got to his new place, he was in a vile mood.

What the hell was he doing? This wasn't his home. This was a derelict building. His home was downtown, near Washington Park, where by all rights he and Angie should have been curled up together in bed. All he wanted right now was to pull into the garage, close his eyes, and let the exhaust fumes usher him off to wherever his wife was now.

He just needed to sleep. Everything would look different after a couple hours of quality REM time. Besides, he wasn't ready to cash in his chips quite yet. He had a 7:00 A.M. engagement that he fully intended to keep.

The place looked marginally better with a fresh application of snow, almost as though nature had decided to spruce it up a little in his absence. The roof was smooth and white, the windows frosted, and the wind had swept drifts up the front, concealing the less sightly graffiti. The snow made the trees look lush and full. Even the chain-link fence somehow seemed beautified by the sparkling application of ice. It was next to impossible to tell that the lot was really an ugly combination of dirt, gravel, and—

Something caught his eye. Nothing overt, but the kind of thing that set off alarm Klaxons in his subconscious.

He was parked facing the gate, his headlights blurred by the falling flakes, his windshield wipers flapping across his vision. He'd been just about to climb out to open the padlock, when the sensation smacked him upside the head. It took his mind several seconds to catch up with his eyes. When he left, the snow had only begun falling. Now there had to be at least three inches on the ground. Faint tire tracks, now little more than impressions, created parallel lines to the middle garage door.

Someone had driven into the garage.

Someone other than him.

38

Mason parked a mile or so up the road at a bend with easy access to the river. The last thing he wanted was to brave the cold again, but he figured it was an acceptable inconvenience if it afforded him the opportunity to finally shoot one of the bad guys.

He attuned his senses to his surroundings until he was acutely aware of every sound, every shadow, every detail. It was almost as though he'd entered a state of hyperawareness, which served to slow down the world around him. He stayed low and moved quickly along the bank of the river, his pistol in a two-handed grip, and surveilled the buildings neighboring his through the dense, snow-blanketed trees. Most of the windows had been broken and boarded up. The chain-link fences remained largely intact and enclosed lots crammed full of stacked pallets, giant cable spools, and unidentifiable objects buried beneath the snow. There were no footprints. No sign that anyone or anything had been through here before he arrived.

A faint glow emanated from behind the trees ahead of him. He crouched and crept closer, scrutinizing the light down the barrel of his Sigma. His building appeared through the branches as little more than a swatch of gray siding. As he neared, he got a clear look at the source of the glow, which was barely bright enough to outline the edges of a sheet of plywood covering one of his windows. It was subtle, but there was no mistaking that there was light radiating from inside a building where he had left no lights on.

The window was at eye level, so he had to believe it was on the main floor. He'd already established that the overhead lights didn't work, so unless whoever was in there had brought his own bulb, the source of the glow had to be a flashlight or some other battery-powered device. He watched it for any change in intensity to suggest movement. If there was any, he couldn't see it.

In the end, he decided that even getting shot would be preferable to kneeling out here in the snow any longer.

The rear of the building was maybe two hundred feet from the overgrown fence. He scaled the chain link, perched on the top, and then jumped.

Mason hit the ground running—right on a patch of ice—and landed squarely on his face and chest. He scrambled to his feet and was up against the back wall of his house in a matter of seconds.

Eased along the siding. Peeked around the corner. Ducked back.

Clear.

He went around in a crouch and sprinted through the snow until he could see the front gate. To his right, he had his pick of garage doors. He studied the tire tracks. The snow had nearly concealed them. He could barely make out the hint of footprints. It looked as though someone had tested the front door, then the first garage door, before finding the middle one unlocked. He'd then opened it and pulled his car inside.

Mason had to assume that both the vehicle and at least one person were inside. He hoped his intruder wouldn't bleed too much. He was in no mood to clean up a mess tonight.

He flattened himself to the ground. Raised the garage door just high enough to roll under. Lowered it silently behind him. He was underneath the fender of a sedan of indeterminate make and model. The melting snow dripped from its undercarriage onto his cheek.

Once his eyes adjusted to the darkness, he crawled out from beneath the car and headed for the lone entrance. He took each step slowly, silently, and found the knob with his left hand. Twisted it. Barreled through. He was in a shooter's stance when the door ricocheted from the interior wall. Took the rebound against his shoulder.

No sudden movement.

The glow was coming from the main room, just around the corner. He was already squeezing the trigger into the sweet spot as he went in fast and low, sighting down the source of the illumination. A laptop computer. Two silhouettes. Their faces unrecognizable chiaroscuros. One of them wore a smile that glowed almost blue from the display on the screen. Mason sighted his weapon just above the teeth and prepared to decorate the wall—

"Christ Almighty, Mace. Would you put that thing away?"

"Gunnar?" His old friend gave a tip of an invisible cap. His dirty-blond hair had thinned slightly since Mason had last seen him, but he still looked just like he always did: same little round glasses, same crooked smile, same face, as smooth as a baby's bottom. Only the suit was new, and he wore it like an aura of power that somehow made him look larger. "I thought you were on the other side of the globe."

He shrugged.

"It sounded like you could use a little help. And Lord knows I need a challenge every once in a while. Besides, what good is being rich and successful if you can't rub your friends' noses in it from time to time?"

Mason smiled, holstered his Sigma, and turned to the other silhouette.

"What?" Ramses said. "I get to rub your nose in my success all the time. Least you could do is show a little gratitude. A guy could die of thirst in this place. It's like the inside of a vacuum bag."

"Like you even know what a vacuum cleaner looks like, Ramses."

"Of course I do. What kind of monster makes his cleaning lady bring her own—?"

"Would you shut up for thirty seconds so we can show him?" Gunnar said.

"Show me what?" Mason asked.

"Come around over here so you can see the screen. Ramses, you do the voice again, okay?"

Mason stared at the small black-and-white image on the screen. He didn't immediately recognize what he was supposed to be seeing. It looked just like any snow-packed road from a bird's-eye view. A satellite, he assumed. Headlights washed over it from the right and a car appeared. A black Grand Cherokee just like his. It pulled up to the gate in a tall chain-link fence he now recognized as his own and sat there idling.

"Was it 'push in' or 'pull out'?" Ramses said in a voice Mason guessed was supposed to sound like his. Based on how hard Gunnar was laughing, he must have been doing a pretty decent job. "Maybe if I concentrate, I can open it with my mind."

"Shut up. I saw your tire tracks and didn't know who the hell was in my house."

"We thought you might have dozed off, you were sitting there so long," Gunnar said.

"I was playing with myself," Ramses said in his Mason voice.

"Those bruises around your eyes are only now beginning to fade, Ramses."

Mason's car backed away from the fence and headed back in the direction from which it had come.

"I can't believe I forgot which one of these crack houses is mine. Maybe if I drive back out and try again, I'll have better luck."

"How *did* you guys know I bought this place?"

"Ancient Chinese secret," Gunnar said. "Seriously. The Chinese are wired into everything. You can't sneeze without someone in a red room saying '*Shang di bao you ni*.'"

"Fast-forward to the good part," Ramses said.

"I get the point," Mason said. He knew exactly where Ramses was going with this.

"What point? This is just for fun. Wait! Hold up. Right there."

Another shot from orbit. A line of snowcapped trees. A shadow scaled a chain-link fence and paused at the very top, then dropped down into the snow.

And fell flat on his face.

Ramses roared with laughter.

Mason did have to admit that it was almost comical how he limped-ran across the lot and pressed himself up against the side of the house, but it wasn't nearly as funny as his wonderful friends seemed to think it was.

"I'm surprised you couldn't hear us busting up through the wall." Gunnar clasped his hands together, made a gun out of his index fingers. "Ramses was humming 'Secret Agent Man' and everything."

"I should have shot you both."

"Then you would have had to deal with our ghosts in this haunted pile of shit," Ramses said.

"It just needs a personal touch."

"What it needs is an arsonist's touch."

"All right, all right." Gunnar's expression became serious in the blink of an eye. "We've had enough fun at our less than gracious host's expense. Time to get down to work. You're poking around in the wrong people's business, Mace. These are men you don't want as enemies."

"What do you know, Gunnar?"

"Something big is coming. Bigger than anything I've ever seen."

39

"Duh-duh-duuhhhh," Ramses said. "Could you be any more melo-dramatic?"

Gunnar shot him a look, and Ramses held up his hands in mock surrender.

"You're familiar with the volatility index—the fear index—on the stock market, right?" Gunnar flashed through a series of windows on his screen and brought up a jagged line graph under the heading "CBOE VIX." "That's what this is. If I broaden the time frame to, say . . . the last twenty years, and we look at it from a historical perspective, you'll see exactly what I mean. This line is essentially a graphic representation of the nation's confidence in our economy. The pulse of the market, if you will. For long stretches of time, the index stays relatively steady, with only mild fluctuations based on variables like agricultural futures, freak natural events . . . the unpredictable things that cause momentary panics and frenzied trading. This means private investors and brokers are feeling good about their portfolios. Now, these spikes you see every so often? That's where things get a little dicey. People are starting to sense that something's not right. A betting man would buy volatility options low and ride these spikes as high as he could bear before selling and cashing out again when confidence in the market returns."

"So the difference between legal and illegal gambling is the amount of money involved?" Ramses said. "Or is it because Uncle Sam gets his cut in the end?"

Gunnar continued, as if he hadn't heard.

"What causes these spikes? In a nutshell . . . fear. When all of a sudden people start moving a lot of money from one place to another, the economy starts to get nervous and the volatility index rises. Slowly at first. As it continues to rise, traders feel something coming and make even more transactions and move even more money. Now the economy's more than a little nervous. Next thing you know, people are pulling enormous amounts out of stocks that were formerly perceived as solid earners, destabilizing the whole foundation. The economy's scared now, and rightfully so. It knows it's only a matter of time before people start bailing out altogether or moving into traditionally low-risk stocks and bonds. We're talking about stocks that have been on the market nearly since its inception—stocks like JPMorgan Chase, General Electric, Agfa-Gevaert, Siemens, Bank of America. And the newer heavyweights like Apple, Microsoft, Walmart, Coca-Cola, PepsiCo. You get the idea. The economy passes the point of panic and goes straight to doomsday mode. And that's when the bottom falls out. The market crashes. Companies and investors alike go down in flames. The value of the dollar plummets. You're following me so far, right?"

"It's a self-fulfilling prophecy," Mason said.

Gunnar gave a crooked smile and tapped the tip of his nose.

"Exactly. The people who have the largest stake in the market, the point zero one percent whose investments are myriad and so diversified that it's impossible to track, let alone monitor . . . they control the market. All it takes is for these guys to shuffle their own financial decks, and next thing you know, the entire market is in chaos and we're all scrambling to get our money someplace where we know it will be safe. And where is that?"

"Right back into the pockets of the people who own those companies."

"The same people who initially caused the furor, then reap the rewards of it, and all without taking the slightest risk. And no one suspects them because—superficially, anyway—they appear to have the most to lose when the stock market crashes."

"And I'm the criminal?" Ramses said.

"Now you have to look not only at the timing of these spikes, but also at the stocks involved." Gunnar touched the screen on each of the volatility spikes in turn. The program zoomed in on them, isolated the chronological points on each upswing where investors lost confidence, and produced a list of the stocks most impacted by the panic. "This huge one here? Black Monday. October nineteenth, 1987. Suddenly there's a lot of money being funneled out of oil. See that right there? You know what happened that very same day? U.S. warships destroyed a pair of Iranian oil platforms in the Persian Gulf, in what most believed to be an unprovoked attack. You probably didn't hear about that, though. I know I didn't. So when oil prices plummeted in response to the aggression, the very same people who had just sold those stocks when prices were high bought them back when the market bottomed out, and made an absolute killing."

"Could be coincidence," Ramses said.

"Really? How about this one? Three years later. August 1990. The price of oil is at a record high; then all of a sudden confidence plummets, people yank their money out of the market, and within a matter of days Iraq invades Kuwait. This next spike here is just five months later. January twelfth, 1991. Congress authorizes the use of military force in Iraq, the price of oil falls, and the same people who sold the stock are snatching it back up again, hand over fist.

"After that there's a long period of relative stability until August of '98, when the Second Congo War kicks off. We're talking about one of the bloodiest wars in the history of civilization. And within days of that, our embassies start getting bombed. Who gave the order? Osama bin Laden. Our former Saudi ally, who three years later takes credit for the destruction of the Twin Towers, and only then do we decide to go out of our way to track him down?

"And how about nine/eleven itself? That's this spike here. Did you know that mere moments before the first plane hit, there was a frenzy of trading by major brokerages like Salomon Smith Barney and Morgan Stanley, which not only placed orders for an extraordinary amount of 'put' options on United and American Airlines stocks, but also occupied two of the towers that fell. You understand what I'm saying, right? Buying put options means they were betting those stocks would tank. Citibank, owner of Travelers Insurance, which stood to pay an estimated five hundred million dollars in damages, experienced forty-five times its ordinary volume of trading in the days leading up to the attack. Six times more 'call' options for a defense contractor called Raytheon were placed on September tenth than in the entire history of the company. A lot of people made a lot of money from a supposedly unexpected terrorist attack. So many, in fact, that the SEC launched an insider trading investigation, which was inherently hampered from the start by the fact that both its office and the regional office of the IRS were located in building seven of the World Trade Center, which fell several hours *after* the attacks. There's even a coalition of architects and engineers that believes it fell as the result of a controlled demolition that was instigated on the ninth floor. And who was the tenant on that floor? The United States Secret Service. The same entity charged with the protection of the very man who ordered the air force to stand down."

"My old partner was part of the investigative team," Mason said. "If there was something underhanded going on, he would have found it."

"How? Not a single one of the hard drives retrieved from the rubble was salvageable. Not one. All proof of potential wrongdoing was destroyed. All of it. And apparently no one thought to actually investigate any of the people who worked in building seven, despite the fact that not a single person died when it fell."

"You realize how you sound, right?"

"Like a total conspiracy theorist. I know. But this is what I do for a living. These are the kinds of threads I tug on to see what unravels. There are aspects of my profession that aren't necessarily pretty. From time to time, I have to utilize leverage—"

"You mean blackmail," Ramses said.

"—to convince people to see things my way. I should say, the way I've been paid to see them. These things I've been telling you? These are facts that are easily corroborated. The paper trails are so easy to follow, it's as though no real effort was invested into hiding them. It's like the people who wield the nation's wealth—the world's wealth—have the government so deep in their pockets that they see themselves as untouchable. I mean, look at this monster spike in 2008. That was an outright cash grab if I've ever seen one. October third. The global financial crisis. The Emergency Economic Stability Act was put into place to resuscitate the economy. Remember good old TARP? The Troubled Asset Relief Program, which instigated all of the bank bailouts? We're talking about *seven hundred billion dollars* in taxpayer funding going straight into the banks, the majority of which found its way into the Federal Reserve's newly formed Maiden Lane Transactions, which consolidated JPMorgan Chase, Bear Stearns, and AIG. All of that money, no less than four hundred billion dollars, funneled into the Federal Reserve itself, and the Fed isn't even owned by the government. The people who own it, the families hiding behind generations' worth of interbred corporations, are the very same people the act was established to bail out! Everything that's happened has been orchestrated to transfer what amounts to nearly a full three-quarters of the world's wealth into the hands of a small group of people. A plutocracy. A global elite, if you will. And this is a group that not only has aspirations to rule the world, but the financial backing to make it a reality. A single global economy with them sitting right on top of it, in the seat of power, from which to pull the strings for a puppet government that serves no other interests than its own.

"These are the same people who supported the United Nations' World Summit on Sustainable Development and the Good Club, entities that are actively pursuing agendas related to population control. The people who formed the League of Nations, the International Congruity

Alliance, and the Global Societal Reform Federation. Patient people who've been gradually building up to whatever's about to happen since the late nineteenth century, when industrialists first dreamed of their own empires. And those are just the financial threads. The threads of power and influence are every bit as intricately woven."

Mason looked at Ramses, who matched his stare for a long moment before raising a single eyebrow and turning back to Gunnar.

"I could run out to the store and pick up some tinfoil to make a hat for you, bro. Keep the satellites from picking up your thought waves."

"You're suggesting this shadow organization, for lack of a better term, is consolidating the world's wealth in preparation for making some kind of global power play," Mason said.

"Look, Mace. You, of all people, should understand that power is a much more valuable asset than money. In fact, when you're dealing with the people who wield significant power, they all have such sizable fortunes that finances don't really even factor into the equation, unless that money is being used for the acquisition of more power. And even then, there are much more effective ways to gain influence and secure loyalties. Anyone who can be bought like a common commodity can be easily co-opted or outright bought again. The key is to find the proper leverage to bend any given situation to your will. That's where I come in. My job essentially boils down to figuring out and ascertaining the desired leverage for whoever's willing and able to pay for my services.

"I know these people because I've worked with them, for them, and against them. I know how they think. I've seen what they're capable of doing. I've unraveled some of the most convoluted paper trails to find things that would flat out blow your mind. These are people who see themselves as some sort of superior race, a worthier class that has ruled the world from the shadows for hundreds of years and has patiently bided its time, waiting for the machinations it set in motion generations ago to reach the prescribed hour of destiny, when they can finally step into the light and assume what they feel is their God-given right to rule not just this country, but the entire world."

"Like Cobra from G.I. Joe?" Ramses said.

"I'd nearly forgotten how maddening it is trying to talk to you."

"Maybe you're right, Gunnar," Mason said.

"Maybe? Haven't you been listening?"

"Hear me out. Let's say that everything you've said is true. Every last word of it. Tell me how it relates to what's happening to me now? How does some global financial conspiracy relate to the smuggling of viruses and the deliberate infection of immigrants in the Arizona desert? To the death of my partner? To the murder of my wife?"

"That's just it, Mace. I don't know. And that's what makes me so nervous. I've been following this since long before you reached out to me. It started slowly, but everything's moving so fast now that I can only assume the finish line is in sight. The sudden surge in trading that's causing the volatility index to rise. The extreme amount of interest certain people have taken in everything going on here. Something earth-shattering is coming, and we don't want to be anywhere around here when it hits."

"Who are these people who've shown an 'extreme amount of interest'? How do you know these things? Quit dancing around it and give it to me straight."

"Why don't I show you instead?"

40

"You have to understand that I've signed legally binding confidentiality agreements with these clients, any violation of which would mean the end of my career for sure, and more than likely a Guantánamo Bay kind of prosecution, with an anonymous deep-sea burial." Gunnar looked at each of them in turn. "You get what I'm saying, right? These people don't screw around. Serve them and you're family; cross them and you're dead. And, believe me, there are many, many people just waiting for me to cross the wrong person."

"Even our government?" Mason said.

"*Especially* our government. You're familiar with DARPA, right?"

"It's a division of the DoD. Defense Advanced Research Projects Agency. What's the connection?"

"In 1969, it commissioned the development of ARPANET, which was a wide-area computer network that connected several dozen organizations. The first of it kind. As technology advanced, so did ARPANET. The U.S. government recognized the massive potential for this level of interconnectivity and designed an application that utilized synchronously orbiting satellites, called SATNET, which was then integrated into ARPANET. But in order to accommodate this expansion, they needed something like a phone number for each, so that one user could call another directly and not the group as a whole. And they needed some sort of gateway between these different networks to compensate for differences in data size and interface specifications. These gateways also needed to check the destination 'phone numbers' and forward the communications to the right recipients. The solution was a kind of software developed by Cerf called TCP, which produced a steady flow of data from source to end user.

"The TCP protocol created a kind of architecture that bridged the connectivity between ARPANET and SATNET. It utilized a system of addressing individual users by employing a standardized numbering system called an IP protocol and routers that served as gateways, and essentially mapped out all of the different users like one big city on a worldwide web to form a single unified network. ARPANET adopted this new TCP/IP protocol and further broke its networks down into local area networks, or LANs."

"You're talking about the Internet, Gunnar. I'm familiar with the concept."

"It's important that you understand its origins in order to follow me through this. Just pay attention. So about the same time DARPA's ramping up its own network, the National Science Foundation looks at what the DoD is doing and decides to explore the impact of this new computer world on science and engineering by creating the Computer Science Network, or CSNET. Now everybody starts getting in on the act. You get BITNET on campuses and mail capabilities on ARPANET. From there, the NSF contracted IBM and MCI to construct a new network to expand the capabilities of CSNET, which it renamed NSFNET, which augmented ARPANET until it was decommissioned in the early nineties. And then, finally, the government figured out a way to profit from it and opened it to commercial usage."

"And porn," Ramses said. "Don't forget the porn."

"So the NSF pulled out in response, and voilà . . . you have the Internet: a computer network with the ability to connect billions of people all around the world. Suddenly, the federal government of the United States of America found itself almost accidentally sitting on unlimited access to every communication, every transaction, made by everyone from private individuals to large corporations, all on a network of its own design and implementation."

"Where are you going with this?" Mason asked.

"What you need to understand is that the Internet is one elaborate platform on an existing network that functions by utilizing a specific software protocol. Think of the network itself as a system of gravel roads that connects an unlimited number of houses. The Internet is the result of turning those gravel roads into highways by using the TCP/IP protocol like asphalt and tar. The cars and trucks and motorcycles that travel on it are packets of data being sent back and forth in continuous streams.

"Now that you have this network in place and the government checking every vehicle that passes through—opening the trunk, searching behind the seats—there's really no way to get anything from point A to point B without someone knowing exactly what you're doing. But you could always fly from one point to the other, right? You could cruise over the road at any altitude you wanted and still follow its course. You could build a subway underneath it. You could construct another highway on pylons directly above the original highway. What I'm saying is that the existing architecture is already there; all you would need is a different operating protocol, a different type of interface, and a discrete addressing system and you could send information across the same existing network someone already went to all the trouble of building for you. Unless whoever was serving as watchdog had access to your protocol and software, he'd never be able to view the information. All anyone would ever detect was a subtle initial increase in bandwidth usage when this new network launched, and after that it would just blend into the background cyber noise."

"Like the dark web."

"Exactly, but designed exclusively for a select group of users."

"And I assume you have access to this alternate Internet?"

"Two of them, actually."

"How did you get them?"

"Directly from my contacts in the government."

"But you just said that the government couldn't—"

"I didn't say 'couldn't' oversee; I said 'didn't.' One of the networks I can access belongs exclusively to the federal government itself. What do you think, the president just calls up the secretary of defense in the middle of the night on an open airwave? Anyone could pluck their conversation right out of the ether."

"You said two. What about the other one?"

"That's where things get interesting." Gunnar smiled and closed all of the windows he had opened. There were probably a hundred different icons on his desktop, most of which Mason had never seen before. Gunnar selected one that looked like a broadsword from which a triangular flag and a rounded flag flew to the right of the blade, near the hilt. When he touched the icon, the screen immediately turned black. "Watch this."

Gunnar used his index finger to draw a vertical line from the top of the screen to the bottom, right down the center. Nothing appeared on the screen, which remained black the entire time. He drew a shorter horizontal line across the first, as though making a lowercase *t*, then used the right end to draw a diagonal line back to the vertical line and a bulge beneath the resultant triangle in the shape of a half circle. It was a simplified version of the icon on his desktop.

"What does the symbol mean?" Mason asked.

"I don't know," Gunnar said, "but this is the cool part."

"What am I supposed to be seeing?"

"Wait for it. Another thirty seconds."

They all stared at the blank screen until a red rectangular frame appeared in the center. Gunnar placed the tip of the middle finger on his left hand in the center of the rectangle and held it there for several seconds. When he withdrew it, the ghostly image of his fingerprint slowly faded away. The red rectangle disappeared and another one with a mint green frame appeared.

Gunnar pressed his index finger to his lips. Mason glanced over at Ramses in time to see him roll his eyes.

"Password," Gunnar said. The digital representation of his voice streaked across the rectangle from left to right. A yellow version appeared behind it and authenticated the green word he had just spoken. The box cleared itself. "The password changes every time someone accesses the system. It's never the exact same thing twice. There are ten different variables, each with fifty-two possible choices, all of which are coded in one of ten different colors to specify the language in which to speak that particular section of the password. That's nearly an infinite number of possible combinations, all verified by voice. And you only have thirty seconds to answer. I guess you could say that no one gets in without an invitation."

A series of ten numbers appeared above the box: green 8, red 43, yellow 51, blue 19, orange 23, purple 32, white 16, pink 27, brown 4, and gray 29.

Gunnar spoke the combination out loud and the digital representation of his voice appeared in the green rectangle, followed by the yellow authenticator.

"*Ha.* Cue, cue. *Wú ài, wú ài. Ess. Dubbel-ve. Te. Kwu. Ah, ah. De. See, see.*"

When he finally finished, the screen returned to black.

"If you mess up any part of that log-in, the program launches a virus that destroys not just everything on your computer, but everything to which it's networked. These guys don't take any chances."

"Who, exactly, are they?"

"I don't know for sure. All of my transactions have been handled through intermediaries, and their chain of command is so long and winding that even they probably don't know for sure, but we're dealing with the kind of finances that limit the field to, at most, a couple hundred possibilities. Maybe even all of them. You guys need to move out of the webcam's range. Now!"

Ramses and Mason took a step to either side as the black screen vanished. A different type of desktop opened. The address bar at the top showed a series of numbers and letters separated by dashes. There were four quadrants below it. The one on the top right was the largest and featured a line chart with numbers scrolling underneath it. There were twenty different graphs from which to choose, and this was number twelve. The bottom right quadrant looked like a chat window, only Mason couldn't decipher any of the names, and their conversations were further encrypted. The bottom left featured a three-dimensional representation of a spinning globe surrounded by what looked like thousands of dots. The top left corner showed a picture of Gunnar from his own webcam, which had been accessed remotely by the program. A gorilla's face was superimposed over his.

"For anonymity's sake," he said, as though reading Mason's mind. The gorilla moved its lips, only with a slight delay. "Try to go anywhere you shouldn't go on here and the gorilla face goes away and security is alerted to your identity and location, which you can see right there at the bottom of the screen in the GPS box."

"Holy crap," Mason said.

"Yeah, tell me about it. This interface uses a variation on the TCP/IP protocol called SPYDRR. Like spiders crawling across the web. This box in the upper right can show all of the world's markets, plus an additional, unnamed market that only those who have access to this site can view. Unlike the others, this one doesn't represent real-time trading. It's almost like a predictive market. It shows the trades that the members here *intend* to make. Considering these are the people who control at least seventy-five percent of the money in the markets at any given time, what they determine here will find its real-world representation generally within a couple of months. But it's fluid, so at any given time it's just a snapshot of what will *likely* happen."

"So the people doing this pretrading here could cause all of the international markets to crash and burn."

"Or skyrocket. By essentially agreeing on a market forecast to which no one in the general public has access, they can not only control the world's economy, but also carve off slices of the remaining twenty-five percent like prime rib. They set the trends that everyone else follows. They pull money out of high-tech stocks, and the rest of the world does the same. They throw money into their own portfolios, and everyone else follows like lemmings. And considering they own all of these companies anyway, all they're really doing is moving their wallets from one pocket to the other, while investors are shoving their money into it as quickly as possible in between."

"When you said that you could tell that something big is coming, this is what you were talking about, isn't it?"

"Exactly. Just look at the names of the stocks scrolling past. These aren't huge trades, nothing to draw a whole lot of attention. But we're talking about the same names every day. I had a few theories, but I didn't put the whole thing together until you said something about a weaponized virus, Mace. These guys are in the process of stockpiling large quantities of several particular types of stocks that on their own don't really raise any red flags, but in conjunction, they scare the hell out of me."

"Quit beating around the bush, Gunnar. What are they stockpiling?"

"Biotech, pharmaceuticals, oil, energy, gold and precious metals."

"Jesus."

Mason felt sick to his stomach.

"So what?" Ramses said. "What's the big fucking deal? That's smart money."

"Think about it, Ramses." Gunnar's gorilla mouth moved on the screen as he spoke. "If something really bad happened, something capable of obliterating the existing societal infrastructure, who would be in a position to step up and take charge? These are the same people who already control the assets in the Federal Reserve and any number of foreign central banks. When they amass the crucial commodities that every individual needs, they'll be in a position to remake the entire world in any image they want."

And suddenly Mason understood exactly what all of this had to do with him. These were the commodities that would be in demand in the wake of a catastrophic, mass-casualty event.

Like a pandemic.

They were going to release the virus.

PART IV

Since I entered politics, I have chiefly had men's views confided to me privately. Some of the biggest men in the United States, in the field of commerce and manufacture, are afraid of somebody, are afraid of something. They know that there is a power somewhere so organized, so subtle, so watchful, so interlocked, so complete, so pervasive, that they had better not speak above their breath when they speak in condemnation of it.

—Woodrow Wilson, *The New Freedom: A Call For the Emancipation of the Generous Energies of a People* (1913)

41

NOVEMBER 15

"Give me the address and I'll get you an eye in the sky."

Mason told Gunnar the address the woman had given him and watched as he enlarged the box in the bottom left corner. As the globe grew larger, Mason realized that all of the pinpricks of light he'd seen surrounding it when it was minimized were actually satellites in orbit.

"Did you learn anything about Global Allied Biotechnology and Pharmaceuticals? GABP?" he asked.

"Very little outside of the fact that it's your brother-in-law's brainchild, which is more than a little disturbing, considering I generally hear about these things long before the groundbreaking stage. Describe the building again."

"I'm telling you. It looked like a mall or a small airport. That's about as well as I can describe it."

"What made you think that, though?"

"The size of the structure for one. The thing was massive."

"And what made you think it couldn't be an office building?"

"The framework provided too much open space. It was much wider than it was tall, which made it nearly invisible from the road, unless you knew exactly what you were looking for. Not what any architect would envision when dreaming up corporate headquarters designed to impress foreign investors. It looked almost industrial. I mean, there weren't even any windows."

"What are you thinking?"

"I'm not sure, but like you said, it's strange that I didn't know anything about it before now, either."

"Victor's a weasel," Ramses said. "Everybody knows that. He's the kind of guy who shows up at a strip club with a dollar bill on a string. He's probably making a grab for his old man's stake."

"I don't see it," Gunnar said. "It's only a matter of time before Paul simply hands over the reins. It's not like Victor doesn't already control all of AgrAmerica's overseas subsidiaries, anyway. And building a behemoth on the back nine isn't necessarily how one would initiate a takeover."

"You may know all this high-finance stuff, but I know people. Victor would cut his old man's throat in his sleep and blame it on his mother."

"I'm not disputing that. All I'm saying is that while Victor may ostensibly be in charge of whatever's going on out there, nothing transpires on the company's dime without Paul's stamp of approval." Gunnar paused. "Mace . . . tell me again what Victor said they hope to accomplish with the GABP venture?"

They were all tiptoeing around it.

"Their goal is to diversify and corner not only the global agricultural market, but biotechnology and pharmaceuticals, as well."

"Which are exactly the stocks that the people in power are snatching up. You thought Victor sounded sketchy about the whole thing, right?"

"Victor was born sketchy," Ramses said.

"That's the truth," Mason said. "He sent my BS meter off the charts."

"And now the billion-dollar question," Gunnar said. "Do you think he's involved with what you believe happened at Fairacre?"

Mason knew exactly what he was asking. If the Thornton family was connected with the horrible things that had taken place in the stalls behind the auction floor, then they'd also had a say in the decision to murder the IRS investigator who'd been nipping at their heels. Their own blood. Victor's half sister. Paul's daughter.

His wife.

He thought about Paul's strange behavior in the Futures building and about Victor's trademark smugness. These were the kind of men willing to do whatever it took to succeed, but did that really include signing the order for the murder of their own flesh and blood?

"I just don't know—"

"Hold up. This can't be right. Mace? Give me that address again."

"What's going—?"

"Just give me the address!"

"Five three two five Wedgewood Circle. Number nine."

"Are you certain?"

"Talk to me, Gunnar. What the hell's going on?"

"You tell me."

Gunnar scooted away from the laptop and gestured for Mason to take a look. He saw snow-covered pines and naked deciduous trees from above. The roofs of at least three different trailer homes were visible through the dense canopy. At least that's what they looked like under the accumulation.

"So you found it. Good job, Gunnar. I don't see the problem—"

"The problem is that when I went to task the nearest satellite, it was already focused on the very same area."

"Son of a bitch," Ramses said.

"They were following me," Mason said. "I led them straight to her."

"The GPS in your car—"

"Damn it! I can't lose her now!"

Mason sprinted for the garage door and leaped down into the darkness, only to find he'd already forgotten he'd left his car parked a mile down the street.

"Get in," Ramses said from behind him. He clicked a button on his key chain and his car's engine roared to life. The headlights struck the wall like lasers.

Mason raised the garage door and climbed into the passenger seat. The sleek black Mustang Boss 302 rocketed in reverse. Ramses jammed the brake and swung the car around in a single maneuver that nearly tossed Mason through the side window. He hopped out, opened the gate, and barely had time to buckle himself into the seat before the car launched down the street.

42

The Mustang undoubtedly would have slid all over the place had its tires actually been touching the ground. Even given how fast they were going, Mason worried they wouldn't get there in time.

"Can this thing go any faster?"

He'd obviously forgotten whom he was dealing with.

Ramses cocked a smile, hit the gas, and reminded Mason why he needed to choose his words more carefully around his old friend. The white landscape whipped past to either side in a blur. Before he knew it, they were on I-70 and firmly slotted in the icy tire grooves.

The Mustang careened down the off-ramp and blew sideways through the red light at the bottom before the wheels caught with a lurch and propelled them uphill to the north. Ramses finally let off the gas. The Peak View Inn was lost in the snow to the right. The trailers they were looking for were to the east, back up in the dense woodland behind the adult bookstore and the hourly motel. She'd been right across the street the entire time.

"Drop me off at the top of the hill and I'll work my way down through the trees."

Mason's cell phone rang. It was Gunnar.

"You have a Bluetooth?" he asked.

"Yeah. Give me a second."

Mason watched the trailer park flash past through the pines, but he could see little more than the backs of the units closest to the road. He hooked the Bluetooth to his ear, pocketed his cell phone, and glanced at the in-dash clock. It was only five o'clock, two hours before their scheduled meeting.

"Can you hear me, Gunnar?"

"Loud and clear."

As soon as they crested the hill, Ramses turned into the vacant parking lot of a strip mall and parked close enough to a twenty-four-hour convenience store that the Mustang didn't stand out any more than it already did.

"You see anything yet?" Mason asked.

"Movement in the trees to the northeast. Downhill," Gunnar replied.

"You want me to go with you?" Ramses asked.

"Stay here. If I'm not back in thirty minutes, call the cops and get the hell out of here, okay?"

Ramses nodded and Mason jumped out into the snow. The cold hit him like a truck. He wished he'd grabbed a heavier coat, but there was nothing he could do about that now.

"Talk to me, Gunnar."

"Still nothing, but I don't dare mess with the view at all. I'll be caught in a heartbeat. As it is, it's only a matter of time before whoever's watching notices I've piggybacked on their feed."

"Then get out of there. I can handle this on my own."

"The hell you can."

Mason ducked behind the strip mall at the first opportunity and used the shadows to conceal his approach. Once he broke cover, he would have to cross a lone street, and then he'd be in the trees behind the uppermost row of trailers, without any idea how many there were or how they were numbered. And without the slightest clue as to what kind of situation he was potentially hurling himself headlong into.

"Where are you now?" Gunnar asked.

"Crossing the road to the south, at the top of the hill." Mason darted across the street and threw himself into the evergreen shrubs on the other side. "Going silent now. Copy?"

"Copy."

He crawled out of the junipers and crouched behind the trunk of a pine tree while he gauged his surroundings. The road to his left was invisible from this vantage point, as were the trailers and whoever might be lurking in the shadows.

"If they're still in there," Gunnar said, "it's only because they haven't found her yet."

That confirmed what Mason had been thinking. Maybe they'd been able to use satellites to follow her back here after the woman abandoned his car, but there was no way they could have known about the proposed seven o'clock meeting, which also meant they had no reason to suspect that he would be here.

The snow fell heavily above him, causing clumps to drop from the overburdened branches. Somewhere in the distance, a dog barked. Everything else was so quiet that his breathing sounded too loud in his ears. He moved downhill. Slowly. Picking his way from behind the trunk of one pine tree to the next. The first mobile home materialized from the storm about two hundred feet to the northeast. There were no lights in the windows, no movement behind them. He used the back of the trailer as cover to get closer to the road. Wedgewood Circle formed a wide, wending S shape that slithered down through the trees toward the river. There were no tracks on the road and the few cars parked along the narrow shoulders were buried under snow.

Mason drew his pistol and eased around the side, taking full advantage of the shadows for as long as possible. He could only see two other units from where he crouched: one cattycorner across the street, behind a tall chain-link fence, and another about a hundred feet to his right at the end of the bend. Neither had mailboxes or anything resembling a house number. He took a deep breath, sprinted across the street, and knelt in the snow against the side of a small truck with rust around the wheel wells.

"Something's happening," Gunnar said. "Whoever's controlling the camera zoomed out a little. And I see movement. To the east. Behind the tree line."

"Give me a landmark. I'm flying blind out here." Mason crept around the front of the truck. Took a quick peek. Sprinted along the length of the fence and ducked down behind some shrubs. "Damn it, Gunnar. I need something to orient myself."

"The southernmost trailer has an old-fashioned TV antenna. The one across the street to the northeast has a basketball hoop in the yard."

Mason crouched and peeked around the side of the tree. He could barely see a thing through the overgrowth of pines and scrub oak.

"More movement to the east," Gunnar said. "No, southeast. They're surrounding the trailer to the east of the one with the antenna."

There was another massive pine tree fifty feet to the east. Mason ran low along the ridgeline and dove behind it. Glanced downhill. He could just barely see the roof of a trailer home to the northeast through the branches. He leaned farther forward and caught a glimpse of the antenna through the blowing snow. The adjacent trailer would be roughly a hundred feet to the east of it, which meant that the movement Gunnar had seen was on the same ridgeline as Mason, maybe two hundred feet dead ahead through the forest. He halved the distance at a low sprint and knelt in a copse of skeletal aspens.

"Movement to the southwest," Gunnar said.

"That's me."

"Someone else noticed. Get out of there, Mace. You're about to have company from the east."

Mason couldn't see anyone coming, but if they were being coordinated from a distance like he was, that didn't necessarily mean anything. He took two quick strides to the north and slid downhill feetfirst. Crashed into the scrub oak at the bottom. Scrambled to the other side. He expected to hear the report of gunfire and bullets tearing up the bushes around him, but no shots rang out. They didn't want to spook their prey.

Just because they hadn't shot at him didn't mean they weren't still coming, though.

"Directly uphill and behind you, Mace. Two more closing from across the street to the north and northeast. Get moving! If I can see you, so can they!"

He crawled out of the bushes and looked toward what he assumed was unit nine. The window screens were torn, the rear deck sagged, and it almost appeared as through the whole trailer was leaning away from the road onto its buckled skirt. He glanced back to his left, toward the trailer with the old antenna. From this angle, he could clearly see the small security camera directed toward him from behind the row of icicles clinging to the roofline.

Clever girl.

"Jesus Christ, Mason! They're right on top of you! Get the hell out of there!"

He could hear his pursuer behind him now. Maybe fifteen feet up the slope, moving through the aspens. He aimed his pistol at the sound and ran to the west, toward the other trailer, then dashed uphill through the densest cover he could find.

"He knows you're there. He's coming right for you!"

Which was exactly what Mason hoped he would do.

He guessed at the angle his pursuer had taken to intercept him, which would force him to pass right through a narrow gap between pine trunks, and barreled straight toward where he expected him to appear. He was already airborne when a man wearing black fatigues shoved through the branches. Mason caught him up high across the chest, knocking him off his feet. The man landed on his back, with Mason's shoulder planted firmly against his sternum. His breath exploded past his lips as they slid down the slope. Mason forced his left hand down over the bridge of the man's nose. The snow rode up over his head, but Mason could still tell where it was. He slammed the butt of his Sigma down onto the man's forehead. Again. And again.

Mason leaped up from the man's chest and pointed the gun right into his face. He wore a black ski mask, which revealed only his closed eyes, and a gas-operated Heckler & Koch model 417 modular assault rifle on a strap across his chest.

"Get out of there!" Gunnar said. "They're coming around both sides of the trailer and the image is focused directly on you!"

He holstered his pistol, commandeered the HK417, and ran toward the trailer with the camera. If nothing else, at least there'd be a record of his death. Maybe he could even buy the woman enough time to get out of there, if she hadn't already. He raced along the back side of the trailer and ducked around the corner. Pressed his back against the siding.

Waited. Pulse pounding in his ears.

They'd send one man from either side. He needed to stay in the middle for as long as he dared before tipping his hand. As far as they knew, he didn't have access to their level of satellite technology, which gave him an advantage, slight though it might be.

"One coming for you along the north face of the trailer, the other along the south," Gunnar said. "Moving low to the ground. Coming in fast."

If Mason went for the one to his right, heading along the north side, he'd be totally exposed to the road and the units on the other side of it. If he went left, he'd be able to scurry uphill into the woods again. It was a no-brainer. Which was why he went quickly around the side to his right, with all of his instincts screaming for him to go the other way.

The man's eyes widened in surprise a heartbeat before Mason lunged at him with the HK417 raised high. He caught the man squarely in the temple before he could get off a shot. He hit the ground hard, shoulder-first. The entire left side of his face was misshapen and blood seeped out from beneath his torn eyelid.

"Behind you! Damn it, Mace! He's right—"

"Drop the rifle and get on your knees," a man's voice said.

"You'd shoot an unarmed man in the back?"

"Don't do anything stupid," Gunnar said. "Ramses is on his way. Just try to stall, okay?"

"Throw it down in the snow," the man behind him said. "Now!"

"How about you tell me what you want with her," Mason said.

"How about you shut up before I put a peephole through the back of your head."

Mason heard a crumpling sound to his right, from inside the trailer. Like someone trying to discreetly transfer weight across floorboards that hadn't been manufactured with discretion in mind.

He threw down the rifle in order to make the loudest racket possible. He needed to keep the man behind him from hearing whatever was going on inside the trailer.

"Your buddy here could probably use a quick trip to the emergency room. I don't think his eye's supposed to look like that."

"He dies, you die. I don't care if you have a guardian angel or not."

"You know who I am?"

"Shut up and put your hands on your head."

"Ramses just turned into the park," Gunnar said. "You need to buy yourself another thirty seconds. If that."

"How do you know who I am? Tell me, damn it! Did you know who my wife was, too?"

Another creak and a groan to his right. Subtle. Close to the front door of the dilapidated unit.

Mason could hear the smile in the man's voice when he spoke.

"She cried out for you the whole time she was burning."

A car engine to the west. Coming in fast.

The sounds of shifting weight inside the mobile home, the click of a hand settling on a doorknob.

The man's words reverberated inside Mason's skull.

His vision turned red and the edges throbbed in time with his pulse. Never in his life had he felt such depths of hatred. He wanted to tear this man apart with his bare hands.

He never got the chance.

Ramses' headlights swept across them as he came hard around the corner in a controlled slide, throwing their shadows up the side of the trailer and onto the door as it opened outward. A dark silhouette emerged, the barrel of a shotgun leveled at Mason's chest.

"No!"

He tried to get his body between the weapon and the man behind him. He needed to know what the man knew about his wife's death.

An explosion of light and sound.

A gust of hot wind screamed past his cheek.

The sting of discharged particles, biting into his skin.

"More coming from the southeast!" Gunnar shouted through the Bluetooth in his ear. "Get out of there while you still can!"

A concussive clap against his eardrum in the other.

Mason whirled around and saw a spray of red where the man's head had been. Streamers of blood unraveled into the night and spattered the hood of the Mustang as it struck the guy's body from the side. He flopped onto the hood, bounced right off of it, and struck the trailer in a starburst of blood.

Someone was shouting at Mason, tugging on his arm. He could only stare down at the heap of humanity sprawled in the wash of Ramses' headlights. The man's blood dribbled down the broken siding and glistened in the light as the Mustang backed away and swung out into the street.

Gunnar shouting, directly in his ear. He couldn't decipher the words from the ringing.

More tugging.

Something whizzed past his face and struck the trailer, throwing sharp vinyl shards in every direction. He was moving before bullets filled the air around him.

Mason saw Ramses through the open passenger door, yelling and waving him in. He wrapped his arms around the woman who'd been pulling on his arm and tackled her onto the seat. The Mustang was already slipping and sliding in reverse before he could even attempt to grab for the door to close it. The window exploded and the door jumped. He managed to maneuver the woman onto his lap so he could close the door. Two men ran down the center of the road, golden flashes dancing from the barrels of their assault rifles. Mason could hardly see their outlines through all the cracks and spattered blood.

"Get down!" Ramses shouted, and accelerated straight toward them.

Bullets ricocheted from the bumper and hood.

The men dove out of the way.

And then the Mustang was around the corner and out of sight.

43

They were barely out of the trailer park when Mason felt something sharp prod the soft tissue beneath his jaw. Warmth trickled down his neck. He didn't even have the energy to try to turn his head.

"Would you get that thing out of my neck?"

"Who is he?" the woman asked.

"Take the knife out of my neck."

"Knife in your neck?" Gunnar said through the earpiece. "What in the name of God is going on there? Are you all right?"

"Not now, Gunnar."

"If you get blood on the seat I'm going to kick both of your asses," Ramses said.

In one swift motion, the girl swung her legs over Mason's shoulder and landed in the backseat without removing the knife from his skin.

She grabbed him around the neck from behind the headrest with her left forearm and pushed harder with the knife in her right. He grimaced and cocked his head as far away as he could.

An impressive move.

"Driver," she said. "Tell me your name."

With the panic came the accent.

"I'm the guy who's saving your skin, in case you didn't notice."

She gave the tip of the knife a twist and Mason nearly came out of his skin. The blood felt like it was flowing freely now.

"Jesus," Mason said.

"Ramses," he said. "Like the pharaoh."

Another twist. Mason bared his teeth. It felt like she was digging into the underside of his mandible.

"For Christ's sake! That's his name!"

She withdrew some of the pressure. Mason knew he could snap her wrist without a whole lot of difficulty, but she could undoubtedly spear his tongue to the roof of his mouth every bit as quickly. She kept her head down and her face concealed behind the headrest. He could only see a lock of jet black hair hanging out from beneath her hoodie.

"Ramses." She pronounced it Rahm-zees. "When I tell you to stop, you are going to pull the car to the side of the road and let me out or I will cut James Mason. Very deep."

"Okay."

"Okay what?"

"Go ahead and cut him."

"Ramses," Mason said.

"Did he just say what I think he said?" Gunnar asked.

"Not now, Gunnar."

"He said his name was Ramses." The woman shoved her knees into the back of Mason's seat and used the leverage to ratchet her forearm even tighter around his neck. "Who is Gunnar?"

"Gunnar's on the Bluetooth in my ear. Ramses is the driver."

She loosened her grip ever so slightly.

"Do what I tell you, driver, and I will not hurt this man."

"Go ahead. Carve him up like a Thanksgiving turkey, for all I care."

"Damn it, Ramses. You're not helping."

"His blood will ruin your seats," she said.

"Can't have that," Ramses said. Mason didn't even see him make a move for his pistol, but it was in his hand all the same, with the barrel nuzzled against her forehead. "His blood, I don't want. I know where he's been. Your blood, I can live with. Now, get the knife out of his fucking neck."

Ramses somehow managed to drive with his left hand and hold his pistol on her with his right, all while hurtling down the icy road at a speed that would likely end the standoff long before they were able to do so on their own.

"You have to trust us," Mason said. Even that little movement sent electrical currents from the blade into his jaw and the roots of his teeth. "I've done everything you asked. What more can I do to prove that we're on the same side?"

"You can let me out."

"That's not trust. That's stupidity."

"I trust no one."

"At some point, you're going to have to," Mason said. "Right now, we're your best hope of staying alive."

He felt the knife relax under his chin. His instinct was to grab her by the wrist and relieve her of the blade, but nothing good could come from it. He rested his hand gently on hers and waited.

Her breathing slowed and took on a rhythmic quality.

Mason reached to his left and lowered Ramses' weapon from her head. Ramses glanced at him with a question in his eyes. Mason nodded to assure him that he knew what he was doing.

"I am so tired," she whispered. "I can not do this alone."

She removed the blade from beneath his chin and he replaced it with the back of his hand in an effort to stem the bleeding.

"You're not alone anymore. . . ."

"Alejandra."

"Talk to me, Mace," Gunnar said. "What in God's name is going on?"

"Everything's under control. Just needed to take care of a little situation."

"One of many, I'm afraid."

"What do you mean?"

"What's he saying?" Ramses asked.

Mason shushed him and tried to focus on Gunnar's words while he adjusted the side mirror so he could see the woman in the backseat. She kept her face well hidden the entire time.

"If they followed you by using the GPS in your car before, they're probably already tracking your cell signal and are on the way to intercept you at your house."

"Then get out of there, Gunnar."

"I logged out and got the hell out of there the moment you were in the car."

"Where are you now?"

"No way. Not over an unsecure line. Just get to someplace safe and I'll find you."

"How do you propose doing that?"

"Come on, Mace. Who do you think you're talking to here? This is what I do for a living. I find things that no one else can."

A click and he was gone.

"What did he say?" Ramses asked.

"He said to go someplace safe and he'd find us."

"We're better off splitting up. At least for a while. Besides, I've got a hunch I want to play, and a federal agent tagging along would kind of complicate things."

Ramses smiled.

Mason had learned long ago that his doing so wasn't necessarily a good thing.

Ramses pushed the Mustang even harder, while Mason did his best not to dwell on the vision of his mangled corpse wrapped around a lightpost in a tangle of American steel. Instead, he focused on finding a way to get Alejandra—if that really was her name—to tell him everything she knew about the monster who had killed his wife, the man with the blue eyes, who at this very moment could be preparing to unleash a deadly virus upon an unsuspecting world.

44

The streetlights all flashed red near the heart of downtown, where a few cars, mostly upscale SUVs, finally joined them on the roads. The skyscrapers seemed somehow both taller and colder and the snow fell an ashen shade of gray. It was bizarre to think that this entire area essentially emptied at night, only to refill in the morning when the suburban migration commenced. It was an existence that flew in the face of millions of years of evolution, and yet one so ordinary that it was entirely outside Mason's realm of comprehension.

They pulled into the parking structure of a generic office building roughly a mile and a half from the one Ramses lived in and passed through two automated security gates. The building wasn't tall enough to qualify as a skyscraper or short enough to call itself a complex. In the grand scheme of things, it was essentially invisible.

The Mustang's headlights contracted on the concrete wall as they headed straight toward a space labeled C42.

"Where are we?" Alejandra asked.

"Does it matter?" Ramses said.

"What are we doing here?"

"Somewhere else you have to be?"

They parked between an older BMW and a newer Audi and climbed out into the dimly lit garage. The sound of their footsteps was amplified tenfold. The only wet tracks belonged to the Mustang; the other cars had obviously been in here since before it started to snow.

"You worried at all they'll be able to link the Mustang to you?" Mason asked.

"I'm sure they followed us via satellite, but there's no way they'll be able to trace the car back to me. It's registered under the name of Anthony Montana at an address on the fourth floor."

"What's on the fourth floor?"

"An undercover DEA shop. Figured they'd get a kick out of the *Scarface* reference."

"They'll know it was you, Ramses."

"You kidding me? They have no reason to suspect me. Besides, I was at Club Five all night. Probably at least fifty different people saw me there."

"We're not dealing with the police, Ramses. These aren't the kind of people who go through the normal channels or worry about things like gathering evidence."

Ramses grinned.

"Welcome to my world, Special Agent Mason. It's been so long since I've thought about the rules that I'm not entirely sure I even remember what they are anymore."

"They'll still come for you."

"I'd be disappointed if they didn't. But trust me on this one, Mace. I move in the same circles as people like this and have a whole lot of friends who wouldn't be happy *at all* if anything were to happen to me."

"These friends. They're the ones who told you about the building where the SWAT guys were killed, aren't they? You're going to have to introduce me sometime."

"Uh-uh. That's not how it works. You, of all people, should know that I don't sell out my friends at any price." Ramses slipped a key off of his key ring and tossed it to Mason. "There's an older-model Ford Bronco parked at the back of the hourly lot two blocks west and two blocks north of here. There's a briefcase under the floor of the trunk that should come in handy. Don't call me. Understand? I'll track you down once the dust settles."

"How do you propose—?"

"Please. It's me. Ramses."

Mason nodded and glanced at Alejandra, who stood with her back to him, watching the ramp leading up to the sublevel above them.

Ramses turned and headed for the door to the stairwell.

"Hey," Mason called after him. He stopped and turned around. "Thanks."

"I didn't do this for you, Mace. I've been thinking about trading in that Mustang for a brand-new Hummer for a while now. If you know what I'm saying."

Mason couldn't help but smile.

"Don't let them get away with what they did to Angie," Ramses said.

"Count on it."

"Not just out there." He made a sweeping gesture toward the world without, then tapped his temple with his index finger. "But in here, Mace. They've got you flying off half-cocked in every direction at once. That's how mistakes get made. If you want to have any chance of nailing them to the wall, you're going to have to choke down that rage and figure out how to get a step ahead of them."

Ramses went through the door with a squeal. Mason heard him say good-bye, but he was fairly confident his old friend wasn't talking to him. He was pretty sure Ramses was talking to the Mustang.

Mason took Alejandra by the hand and pulled her toward the opposite set of stairs, which he guessed would let out onto Larimer Street to the west. They needed to get moving. There weren't a whole lot of pedestrians out there in the storm with whom they could blend.

"Time to go," he said.

Alejandra jerked her arm out of his grasp and stumbled backward. She tripped over a seam in the concrete and went down hard on her rear end. Her hood fell back from her head in the process.

"Do not touch me!"

She looked up at Mason, and he had to concentrate to keep his expression from betraying his shock. He suddenly understood why she did everything in her power to conceal her face.

"Okay. I won't touch you again. But I need you to listen to me. We need to go. Right now. They could be here any second, and we want to be long gone when they arrive."

She pulled her hood back over her head and led the way toward the stairs.

"Where are we going?" she asked.

"The last place they would ever expect us to go."

45

The Bronco had been right where Ramses said it would be, only a whole lot harder to find buried under eight inches of snow. It started right up despite the cold, as though someone routinely performed maintenance on it. Mason had to wonder if he had any idea of the full extent of Ramses' extracurricular activities. Nightclub owners who dealt in vices of the more innocent variety tended not to need getaway cars stashed within walking distance of a garage where a space was leased under a false name, and the nose of the DEA. The bottom line, though, was that he'd driven into the middle of a situation where he could have easily gotten himself killed to save Mason's ass. Whatever else he might be, Ramses was just about the best friend he had right now. He and Gunnar—wherever in the world he was by now.

Lord knows Mason could have used Trapp's help, too, but he'd already put his partner in a bad-enough situation without asking him to risk his badge. Without his, Mason was operating in the gray area of legality, but he no longer cared about the consequences, at least not professionally. The man with the blue eyes was out there somewhere, and he fully intended to make sure that he and his entire organization burned. Only this time, there would be no hope of rising from the ashes.

He stopped at a twenty-four-hour convenience store, where he picked up some beef jerky, a blueberry crumb cake, an armful of energy drinks, and two disposable cell phones with wireless Bluetooth capability. All of it was on Ramses, thanks to the roll of bills in the suitcase under the trunk, where Mason also found an Infinity high-capacity titanium Tiki .40-caliber semiautomatic pistol with an under-barrel light and enough ammo to shoot his way out of just about any situation.

Feeling somewhat reinvigorated, he hit the road again, heading north. Alejandra sat next to him, her legs drawn up to her tiny frame. She seemed so small just sitting there with the buildings crawling past beside her. It was almost impossible to believe that she had survived

Fairacre, which he might have been disinclined to believe had he not seen her face.

"Are you going to tell me about it?" he asked.

She didn't speak for several minutes. She kept her features hidden beneath her hood, so he couldn't even begin to guess at the thoughts going through her head. When she finally spoke, it was in an almost resigned voice.

"What do you want to know?"

Mason had a million questions, all fighting to be asked at the same time. He decided instead to have her start at the beginning, to let her tell her story in the way she saw fit, in hopes that she would divulge details about which he didn't even know to ask.

He watched the icy road through the blowing snow, which whipped first one way and then the other. It was all he could do to keep the Bronco's tires aligned with the tracks the few cars out on the roads had laid for him. He glanced at the rearview mirror. At the vehicles that had slid onto the shoulders and off the road into the adjacent fields. At everything except the woman in the seat beside him as she spoke of horrors that convinced him that man's capacity for evil truly knew no bounds.

"My name is Alejandra María de Yautepec Vigil." Her voice was soft, distant, and carried a palpable note of sorrow. "I am from San Bartolo, Oaxaca. A village of only six hundred people, in the mountains near the Gulf of Tehuantepec. My family has grown coffee beans on the same land since before my great-grandfather was born. We lived in the house where he was raised. All of us. My parents and brothers. My grandmother. My aunt and uncle and their children. One big family."

Despite being unable to see her expression, Mason could tell she was wearing a wistful smile. Her eyes had turned inward to the time and place she retreated when there was nowhere else to hide.

"Sounds nice," he said.

"It is. Was, anyway. Before the economy collapsed. One day we woke up and our entire harvest was worth half of what we needed to survive. We could no longer even afford to buy food. The struggles of my village were noticed by a Catholic missionary group. They promised they would show us how to make ten times as much money for the same beans we were already harvesting, if we were willing to work for it. They sent our men—among them my father and my older brother, Pablo—to Agua Prieta, fifteen hundred miles to the north, to learn about modern roasting methods and organizing co-ops from other successful villagers, who would teach them the trade in exchange for one year of their labor. They would even be given their own roasters and packaging materials. Everything would have been so perfect. . . ."

Her voice trailed off. Several miles passed in silence while he waited for her to continue. The mere fact that she was sitting here with him now meant that something had gone terribly wrong. When she finally spoke, he could tell she'd been crying.

"My father and the other men . . . they never made it home."

"What happened?"

"One of the men from San Carlos, a village twenty miles away. This man. He found their bus. It was off the road. In the river. There was no one inside. He said . . . he said it looked like it had been there for a long time. And inside . . . inside there were holes. Bullet holes. And blood. The seats . . . they were covered with it. Everything our men had brought back with them. Everything they had worked for the last year to earn. The future of our village. It was all gone."

"One of the cartels?"

"Who else would have done such a thing? These *narcos*. They are not men. They are animals. They took everything from us and left us to starve. My grandmother, she gave the food from her plate to my sister, Gabriela, and me. We watched her waste away and die. *Mi abuelita*. She gave her life for ours. It was then that I decided to leave. I would not take food from the mouth of another. I would make as much money as I could and send it back to help my family. And I would find a way to make the *pinche* narcos pay for what they had done to us."

"What did you do?"

"There are only so many things a woman with few skills and little education can do in Mexico. I could either sell my body or join the army. To them I was just another *guacha* to fight and die in a war we could not win. They trained me and, most important, paid me to fight in the streets of my own country. And when they saw how good I was at killing narcos—how much I enjoyed doing so—they promoted me to Cuerpo de Fuerzas Especiales."

"Special Forces? That would explain a few things."

"They assigned me to the Second SF Brigade and sent me to *San Miguel de los Jagüeyes* to train in urban combat. Taught me how to blend in with the people around me. Go places others could not go. Gather information to be used as blackmail. Get close to targets others could not reach. No man fears a woman so small until she has a knife to his throat."

Mason had learned that lesson the hard way. He wouldn't make the same mistake twice.

"I was part of the team that captured Omar Treviño Morales and brought Los Zetas to its knees. It was not long after that raid, while I was still in Monterrey, that I received a letter from my sister asking for my help. All communications were routed through a central address, so it was already three weeks old when it arrived. By the time I returned home, my sister was gone. I found the coffee fields burned and *mota*—marijuana—growing from the soil. While I was on the other side of the country fighting Los Zetas, the men of Cártel de Jalisco Nueva Generación took my village. They dragged the missionaries into the streets and killed them for all to see. They bribed *federales* to guard the fields and look the other way while they abused my people. I can only imagine the things they must have done to my little sister."

He had to slow the vehicle to combat the worsening roads. It wasn't snowing as hard as it had been, but the wind had gathered strength in its stead. At least Ramses had given him a tank like this old Bronco.

"Gabriela was only sixteen years old. I was not there to protect her when she needed me, and my mother was too scared to try. It is no wonder she ran away. And while I had been of age to join the army, she had not, which left her with even fewer choices. She did not know where to find me, and I knew she would not run away from abuse only to sell herself into it. As children, we had heard the stories of America and promised each other we would go there one day. I was certain that was where she had gone. I swore to my mother I would not return without Gabriela. . . . I have not spoken with her since the night I left."

Mason knew better than to ask why. Her sister's absence was answer enough.

"So you went after her."

"It did not take long to find the man who took my sister north. He called himself 'Papi.' Everyone knew that for two thousand pesos he would take them as far as Altar." Mason was familiar with the small Sonoran town. It was a common staging ground for migrants preparing to make a run for the border, a place where desperate men and women negotiated deals with human smugglers and embarked upon the grueling trek into the scorching desert. "So I went there and showed her picture to everyone on the street. To all of the people sleeping outside the *maquiladoras*, hoping to find work on the assembly lines. To all of the vendors selling supplies from their stalls. I finally found a man who recognized her in one of the *hospedajes*, a guesthouse where he shared a tiny room with fifteen others. He said it had been close to a week since last he saw her. In the plaza. Talking to a man everyone knew was a coyote. He said I would recognize this man by his cowboy hat and snakeskin boots.

"I found him near the fountain in the center of town, selling his services. He was handsome and charming and called himself 'Vaquero.' Cowboy. He remembered Gabriela. She had been desperate to reach America, but she had been unable to pay, so he had taken her to men he knew would help her. If she was willing to carry something across the border for them."

"Drugs."

"That is what I thought. At first. I wanted to kill this Vaquero for handing my sister over to the narcos, but he was nothing. Less than nothing. Men like Vaquero paid Cártel de Sinaloa for the privilege of running their businesses. And helped them find mules when they were approached by people who had no money. I realized that if I wanted to find Gabriela, I was going to have to do exactly what she had done. So I told him I wanted to meet with these men who could help me get across the border. That I was willing to do whatever they asked. And then he smiled. I knew I was making a terrible mistake, but I would have done anything to find my sister."

She paused for several seconds. When she spoke again, it was in a voice so soft, Mason could hardly hear her over the rumble of the tires on the ice.

"Anything."

46

Alejandra didn't speak for so long that Mason thought she might have fallen asleep. He could sense she was to the part he was waiting to hear, but he didn't want to push her too hard. At the same time, though, he needed to find out what she knew.

"What did he do to you?"

"Vaquero?" she said. "He did nothing to me. The man he gave me to, though . . ."

He waited her out.

"Vaquero took me to an area of town where no one goes. Past the *maquiladoras*. Into the barrio. There was an old building. It looked like all of the others. Like it would soon fall down. It was dark inside. He pulled me by the hand to a set of stairs leading underground. The room at the bottom was small. There were other people, too. People like me. I could not see them, though. It smelled bad. Like frightened animals. There was a hole in the wall. At the back. A hole that led to a different building. Vaquero told me to step through. I heard him collecting money behind me. Vaquero, he sold me to these men in the dark."

"Who did he sell you to?" Mason asked. "What do you remember about them?"

"The men. They wore black ski masks with *respiradores*."

"Respirators?"

"Like we wore in the army when we used tear gas. At the time, I thought it was because of the smell. It was so strong. They used their flashlights to direct me through another hole in the wall. There were candles on plates. On the floor. And a man sitting at a desk in the middle of the room. He did not have a mask or a respirator. He wore an old-fashioned suit, like men wore a hundred years ago. Black, with thin lapels. A striped vest and a string tie. And a hat, like a sombrero, only much smaller."

Mason's heartbeat accelerated. He recalled his encounter in the quarry with the man with the blue eyes. He'd been wearing an old suit then, too. Beneath a butcher's apron smeared with blood.

"There was a chair in front of him," she said. "I sat across the desk from him. The men in the respirators left me alone with this man. When he smiled, the corners of his mouth went all the way back to his ears, showing all of his teeth. Like a crocodile."

"Was his skin scarred?"

"Not yet." Mason heard the smile in her voice, but it wasn't the kind meant for others. "It was his eyes that I remember most."

"A deeper blue than you've ever seen on a human being before."

"Bluer even than the ocean near my home in Oaxaca. I told him my sister had come through here, that I was trying to find her. He just smiled, said I would be with her soon, and placed his hand on the table, palm-up. I placed mine in his. For a moment, I thought everything was going to be all right, and then he pulled out two small cases. He set them on the desk before me. He opened one, then the other. He showed them to me. Both had *jeringas* . . . syringes, with short needles. They were half-full. He took one out of each case. Then he said, '*Necesita vacunas si desea ir a los Estados Unidos.*' 'You need vaccinations to go to the United States.' He walked around the desk. So close I could feel his heat. Smell the sickness on his breath. Like he was rotting on the inside.

"I told him I would not let him stick me with his needles. '*Está bien,*' he said. '*Eres libre de irte.*' 'That is fine. You are free to leave.' He closed his cases, returned to his chair, and called for the men to take me away. I said for him to wait, and he waved them off. When I looked at him again, he was smiling. He already knew what I would do and had the syringes ready. I watched him walk around the desk. Looked up into his eyes as he stood over me. He uncapped the first syringe and stuck it in my shoulder. He did the same with the second one. It hurt all the way to the bone. Like he had struck me with a hammer."

"You let him inject you?"

"I told you I would have done anything to find my sister. I would have let him do a thousand times worse. Besides, I had no reason to suspect there was disease in the needles. I thought they were drugging me, so I would not see where they were taking me."

"You should have killed him right then and there."

"It would have been easy. We were alone and he did not fear me. I could have broken a plate and slit his throat. Used the chair I was sitting on to crush his skull. But I did not. I needed this man to help me find my sister."

A green highway sign glided past on the right, its face rimed with snow and ice. Mason had already driven past it once in the last twenty-four hours. He knew what it said: BRUSH 14 MILES.

"The man took me to another room. It was dark, but I could hear other people. This room, it smelled of vomit. I was relieved when the men with the respirators finally came. They put eight of us in the trailer of a small truck. It was so hot. I do not know how far we drove or in which direction. All I remember is dust. The taste. The smell. And the red of the setting sun when the truck stopped and the men opened the doors. It was so bright, we had to cover our eyes with our hands. We were surrounded by cacti and briars. There was nothing but sand for as far as we could see. And a fallen barbed-wire fence. I knew esxactly what was on the other side. I just had no idea how far we still had to go.

"One of the men spoke to us in Spanish, but his words were hard to understand with the respirator. He told us to head north toward the mountains we could barely see against the horizon. That was where we had to go. He said we would walk thirty-five miles and it would take three days. We would travel at night, he said. When the sun was down and it was cooler. There would be a vehicle waiting to take us to a welcome center when we got there. I asked if my sister would still be there when we arrived. He said she would definitely still be 'hanging around.' It was a strange choice of words, but I blamed it on his poor Spanish. We all just stood there, watching him unload cases of bottled water, bags of protein bars, and packages of tuna. And then we watched him drive away. When the dust settled, we divided up the food and water and started walking.

"We did not exchange names, only where we came from. It was

strange. We were together and apart at the same time. The others were excited. They were in America. They made plans for where they would go and what they would do. They ate and drank nearly all of their rations. They talked about the future. But they were fools. The heat the next day was more than any of us could bear."

Mason nodded. He remembered how hot it got in that desert. It might have been a while, but it wasn't the kind of experience he was likely to forget.

"The sun burned through us. Made our sweat turn to salt. It dried our eyes and made it hard to blink. Made it *hurt* to blink. Our lips chapped, then peeled, and then bled. We ate the cactus for its fluid. We had needles in our lips and tongues and inside our cheeks. We ate the few agave we found. We ate the lizards we could catch. We walked until our feet bled inside our shoes and until our hands and knees were skinned from falling on the slick rocks. And on the night of the second day, we prayed. We prayed to any god or saint who could hear our words. And we walked.

"On the third day, the heat was even worse. The blisters on our feet burst. The cactus needles pierced our soles. There was no shade. We developed fevers. We thought it was because we could not cool off. At first, anyway. Until the woman from Puebla screamed. Her sister had fallen and was gasping for air. When she rolled over and looked up at us, it was obvious something was very wrong. The woman knew she was going to die. The veins in her eyes burst and the whites turned red. We barely had the strength to walk on our own, but we carried her as far as we could. It was a mercy for all of us when she finally died.

"It was not long before the man from Tabasco passed out. He stood up, walked a little farther, then collapsed again. We could hear the fluid in his lungs. There was so much, he could not get even a single breath. It was then that we realized what the man with the blue eyes had done to us. The woman from Apaxtla cried so loud that the rest of us tried to get as far away from her as we could. The sound was so horrible, so . . . *lamentable*, I wanted her to die. She lasted longer than most of the others. Longer than the man and the woman from Zacatepec. Longer than the man from Guerrero. I was dying, too. I knew this, but I could not allow myself to give up. I prayed. . . . I prayed to God that Gabriela had not been infected. That if she had, she had not suffered as I was suffering. But God did not hear my prayers."

There was nothing Mason could say. If ever he'd harbored any doubt that the people responsible for doing this to her were deeply and truly evil, he no longer did. There were simply people who were different from the rest of humanity, people who not only embraced the evil inside of them, but wallowed in it.

"The woman from Apaxtla was the last to die. I crossed her arms over her chest, closed her eyes, and said a prayer to San Toribio Romo. And then I was alone and the only thing I could think to do was run. I ran as far as I could. Until I, too, collapsed. It was so hot. My chest was tight. I could not breathe. I could feel the fluid in my lungs. Feel it deep down. I tasted blood and I knew. . . . I knew it was my turn to die. But I did not want to die there. Not like that. So I crawled up onto the rocks. Through yuccas and cacti and paloverdes. I crawled with needles and thorns in my hands and in my face until I finally found shade. And then I closed my eyes. . . ."

Mason waited her out.

"But I did not die. A man wearing a respirator dragged me from the shade and into the awful heat again. Pulled back my eyelids and shined a light into my eyes. Stuck a needle in my arm and gave me fluid from a bag. Carried me back to his vehicle, where the bodies of the others were already piled. The skin on their faces was purple and black and crawling with *moscas*—"

"*Moscas?*"

"Flies. They were covered with flies. The men fanned them away as they loaded the bodies into a trailer. I understood then that even death would not be the end."

She was silent for so long that Mason feared he had pushed her too hard.

"It was only the beginning."

47

Alejandra visibly tensed as they neared Fairacre Ranch Surplus and Auction. Mason watched her the entire time from the corner of his eye. There had to be something he was missing, and there was no better place to start than where all of the threads converged.

Ground zero.

The telltale silhouettes of the house and the outbuilding materialized from the storm against the western horizon.

Alejandra's breathing grew faster.

"Why are we here? I did not ever want to come back."

"I was hoping you might remember something crucial. I don't know what to do from here. Maybe there's something I missed earlier. Some piece of evidence they didn't properly destroy."

"You do not understand what they did here."

"Then tell me."

Mason parked by the house and climbed out of the car. The wind blew across the fields from the west with such velocity that the snow didn't have much of an opportunity to stick. It was maybe four inches deep where the tall weeds had been flattened and swept into drifts against the structures.

He heard the passenger door close behind him.

What little remained of the roof of the auction house sagged under the weight of the snow. A drift had formed against the interior wall, partially concealing the open area where the auction floor and the corrals behind it had once been.

Mason turned around at the sound of footsteps. Alejandra somehow looked even smaller, despite the oversize parka. He watched her eyes for signs of recognition, but she caught him looking and tugged her hood down.

He needed her to help him figure out why whoever bought the Fairacre shelf corporation had gone to such great lengths to prevent anyone from investigating this property if there was nothing incriminating here. This was the piece of the puzzle he couldn't quite make fit, and yet it was the discovery of this property that had started the chain of events that culminated in the deaths of his wife and a federal prosecutor.

"This is the place." Alejandra's soft voice was swept away by the wind. "I remember the smell. It was the first thing I noticed when they unloaded me from the truck."

"How long were you here?"

"I do not know for sure. A week? Two?"

Mason stood back and let her lead the way into the back area, where stalls had once lined the rear wall. He followed her eyes up to the rafters from which the chains and hooks had once hung, then quickly back down to the ground.

"'Scream all you want. No one will hear you.' That is what one of the men said to me. 'Scream all you want.' And for the first few days, I did just that. I screamed until I had no voice left and the pain in my throat was too great. When I learned that my cries gave them pleasure, I stopped. I would give them no more pleasure."

"Did they . . . ?"

"Rape me? No. That is a sick pleasure, but it is the pleasure of men. The people here, they were monsters. Their pleasures were twisted . . . *sádico*."

"Did they bring you straight here from the desert?"

"I do not know. I was asleep most of the time. The crossing nearly killed me. I remember being pushed from the truck into a muddy field with an old fence. It was night, but I could tell there were no mountains. No trees. No ocean. Nothing. They shoved me up a wooden ramp. Into a room that smelled of animals. It was an old smell. Like it is now. There was another smell, too. One I could not place. Not then. Chemicals, I later learned. The chemicals they used to clean up the messes they made. That we made."

She walked past where the row of stalls had stood before the fire consumed them.

"How many of you were here?"

"Ten. I think. It was hard to tell. People came and went so quickly."

"Went? Where did they go?"

"They died. I listened to a woman die that first night. After they locked me in the darkness."

Alejandra stopped at the end of the row, near where the rusted cattle gate was wedged in the mouth of the chute. She turned in a half circle, then dropped to her hands and knees. She scooped away the snow and scraped at the hard dirt.

"They already sanitized this place," Mason said. "They didn't leave anything behind. Trust me, I"—he caught a glimpse of dark metal, maybe iron, beneath the dirt—". . . already . . . checked. . . ."

He knelt opposite her and chiseled the dirt away as fast as he could. They exposed the seams. The corners. The notch where someone could insert the end of a rod and lever it open like a manhole cover. When it was fully revealed, he sat back on his haunches and stared down at it. He never would have found it. He'd probably even walked right on top of it.

"Help me lift it." She clawed at the edges, searching for any kind of grip. "There has to be . . . has to be a way."

"Hang on."

Mason ran back through the snow and opened the trunk of the Bronco. He found the tire iron under the false floor beside the emergency case, right where he remembered seeing it. He popped the case, grabbed the Infinity, and tucked the pistol under his waistband. He had a hunch the under-barrel light might come in handy. Besides, there was no such thing as having too much firepower.

By the time he returned, Alejandra had scooted back against the rear wall, where she sat motionless, her face concealed within the shadows of her hood. He stepped in front of her, wiggled the end of the tire iron until it caught the notch, then lifted it with a scream of rusted hinges.

She crawled forward and peered down through the swirling dust into the darkness. The odor was one of disuse, of the faint traces of chemicals beneath the overriding scent of age. He dropped the tire iron, drew the Infinity, and switched on the LED light. The beam illuminated a staircase leading underground.

"What's down there?"

"Hell."

48

Mason cautiously descended into the darkness. The wooden stairs were old and warped and creaked loudly enough to echo from the subterranean structure, which, judging by the sound, was much larger than he initially suspected. He reached the bottom and found the floor was made of bare concrete, treated with the kind of sealant he associated with industrial garages and zoos, the kind designed to be hosed off into drains. The rest of the structure was obviously much older. The wooden cribbing was so ancient, it looked almost petrified. This must have been a storage room during Prohibition. Or maybe it had always been a vile place hidden even from God's sight.

Mason was almost surprised when he heard Alejandra's footsteps on the stairs behind him.

The pistol's beam guided him deeper into the darkness. He walked in a shooter's stance, allowing the surprisingly strong light do the exploring for him. There were six enclosures on either side of the central aisle. A dozen in all. As above, they appeared to have been designed for animals—animals of a different kind, however. They were maybe six feet wide and eight feet deep, with locking gates. The drains set into the floor were red with rust.

"This is where they kept us," she whispered. "When they were not hurting us."

She stared into the cages to the right as she walked past, as though searching for one in particular. He heard the hesitation in her footsteps beside the fourth stall and could only imagine the thoughts going through her head.

Past the final cage on the left, a short corridor led into a room nearly the size of the auction house above it. The floor and the walls were made of the same polished-looking concrete. There were drains every ten feet or so. No interior walls or subdivisions of any kind. Just a giant open space with spigots low on the walls for hoses, and showerheads mounted above them. He wasn't actually sure what the rest of the pipes that ran along the ceiling had been designed to carry, but they looked a whole lot more like gas lines than water pipes, and the downward-facing nozzles appeared better suited to the dispersion of an aerosol than water.

"There used to be long metal tables," she said. "They had holes in them. At the ends. So things could be hosed into them."

"Drains. They had tables with drains?"

Mason imagined autopsy tables set up down here. He could still see the copper conduits they'd used to run the electricity across the ceiling to power the lights and the implements.

"They took our blood every day. Put it into different machines. There was a constant humming sound. Sometimes there were animals. Monkeys, mostly. We listened to them die. Screaming."

There was a fine layer of dust on the floor, just enough to prove that theirs were the only footprints that had disturbed it.

"Every day it was the same," she said. "The first person to awaken would begin to cry. Then someone else would join them. The crying turned to screaming. People threw themselves against the doors of their cages. They were like animals. And I was like them. Until the men in the white suits came with the mist. Not mist, exactly." She rubbed her fingertips together. "Powder. Dust. It did not smell of anything. It just made us tired. So the men could come into our cages. They kept me alive with tubes in my arm. I was always thirsty. They stuck needles into my belly. Into my neck. My back. They swabbed my mouth. Put strips of paper under my eyelids. A tube in my vagina. They took everything from inside of me. The men in the white suits. And then they took me upstairs. . . ."

Mason knew what had happened upstairs. He had seen the framework of the stalls here and the occupied ones in Arizona. If he was right, the man with the blue eyes had injected people like Alejandra and her sister with a virus and an experimental vaccine—or two pathogens, or maybe a single virus in two parts—and then sent them into the United States through the desert, along the route of least resistance. These men and women, these undocumented aliens, for all intents and purposes, simply didn't exist. There was no record of their travel itineraries. No one who would miss them back home. No one would file a report when they didn't reach their destinations. They had been selected for just that reason. Those who survived had been consigned to a painful death sentence, which had been enforced down here with invasive medical testing and executed on the hooks hanging from the rafters. But to what end?

Darkness emanated from everything around them. The things the men responsible had done to these poor people. What they intended to do to everyone. Not since the days of Josef Mengele and his Nazi ilk had such horrors been visited upon innocent men and women. The monsters responsible for these atrocities needed to be exterminated and the entire earth cleansed of anything they might have touched.

He followed Alejandra back up the stairs and into the lone remaining section of the stall area, where the wind blew the snow into a drift in the corner.

"When they were done with me . . . when it was my time . . . they brought me up here. I had no strength left to fight. I thought for a moment they were going to release me. Maybe God had decided to take mercy on me after all. And then they dropped me on the ground. Rolled me onto my chest. I could taste the dirt. And I knew. I knew this was where I would die. In this horrible place. Here was where I would rejoin my sister."

The wind wailed, causing the walls to shake. Mason thought for a second he might have heard a car in the distance.

"Then came the pain. Worse than anything I had ever felt. The hooks. I felt them go into my skin. Through my skin. Felt them in my back. Beside my shoulder blades. They scraped the bones inside of me. The men told me I should not be feeling the pain. But I did. I felt the other hooks go into my sides. Felt them tighten, then lift me from the ground and hold me there. I screamed for them to kill me. To end my pain. I told them I would give them anything they wanted if they would just . . . kill me. But instead, they left me. They left me hanging all alone. At least I thought I was alone, until I saw the others. They left me hanging with the dead. Where I could scream all I wanted because no one would hear me."

She was reliving it as she spoke. He could hear it in her voice.

"I recognized the man from the cage across from mine. The woman who took his place after they were done with him. A man I had seen only once when they dragged him past my cage the night he arrived. And I saw my sister. *Mi hermana pequeña*." She drew a shuddering breath and continued in a flat, emotionless tone. "She survived the desert and the disease, only to die in this horrible place. My Gabriela. The last thing she knew in this world was hanging from these hooks. Alone and afraid. They left her hanging here to rot. Until even I could hardly recognize her. I felt anger, not sadness. Anger even stronger than the pain."

There it was again. Was it a car? Mason couldn't be sure. He couldn't even tell if there really was a sound beneath the wind. He peered around the wall, but could barely even see the house fifty feet away through the storm, let alone the road a quarter mile past it.

"That was when the man came," she said. "The man with the blue eyes. He stood in front of me and looked into my eyes. He smiled and said, '*Tuve una sensación acerca de usted.*' 'I had a feeling about you.' That was what he said to me. 'I had a *feeling* about you.' This man with the awful blue eyes. Standing there in his old-man suit and his old-man hat. Looking up at me with pride. As though everything I had endured . . . everything I had survived . . . had been a game to him. I prayed to God for the strength to kill him."

Mason exchanged the pistol from the case in Ramses' Bronco for his Sigma. If he was going to have to use it, he wanted a gun he'd taken care of himself. He still couldn't be certain he heard a car, but the fact that he still heard *something* wasn't a good sign.

"He said to me in Spanish, 'Do not worry, child. Your sacrifice is not in vain.' Then he reached up and stroked my cheek. When he spoke next, it was in English. I did not let on that I understood. I watched him open a case full of syringes. Like the ones from Altar. Watched him smile as he picked just the right one. 'There's just one problem we haven't solved,' he said. 'How do we dispose of all the bodies?' And then he took my hand. Gently. Rolled it so he could see the vein on the side of my wrist. He slid the needle inside me. I felt the heat. It crawled up my arm and into my shoulder. Spread through my chest. I tasted it in my mouth. Like pond water. Or mold from bread. And then I was . . . *convulsionar*— convulsing. My body jerked. My ribs broke with a loud snapping noise. There was blood. So much blood. And more pain than I could bear. My skin tore and I fell from the hooks. I landed on the man. He shouted at me. Shouted and cursed. Knocked me off of him, and I saw it. The needle. It was sticking out of his neck. Under his chin. His mouth was open and he was choking. He pulled on the needle, but he could not get it out. The veins in his face darkened. Spread through his eyes like lightning."

Louder now. One car. He was certain of it. Moving slowly. Away from the road. Toward them. The wind rose and stole the sound once more.

"We need to get out of here while we still can," Mason said.

"So I ran. I ran as far and as fast as I could. I never looked back. I lived on the street. Suffered from my wounds until they healed well enough that I could find other people like myself. Other illegals, other deserters. They gave me what little money they could spare, but they would not help me. They knew what would happen to them if they got caught. There was nowhere to go. Nowhere to hide. Not after what they did to me. To my face."

Mason understood now. The final injection had produced the disfiguring effect. That was the reason her left eye was milky, the lid immobile. Why she used her hair and her hood to conceal her features. And why what looked like burns covered the left half of her forehead, cheek, and jawline—the same kind of scar tissue that covered the face of the man with the blue eyes.

There's just one problem we haven't solved.

He could hear the car clearly now. Even over the wind. It was on the lone driveway leading to the main house.

They were running out of time.

How do we dispose of all the bodies?

"All of what bodies?" he whispered to himself.

The sound of the engine died.

He was wrong.

They were already out of time.

49

Mason grabbed Alejandra by the hand and pulled her toward the cattle chute. Kicked it several times to widen the gap beside it. A series of rickety ramps led back to a maze of blind wooden corridors and holding pens. If she weaved through them and sprinted in the opposite direction of the house, she'd be able to vanish into the storm and the adjacent farmland.

"Run as far as you can and find a place to hide," he whispered directly into her face. "If I don't make it, go to Club Five in Denver. Find Ramses. He'll take care of you. Now go!"

She scurried through the chute without a word. The moment he heard her footsteps on the wooden ramp, he crawled through after her.

The men hunting them were undoubtedly already moving to outflank them. One of them would approach from the path beside the main house, while the other would come around the charred auction house from the eastern side, closest to the turnaround where they'd presumably parked by the Bronco. A third man would provide a variable for which Mason couldn't entirely account. He could be posted by the cars to block their escape should they get past the other two men, or he could be taking up position on the roof of the house with a high-powered rifle at this very moment.

Alejandra had already disappeared into the blowing snow by the time Mason scrambled down the decrepit chute. She'd escaped from this place once; he had no doubt she could do so again. He made a mental note of the direction she'd gone and then crawled under the ramp, worked his way into the snow, and flattened his back to the ground. If the second man took a diagonal path from the east to intercept them, he would walk between two pens, right through Mason's line of fire. If the man approaching from inside the structure came out through the chute, Mason would be staring straight up at his underside through the gaps between the weathered planks.

He focused on slowing his heartbeat. On attuning his senses to even the slightest sound beneath the screaming wind. He adjusted his grip on his pistol and took aim at the corner of the building.

Waited.

The wind slowly obliterated Alejandra's footprints. And still no one came.

What were they waiting for?

A creaking sound overhead.

Subtle.

Mason rolled onto his back and looked up through the narrow

cracks between the boards. A dark shape climbed out of the chute. He saw the thick rubber tread of a large boot. The man shifted his weight again and he was all the way out. Moving in a crouch. Pistol in a two-handed grip.

The man crept forward.

Slowly.

Quietly.

Mason could have easily fired a full clip up through the boards, but he couldn't afford to sacrifice whatever information he might be able to get out of him.

As soon as the man was completely past him and near the end of the ramp, Mason rolled out from underneath and lunged to his feet. The man made no indication that he had seen or heard Mason as he studied Alejandra's vanishing tracks leading toward the distant fence to the north. Mason had the back of the man's head sighted down the barrel of his Sigma when he spoke.

"Drop the weapon."

"Mason. I hoped I'd find you—"

"Drop the weapon and hold your hands away from your body, where I can see them."

"This is a simple misunderstanding. We can clear this up with a single phone—"

"Drop the goddamn pistol and show me your hands!"

The man held a .45 auto Glock 21 away from his body with his left hand and let it dangle from his finger by the trigger guard before dropping it into the snow. He slowly extended his arms to either side and fanned his fingers. He was wearing black boots and black cargo pants. His jacket was black and was the kind made almost exclusively of pockets. He wore a baseball cap facing forward. It was the kind of field utilities SWAT guys wore. Or federal agents. Mason had an outfit just like it himself.

"You're making a mistake, Mason. Christensen sent me to see what I could do to help you. Call him yourself if you don't believe me." The ground felt like it fell out from beneath Mason when he recognized the man's voice. "Why don't you let me turn around, so we can talk this over like civilized human beings? You know . . . without you aiming a gun at my back?"

"Technically, I'm aiming at your head, but now we're just splitting hairs."

"Come on, Mason. You wouldn't shoot an unarmed man in the back."

"We've been over this already. I'd be shooting an unarmed man in the head. Now keep your hands where I can see them and turn around. Slowly."

"How about this, then?" The man turned around, arms out to his sides as ordered. "You wouldn't shoot your own partner, would you?"

The wind blew the snowflakes into Special Agent Jared Trapp's face. They deflected from his sunglasses, which might have hidden his eyes themselves, but not the bruising or the stitches above his left eye.

"Yes." Mason lowered his aim and shot his partner on the outside edge of his left knee. "I would."

The report thundered across the plains.

Trapp dropped hard into the snow. He bared his teeth and pressed his hands to the wound to stanch the flow of blood.

"Jesus Christ, Mason! Why the hell did you do that?"

"It's just a flesh wound. For now. I have another sixteen bullets in the magazine and would be happy to go get more if I run out. Tell me what you know, or I swear I'll take my time—"

"For the love of God! You just *shot* me!"

Mason shifted his aim to Trapp's right shoulder.

"I'm not going to ask you again. I know you were at the trailer last night—and, by the way, that eye's really not looking so good—and now here you are again. Start talking or there won't be a third time."

"She's a fugitive, Mason."

"So you're a bounty hunter now? The FBI doesn't send a team armed with HK417s for one little girl in the middle of the night . . . *partner*."

"Maybe you're right. But tell me, if you're so fucking smart, why in the world would you think I'd come alone now?"

Mason watched the smile form on his partner's face. He glanced up and to his left and realized his mistake. He hadn't thought what little was left of the roof of the auction house would be strong enough to support a man's weight. He dove to his left as bullets struck the snow behind his heels. Twisted in the air. Lined up his shot down the length of his body, between his feet. Pulled the trigger repeatedly as he slid on his back through the snow.

The man on the roof bucked. Toppled backward. He was still sliding down the roof in the crimson slush when Mason lunged to his feet and bolted for the cover of a cow pen.

The crack of gunfire. A bullet sang past his ear.

Mason didn't know how many of them there were or where they might be. If they had someone coordinating their movements via satellite, the storm would work to his advantage. There was no way a satellite would be able to penetrate the dense cloud cover. And the advantage was his on the ground. They couldn't shoot him if they couldn't see him.

Another round of gunfire and the snow kicked up at his feet.

He turned and fired off a few shots. Dove over the split-rail fence. Rolled back to his feet. He needed to lead them away from Alejandra. And he eventually had to find his way back here for a vehicle. He'd be too easy to track across the open fields. Besides, where could he possibly go?

The trees.

He remembered the line of dead cottonwoods filled with crows the first time he'd come here. They ought to at least provide temporary cover.

Mason veered to his left and ran straight across the field to the west. His leg muscles already ached from fighting through the accumulation. He kept anticipating shots that never came. Either someone had a visual bead on him or they intended to track him by his footprints.

The trees wavered in and out of the storm. There and gone again. There. Gone. By the time he could see them clearly, he was just about standing underneath them. They were old and gray. The termites had already felled several and cored holes through the others. Undoubtedly a consequence of the neighboring farms shunting the water from the irrigation ditch on the far side of the tree line when Fairacre was abandoned. The ditch itself was maybe six feet deep and twice that distance across. More skeletal cottonwoods stood sentry over the opposite side.

He cleared the near lip and jumped down into the drainage ditch. There was hardly any snow on the slope of the western bank, largely due to the enormous drift the wind had created on the eastern side. It looked like a great white wave preparing to crash down on him. The upper layer was crisp with ice.

Mason ducked and sprinted to the south.

If he overshot the house, he could work back toward it from the far side. With any luck, he'd be approaching from their unguarded rear.

He heard his name called from a distance. Between the wind and the echo, it was impossible to divine its origin, but there was no mistaking the anger in Trapp's voice. The pain. Mason had allowed the enemy to infiltrate his life in the guise of his partner without so much as suspecting duplicity. He should have been paying closer attention. He should have seen this coming.

"Maaaasssoooooooonnn!" His name echoed across the field. "There's no point in running! There's nowhere to go!"

The sound originated from somewhere between the pens and his current location. Either Trapp had guessed he'd head for the ravine and guessed again that he would head south—the odds of which were, at best, one in six—or they were somehow remotely tracking him.

He glanced up. The clouds were low and dense. No, they didn't have a clear image of him. They had to be using a satellite equipped with thermal-imaging capabilities. In which case, he was pretty well screwed. He'd stand out against this sheet of fresh snow like a red-and-gold supernova.

"Why don't you come on out of there? Let's talk about this! We're on the same side!" Mason thought he heard Trapp chuckle. "You just don't know it yet!"

It still sounded like he was charting a course that would intercept Mason's. And after what he'd done to Trapp's knee, he should have easily distanced himself from his partner by now.

If he continued running due south, they would have someone waiting for him. Veering east toward the house would lead him straight into the teeth of his pursuit, but at least he might have a chance of catching them off guard. Surely they'd closed off his direct route of retreat, and there was nothing but an eternity of flat land to the west.

A mound of earth appeared from the storm ahead of him where the drainage ditch ended. Once he broke cover, he'd be an easy target. As he neared, he saw that it was actually a road that connected the field to the east with the field to the west. And the water would still have had to flow through it somehow. . . .

There!

He could barely see three inverted crescents of darkness over the top of the accumulation. A trio of ribbed culverts that allowed the water to pass under the road, any one of which would extinguish his heat signature beneath five feet of dirt and nearly a foot of snow.

Mason scurried into the first one, crawled all the way inside, then back out. He did the same thing with the other two. They wouldn't be able to tell which one he was in by his tracks, and he was counting on the satellite's thermal spatial resolution not being smaller than the standard three-foot-square pixel.

A scream from somewhere to the north.

A woman's scream.

The acoustics were odd, hollow, like she was screaming from inside a deep hole.

"Get her out of there."

A man's voice. Not Trapp's. Closer than Mason expected. Maybe a hundred feet behind him. A loud cracking sound of breaking wood and Alejandra screamed again.

She'd crawled inside one of the dead, termite-ravaged trees, which all but confirmed his theory about thermal imaging.

Her cries reverberated all around him.

Scream all you want. No one will hear you.

Mason backed away from the three holes, appraised his work, and prayed they wouldn't see through his ruse too soon. He turned around and ducked under the overhanging drift. If he could somehow burrow into the windswept snow, he'd be able to conceal his thermal signature from the satellite. The layer of ice on top would maintain the integrity of the drift and keep the whole thing from collapsing on him and giving him away. No one would be able to tell where he had gone without investigating on their hands and knees.

Or so he hoped.

He dug into the drift until he'd created a hollow large enough to crawl inside without making the whole white wave collapse. Contorted his body until he was all the way inside. Dragged as much snow in front of him as he could, sealing off the light.

And waited for Trapp to come for him.

50

"Mason . . ." Trapp's voice sounded like it came from miles away through the snow packed all around Mason's head. "We have . . . girlfriend . . . got to say . . . not nearly as attractive as . . . last one. Things didn't work out . . . well for her, did they?"

His pulse thudded in his ears. It was all he could do to keep from exploding from the snow with both guns blazing. He maneuvered his body so that his feet were flat on the ground and his knees were bent. Compressed himself like a spring. The snow in front of his face turned to ice. He was recycling the carbon dioxide from his exhalations. It wouldn't be long before he started to get dizzy.

"He . . . under there." A third voice.

"One of . . . go around . . . other side . . . road." Trapp.

". . . which culvert . . . ?"

"Does it matter?"

Mason pictured three adversaries. Trapp and the man restraining Alejandra on this side of the road. The third man on the far side.

A thump right beside him. Snow fell down around his face.

Heavy tread in the accumulation. Coming closer.

Another footfall, followed by yet another, more labored, thump.

They were directly beside him now.

"Don't make . . . harder than . . . needs to be," Trapp said. "Why don't . . . come out on . . . own so we . . . discuss . . . like adults?"

"No tracks . . . the other side." The second voice. Farther way.

"Take up position . . . top of . . . road."

Mason maneuvered his Sigma into his left hand and drew Ramses' Infinity with his right. Crossed them over his chest. He was only going to get one shot at this.

Alejandra continued to scream. At least he knew where she was, but she was making it hard to determine exactly where the others were. If he had any chance of pulling this off, he was going to need to aim before he even saw them.

"Shut her up," Trapp said.

A sharp *crack*. A thud on the ground beside him. More snow fell onto his face. He was already feeling the oxygen deprivation in the tips of his fingers and toes.

". . . running out . . . patience, partner. If you come out . . . own . . . let you live, but if . . . make me . . . come in there after you . . . not going to like . . . consequences."

Why hadn't they just started shooting into the culverts?

"There may . . . people who want you . . . survive this, but . . . number's growing smaller by . . . minute. They won't be able . . . protect you forever."

"Let's just shoot . . . both and get . . . hell out of here." The third voice. Ten o'clock. Maybe ten-thirty.

"Fine." Then louder. "Richards? If you will . . ."

The prattle of automatic gunfire mere feet from Mason's head. The pinging sound of bullets ricocheting from the inside of one of the culverts and careening off into the distance.

"One down, Mason. Odds . . . fifty-fifty. What . . . you say? Come on out . . . be done with it." Then softer: "Be ready. He's going . . . shoot back at us . . . then bolt . . . opposite direction."

"Middle or end?" The second voice. To his right. Two o'clock.

He had them all now.

Mason tensed his legs. He could already feel the lactic acid building in his muscles. It was now or never. He just needed all of their attention focused on the remaining culverts.

"Your choice . . . might . . . fun to drag . . . out a little while longer."

The second he heard the crackle of gunfire, he drove with his legs, straight up into the drift. The uppermost layer was hard and crusted and felt like it tore open his scalp when he burst through it. He uncrossed his arms as he emerged, aligned the Infinity with the closest man, to his right, and his Sigma with the man up on the road. The HK417 bucked in Right's hands, spewing sparks and bullets into the middle culvert. Left was leaning over the far end of the hole in anticipation of shooting Mason in the back of the head when he crawled out from under the road.

Neither of them ever saw him.

He took Right with a point-blank shot that sprayed the contents of his head straight up the western slope of the ditch and into the trees. At the same time, the first shot from the Infinity hit Left in the flank, the second between his shoulder blades. The poor guy might have survived had Right not still been squeezing the trigger as he toppled sideways, his bullets chewing up the hillside to the road and lifting Left into the air.

Mason turned toward Trapp just in time to see the surprise register on his face. He sighted the barrel of the Infinity between his partner's eyes, then swung his Sigma around to join it.

"Drop the gun!"

"Mason . . ."

He fired a shot next to Trapp's right ear.

"Motherfucker!"

He dropped his gun as if it were on fire. Red welts were already swelling on his ear and cheek where the discharge had burned him.

"How many more?" Mason shouted.

"Jesus! Get those things out of my—"

"How many more of you are there?"

"None. Christ! None! There were four of us. That's all!"

"Tell me what's going on before I put a bullet through—"

Trapp cut him off with a laugh. Mason was able to resist shooting him in the face, but just barely. He kicked him squarely in the left knee instead. Trapp went down hard with a shout of agony. He rolled over and looked up at Mason, tears streaming down his red cheeks . . . and started to laugh again.

"You mean you haven't figured it out yet? How stupid can one man be?"

"I could ask you the same thing. You're talking to the man who just killed your entire team and is currently aiming not one, but two guns at your head."

"If you were going to kill me, you'd have done so already."

"In case you've forgotten, I have no qualms about shooting you in all kinds of painful places if that's what it takes to make you talk."

"You don't have it in you."

Mason lowered the pistol in his left hand, looked Trapp squarely in the eyes, and shot him in the other knee.

Trapp bellowed and clutched the wound.

Alejandra stirred on the ground. The butt of the dead man's rifle had split her scalp near her right temple. Rivulets of blood were already freezing to her cheek and around the corner of her mouth.

"You can die with the rest of them, for all I care," Trapp said. "There's not a damn thing you can do to stop it anyway."

"Why are you doing this? You were my partner. My friend."

Trapp laughed again.

Mason kicked him upside the head.

Trapp toppled onto his dead partner, losing his cap in the process. He looked up at Mason with blood pouring down his forehead from above his already ruined eye and tossed his broken shades aside. He rolled over onto his side and spat blood into the snow. His right hand disappeared underneath the dead man.

"Don't even think about it."

"It appears as though you need me a whole lot more than I need you. How far are you willing to take this?"

"Just tell me where to find the man with the blue eyes and we can end this. No one has to know. I can protect you."

"You don't get it, do you? This is far bigger than either of us. Events have already been set in motion and there's nothing you can do to stop them."

"You obviously don't know me as well as you think you do."

Trapp's right arm tensed and Mason heard a faint clattering sound from under the body. This wasn't going to end well.

"Why don't you ask me what you really want to know? Come on, Mason. Ask me about that sweet little wife of yours. Ask if she begged at the end. Ask about the sounds she made when her hair caught fire. Ask about how she clung naked to that prick Martin while they both burned."

The muscles in Trapp's shoulder bunched. There was no stopping what was about to happen.

"Damn it, Trapp. Don't do this."

"Or maybe I should ask you, *partner*. How does it feel to know that your wife died in the arms of another man?"

Trapp rolled to the side and drew the assault rifle from beneath the body in one swift motion.

Mason pulled both triggers at once.

The top of his former partner's head disappeared in a crimson burst that spattered the snow around him. His body snapped backward and landed in an awkward twisted position.

The echo of the combined reports boomed across the plains.

51

Mason quickly searched all four dead men and found exactly what he'd expected to find.

A whole lot of nothing.

He had a feeling he'd seen one, maybe two of them before, but he couldn't recall where or under what circumstances. They were all in their late twenties or early thirties and had the look of military men. They wore matching utilities and carried nothing of a personal nature. No IDs of any kind. They each had comlinks that fit snugly inside their ears. He took one from the man he'd shot on the road above the culverts, as it was the only one not covered with blood. Whoever had once been on the other end was long gone, though.

Alejandra followed him back to the Bronco. Her pupils were sluggish in their reactions and she occasionally swayed as she walked, but she didn't once complain. The only way he could actually tell that the injury bothered her at all was because she pressed a snowball to her forehead.

Whoever had been coordinating the men was probably staring at a computer screen displaying their complete lack of movement and rapidly fading thermal signatures. He'd surely dispatched another team, which meant that Mason was already on borrowed time, but he wasn't about to leave without searching their vehicle first.

The men had parked their black Ford Explorer behind the old Bronco. It was the same model as the green-and-white Border Patrol vehicles in Arizona, one routinely used by any number of government agencies, the FBI chief among them. It was a pool car, so Trapp would have needed a requisition to check it out, and that requisition had to have a signature on it. Someone in a position of authority at the very agency to which Mason had dedicated his professional life had given the order for them to track him down.

Someone inside the FBI had signed his death warrant.

There were no receipts in the glove compartment. Nothing to link the occupants of the vehicle to the Bureau, outside of the VIN number, which could be easily altered in a computer database the moment anyone started asking questions. There was no dirt on the floorboards. No trash. No cups from which to pull prints, even if he could somehow gain access to the crime lab and the NGI.

Mason did find something on the backseat itself, though.

He pinched it between his fingers and held it in front of his face to get a better look.

It was a short, coarse hair. Black. Barely distinguishable from the dark upholstery.

He smiled and let it drift away on the breeze. Now he remembered where he'd seen one of the men before. He wished he could say he was more surprised.

"Your phone is ringing," Alejandra said.

She was already sitting in the passenger seat of the Bronco, eager to get away from this place.

As was Mason.

He climbed into the car and answered as he started the engine.

"Get out of there, Mace!" He recognized Gunnar's voice immediately. "They're already locked onto your position. Your pursuit is maybe fifteen minutes out. Coming in fast from the northwest. And there's an eye in the sky on you even as we speak."

Mason drove around the dirt island and pinned the gas on the straightaway.

"Talk to me, Gunnar."

"You've got at least two vehicles closing on you by road and a freaking helicopter streaking overland."

The Bronco bucked from the ruts and barely stayed on the road. He tossed the phone to Alejandra so that he could use both hands on the wheel. She put Gunnar on speaker.

"How did you find us?"

"It took all of about three seconds to figure out where you were going, which, in case you didn't notice, fooled absolutely no one. From there it was less than a minute's work to isolate the lone cellular signal within a ten-mile radius."

The Bronco slid sideways out onto the main road. The tires barely caught in time to keep them from firing straight through the barbed-wire fence and into the field on the opposite side of the road. They headed south as fast as the car would go.

"Was there a reason you called, Gunnar? If all you want to do is criticize, then I should probably let you know I've got my hands kind of full at the moment."

"Listen to me and listen good. Roughly ten miles south of your current position is a bridge spanning the South Platte River. A mile and a half to the west is a grove of trees. Beneath those trees is a farmhouse. What you need to do is run that car off the road and into the river. They'll have to confirm that you were in it, which ought to buy you a little more time. Find a way to get to that farmhouse. And make sure you sell it, Mace. If they catch on too quickly, you're in big trouble."

Gunnar disconnected without another word. Mason debated throwing the phone out the window, but there was really no point if his adversaries already had a bead on his location. For the life of him, he couldn't figure out how he was supposed to pull this off. If the men tracking him were using thermal surveillance, they'd see him and Alejandra the moment they got out of the car and it would be impossible to miss them trudging through the deep snow. And there was no way he and Alejandra would be able to run a mile and a half through shin-deep accumulation in fifteen minutes. All the men would have to do is take whatever road led to the farmhouse and they'd overtake them. He didn't know what Gunnar had hoped . . .

"Oh no," Mason said. "He can't be serious."

"What?"

Alejandra braced her feet against the dashboard and clung to her seat belt like a life preserver.

"I need you to crawl over the seat and get into the back for me."

"What do you—?"

"Hurry up! Please. Please hurry." Mason had to remain calm. He needed her to do exactly what he said, when he said to do it. No hesitation. If she thought for a second that he'd lost control of the situation, they were both dead. "I want you to grab the silver case from the trunk and bring it back up here."

She was already unbuckled and climbing into the backseat by the time he finished the sentence. The snow was blowing sideways across the road, limiting speed as much as it did visibility. He caught the occasional glimpse of trees in the distance. They were running out of time and road.

Alejandra scurried over the rear seat and landed in the trunk with a thump. A silver flash in the rearview mirror and the case was on the seat behind him. He drew his Sigma and passed it back to her.

"Put this in the case with the other one." He'd returned the Infinity when they first reached the car. "Now take off your clothes and—"

"What?"

"Listen to me. Take off your sweatshirt and your jacket and your jeans and put them in the case. These, too." He shed his layers as fast as he could and handed them back to her. Getting out of his pants and shoes without sending them careening into a field was a considerable feat. By the time he was down to his boxers, he was already shivering. "I need you to make everything fit inside and close it tight, okay?"

They couldn't have been more than two miles from the bridge. He could think of nothing in the world he wanted to do less than what he was now mentally preparing himself to do, but there was no other option. No other way to simultaneously beat the thermal imaging and keep from leaving a trail through the snow.

"Now, climb back up here. And bring the case with you."

She slipped into the seat beside him, wearing nothing but a T-shirt and panties. They were nearly upon their destination. He unbuckled his seat belt.

"Roll down your window, Alejandra."

"This is not going to work."

"Then they'll owe us a thank-you card for saving them the cost of ammunition."

Mason thought about the river behind his new home—the very same one toward which the Bronco was now hurtling—maybe a hundred miles to the southwest. Several feet of ice had already formed along the banks, but the center had yet to freeze. He prayed this section was in the same condition. More important, he prayed it was deep.

Trees through the snow. All in a line, on either side of the road. A wall of them.

"Crawl out the window as fast as you can. The water will be so cold that it will physically shock you the moment it touches your skin."

A warning sign. A yellow diamond. Its face partially crusted with snow. BRIDGE MAY BE ICY.

"Swim away from the car. Don't let it pull you under."

She braced her feet against the dashboard again.

"*Estás fuera de tu mente.*"

"Focus on your breathing. Your body will start to shut down. You can't let it."

He could clearly see the trees now. Cottonwoods. Evergreens buried under snow. The metal guardrail. Circular orange reflector disks.

"Turn your back to the current. Keep your feet in front of you to fend off the rocks. Whatever you do, keep your head above the water."

Icy bridge straight ahead. Steep drop-off to the right.

"*Nos vamos a morir.*"

He couldn't see the river.

"Damn it!"

Was there even water down there?

Alejandra's bare calves flexed in his peripheral vision. She made a low-pitched humming sound from the back of her throat.

He pulled the case onto his lap and positioned it in front of his chest in hopes that it would absorb the impact with the steering wheel and remain close enough that he could grab it on his way out.

"A mile and a half. Grove of trees. Do you understand?"

Mason readjusted his grip on the wheel.

And make sure you sell it, Mace.

His pulse in his ears. Deafening.

The wind rushing through the open window. A sound like thunder.

The guardrail.

Water off to the right.

He slammed the brakes.

Cranked the wheel.

Impact.

Shearing metal.

A scream.

Cracks raced across the windshield.

Beyond it, the hood buckled.

Treetops. Gray sky.

The entire windshield spiderwebbed.

Tree trunks. Steep bank. Rocks covered with snow.

Weightlessness.

Balls of glass. All around them. Frozen in midair.

Black water.

52

Mason was still drawing a deep breath when the frigid water struck him in the face. It was even colder than he'd expected. Paralyzing. His limbs stiffened. Chest tightened.

The hood bobbed up just long enough to offer him a final look at the trees, and then down it went. Water poured over the dashboard and in the blink of an eye the car was full. Submerged. Tumbling. Upside down.

He shoved the suitcase up over the steering wheel. It went right out the gaping hole where the windshield had been and took him with it. His feet found the sharp rim of broken glass and he shoved off with all his strength. He could already feel his body starting to shut down.

Vision constricting.

Heartbeat slowing.

He broke the surface and gasped for air. Turned his back to the current. Stretched his legs out in front of him. Hung on to the suitcase for everything he was worth. Looked for Alejandra.

Glanced behind him. Nothing.

Ahead? Tires jutting above the surface, still spinning. The Bronco moving downriver ahead of him. It stopped abruptly. The sound of wrenching metal. The rear end swung around toward him. He bent his knees. Braced for the collision. Slammed into the rear quarter panel, spun around the side, and went under.

A tug on the collar of his T-shirt and his head broke the surface. He turned to see Alejandra. She barely managed to keep her own head above the water. Her lips were the purple of a deep bruise and her face had taken on such a pallid cast that her white eye nearly blended in. Her black hair was already crystallized with ice.

She let go and outpaced him on the current.

Mason clung to the suitcase. It wouldn't matter if they survived the river itself if they lost the case. Without dry clothes, they were dead regardless.

The river wended to the right, working its way back toward civilization. The ice encroached from either bank. Chunks floated past him beneath the surface. Two months from now, the entire river would be choked with ice.

It might not have been much of one, but a break was a break and he was happy to finally catch one.

Mason could feel himself sinking lower and lower, and yet there was nothing he could do to stop it. He didn't know how much longer he'd be able to keep his chin above the water.

He momentarily blacked out. Jerked involuntarily when he inhaled a mouthful of the cold water and nearly lost the case in his panic to reach the surface. He emerged, coughing and sputtering.

There were trees all around him now. Their heavy boughs hung over the water. Alejandra was to his right. Crawling across the ice toward the shore. Breaking through it with even her slight body weight and then climbing back on top, only to fall through again. He wondered why she didn't just stand up until he tried to do so and couldn't find the ground. He barely managed to transfer the case to one minimally responsive hand. Struggled to swim toward the shore. He was twenty feet downriver from where Alejandra had crawled onto the snow-covered bank when his feet finally touched the bottom. Another fifty before he was actually able to gain any sort of traction on the slick, rocky bed.

Breaking through the ice was physically the hardest thing he had ever done. He was frozen to the core, exhausted, and shivering so hard, he could barely control his limbs. It was all he could do to crawl into the snow and collapse onto his chest. Every inch of his flesh positively hurt from the cold.

His arms shook when he pushed himself to all fours. His shirt was already crisp with ice when he pulled it off. His skin was marbled pink and white and pale blue. He could hardly force his trembling fingers under the waistband of his boxers to slip them off. He turned to see Alejandra doing the same. She was maybe ten feet up the bank and rubbing her bare flesh for warmth. He hoped he didn't look even half as bad as she did. Her skin was so pale, it was almost translucent. Her hair was white with ice and snow and her body was already barely steaming. She took a step. Fell. Rose. Took another step.

Mason opened the case and dumped out all of the clothes. Alejandra stumbled closer and fell to her knees beside the pile. She had the wings of an angel tattooed on her back. The scars they'd been designed to cover were obvious in this light. They were fat and puckered and rippled where the skin had torn. She was so thin, he could see the knots where her broken ribs hadn't healed properly.

They dressed as quickly as they could, buried their wet clothes in the snow, and ducked under the canopy just in time to hear the mechanical thunder of a helicopter speeding in their direction. He pulled Alejandra into the snow-packed branches of a juniper as the sleek body of a Bell OH-58 Kiowa raced past, just over the treetops.

Their heat signatures were undoubtedly rising. They needed to get out of the open before whoever was monitoring the satellite detected their deception or the men broadened their search from the immediate vicinity of the crash site. If they hadn't already.

Mason led Alejandra through the trees. They found the house roughly a quarter mile to the northwest. Whatever buffer their little dip had bought them was undoubtedly spent. He could hear the chopper in the distance. Not well enough to pinpoint its position, but at least well enough to tell that it seemed to be hovering over a single location, presumably that of the submerged Bronco.

The house itself was a ranch-style home that looked like it had originally been built sometime during the forties or fifties. There was a livestock shed behind it, but not an animal in sight. Probably built for cattle. They rounded the front of the house. No movement through the windows nor any sound from inside. A single trail of footprints, little more than dimples now, crossed the yard from the house to a large barn to the northeast. A pair of wide tire tracks led away from the left door of the barn and into the field to the north. Bits of straw tumbled across the accumulation. Mason's best guess was that someone had left the house two, maybe three hours ago, loaded some hay into the bed of a truck, and drove off to feed the herd.

He wasn't entirely sure what he was supposed to do from here.

They could hide in one of the buildings, but it wouldn't be long before the men found them. And neither of them would last long out here in the elements. Despite the dry clothes, if they didn't warm up in a hurry, they were dead.

He was starting to think that Gunnar had consigned them to their fates, when he heard the rumble of an engine from inside the barn. He glanced at the sheet of snow that separated the barn from the house. Still only one set of tracks, leading out. This didn't fit at all with the scenario he'd crafted inside his head.

Mason knocked on the barn doors. They were held in place by a locking mechanism. From the outside. He knocked again. Waited. He finally had no choice but to unlatch the doors and swing the right one outward into the snow, just far enough to admit a column of light into the dark barn. It smelled of desiccated hay, grain dust, and old manure. The truck had been backed inside, as though to make it easier to load whatever was in the rear portion of the building. It was a GMC Suburban. There was a conspicuous gap next to it where the truck that was now out in the field had bled oil onto the straw.

He dropped the silver case, held up his hands, and spread his fingers in an effort to look as nonthreatening as he could. The Sigma in the holster under his arm undoubtedly gave lie to the illusion, though.

"My name is James Mason. I'm a special agent with the FBI."

He approached the driver's side door slowly. There was dust on the windshield, but not so much that he shouldn't have been able to see the driver. The backseat and trunk were stuffed full of what looked like handcrafted furniture.

"There is no one in it," Alejandra said.

"Then why is it running? It's not like you can start . . ." He smiled. "Hurry up and get in."

Mason slung the case behind the driver's seat, climbed in, and hit the lights.

"Thank you, OnStar."

All newer-model vehicles from General Motors came fully equipped with OnStar, the magical technology that, with the touch of a button, connected the driver to any number of emergency services. In addition to allowing you to unlock your vehicle remotely and make your lights flash and your horn blare when you forgot where you parked, the service had also added security features, giving you the ability to disable the ignition in cases of theft and power down the engine should the car be involved in a high-speed chase. It also enabled the owner—or someone skilled enough to subvert OnStar's firewalls—to start the engine with a simple app that could be downloaded to any cell phone.

Alejandra had the heater blowing full force before she even closed her door.

Mason was so cold that the air positively burned, but he wouldn't have traded the sensation for anything in the world. He pulled out of the garage and drove as fast as he dared; he didn't want to attract any more attention than absolutely necessary, especially in a stolen vehicle.

The driveway wound through the trees and back to the main road, then headed north. He rolled down his window and listened to the chopper blades thupping to the south, near the river.

Right where he hoped they'd be.

53

It took Mason several minutes to realize that the GPS display was directing them to a specific point in the town of Brush. Considering the owner of the Suburban surely knew his way around a city that small, he figured the directions had been programmed for them specifically. They didn't have long before they'd have to ditch the car, anyway. As soon as either the owner noticed it was gone or the men who were after them picked up their trail, they'd be able to locate the vehicle and remotely power down the engine. He intended to be far away from it when that happened.

The computer voice guided them into the parking lot of the bar on the main strip, the Drink King. He parked around the side of the building, behind the Dumpster. The decision to climb out of the saunalike interior and into the bitter cold caused him physical discomfort. He unloaded the case and waited for Alejandra before crossing the lot toward the adjacent alley. This was an ideal place to dump the Suburban. There were several other large vehicles, which, judging by the amount of snow on their hoods and roofs, had been parked in the lot for at least a day. He'd have loved to hop in and hot-wire one of them, but that was a skill he simply didn't possess.

"What are we supposed to do now?" Alejandra asked.

They'd reached the end of the alley, and an obvious solution had yet to present itself. Mason was debating whether he should turn around, when headlights flashed from the side of a convenience store diagonally across the street. It was an older-model red truck with a camper shell on the bed. The windshield wipers arched across the glass, through which he could see little more than the vague outline of the driver.

Regardless, they hurried across the street. Gunnar climbed out as they neared, went around to the back of the truck, and opened the camper door. Mason tossed the silver case inside, on top of another case, which he recognized as the one Ramses had given him—the one with the bush beater that he'd left in the trunk of his Cherokee. Both his laptop and his wife's were up on the sleeping bunk. The camper itself wasn't long enough for a grown man to stretch out to his full height, but it looked as though someone had been living inside. It smelled of sweat and roasted chili peppers.

"What do you think?"

Gunnar gestured toward the interior before closing the camper door.

"It's definitely . . . used," Mason said.

"I was so hoping you'd like it. After all, it's yours. The gentleman who owned it seemed genuinely pleased to take your Jeep in trade."

"I'm sure he did."

Mason walked around to the passenger side and climbed inside. Alejandra reluctantly scooted over and made room. He had to hold Gunnar's laptop on his thighs.

Gunnar closed the door and struggled to force the stick between Alejandra's knees into gear.

"I figured this beast would look perfect parked in front of your new place."

Unfortunately, he was probably right.

"I owe you one, Gunnar."

"I'll put it on your tab. Now, if you'd be so kind as to introduce me to your lovely companion . . ."

"Gunnar . . . Alejandra. Alejandra . . . Gunnar."

She offered her tiny hand, but kept her face hidden behind her hair.

"Charmed," he said, and kissed the back of it.

"Eyes on the road," she said.

"Have you learned anything more about AgrAmerica's holdings?" Mason asked. "What about GABP?"

"In case you didn't notice, I was kind of busy driving halfway across the state—through a blizzard, I might add—to save your life not once, but twice. Or was it three times? It's all a blur. Saving lives can be like that. Some might even call such selfless actions heroic."

"I must have missed the answer to my question somewhere in there."

"No, I have not. But not for lack of trying. These guys have done an amazing job of shuffling their financial deck. If I didn't know better, I'd think they were sheltering their assets under someone else's umbrella."

"What do you mean?"

"I'll put it in hockey terms so you can understand. Your brother-in-law's devious, for sure, but when it comes right down to it, he's still a recent call-up from the minors. His old man's barely clinging to his position on the fourth line because he's a scrapper, you know? Both of them are role players, at best. There are other people who're a lot better and who've been playing the game for a whole lot longer. The guys who do all of the scoring. You have to have the role players to support them. The enforcers do the fighting so that the scorers don't hurt their hands. The grinders wear down the opponent's top line in the defensive zone. All to keep a few top players happy and healthy so they can continue putting points on the board. So they can make the big bucks and remain untouchable."

"Someone's controlling Victor."

"Exactly."

"So who's pulling his strings?"

"That's the thing. I don't think it's that simple. I'd be able to find one name. I think we're dealing with several different entities that are exceptionally adept at playing the shell game when it comes to hiding assets. I will figure it out, though. I assure you."

"So that's it? We wait?"

"What you have to understand is that the traditional rules don't apply to this game. Think of yourself as a tourist in the Vegas of high finance. There may be many games in town, but the house invariably wins them all."

"I don't care about their games. No man is above the law. Some just have farther to fall than others."

"Your law, huh? Last I knew, you didn't even have a badge. *That's* how they play the game, Mace. Whatever you do now, you're on the wrong side of the law. In real-world terms, *you* are the bad guy now."

54

Mason leaned his forehead against the cold glass and stared out the window. The snow had slowed incrementally, but visibility had dramatically improved. Flat white fields stretched off into eternity on either side. Other cars had joined theirs on the highway, primarily interstate tractor-trailers painted with dirt and trailing swirling slipstreams of snow from the accumulation on their roofs.

Alejandra's breathing had grown slow and measured. He wondered how long it had been since she'd last slept, or if it was even a luxury in which she allowed herself to indulge. All he knew was that he was perfectly happy not dreaming her dreams.

"Can I ask you something?" Gunnar said.

"Of course."

"How does one man survive multiple explosions that kill pretty much everyone else and any number of confrontations in which he's outnumbered and outgunned?"

Mason remembered what the masked man outside of Alejandra's trailer had said.

He dies, you die. I don't care if you have a guardian angel or not.

And what he had heard his former partner say while he was hiding in the snowdrift, moments before he killed him.

There may . . . people who want you . . . survive this, but . . . number's growing smaller by . . . minute. They won't be able . . . protect you forever.

"My father's not involved."

"There are few people on the planet who wield so much influence and keep such powerful company."

"My old man might be ambitious to a fault, but he's not a monster. He'd never support any agenda that risks the life of a single registered voter, let alone what little family he has left."

"I'm sure you're right, but I'll lay odds he's at least on a first-name basis with the people responsible. Political currency will buy someone— even a senator's son—only so much rope before they hang him with it."

Mason conceded Gunnar's point with a nod. While he was confident his father had no knowledge of what these men had planned, they undoubtedly knew who he was and recognized the amount of influence he exerted. They'd taken a huge risk by killing the vaunted J. R. Mason's daughter-in-law. Putting his son in the ground would all but guarantee he'd find a way to unleash the wrath of God upon them.

That is, if Mason didn't do so first.

They rode on in silence, watching the mountains slowly rise from the horizon through the waning storm as they headed west. They passed Greeley before veering north toward the town of Windsor, which had evolved from a single railroad station into a flourishing agricultural mecca around the turn of the twentieth century. The soil conditions were perfect for the cultivation of sugar beets, so when a processing and refining factory was built, people flocked from far and wide to gamble on the future—most notably among them, a large number of ethnic German immigrants from Russia.

The truck wound through an older historical district filled with turn-of-the-century Victorians and into a neighborhood with estates set back from the narrow road and surrounded by fifteen-foot wrought-iron fences. Gunnar slowed as they rounded a curve and peered past them and up the hill to the right, where a sprawling mansion sat like a crown adorned with evergreens and elm trees. Mason couldn't help but notice the security cameras mounted along the perimeter. They weren't the kind meant to be seen or to serve as a deterrent. Only a trained eye would recognize them, which meant that not only was there something of considerable value inside, someone was actively watching the feeds from those cameras. He was proved correct when the gates started to open even before they pulled up to them.

Alejandra sat bolt upright in the seat.

"Don't worry," Gunnar said. "We'll be safe here."

"Nice digs," Mason said. "Who lives here?"

"A guy I've done some work for in the past."

"What kind of work?"

"Pretty tricky financial stuff, mostly, but a surprising amount of historical stuff, too. Like the pictures I found for you, especially the one from Egypt. I emailed it to him to get his thoughts. He got right back to me and suggested we meet in person."

"You think he knows something about the man with the blue eyes?"

"I guess we'll find out soon enough."

The heated driveway was lined with snow-blanketed shrubs that looked like marshmallows. There was a turnaround at the top, in the center of which was a fountain that had been allowed to freeze with the water running to create an enormous ice blossom. They rounded it and parked at the foot of a wide portico.

The house itself had been built in the Georgian Revival Style, with decorative cornices, rectangular windows, and doors with crown pediments and overhead fanlights and sidelights. The exterior was gray slate, which had probably been quarried from the ground beneath them. Twin chimneys framed a roofline broken by peaked dormers.

The engine ticked for several long moments before Gunnar finally killed it and opened his door.

Mason felt eyes on him the moment he stepped from the car. There was one man in the shadows to the northeast of the detached garage. Another behind a hedgerow on the southwest side of the house. A third in one of the windows on the upper story. A fourth behind him. These were well-trained men, not your run-of-the-mill hourly rent-a-cops. He never saw more than the faintest silhouette of any one of them, and had no doubt whatsoever that had their instructions been to prevent them from entering the home, they would never have gotten this close.

The front doors swung inward as they mounted the steps. A grandfatherly man greeted them with a broad smile on his face. His white hair was combed back from his forehead and formed natural points on either side. His chin and nose were both blunted and ruddy. The wrinkles on his face proved the smile wasn't just for their benefit. He wore powder blue linen pajamas that could have come from any department store, a red-and-black flannel robe, and a pair of sheepskin slippers.

"Ah, Gunnar, my friend." He shook Gunnar's hand with sincere exuberance. "At last we meet in person. It is my distinct pleasure to finally have the opportunity to do so. Now please. Please do come in from the cold."

He held the door open and gestured for them to enter. He maintained both the smile and eye contact with each of them as they passed. Mason read him as a genuine individual unaccustomed to presenting a facade for anyone, which struck him as completely at odds with the security presence. A wide hardwood staircase with ornate hand-carved banisters led upward to a landing, where narrower flights branched to either side. The display case on the landing held a dirty hand spade encased in Lucite, above which hung a large painting of fields filled with wavering grasses and grazing bison, clearly a depiction of this area before any of the houses rose from the soil. While outwardly ostentatious, there was simply something unassuming about the house, as though it had been built for the people who lived inside it rather than for those they wanted to impress.

Mason liked this man already.

"Please make yourselves at home. May I offer you tea or cocoa? I myself prefer the dark chocolate with those tiny little marshmallows."

"Anything warm would be great," Mason said. "Thank you."

"I must apologize for not offering coffee, as is the custom. I do not entertain guests so much anymore. Besides, an old man like me prefers to have his pulse quickened the old-fashioned way. Speaking of which, who is this divine creature?"

"Alejandra."

Although she kept the scarred half of her face concealed by her hair and hood, she couldn't hide her smile as he bowed and kissed the back of her hand.

"A beautiful name for a beautiful woman. I am enchanted, my dear. May I take your jacket?"

Mason's jaw dropped when she allowed him to remove it from her shoulders. He draped it over his left arm and proffered his right hand to Mason.

"Johan Jakob Mahler."

"James Mason." The old man's grip was remarkably firm. The skin on his palms was coarse, as though he had spent more time in the fields than in a boardroom. "We appreciate your hospitality, Mr. Mahler."

"Please, please. There are no formalities in this home. Call me Johan. And I shall call you James. You must forgive me for supporting your father's opponent in the last election. And all of the others before that."

Mason smiled. It was a nice change dealing with someone who seemed so open and honest. He had to remind himself of the security force and the fact that they wouldn't be here if Mahler didn't know something about the man who'd killed his wife and partner.

"Gunnar told us he's done some work for you in the past," Mason said, prompting.

"Your friend here is an exceptional individual who provides services that never fail to exceed my expectations. And considering my business now is of a more personal persuasion, I deal only with people of high character. I would never think of denying any of them a favor when they ask." Mahler guided them deeper into the house. They passed a large but homey kitchen, where a man in a cardigan was already preparing a tray of steaming mugs. The bulge under his left arm didn't escape Mason's notice. "One of the benefits of reaching my age is that you no longer have to spare a thought for what people think of you. I get to choose my attire based on what makes me feel good. An added benefit is that I've found people tend to let more of their real selves show when they think you've gone a little batty. My dear wife, Dolores—God rest her soul— would never have allowed it. I eagerly anticipate the eternity she will have to chastise me for it."

They passed through a sunken family room with bookcases built into the walls, furniture that appeared to have been chosen for comfort over formality, and a hearth large enough to accommodate an entire pine tree, then entered a hallway adorned with portraits of children through the generations.

Mason had already identified six security cameras, two in this corridor alone.

"My grandchildren." Mahler nodded at the wall to his right, where pictures of dark-haired children with light eyes smiled back at them with various amounts and configurations of teeth. He slid aside one of a girl who looked to be about twelve or thirteen to reveal an access panel, then tapped in a combination. A section of the wall opened, revealing a well-lighted staircase. He continued talking as he led them down. "I have six in all. Every single one of them happy and healthy. Knock on wood."

At the bottom of the stairs was another short hallway, which terminated against a stainless-steel door with a digital keypad. Johan tapped in a seven-digit combo and the door popped inward with a hiss of escaping air.

"We keep the substructure hermetically sealed to maintain the proper pressure, temperature, and humidity necessary to preserve the documents. Do be a dear and hit that button beside the door once you're through." Gunnar did as he was asked and the door sealed behind them. The corridor was dark and narrow and revealed absolutely nothing. Mason heard a series of beeping sounds as Johan entered another series of numbers, then the hum of hydraulics as the final door opened before them. "They're all original and represent a lifetime's work for both my father and myself. Some of these artifacts are more than a hundred years old."

A clicking sound, then the *thoom-thoom-thoom* of large banks of overhead lights turning on. The pale whitish blue glow gave the distinct impression of being underwater.

"Welcome to my archives," Johan said.

He stepped aside and gestured toward a massive room that had to be the size of the entire structure above it.

Suddenly, Mason knew exactly why this house required so much security.

55

The armed man in the cardigan appeared in their midst, served mugs of cocoa from a silver tray, and disappeared again without a word. They sipped the steaming brew while Johan gave them the tour. He claimed that to truly comprehend the significance of the substructure, which filled nearly the entire hillside upon which his house had been built, they needed to understand how it had come into being.

"My father, Abraham Jakob Mahler, commissioned the construction of this sublevel in 1947," he said. "His father and my grandfather, Jakob Ephraim Mahler, was the eldest of six children by a solid decade. His mother died during childbirth and his father sent him to Prussia to live with his maternal grandparents on their farm. These were different times, you must understand. It was just how such things were done. Years later, he was reunited with his father, his father's new wife, and their children. Despite the differences in age, he was very fond of his new brothers and sister. Two of his brothers worked for the Reichsbank. Another served as a representative to the Bundestag, and the fourth as a chemist for Bayer, and ultimately for IG Farben. His lone sister, May, had three children with an aviation engineer. And yet he did not envy the success they had achieved. Instead, the eldest son of what had become a prominent German banking family in his absence sought his fortune in the New World. He joined the mass migration to Manitoba, and eventually found his way down the Great Plains into Colorado."

Johan's words reverberated inside Mason's head as he tried to rationalize the existence of this enormous basement, which was completely at odds with the house above it. Where the upstairs was warm and bright, down here it was cold and clinical.

"He harvested sugar beets with the rest of the immigrants, his wife, Helen, and their three sons, my father, Abraham, among them. He saved every cent until he was able to buy his own land—the land upon which we now stand—and worked it, with his entire family, every single day. They built their own refinery and turned what had once been a vast swath of grassland into an empire. And then, with the help of his brothers overseas, he invested his fortune to establish the First Prairie Bank of Colorado, and seemingly overnight he became one of the twenty richest men in America. But for all his money, he couldn't stop the inevitable."

The main portion of the substructure was filled with computer stations and banks of servers. Detailed maps from all over the world covered the walls. It almost reminded Mason of a military command center.

"When the Nazi Party rose to power, his brothers at the Reichsbank sensed trouble brewing and transferred the family's liquid assets into Jakob's Prairie Bank as a precaution, but even in their worst nightmares, they could not have imagined what was to come. The Mahler family went from being one of Germany's premier banking families to its premier *Jewish* banking family. His brothers and their entire families vanished, along with all of their remaining assets. His father and stepmother were taken from their home in broad daylight as their neighbors looked on. His brother-in-law sent Jakob's sister and nieces to Poland before being beaten to death in the street. His lone brother who remained free continued his research at IG Farben clear up until he earned the right to test an experimental pesticide called Zyklon B.

"Jakob knew none of this at the time, though. From his perspective, his family had simply fallen out of contact during a period when the newspapers were filled with stories of the war in Europe. All three of his sons took up the flag and returned to the Fatherland as its liberators. Only Abraham—my father—returned, and just in time to bury my grandfather, whose heart had been strong enough to carve a fortune from the rocky ground, but ultimately was unable to withstand the loss of his parents, five siblings, two sons, and his wife, who had succumbed to pneumonia the previous winter."

Mason couldn't figure out what Gunnar could have possibly done for this man. Judging by the expression on his old friend's face, he seemed to be struggling to put the pieces together, too.

"My father was overwhelmed by all the changes in his life. His entire extended family was dead. The wife he'd left behind was a different woman and his child was now nine years old. He had more money than he could spend in ten lifetimes, a thriving enterprise he had no desire to run, and more grief than one man could be expected to bear. So he took a step back and prioritized his life. He hired a management team, sold off the less wieldy portions of his holdings, and retired from the business world to take care of what little family he had left. It was then that he commissioned the construction of this sublevel and came down here every day as if he were going to work."

"What did he do down here?" Mason asked.

"I wondered the same thing for many years. Until my fifteenth birthday, when he finally showed me. I remember descending the stairs, which had always been off-limits, even to my mother, into a dark room that smelled of dampness and mildew. At the time, there was just a single overhead bulb. He pulled the string and illuminated walls covered with photographs and maps and newspaper clippings. He told me how it had taken him more than five years, but he'd pieced together the fates of our German relatives. He'd acquired thousands of articles and reports and obituaries and documents on the postwar European black market. He'd paid enormous sums for bills of lading and receipts of all kinds, for passenger manifests on railcars and ships and passports stamped at various borders. He'd amassed a collection of the numbers that our people had been reduced to after being stripped of their identities and herded like cattle into concentration camps. And he'd become part of a larger group that was determined to put a name to every one of those numbers."

Johan led them through a narrow doorway into a room that served as a memorial to his extended family. There were portraits of men and women in gilded frames, all displayed with reverence. This was a sacred place, a family crypt of sorts. He gestured to each of the pictures in turn as he walked past.

"My great-grandparents died in an overcrowded railcar bound for Dachau. Their two banker sons, Joseph and Heinrich, were executed in that same concentration camp by the gas their brother Wilhelm had helped to create. Their youngest son, Erich, was shot and killed before ever arriving at Auschwitz, where my grandfather's sister died after having failed to cross the Polish border. One of her children survived. One. Of the twenty Mahlers in Germany at the start of the war, only one survived. My father had devoted every free second to finding out what had happened to them, like my grandfather would have wanted, only once he had, he still felt empty."

The doorway at the back led to a shrine of a completely different nature. Mason felt a chill when he entered that had nothing to do with the temperature of the room.

"My father called this his 'Trophy Room.'" Johan positively swelled with pride. "He tracked down the personnel records from all of the concentration camps. He got the names of every man and woman who ever served as a guard, every person who ever took up arms for the Nazi cause. From the most lowly *Sturmmann* all the way up to his *Reichsführer*. He collected all of the pictures he could find of each of them, hung them on these very walls, and then he started hunting them."

The people staring at them from the old photographs looked no different from anyone they might pass on the street, save for the swastikas and runic insignias on their uniforms. Human beings like any others. Men and women who had gotten swept up in a movement that promised an end to their hardship and suffering, and all they'd had to do was step across this one little line in the sand, then just one more, and one more still, until mass murder became patriotic.

"It was our shared obsession," Johan said. "We tracked the ratlines all the way to South America. We followed the flow of money from German banks to international banks owned by Nazi sympathizers. We pooled information and resources with other people like us from all around the world. We built an entire network dedicated to tracking down the war criminals who'd slipped through Nuremberg's net. And once we found them, we did something about it."

Mason glanced at Gunnar, who wore the same expression of shock he could feel on his own face. Alejandra, however, betrayed nothing.

"This was the first one," Johan said.

There were two pictures on a single placard, mounted side by side, both in black and white. They featured the same subject; of that there was no doubt. The image on the left was of a smiling man. His head was framed by an out-of-focus coil of razor wire. A rifle leaned against his shoulder. The picture directly beside it was of the same man, only a little older. There were creases around his eyes, which stared blankly at the camera. His lips were parted and his skin was waxen, and in the middle of his forehead was a silver coin. It had been used to cover the entrance wound of a bullet from a small-caliber pistol, judging by the powder tattoos around the coin and the almost nonexistent spatter on his nose and cheeks.

There was a small brass label engraved with the numbers 04-092 above the name Rottenführer Abel Ahrens. It was old and faded and the engraving had almost been worn smooth from Johan doing exactly what he was doing now, running his fingertips across the discolored metal.

"I remember my father standing behind me with his hands on my shoulders while I looked from one picture to the other for the longest time. Searching this man's face for the demon inside of him and in the end realizing that there simply wasn't one. This was just a man who had committed horrible crimes because he had chosen to do so. A man who had tried to get away with what he had done. And this picture on the right? This was merely the execution of the sentence he would have received had he stood trial before the International Military Tribunal."

Gone was the grandfatherly figure who had welcomed them into his home. This was a different person entirely, one with a faraway look in his eyes and the ability to stand in a room filled with the pictures of men he had sentenced to death and speak of them with the same detachment they must have felt when they did the very same thing to his relatives.

The walls were positively covered with displays just like the one for 04-092. Men reduced to numbers and their lives reduced to photographs. And Mason realized that evil wasn't merely the symptom of a disease; it was a condition of normalcy, one that everyone denied was inside them until the very moment they embraced it.

The man in the cardigan, who'd brought their drinks, appeared from nowhere to whisk the empty mugs away. He'd been watching them so closely, he'd been able to tell when the last of them took a final sip.

Gunnar had noticeably paled. Considering his skill set, Mason could only assume that he had unknowingly helped track down some of these men. Their blood was on his hands.

"They're all dead now," Johan said. "Nearly all, anyway. Time has taken care of most everyone we missed. Justice has been served. The problem now isn't that evil still exists, but, rather, that it has bred. It's like pulling a weed, but missing the roots. They lie dormant for long periods of time before emerging at some new location and at some unforeseen time. Now we're no longer dealing with an evil ideology or a prejudice against a single group of people. That was just the weed that was Hitler. The roots, though . . . the roots survived and new weeds are popping up everywhere you look. They hide behind their money and their power and have such strong allies that they're nearly impossible to identify. Which is where you come in, Gunnar. Your services have proven invaluable, my friend. Speaking of which, you mentioned you have something to show me?"

Gunnar looked at Mason from the corner of his eye, as though giving him one final opportunity to change his mind. And while the thought had occurred to Mason, he quickly dismissed it. They were talking about the man who had killed his wife and his partner. If Johan, with his proudly displayed pictures of men whose murders he had commissioned, could help him find the man with the blue eyes and bring him to justice, regardless of the method, then Mason had every intention of using him to do so. It turned out that he was more like this man, who had staged one of the largest serial-killing rampages about which the world would never know, than he cared to admit.

He nodded.

Gunnar removed his laptop from beneath his arm, opened it, and turned it around so Johan could clearly see the screen.

Mason watched Johan's eyes. Watched the reflection of the image on his corneas. Watched the spark of recognition form. His eyes looked just like those of 04-092.

"You know who this man is, don't you?" Mason said.

"Where did you get this picture?"

"Tell me what you know first."

"When was this picture taken, damn it? How long ago?"

"Tell me what you know."

"You don't understand, do you? This is a catastrophic development. I need to know when this picture was taken and where!"

"Just over three weeks ago," Gunnar said. "Denver."

"Dear God . . . It may already be too late."

Johan turned without explanation and passed from the Trophy Room into the final chamber, which was divided in half by a wall covered with dry-erase boards. There were at least twenty of them, all the size of blackboards, and all turned on their sides, so they went from floor to ceiling. At the very top of the center panel were two words written in bold capital letters: MOST WANTED. Each board was dedicated to a specific individual. At the top were pictures of the subject from every available angle, however few. Most showed little, if any, detail. These were men and women who had learned how not to be captured on film. Below each collection of pictures was what Mason assumed to be a code name. Some had real names written beneath their code names. Most didn't. All of them had numbers he initially guessed were their rankings in the top twenty. Some of the numbers were duplicated, and some subjects had multiple numbers beneath them. He found his guy right away. His eyes made him impossible to miss. As did the fact that he had more pictures than any of the others, and he was the only one with pictures more than a couple decades old, let alone half a century.

There had to be thirty or so of them, all enlarged as far as the resolution would allow. Mason recognized the pictures he already had, although the ones in this display were either originals or created directly from the negatives. They were each labeled with the date they had been taken and covered a span from 1918 through 2017. There was a single code name, a dozen names he assumed to be aliases, and two numbers: 2 and 10.

"He calls himself 'the Hoyl' to taunt us," Johan said. "The Hoyl is the magical bird of Jewish lore that refused to taste the forbidden fruit when Adam offered it, and thus was never subjected to the punishment of expulsion from the Garden of Eden. Or mortality. It is almost like the phoenix, in that sense. It burns hot and fast, but rather than rising from its ashes, it becomes an egg from which it can be reborn. Just like the man who bears its name, whom we have already killed twice."

Johan tapped two different pictures: one in black and white, and the other the faded color Mason associated with his youth. Both featured the face of the man who called himself the Hoyl, but there were distinct differences. The black-and-white image depicted a man who had to have been in his seventies. His face was wrinkled, his bared teeth yellowed, his nose bulbous and veined. Not his eyes, though. They were neither young nor old. The only word Mason could summon to describe them was *eternal*. He, too, had a silver coin on his forehead, which concealed the entry wound of the bullet that had killed him, but not nearly as well. The skin had torn away from the exposed bone and appeared singed at the edges. There was blowback spatter all over his face.

The other image showed a man who couldn't have been much beyond his mid-fifties. The wrinkles were just starting to come in, and were doing so in a slightly different configuration. His front teeth appeared longer and whiter, as well. There were enough differences up close that it was obvious they were two distinct individuals from a shared lineage, undoubtedly father and son. Only their eyes were exactly the same. And the fact that both had silver coins covering the entry wounds on their foreheads.

And yet still the sightings continued, clear up until the facial scarring appeared. Mason glanced at Alejandra, who had been silently trailing in their footsteps. She was staring into the face of her own personal demon with an expression he couldn't interpret.

"He's gone by many aliases, but we believe his family name is Fischer. Unfortunately, it's also the fourth most common surname in Germany. There are more than a quarter of a million Fischers in that one small country alone." Johan tapped a picture that looked similar to the one Mason had from Egypt in 1939. It was of some sort of army company in 1934. Very formal. Twenty-two serious men staring at the camera. Someone had drawn red Xs on the chests of seventeen of them and written first names above the heads of the remaining five, scratched them out, then written different names. Only two of the five currently had names. "There were five Fischers in his battalion alone. Division z.b.V. *Afrika*. A special ops unit created for a specific goal in Africa *prior* to the war. We've only been able to match two of the men to verifiable casualties. The other three are all listed as 'missing in action, presumed dead,' which means no bodies were ever recovered. Their names were Fritz, Leopold, and Martin. We have no idea which belonged to the Hoyl. And that's where the paper trail ends. He's used a dozen different identities through the years. Nearly everything we know about him is anecdotal. But there is one thing we know about him for sure."

Johan looked at Gunnar and then directly at Mason.

"Whenever he appears, people die."

56

Lines had been drawn from the various pictures of the Hoyl to different handwritten paragraphs. There was a definitive time line to them. The first instance was the same photograph Gunnar had found of the man with the blue eyes in the tent in France, 1918. Johan tapped the picture.

"This is the first recorded sighting, nearly twenty years prior to the picture taken of a younger version with the z.b.V. *Afrika* Division. We call this man Fischer F One, for first generation. Patriarch of the clan Hoyl. This picture was taken roughly two months prior to the outbreak of the Spanish influenza during World War One, which claimed an estimated fifty to one hundred million lives."

"You're suggesting this man is responsible for a global pandemic," Mason said.

"I'm not suggesting anything. Bear with me. This man here is Fischer F Two, whom we believe to be the son of F One. We don't know why or how successive generations look nearly identical. Eugenics. Selective breeding. In vitro fertilization. Maybe just strong genes. Regardless of the means, they are bred and raised to continue the diabolical work of their forebears and perpetuate the illusion of immortality. This is him in 1942. Egypt. He's photographed here and . . . here with various high-ranking officials at both Nazi Party headquarters and IG Farben, the company responsible for the development and production of chemicals, pharmaceuticals, and early biotechnology. Farben subsidiaries manufactured the various nerve agents that killed millions of my people and that monsters like Mengele used in concentration camps to perform human testing on unwilling subjects. They turned the country into their own private lab while the German forces were divided among three different fronts. One of them in the deserts of Africa, where, in 1942, an outbreak of malaria—a *tropical* disease—claimed thousands.

"And here. China, 1956. An older F Two is again photographed at the epicenter of a pandemic. The Asian flu—H2N2—started right here in the heart of the Guizhou Province and killed more than two million worldwide." Johan grew more animated as he talked. "Here. Hong Kong, 1968. Photographed just days after the first recorded case of the Hong Kong flu—H3N2—which killed another million.

"Now along comes F Three—distinguished by this mole you can clearly see below his left eye—and a change in modus operandi. Enter the violent age of hemorrhagic fevers and viruses that attack the immune system. Zaire, 1976. The first cases of the Ebola virus, a horrible disease with a ninety-plus percent fatality rate. The Ubangi River Basin in the Congo, 1981. Later determined to be the origin of the AIDS epidemic."

Mason found it hard to swallow that one small group of men with the same lineage could be responsible for the deaths of more than a hundred million people, but he was positively choking on the sheer amount of coincidences.

"Enter F Four. September 1994. The Gujarat State of India. A suddenly younger version of the Hoyl is photographed in Surat during an outbreak of the plague. The Black Death, mind you. A disease that had been considered controlled for more than eighty years. China, 2002. The SARS coronavirus. The first of what one might consider the highly contagious 'designer influenzas.' It may have killed fewer than a thousand people, but it generated more than one hundred million dollars in revenue for the pharmaceutical company that just *happened* to be sitting on an 'experimental' vaccine."

"You're claiming collusion with big business? That this is all about money?"

"*Everything* is about money," Johan said. "There have been more outbreaks of various epidemics since the start of the twenty-first century than there were in the previous century and a half, despite all of the advances in sanitation, hygiene, and medicine. Nasty, nasty diseases, too. Dengue fever, Ebola, cholera, the plague. Now we're talking about things like mad cow disease and prions. Nature knows how to adapt, but she isn't capable of working at such staggering speeds. Somewhere there are men cooking up our ultimate demise in laboratories flying corporate flags, funding their research by profiteering from the vaccines for the very diseases they create. Did you know that the top ten pharmaceutical companies in the Fortune Five Hundred gross more than the other four hundred and ninety companies *combined*?" He tapped the picture of the man with the blue eyes standing behind the rack of slaughtered pigs hung by their hooves. "Look here. F Four. Mexico, 2009. H1N1, just another minor variation on the same flu virus. The swine flu vaccine brought in more than three point three billion in revenue and was used to dose nearly every government, military, and health-care employee—whether they wanted the *mandatory* vaccine or not—and the droves of civilians who lined up to deplete the 'limited' supplies, which, again, just happened to be ready and waiting.

"This one Fischer bloodline alone helped create a global environment of fear and the complete reliance on pharmaceuticals, which one could consider the twenty-first century equivalent of eighteenth-century gold, nineteenth-century steel, and twentieth-century oil. We're talking about an industry that routinely charges markups of ten thousand percent or more, which by itself is driving private health insurance and hospitals to the brink of ruin. And the only theoretical means of salvaging the system is by government intervention and a national system of socialized medicine, which plays right into their hands. Now you have the IRS monitoring every cent you make or spend, a Department of Health with every detail of your personal medical history, a Department of Homeland Security with unlimited power to search and detain under the Patriot Act, the most powerful army the planet has ever seen, and all of the country's finances held in a privatized Federal Reserve controlled by the very same interests that initially financed and implemented the very same model in Germany following the end of the First World War. The Gestapo, the health division of the Reich Interior Ministry, the Shutzstaffel and Sturmabteilung, the Wehrmacht, and the national, privatized Deutsche Reichsbank—different names for exactly the same thing. And now . . . violà. National socialism. The Land of the Free becomes a military state that no longer functions to serve the interests of the masses, but, rather, the financial interests of the few who are suddenly one step closer to the global rule they desire. And this man—" *Tap-tap-tap.* "This man is their key to doing it."

Mason caught movement from the corner of his eye. He turned and saw that Alejandra had removed her hood and was gently tracing the scarring on her face with her fingertips. He recalled the words she had committed to memory through her desperate escape and her years in hiding, the words spoken by the most recent incarnation of the monster whose face adorned the wall before them now, the great-grandson of the man who first took up the mantle on a battlefield in France. The monster who called himself the Hoyl.

There's just one problem we haven't solved. How do we dispose of all of the bodies?

When Johan spoke again, it was in a tired voice, one that betrayed a lifetime spent chasing shadows.

"So I ask you again. Please, James. Please tell me how you got this man's photograph."

Mason turned to face Johan so he could watch the old man's eyes.

"It's a digital enhancement of a reflection. The reflection on the lens of my wife's sunglasses on the day she was killed."

"*Your* wife? That can't be right. That would mean . . ."

"What aren't you telling me?"

"You must go now. I have much work to do."

"Tell me what you know."

As Johan started for the doorway, Mason grabbed him by the sleeve of his robe. Two men appeared from nowhere and seized Mason by either arm.

Johan shrugged back into his robe, straightened the lapels, and turned to face them, composed once more.

"I told you what you came here to find out. You know enough now. There are some things you are not yet ready to learn. For now, there is one goal upon which we must focus all our energies. Everything else is extraneous. We need to figure out what the Hoyl plans to do and where he intends to strike."

He whirled and strode toward the Trophy Room.

"I've seen him before, you know," Mason said.

Johan froze like a statue, his back to them.

"What do you mean, you've *seen* him?"

"The statement is fairly self-explanatory."

"Where?"

"Arizona. One year ago."

Johan gave a slight wave with his right hand and the pressure on Mason's arms abated. The men stepped back just far enough that he wouldn't be able to forget they were there.

"Very few men have seen him in person and survived the encounter."

"I have."

"Tell me about it."

He kept his back to Mason so the younger man wouldn't be able to read the desperation on his face, but Mason knew it was there. He could hear it in the old man's voice.

"You first."

Mason felt the men behind him move subtly closer. Johan took a long time to formulate his words.

"That they killed your wife is a bad sign. They would have done so only as a last resort. It was my understanding that her death was unrelated. Now it's your turn."

"Not until you give me something I can use. Tell me what you know about my wife. Is her family involved? Why did they kill Angie?"

Johan sighed and turned to face him.

"You have my sympathies, young James Mason. I, too, know the pain of losing a wife. There is no greater sorrow a man can endure." His expression hardened and he finally revealed the true face of the man who could sign the orders to hunt down and kill the men in the Trophy Room. "Now you must become her avenging angel. Let no man stand in your way. Yes, I am certain your wife's family is involved."

Mason thought of Paul's uncharacteristic mood and had no doubt that he had been party to the decision to murder his own daughter.

"It was at a rock quarry on the Tohono O'odham Reservation, not far from the border. We tracked him there—"

"He led you there."

"It was an ambush. Nearly my entire team was killed, including my partner. I found the man with the blue eyes—the Hoyl—in a room filled with corpses, all of them hanging from the roof by chains. I looked him squarely in the eyes through the smoke and the flies and I . . . aimed my gun at his head . . . and I . . ."

"You must not hesitate again."

"Not a chance."

"These corpses?"

"All in various stages of decomposition."

"Did you recognize any telltale signs of pathology? Sores. Bruising. Bleeding. Lesions on the skin."

"I didn't get a very good look. I was a little preoccupied with the man holding a gun to my partner's head and the fact that the entire building was on fire around me."

"Did he say anything?"

"No," Mason said, and looked pointedly at Alejandra. "At least not to me."

Johan followed his stare. Recognition dawned in the old man's eyes.

"What did he say to you?"

"He said, 'There's just one problem we haven't solved. How do we dispose of all the bodies?'"

Johan furrowed his brow. Then, with a flash of flannel, he was gone. The shuffling sound of his slippers followed him through the sublevel.

"I take it we're done here," Mason said.

"We would be happy to escort you to the door, sir," the man in the cardigan said. "And make no mistake, we *will* be following your investigation with great interest."

His accent was distinctly Middle Eastern, filtered through a formal British education. Dark hair, bushy eyebrows, light skin, an abundance of moles. He gestured toward the door with a half bow—as though he were a maître d' seeing them to their table, rather than an enforcer whose cardigan shifted just enough to expose the butt of an Israeli Jericho 941 semiautomatic pistol—and led them up the stairs, through the living room, and to the front door.

He stood on the porch and watched them climb into their truck and drive away. The gate was already closing behind them when they hit the street.

"Where do we go from here?" Alejandra asked.

The truth was, Mason simply didn't know.

He was just about to close his eyes and succumb to exhaustion, when he caught a glimpse of the smile forming on Gunnar's face.

And then he realized why.

The Thorntons had gone to great lengths to make sure no one knew about their new windowless corporate headquarters on the AgrAmerica lot, which meant there was undoubtedly something inside they didn't want anyone to see. He had a hunch they weren't about to offer him a personal tour, so he was just going to have to arrange one for himself.

It was time to find out what they were hiding.

PART V

The real truth of the matter is, as you and I know, that a financial element in the larger centers has owned the government ever since the days of Andrew Jackson.

—Franklin D. Roosevelt, letter to Col. Edward Mandell House (1933)

57

Greeley, Colorado

NOVEMBER 16

Alejandra and others like her had been injected with various pathogens and used as mules to carry them across the border. They were undocumented aliens. There was no record of their existence. For all anyone knew, they'd simply wandered out across the red sands and vanished into thin air.

Neither the risk nor the exposure was great at all for those responsible—unlike just about every other option. The CDC had installed quarantine stations in all of the major international airports and screened passengers for a host of symptoms. There was also the distinct possibility of uncontrolled exposure. Any vehicle, whether a car or a boat, could be subjected to a random search at the border. The only way of guaranteeing acquisition of the test subjects was by funneling them through a dangerous, uninhabitable desert wasteland those responsible had arranged to leave unguarded and unfenced.

But what was their ultimate goal?

Were they testing the afflicted for antibodies, determining the level of lethality, or did they simply want to find out what would happen? Mason could only assume that the entity the Hoyl represented was collecting these diseases in the wild and working on them somewhere out of the country, away from oversight.

If everything Johan said was true, then in addition to the plague, cholera, Ebola, and dengue fever, these men had access to several different and largely fatal varieties of influenza.

Mason still couldn't see the endgame, though. Was it possible that Johan was right and it was all about money? That someone, somewhere, was sitting on the vaccine, just waiting for the outbreak so he could make billions from the cure for the disease he had created? That theory definitely fit with Gunnar's feeling that something big was on the horizon, especially when you factored in the specific stocks being traded.

The most pressing question was, where did they propose to release it? Some village in the middle of nowhere or right in the heart of Times Square?

And how did the trap in the administrative building out by the old airport, where the SWAT team had been killed, fit in? The small chamber had been sealed with plastic sheeting, and some sort of biological agent had obviously been released inside. It had the feel of some sort of deal, but were the dead men lying on the ground inside the purveyors of the disease or the cure? Or was it just another test? And why leave the evidence there to be found when the ultimate goal had always been to incinerate it?

Most important, why kill Angie when all she potentially had to go on was the blackened ruins of Fairacre and the hidden subterranean chamber she likely would never have found underneath it, especially considering all of the equipment had been removed or destroyed?

The only thing Mason knew for certain was that regardless of the angle at which he looked at the problem, he ended up looking at Paul and Victor. He just couldn't figure out why. If they were buying their way into the world of pharmaceuticals, then popping up out of nowhere with the cure for some terrifying new virus would definitely put them on the map, but nothing in that line of logic necessitated the death of their daughter and sister, respectively. Mason's wife.

The fact that Angie hadn't known her family was investing a fortune into building a new corporate headquarters for an entity her father had never once mentioned to her didn't sit well with Mason. Nor did Gunnar's lack of knowledge about the Thorntons' new venture, Global

Allied Biotechnology and Pharmaceuticals. They both made it their business to know such things, which meant that considerable effort had been invested in concealing that information, not to mention the enormous structure being raised on AgrAmerica's back nine. There was something crucial he was missing and only one place he could think to look.

They weren't going to let him just waltz through the front gates this time, though.

There was enough activity around the construction site that he probably could work his way into the crowd, but if anyone recognized him, he was screwed. Their only real option was to wait for the place to empty out for the night. The flaw in that plan was that the entire complex would be on heightened awareness because of the morning's events at Fairacre. Fortunately, he'd already dealt with at least part of Paul's security force while he was there.

Gunner proposed the idea of going in right at quitting time, during the mass exodus of bodies and vehicles. Security would still have to search the cars on the way out, and they'd be on high alert for any incoming traffic. They would be expecting Mason to come under the cover of darkness, if they even suspected such a bold move at all. Five o'clock. That was his magic window. He needed to be in the building before everyone else was out and security tightened the cordon around it. The challenge from there would be getting out, but Gunnar assured him that he had everything under control.

"Easy for you to say. You'll be miles away from the action."

"You're not the only one with his neck on the proverbial chopping block. Their cybersurveillance team is undoubtedly already at maximum readiness. If they so much as sense I'm attempting to gain access to their system, they'll initiate whatever active defensive countermeasures they employ and shut down their entire network. Any potential intrusions will stand out like beacons. They'll be able to cut through my web of proxy servers and VPNs and isolate my IP address in a matter of minutes."

"Have you ever been caught?"

"Of course not. You?"

"The FBI tends to frown upon the whole breaking-and-entering thing."

"When it suits its purposes." Gunnar smirked. "You're burning daylight."

"He is right," Alejandra said. "This is our only chance."

Mason nodded, climbed out of the truck, and sprinted toward the tree line. He watched the old pickup drive around the bend from where he crouched in the shrubs before turning his attention to the southeast and the distant compound. They'd stopped at Walmart, where he'd bought a new Bluetooth, a canvas tarp, a box of antiviral face masks, and a white hooded sweatsuit large enough to fit over his black clothes.

They'd settled on a drop-off point just southwest of the small community of Ault, behind a warehouse on the outskirts of town. From there, it was roughly six miles across largely open terrain to the northwestern corner of AgrAmerica's perimeter. He'd be able to cling to the cover of the trees through an expanse of frozen wetlands for a good portion of that distance, but he'd be completely exposed during his final approach.

At least the weather had seen fit to do him a favor. The storm, which had taken a breather for several hours, had found its second wind. The flakes were the size of moths and fluttered on the attenuated breeze beneath the canopy and outright swarmed in the clearings. Visibility was limited, for which he was extremely grateful. He was also counting on there being no satellite surveillance of the complex. If he was right, the Thorntons didn't want anyone to get a good look at whatever they were doing back there. It was a gamble, though. If he was wrong, anyone watching the feed would be able to see him the moment he broke cover and started for the fence.

From there, he was depending on Gunnar to work his magic.

Mason didn't have any idea what he would find in the new building. He remembered how Victor had steered him away from it and back to his car. Victor wasn't the kind of guy who did anything without a reason, and Mason certainly couldn't remember another time when his brother-in-law had thrown his arm over his shoulders like they were friends, let alone family. There was definitely something inside that building, and it was high time he figured out what.

He made his way through the marshlands as quickly and quietly as he could, clinging to the edges of the cattails and staying beneath the cotton-woods and pines, until he finally broke cover about a mile and a half from his destination. The cattails continued along the edge of the marsh for another couple hundred yards, beyond which he could see little more than a seamless stretch of whiteness through the sheeting snow.

Mason tapped his earpiece to connect to Gunnar.

"How does it look from here?"

"The imagery I have to work with is a year old, but it looks like there's a fieldstone retaining wall just to the west of the marsh," Gunnar replied.

"It'll have to work. Are we clear of any satellite?"

"If there's one overhead, I can't find it."

"Is that a yes or a no?"

"We'll find out soon enough."

"Very reassuring. What's the status of security?"

"I'm in their system now. So far, no alarms have been raised. I have audio on the security forces on the grounds, video inside the compound, and access to the perimeter alarms. This isn't your run-of-the-mill corporate security system, Mace. It has all the bells and whistles. We're talking motion sensors and outward-facing infrared cameras along the entire fence line. You trigger any of those sensors and those cameras will zero in on you."

"You're sure you can handle them?"

"Piece of cake," Gunnar said. "Just keep your eyes open."

Mason started forward at a crouch, then stopped.

"Gunnar?"

"Yeah?"

"Why are you doing all of this for me?"

"You're not the only one who has a personal stake in taking these guys down."

"What's that supposed to mean?"

"Let's just say I don't take kindly to being manipulated," Gunnar said. "Now get moving. I'm already starting to see an increase in traffic exiting the gate."

Mason charged through the edge of the cattails. The muscles in his legs were already burning and he had a long way to go in a short period of time. He found the retaining wall without much difficulty. It was old and had fallen in spots, but what remained was just high enough to obscure his approach until he was within range of the complex.

The perimeter fence alternately appeared and disappeared through the storm. It was maybe three hundred feet away, across the open terrain, with nothing resembling cover in between.

"Talk to me, Gunnar."

"We've got a ton of activity at the main gates, but that's about it."

"What about the cameras and motion sensors in the northwest corner?"

"Prepared to loop the feed from the cameras and disable the motion sensors on your mark."

He could barely see the silhouette of the new building through the snow. There were still cars in the lot, judging by the diffuse glare of headlights. There was no sign of anyone lying in wait for him, though.

"Now would be a good time, Gunnar."

"How long do you need?"

"Every second you can give me."

Mason dropped to his hands and knees and crawled out from behind the wall. The accumulation came halfway up his thighs and nearly to his elbows. He stayed as low as he could to minimize his profile. While he was confident that with the ferocity of the storm no one would be able to separate him from the surrounding snow at a distance, his shadow would be a dead giveaway. As would the trail he was leaving behind him.

He reached the fence without incident and flattened himself to his chest to covertly survey the complex. There were only a few headlights still in the lot beyond the snow-blanketed mounds of dirt, construction materials, and earthmovers, which would serve to conceal his final sprint to the building itself.

He removed the folded canvas tarp from underneath his jacket. This would be his moment of greatest exposure. His heartbeat thudded in his ears, a counterpoint to the screaming wind.

"Ready on that fence?"

"You're a go on my end." Gunnar paused. "Don't get yourself killed."

Mason jumped up from the ground and used the momentum to unfold the canvas. He gripped the chain link with his fingers and toes and crawled upward for everything he was worth. It took several tries with the wind working against him, but he managed to flop the tarp over the coils of razor wire. It didn't work perfectly, but well enough to prevent the sharp barbs from disemboweling him when he leaned on top of them, tucked his head, and pushed off. A moment of weightlessness and he struck the snow flat on his back.

He rolled over onto his belly and scrutinized his surroundings. The moment he was certain no one had seen him, he tore down the tarp, pushed himself to his feet, and ran at a crouch toward a dump truck. Pressed his back against it. Peered around the hood.

Clear.

Dashed toward a mound of earth. Rounded it. Stayed low all the way to the rear of a construction trailer. Listened for any noise inside. peeked through the dusty windows.

Nothing.

Crept along its length, around the side.

The grand international headquarters of GABP was just on the other side of the dirt lot. Maybe a hundred feet. Five, six seconds at a sprint. Still cars to his left. Not many, though. The majority of the headlights had become the red glare of taillights.

It took him closer to eight seconds to reach the building. He hadn't taken into account the choppiness of the ground beneath the snow from all of the deep tire ruts.

"There's a second entrance on the northern side," Gunnar said. "Get moving."

He ran low and kept his shoulder against the building. It was bare gray concrete, which, presumably, would soon enough be hidden behind some sort of ornate bricks or stones. He grabbed the handle of the steel door and gave it a solid tug. It didn't budge. He glanced beside it.

"Door's locked, Gunnar. There's a standard ten-digit keypad—"

"I'm on it."

The tiny red light turned green. He had the door open and his entire body inside before the beeping sound died. The darkness closed around him like a fist. While he waited for his eyes to adjust, he slipped off his white sweatsuit, folded it neatly, and tucked it up under his jacket. He drew the Infinity from its holster beneath his arm, clicked on the light, and crept down the corridor. The inner walls and floor were made of the same smooth concrete as the exterior. All of the electrical and plumbing lines had been run across the ceiling and bracketed in place. The entire building had a distinctly industrial feel to it, which didn't mesh at all with what Victor had told him.

Mason advanced slowly, listening for even the slightest sound. Swept the beam from one side of the hallway to the other. Passed through a section where it looked as though they were installing an air lock or hatch of some kind. There were no doors on either side, only a single opening dead ahead. He clicked off the light as he neared the terminus, pressed his back against the wall, and moved as stealthily as he could. The corridor opened onto a landing. Beyond the railing he could see only darkness. An elevated walkway led to either side. His first impression was of being on the upper level of a shopping mall, but that quickly faded when he factored in the height of the building and how many levels there must be above him, all of them built surrounding an open courtyard of some kind. More like a hotel.

He leaned over the railing and peered upward. There were three more levels up there. Another one below. There were rooms or offices on every level. Large windowless cubicles, the interior walls of which he assumed would eventually be lined with glass. He found a staircase to his right and descended to the lower level.

The open space was vast and cavernous. He risked turning on his light and shined it across the bare concrete, which was littered with sawdust and dirt and construction scraps. There were four small trailers that looked like they could be hitched to the back of pickup trucks. Each supported a large array of domed spotlights, the kind highway crews used for night work. There was no hint at all as to what his in-laws intended to do with the space. He was sure that if Paul had his way, the entire thing would be filled with his various pet projects growing all the way up to the sky. But there was no skylight up there to admit the sun.

He turned his light in a circle. Nothing about the structure made any kind of sense. It almost reminded him of a—

And then he saw it.

"What the hell?"

58

"Talk to me, Mace," Gunnar said. "What's going on?"

Mason walked slowly toward the southern wall, beneath the balcony, and stood in the mouth of a great dark hole. He traced the circular edges with the under-barrel light and then shined it inside. The beam terminated long before encountering any resistance.

"Answer me, Mace! Are you all right?"

He was incapable of formulating a reply as he stared into a concrete tunnel. Not bare soil or wooden cribbing. This was no temporary construct or mine shaft that predated construction of the structure above it. This was new and it was supposed to be here. There were recessed light fixtures in the ceiling, what looked like narrow elevated walkways to either side, and a wide trench right down the center.

"You are not going to believe this."

"Believe what? Is everything all right?"

"Yeah, Gunnar. Give me a few minutes, okay? I have a feeling I might lose my signal."

"If you do, you're on your own. I can't deal with security if I don't know where you are."

Mason nodded to himself and started walking. He was heading maybe five degrees east of due south—toward the city of Greeley, which was still a solid seven miles away. The tunnel wasn't wide enough to accommodate a car, and that distance was simply too far to walk comfortably. If the tube had actually been designed for any sort of underground transit, then you'd need—

His beam glinted from the central rail, running right down the middle of the trench. There was just enough room for the horizontal wheels that fit between it and the concrete sides, as evidenced by the black stripes of discoloration from the rubber tread. More rails were stacked on either side, ready to be laid.

The track was too narrow for anything as large as a subway car. More like the shuttles they used at large airports to connect the remote terminals. Small passenger trams that moved at high rates of speed. Something like that could cover the distance between Greeley and the GABP HQ in roughly ten minutes. But what would they need to transport that couldn't simply be driven down the road? Neither Victor nor Paul would have gone to such great lengths and even greater expense to provide a mass transit system for a workforce they bussed in from south of the border. Nor would they have designed it to let out in the middle of their brand-new global headquarters.

He was missing something critical.

The Bluetooth crackled with static. Another couple of steps and he completely lost the connection. Even his lightest footsteps echoed. He passed the occasional access panel on the wall. Electrical conduits traversed the distance between them. Rounded forks branched off to either side, only to rejoin the main passage a couple hundred feet later. Everything appeared to age before his eyes. Water stains appeared on walls no longer perfectly smooth and gray. Construction of the tunnel had obviously commenced long before they'd broken ground on the new building, but how could they have pulled it off without anyone knowing? Earthmovers and trucks driving in and out of the complex all day and night wouldn't have gone unnoticed, and surely Angie would have discovered such massive expenditures when she reviewed AgrAmerica's taxes, which meant that another entity must have been financing the construction, and had been for quite some time.

If there were security cameras down here, he was already screwed. There could be men closing in on him from both sides at this very second. He figured he'd be better off forcing a confrontation with one group rather than both at once, so he started to jog beside the rail, his light swinging in front of him, casting eerie, shifting shadows.

He pondered the building falling rapidly behind him. Maybe they were going to lay marble over the concrete and install full panes of glass for the front walls of the cubicles. And maybe they would build a fountain and plant trees in the courtyard. Maybe he simply lacked the vision to see the glorious design as his in-laws envisioned it, because to him it looked almost like you could fashion bars across the open units with their bare concrete walls. Like you could transport whoever you intended to keep inside of the cells in trams that traveled underground, where no one could see them. The kind of place where they were installing air locks in the entry corridors to prevent something inside from reaching the outside world.

Mason was still jogging nearly due south when he came upon the first access chute. Rungs were bolted to the wall and led upward from the walkway into a round chimney. He'd been jogging for what felt like about twenty minutes. At roughly six miles an hour, that put him approximately two miles from the building, well clear of the outer perimeter. He figured now was as good a time as any to poke his head out and see where he was.

He wasn't about to relinquish his pistol, so he climbed one-handed. There was no light above. He was maybe twenty feet up when he saw why. There was a hatch on the chute, maybe another fifteen feet higher up. It had a wheel on the underside like you'd find in a submarine. It spun easily and opened into darkness every bit as complete as that below.

He tapped his earpiece to connect with Gunnar again.

"For the love of God, Mace! Get the hell out of there!"

"What's wrong?"

"You've been in there too long. You're already on borrowed time. Get out of there while you still can. *If* you still can. The last of the traffic is passing through the main gate and security's already begun to fan out into patrols. And other than the main door on the east and the one you entered through, I can't find any other way out of that building. Damn place is built like a fortress."

"That's pretty much exactly what it is." Mason crawled from the hole and slowly turned in a circle. He was inside a small cube that couldn't have been more than four feet wide and four feet high. There was a small door set into the wall. He tried the handle, but it wouldn't budge. "Can you triangulate my location?"

"You're inside a building. Open your eyes and look around."

"Just do it, Gunnar."

Mason focused on a point just to the right of the doorknob. Kicked it as hard as he could. There was a loud cracking sound. He kicked the same spot again. The door popped open three or four inches. The frigid wind raced through the gap and buffeted him with snowflakes. He crawled outside into the accumulation to get his bearings.

"How'd you get all the way out there?" Gunnar asked. "I'm showing you just under two miles *outside* the perimeter."

"Do me a favor. Draw a straight line from the building, through my current location, and to whatever it intersects in Greeley, okay?"

"What am I looking for?"

"Where the tunnel lets out."

"What tunnel? There's no tunnel on any of the security schematics."

"That's kind of my point, Gunnar."

Mason stood outside a small concrete access building, the kind they built along railroad tracks or beside highways. The kind you saw everywhere with such frequency that as you grew up, you ceased wondering what secrets they held, and eventually stopped seeing them altogether. Just a tiny, essentially invisible building in the middle of a field, undoubtedly overgrown by sunflowers or cornstalks in the summer.

"The line intersects with a commercial plot on the northeast corner of Eighth Avenue and Seventh Street," Gunnar said.

"Which building specifically?"

"A feed and tack shop. Flying W Ranch Supply. What are you thinking?"

"That the tunnel will take me directly there."

"It could bend in any number of directions long before then. Or it could stop altogether."

"They've already laid rails down there, Gunnar. A track for some sort of transport vehicle that goes all the way into the new building itself. Through tunnels that aren't on the blueprints."

"Why would they need something like that?"

"To move something they don't want anyone to see."

"Like what? Their new top secret cash crops? A herd of supercattle?"

Mason ducked back inside, out of the wind, and stared back down into the darkness. It smelled of dust, motor oil, and grease.

"I think it's designed to move people. I don't think the building was built to be the envy of the corporate world like Victor said, but, rather, as some sort of long-term housing arrangement. I'm just not sure whether or not the intended occupants will be there of their own free will."

He heard Alejandra's voice, but couldn't make out her words.

"Was it like the other place? Where they took Alejandra? She says you'll know what she means."

"I don't know. All I can say is that it looked like they were installing an air lock in the entry corridor, and the hatch I just crawled through was airtight. It's like they want to prevent airborne particles or contaminants from getting in. Or out."

"So what's the plan from here?" Gunnar asked.

"How's it looking at AgrAmerica? Did I set off any alarms?"

"Negative. It doesn't sound as though security has any idea you were there."

"Then I'm going back down." Mason closed the door behind him and sat with his legs dangling over the nothingness. "I need to see where the tunnel takes me."

"I can't help you if you don't have a signal."

"Just meet me at Flying W, okay? But keep your distance until you hear from me again."

"There's no way someone could build a tunnel underneath downtown Greeley without anyone noticing. Something like that would be impossible to miss."

"Which means that at least some portion of it was already there."

"I'm not sure whether I hope you're right or wrong."

The signal dissociated into static before he even sealed the hatch above him. He shined the light toward the ground to make sure there was no one sighting him down the barrel of a rifle, then hustled down the rungs.

He listened for any indication that he wasn't alone in the tunnel before taking off at a jog.

The Thorntons had somehow built a tunnel under miles of farmland without anyone knowing. It was a monumental task that would have taken years, and had surely been designed with a specific goal in mind, one his in-laws had been planning for a long, long time. And they were finally close to seeing their plan to fruition. He needed to figure out what they were hiding, and how it could possibly be more important to them than the life of one of their own.

Mason found a pace he could sustain and settled into a rhythm. He needed to pace himself if he was going to cover five more miles in a reasonable amount of time. As it was, there was only one thing he knew for sure: He had a long night ahead of him.

59

Mason passed several more surface-access chutes along the way. There were maybe half as many short, semicircular branches designed to allow railcars moving in opposite directions to pass each other without slowing. The under-barrel flashlight beam diminished in strength as the smell of decaying wood and earth increased. It was a distinct scent, like that of a ghost town.

The tunnel widened, subtly at first. Water dribbled down the rust-stained concrete from the exposed pipes and formed puddles at the base of the walls. He slowed to a more cautious pace. There was no doubt he was underneath the city now, and he could stumble into another secured zone at any time.

He walked in a shooter's stance, allowing the Infinity to lead him. He couldn't quite picture the configuration of streets above him and wished he'd paid closer attention any of the dozens of times he'd driven through. The city civic center, or what most just called "old downtown," was on the northeastern edge of town. The town spread to the southwest from there, toward the distant mountains. The courthouse and city hall were a couple blocks away.

The signs of the district's age showed through. Despite renovations every generation or so, a decision would have to be made in the not-so-distant future either to designate it a historical landmark or raze it to the ground. The buildings deteriorated quickly heading east from there, almost as though the face-lift to the civic center itself served the dual purpose of hiding the unsightliness of the warehouses and run-down stores that had serviced the Denver Pacific tracks a century ago.

The ceiling of the tunnel rose as the walls receded. He had to be getting close. The smell of age grew stronger with each step, until finally the tunnel opened into a man-made cavern of sorts. Modern pillars supported an aged concrete dome that showed signs of recent patching. His best guess was that directly above him was an intersection, one that had partially collapsed during a storm not so long ago. The patch job reflected the pride and craftsmanship of a city employee, unlike the rest of the artisanship around him, which was positively breathtaking.

It was like a city beneath the city, only one that hadn't seen use in many, many years. He was at a crossroads, where once men and women of wealth and prestige had moved unseen between theaters and brothels and speakeasies while their reputations remained intact aboveground. He wondered how many people had been aware of the existence of this place at the time, let alone now.

To his right, a broad staircase led upward to a semicircular landing framed by ornate stone balustrades upon which gargoyles perched. The grand facade was of the American neoclassical style favored for capitol buildings and courthouses, with ornate Corinthian columns, cornices, and bas-reliefs. He recognized the Latin words carved in the frieze. *Audaces Fortuna Iuvat*: "Fortune favors the brave." Virgil, from *The Aeneid*. The benefits of a classical education.

Adjacent to it, across a narrow alleyway engulfed in darkness, was a similarly elaborate facade, only of a different architectural period. The design was of the classic Renaissance style, with Doric pilasters, arches, and entablatures. Above the cornice, the words *Nulla Poena Sine Lege; Nulla Regula Sine Exceptione* had been inscribed. "No punishment without law; no rule without exception." Marble stairs led up to a door that didn't look as though it had been opened in a century.

The structure immediately to his left showed much more recent signs of use. It was Gothic in style, as though yet another stop on the underground tour of European architecture. It was made of limestone that had taken on a dirty cast through the years, which added to the gloominess of its lancet arches and blind arcades. The words *Disce Quasi*

Semper Vivam, Si Vivet Non Morietur had been carved above the threshold. "Learn as if you'll live forever, live as though you'll never die." The door had been removed, and his light revealed just the faintest hint of a staircase leading upward.

The adjacent building was hidden behind a framework of platforms and plastic sheets. Someone was still working on whatever was behind there, although at this point he could only wonder why.

Mason had expected the track to end here, to encounter the tram that serviced the two stations, but he was wrong. The tracks went on indefinitely into the pitch-black tunnel for Lord only knew how long.

He'd run out of steam. His body had passed the point of exhaustion somewhere around the six-mile mark on the seven-mile jog. As had his mind. He couldn't remember the last time he'd either slept or eaten. He somehow managed to climb the staircase under what he was certain was Flying W Ranch Supply. There was no door at the top. The stairs dumped him into a vast basement metered by pylons. The concrete walls were striped with rust. He figured this was where they'd kept the booze once upon a time, when crime was organized and criminals didn't even try to pretend they were like everyone else.

Another staircase on the far side of the room led up to a massive warehouse that looked a whole lot more like a lumberyard than any sort of granary. There were mountains of two-by-fours and bags of cement, sheets of plywood and steel I beams, massive spools of cable and bundles of conduits, and a forklift parked beside a stack of rails that probably could have formed a line to the moon and back. The enormous garage doors were locked from the outside, forcing him to work his way through the maze of narrow, claustrophobic aisles until he found a single door that opened onto the actual storefront.

Mason passed aluminum troughs full of chicken scratch and cracked corn and seed mixtures of all colors and varieties. There was a whole selection of horse-related supplies to his left. A lone cash register with large buttons sat on a counter beside a discolored section where the melamine had worn away through the years. All he had to do was turn the lock, open the door, and—with the jangle of a bell—walk out onto the street once more.

Despite the snow and the ferocious wind, he was happy to be topside again. He walked through a parking lot that looked like any other, away from a building that could have been any building in any American city, and across a street people traveled every day without being any the wiser. He shoved aside the snow and plopped down on a bus bench. His in-laws and whoever else was responsible for the construction of the tunnel were so unconcerned that their plot would be discovered that they hadn't even set an alarm. The authorities were obviously bought and paid for. Hell, the entire city was. He wondered if his father, the senator, had any idea what was going on in his state while he was away in Washington. There was no way he'd stand for any of this. His father and grandfather had helped to make this country what it was by imposing the will of the law on a largely lawless land. They'd be sickened to learn that everything they'd built had been disassembled by men wielding their pens and checkbooks like swords and shields.

Mason tapped the Bluetooth and connected to Gunnar.

"I was starting to think you'd decided to take a nap down there."

"I could use a lift," Mason said.

He stared down the road to the east, past the railroad tracks and the distant groves of trees, toward the stormy sky and the end of the world beneath it.

"You okay?" Gunnar asked. "You don't sound like yourself."

Mason had debated the merits of feeding starving children with a father capable of giving the order to murder his only daughter, and had discussed global expansion with a businessman complicit in a plot to release a deadly disease upon an unsuspecting world. He'd looked them in the eyes without sensing so much as a hint of the true depths of their depravity, or the kinds of horrors they intended to smuggle through those depths and into the windowless structure on the back side of their property. These were men he'd considered family, yet they'd robbed him of the one thing in his life that mattered. And all for what? Money?

"Yeah. I'll be fine."

But when it came right down to it, he wasn't sure anything would be fine ever again, not as long as there were men out there like the Thorntons and the Hoyl, who wanted nothing more than to watch the world burn.

60

"No one's actually sure why the tunnels were built," Gunnar said. He'd utilized his time while Mason was underground to do a little digging into the matter, in hopes of discovering something useful. Judging by the glint in his eye, he had, but he was certainly taking his sweet time getting to it. "That intersection specifically—Eighth Avenue and Seventh Street—was the center of commerce around the turn of the twentieth century. On one corner you had the grand Oasis Hotel, where people like Charles Lindbergh stayed. Across the street were the Jackson Opera House and the Chief Theater. Catty-corner to them was Farmer's Supply and Machinery, which was pretty much the sole rancher's supply store within a fifty-mile radius. The lot across from it, at one point or another, housed a hardware store, a sporting goods store, and half a dozen grocery and mercantile stores."

This time, Mason did the driving, freeing Gunnar to work with his laptop on his thighs. They'd filled up the old gas-guzzler and grabbed some food and coffee while they were at it. He was starting to feel more like himself already. The truck idled in the parking lot of the old train station, now the Chamber of Commerce, while he finished off his first cup and started on the second.

"Most people believe the construction of the tunnels wasn't initially meant to be secretive at all. The most benign explanation for their existence is that the buildings shared a common source of forced-air heating and the tunnels were used to distribute it from a central coal furnace. There are all sorts of rumors, too. Everything from theater actors sneaking under the street to rendezvous with groupies in the hotel to entire underground networks of gambling and bootlegging. People have found tunnels throughout this entire area—beneath houses, under the bank, in the middle of streets. But, for whatever reason, they just got closed up, and no one mentioned them again. They even found one right beneath where we are right now, which connected the train depot to the old Farmer's Supply, presumably to move liquor from the arriving trains into the city. Tunnels have been discovered as far as five blocks away, including what some claim to be a whole network designed to evade hostile Indians."

"So they already had an existing infrastructure of primitive tunnels to build upon."

"More than that," Gunnar said. "We're not just talking about holes dug in the dirt with lanterns hanging from the old cribbing. These tunnels were constructed with brick and mortar. Real solid, arched numbers. My point being that they weren't made by your average smugglers. Bootlegging was a serious business, but not one anybody thought would last forever. An enormous amount of money had to have been invested in the construction, right? You don't hire crews and spend years creating an entire subterranean labyrinth when repealing Prohibition would immediately make it obsolete. You don't throw down piles of cash just so some stage actor can shag a farmer's daughter, either. And if you're too cheap to heat your buildings individually, then you're not going to blow exorbitant sums on the connecting tunnels, knowing full well they're going to be covered with a foot of soot in no time flat. You have to take a step back, factor the equation down to its simplest financial components, and evaluate it in a historical context. Essentially what I do for a living, only in this case, it's for companies that no longer exist, and using business models that were outdated a century ago.

"Bottom line. Why does anyone do anything? Sex, money, or power. It didn't take a whole lot of money to buy sex back then, and even minimal power has always been enough to pretty much guarantee a steady stream of action. So we're left with money and power. Who has them and who wants them? In a colony full of religious teetotalers and moral idealists, only one man stands out. Wesley Thornton. Your wife's great-grandfather. By 1900, he'd snatched up nearly two-thirds of all of the active ranches in the area. He had the trade cornered. He'd expanded his kingdom as far as it could go. And anytime something like that happens, the only thing left to do is conquer another kingdom, which he did in the form of entering the railroad game. He bought controlling interest in the small Cache la Poudre Line, leveraged it to outright buy the depot behind us, as well as a dozen others along the line, and then sold his interests in the railroad itself to Thomas Elliot Richter, who eventually traded it to R. J. Mueller in a deal that allowed him to monopolize the oil trade.

"Superficially, not much there. Thornton cashed in on a commodity and increased his fortune. On the practical side, he now controlled access to the Rio Grande train line from just north of the Wyoming state line all the way down through Denver."

"You said he sold the railroad."

"But he kept the depots. Think of them as seaports and him as the harbormaster. He determined what got on and what got off and how much it cost for each item to do so. Now, in 1908 he entered into a partnership with a company called StockCo Holdings and bought a large plot of land in an area that came to be called Island Grove, seven blocks north-northwest of the train depot. A heavily wooded lot near the river. The stated mission of this partnership was to establish a hog farm that would revolutionize the industry and bring it in line with the standards and profitability of cattle production. This side venture was snakebit from the start, though. Dozens of hogs died the first month, as did two of their hired hands. By the spring of 1909, they'd lost more than two thousand head. And four employees. All from pneumonia. Or at least that's what was reported. There's even a picture here from the Colorado Historical Society."

Gunnar turned his computer so that Alejandra and Mason could see. The image had obviously been scanned from a photograph that had seen better days. The emulsification was spiderwebbed with cracks, but Mason could still clearly see the subject: a broad expanse of mud partitioned into pens, riddled with bloated white carcasses. The picture had been taken from a distant vantage point, through trees that framed the corners with blurry leaves. The focus was the sheer amount of carnage, the dead pigs everywhere. Not necessarily the men picking their way through the remains in primitive gas masks and baggy white gowns.

He looked up at Gunnar, who smiled at the recognition in his eyes. He could see where his old friend was going with this line of thought, could practically hear the tumblers falling into place.

"With their hogs dead, AgrAmerica and StockCo were forced to cut their losses and abandon their shared venture. In exchange for the cleanup, the land was given to the city and the families of the deceased employees were compensated. But they weren't the only ones. StockCo reimbursed AgrAmerica for its purchase of the now-dead livestock in the form of corporate shares, which, considering the colossal failure of the hog farm experiment, were worthless on paper. However, when StockCo's parent company rolled it back and merged it with a more successful subsidiary, those shares carried over to the sister company and were suddenly valuable again. In fact, great-grandpa Wesley leveraged them into a seat on the board of the parent company, traded them in small amounts on the open market until their value peaked, and then cashed them in to the tune of forty-three million dollars. His initial investment in two thousand dead pigs was reimbursed at a rate of more than *twenty thousand dollars* a head at a time when a hog cost less than five bucks. Are you following me so far?"

Mason could only nod and stare at his coffee, which was growing cold in his hand.

"In 1912, construction workers discovered a tunnel beneath a property two blocks to the north-northwest when part of the site collapsed, revealing what they believed to be a section of this mythical 'Indian tunnel,' but if you look at the map, it falls right in line with the tunnel you were just in. The city paid for the ground to be closed up once more. One of the workers was quoted at the time as saying it smelled like something had died down there. Later that same year, Wesley began selling off all of his railroad depots."

"Get to the part about the owner of StockCo," Alejandra said.

"Right. StockCo was absorbed by its sister company, Western Agricultural Consortium, which, until 1908, was a wholly owned subsidiary of Mueller Steel, who sold it to Tectonic Shale & Oil, whose parent company was—duht-duh-duh-dahh—Great American Oil. Your in-laws shared a forty-three-million-dollar mess of dead pigs with Thomas Elliot Richter, the richest man in the country. And it gets better. The Richter Foundation—the charitable arm of the corporate juggernaut—was the largest contributor to the research that resulted in the formation of Unified Pharmacopeia, a joint venture between Mueller Steel and Great American Oil. Unified then bought all of Bayer AG's patents and holdings, which were seized under the Trading with the Enemy Act in 1917. The act itself was repealed just long enough for those assets to be auctioned off, chief among them the patent to a revolutionary new drug called aspirin. Unified immediately commenced mass production of the most powerful medicine the world had ever known and amassed stockpiles large enough to treat the millions afflicted with the Spanish flu *the following year.* Unified made nearly a billion dollars in the process. And what did research scientists learn in 2009 when they exhumed several victims of the pandemic whose bodies had been frozen in the Alaskan ice? That the Spanish flu was a variation of the influenza A virus, H1N1 specifically, which began its life as an avian flu that was passed to humans with one slight detour in between. Care to wager a guess as to what?"

"Pigs," Mason said.

"You got it. The most deadly pandemic in the history of the world started as a cough in a duck and mutated into something far worse in a field full of dead hogs. And the company that profited most from it was an early pharmaceutical company selling aspirin, using a recipe it had ripped off—with the government's help—from Bayer. A company half-owned by Great American Oil, the charitable foundation of which took a sudden interest in the treatment of those afflicted, as evidenced by—"

"The photograph from the Library of Congress. The one with the man with the blue eyes, a doctor with the Richter Foundation, treating casualties in a tent in France during World War One. The first known appearance of the Hoyl."

"A century ago, Mace," Gunnar said in little more than a whisper. "They've been doing this for so long, they've got it down to a science."

"Then it is time someone stopped them," Alejandra said.

"Exactly what I was thinking," Mason said. "Do me a favor, Gunnar. Extrapolate the course of the tunnel in both directions and compare the properties situated along its projected course to any of AgrAmerica's or GABP's current holdings. There has to be a match. Whatever lies at the far end of the tunnel is the key to understanding what's happening now."

Gunnar's fingers flew across the keyboard, as though the computer were an extension of himself.

"Nothing here. At least nothing on a direct line."

"Try properties that list the same corporate address as Fairacre."

Mason felt the connection even as he said it. This was where every-thing came together. This was the reason his wife had been killed. He closed his eyes and saw Angie's face, watched a smile form on her lips. He would have given anything to cling to that image forever.

"There it is. Steerman's Meat Processing and Packing. Fifteen miles south-southeast of here. Nine miles north of Fort Lupton. Middle of freaking nowhere. Give me a second." His fingers buzzed across the keys. "It was originally family-held, owned and operated by Angus T. Steer-man. Seriously. That was his real name. It was in his family for three generations. Started by Delbert Chester Steerman in 1919, following his return from the war. Grew the business to a couple thousand head and made a comfortable living. Turned it over in 1953 to his three sons, who promptly converted it into a commercial slaughterhouse and pur-chased a fleet of semis with freezers to distribute their products. Made a killing through the mid-eighties. Grew complacent. Made some bad in-vestments and even worse business decisions. Turned the company over to their combined eight children, who ran it into the ground in a matter of years. Angus bought out his two sisters and all five cousins in an at-tempt to make a go of it on his own. He lasted until 1994 before filing Chapter Seven and liquidating all of the assets in a fire sale. The freezer trucks went to Safeway for pennies on the dollar, the cattle sold by the head, and the physical property was obtained by a company named Mountain States Land Development. Now Mountain States, you'll be surprised to learn, had only one other holding, a penthouse suite in a nonexistent office building in Commerce City, which it sold, along with the Steerman land, to an international agriculture consortium with of-fices in Switzerland. And who would you imagine sits on this Swiss com-pany's board?"

"My dear brother-in-law, Victor, who was there mere days ago."

"It's like you're psychic."

"Then this is where we must go," Alejandra said. She knew even better than the rest of them what—or, more important, who—they were likely to find there.

"Without a doubt," Mason said. "Can you get us the blueprints for that place, Gunnar?"

"Already on it."

"What about satellite?"

"We don't want to tip our hand. If I task a bird to that location, they'll know it."

"Then I'll be going in blind."

"Not necessarily."

The left corner of Gunnar's mouth curled upward into the hint of a smile.

His phone rang. The song was "Walk Like an Egyptian." Mason had a pretty good idea to whom the ringtone had been assigned.

"It's about time, Ramses. Are you certain this call isn't being traced?" Gunnar rolled his eyes at the answer. "Yeah, yeah. I know." A sigh. "Yes. He's right here with me." A pause. "Hang on a second. Just a sec— Hold on, for Christ's sake. I can't ask him if you don't stop talking. . . . Okay, okay. Just a second. Mace, Ramses wants to know how you're coming with that Hummer you owe him."

"Tell him I've been kind of busy."

"He said to tell you he's been kind of— Fine. Hang on." Gunnar put the call on speaker and set his phone on the dashboard. "There."

"Are you there, Mace?" Ramses asked.

"Yeah," Mason said. "But your Bronco didn't make it."

"You're killing me, man. This is the reason why nobody helps each other anymore. Between you destroying all of my cars and your old man calling my clubs, I'm starting to think you're trying to give me an aneurysm."

"*My* old man? Why in the world would my dad be calling you?"

"That's what people around here are starting to ask. There's no good reason for a man in my position to be talking to a United States senator, especially one who sits on any number of subcommittees whose sole focus is the ruination of the majority of my business contacts."

"Did he say what he wanted from you?"

"From me? You kidding? There's nothing he wants from me, shy of my head mounted on his wall. He just wants to make sure his baby boy is okay, because Son of the Year isn't returning any of his messages and no one seems to know where he is."

The wind shifted direction and lifted the settled snow back into the air, momentarily obscuring the old depot.

"What did you tell him?"

"You're not listening, are you? Nothing! The hell if I'm talking to him. He's always had that way of seeing right through me. You know that. He's your problem, man. Not mine."

"Did those friends of yours have any useful information?"

"These things require some serious finesse. Everyone knows that Ramses doesn't ask for favors, he grants them, so all kinds of red flags go up the moment he does. Ask the wrong person and next thing you know we're all being fitted for toe tags."

"You could have just said no."

"You get some sort of perverse pleasure out of pushing my buttons, don't you? Let's just say it's still a work in progress. I should have something by the time I catch up with you."

"How do you know where—?"

"I ended up having a little chat, in a roundabout kind of way, with the personal assistant of an elderly gentleman, who, as it turns out, feels something of a kinship for you."

The idea of Ramses having any sort of connection to Johan came from so far afield that it took Mason a second to catch up with the conversation.

"You talked to Mahler's man?"

"He goes by Seraph, but his name's actually Asher Ben-Menachem. Turns out we bumped elbows in Uzbekistan. He was a battalion commander in the Golani Brigade of the IDF back when I was playing G.I. Joe. I'm on my way up there right now to have a little powwow with him. Don't start the fireworks without me."

"Might want to push it a little harder, then. If I'm right about where we're going and what we're about to walk into, the show's about to begin."

"It'd be a whole lot easier if I still had my Mustang."

"Point made."

"Let me talk to Gunnar."

"He's sitting right here."

"I mean in private."

Gunnar killed the speaker and brought the phone to his ear. Mason watched him from the corner of his eye as he pulled out of the lot and headed back toward the highway. A few more cars had joined them on the road, but not many. The sand trucks were already out and about, plowing through the accumulation, gravel bouncing in their wake.

"Not yet," Gunnar said. He instinctively peeked past Alejandra at Mason. "Now's not the time, Ramses. I—"

Mason watched the road and tapped a tuneless rhythm on the steering wheel with his thumbs. Whatever the two of them were discussing made Gunnar uncomfortable in a way that recalled his more awkward youth.

"You know damn well I didn't deliberately do any—" Gunnar lowered his voice. "Of course I want to make things right. You know every bit as well as I do that—"

"Do you think that monster will be waiting for us?" Alejandra asked.

"I'm counting on it," Mason said. "It's time to end this once and for all."

Whether the Hoyl knew it or not, today was his last day on this earth.

"Fine, Ramses," Gunnar said. "You know what? Ramses? Ramses. No, you . . . Just wait . . . Hold—hold up. . . . Check your email. . . . No, not that one. You know which one I'm talking about. You think I want this broadcast for the whole world to see? Are you even listening to me? Ramses. Ramses?"

Gunnar terminated the call and tapped some keys.

"Are you going to tell me about it or are we just going to pretend I didn't hear any of that?" Mason said.

"Now's not the time, Mace. Believe me."

"How are we going to get into this place?" Alejandra asked. "We cannot just walk up and knock on the door."

Mason thought about the bush beater Ramses had given him earlier. He figured it would probably work quite nicely as a door knocker, too.

"Yeah," he said. "That's exactly what we're going to do."

61

The Steerman complex was situated at the southeastern corner of a 963-acre parcel, the majority of which had been divided into stockyards that provided a steady supply of meat for the grinders. All that remained now was a ruined framework of fallen fences overgrown with weeds. The most recent satellite images Gunnar could find were already two years old. They were just going to have to hope that not very much had changed in that time.

The core of buildings formed a nice tight cluster maybe a mile and a half in from the main dirt road. Tall weeds grew from the cracked asphalt of the tarmac. The family homestead sat off to the east, away from the commercial operations, surrounded by several large outbuildings, one of which appeared to have fallen to the ground. The commercial zone was deeper into the property to the northwest, at the heart of the maze of stock pens and cattle chutes that wended their way up to the largest building, which was the size of a department store. It had a multitiered roof connected by metal ladders and several tall industrial chimneys. Roads led from either side of the main building through the curved cattle funnels—or races—and the crowd pens, which were barely visible through the overgrowth.

For as much information as they could glean from the old satellite images, there was even more they couldn't. They hadn't been able to find blueprints for any of the buildings. All they had to go on was a generic floor plan for a modern industrial slaughterhouse, which meant that Mason needed to familiarize himself with the basic layout and the function of each of the various rooms so that he wouldn't be walking in there completely blind.

The cattle would have been led from their stock pens into smaller crowd pens, funneled through a series of races so narrow that they couldn't turn around, and then up a ramp, through a chute, and into a cage called a knocking pen, where a guillotinelike device colloquially termed a *neck crush* was used to immobilize the animal's head so it could be percussed by a captive-bolt gun. From there, the carcasses were skinned, decapitated, and carried along an overhead conveyor down the butchering line from the precooler to the cooler to the preparation room on their way to either the freezers or the docks.

And that was just the killing floor.

There were offices and locker rooms and lounges and bathrooms and storage rooms and any number of facilities now considered obsolete. Boiler rooms, furnace rooms, scalding rooms, elevated walkways for constant supervision. Not to mention the entire second and third levels. And, of course, there was a tunnel leading right up to it from beneath the barren fields.

In other words, he was really little better off now than he'd been before, but at least he'd be able to recognize where he was as he stumbled blindly from room to room.

He hoped.

Then again, they could always arrive and find the whole place burned to the ground.

He doubted it, though. It felt like everything had been building up to this. From the discovery of the flu virus and the death of his partner in the Arizona desert to the reappearance of the Hoyl and the subsequent murder of his wife, whose investigation had exposed the solitary weakness in the conspiracy, a financial trail that led from a shelf company in Commerce City to the Fairacre property on the eastern plains to a tunnel hidden inside a windowless building on the AgrAmerica lot. It had all brought him to where he was right now, crouched in the snow beside a concrete access building roughly two miles north-northwest of Steerman's slaughterhouse.

Mason's watch read 3:40 A.M.

He crawled through the small door and out of the storm. The wheel of the hatch took some serious torque, but he managed to open it. He lost the cell signal to his Bluetooth before he was even halfway down. Thirty seconds later, he was kneeling on the cold ground, listening to the darkness around him. Judging by the smell, this section of the tunnel was newer than the one under downtown Greeley. He risked turning on the Infinity's under-barrel light. The LED output had already dimmed significantly, which meant he was going to have to use it sparingly.

The tunnel looked exactly the same as it had fifteen miles to the north: smooth, rounded concrete with electrical boxes and conduits traversing the walls and the ceiling. The only real difference was the scoring on the rails. These tracks were in use and had been for some time, if sparingly. He took a mental snapshot and killed the beam. The resultant darkness was complete.

Mason leaned his right shoulder against the wall beside him and used it as a guide to help him travel as fast as he could. He had a pretty good mental odometer, and at this pace it wouldn't take him much more than half an hour to cover the two miles. The problem would be finding what he was looking for once he was inside.

He was walking into a trap and he knew it. The element of surprise would work to his advantage, but what he was really counting on was what the men had said about someone looking out for him. His guardian angel. A second's hesitation was all he would need, as he had no such angel sitting on his shoulder.

The mile mark came and went. He was starting to get edgy. He carried the pistol higher and in a two-handed grip. His eyes had adjusted to the darkness, at least as well as they were going to. He could make out the faintest hint of the rail to his left, and he was coming to anticipate the turnoffs by the changing intonation of his footsteps. He slowed at a mile and a half to minimize the sound of his advance. He didn't risk using the light at all. Another quarter of a mile and he was in full shooter's stance, his heart pounding in his ears. He focused on slowing it, on metering its rhythm. Opened his mouth to quiet his breathing.

He could positively taste it now. This was it.

A sour scent joined that of the dust. A biological stench. A taste as much as a smell. He remembered it clearly. It was the same one he'd followed through the burning building in Arizona a year ago.

With those memories came others. The plastic sheeting melting up to the ceiling, dripping smoldering liquid. Smoke swirling all around him. Flames consuming the wooden walls. Dark silhouettes dangling from chains. The reek of decomposition and the buzz of flies. The man with the blue eyes, smiling behind his respirator. Kane emerging from one of the stalls, shouting for Mason to take the shot. The man holding a gun to the base of his partner's skull, his head snapping backward as his forehead burst. Again, those horrible blue eyes, staring at him down the barrel of his pistol. Mocking him. Then heat and light, which faded into a vision of his wife.

Angie looked up at him and he recognized the longing in her eyes. The longing for him to return from wherever he'd gone, to rejoin her in the land of the living. He saw the hope in her expression, which told him that her heart was his, for better or worse, and that it was up to him to make things right between them, that she would wait for him until the end of time if she had to. Then she donned a pair of sunglasses and he saw the face of the man who had stolen her from him. Saw his inhumanly blue eyes and his horrible smile. And then he saw only flames.

Mason would not fail them again.

The sound of his footsteps changed. Slowly. If there was such a thing as the note of finality, it was the echo of footsteps dying against a concrete wall. A flat noise with no depth. It was the sound of the end.

He clicked on the light and shined it ahead of him. The beam reflected from a large slanted rectangle maybe three feet up from the tracks. It was a sheet of Plexiglas, through which he could see thin vertical posts, chain-link fencing, and maybe the hint of a doorway in the rear. It was a tram, as he'd initially guessed. There were four cars in all, with sliding doors that opened on both sides. They were closed, but there was no missing the subdivisions inside. The cages. It was a prison transport vehicle. Backed right up against a bare concrete wall, which was a slightly lighter shade of gray than those surrounding it, a more recent addition.

There had to be an ingress nearby.

Right there. At the end of the tunnel, nearly abutting the wall. A heavy steel door.

Mason scanned the edges. No wires or infrared or any other devices on this side. The door opened outward, toward him. He'd be able to see inside before entering. For whatever that was worth. If it was alarmed on the inside, there would be no way to avoid setting it off. It didn't matter now anyway.

They'd know he was here soon enough.

He switched off the light, stood in the darkness while his eyes adjusted, then took hold of the handle.

The metal was cold in his grasp.

He focused his senses, steadied his breathing, and turned the knob.

62

The smell hit Mason squarely in the face. It took all of his concentration to keep from vomiting. He closed the door behind him as quietly as he could. It was every bit as dark inside as it was in the tunnel, only about twenty degrees warmer. And much more humid. The sweat was already flowing under his multiple layers. He held his gun in his right hand and used his left to guide him along the wall.

Beneath the smell of death was something else. Desiccated straw and manure. Maybe earth and mildew. And the faintest hint of chemicals, fuel of some kind. Considering the Hoyl's proclivity for fire, he had a pretty good idea what it was for.

The walls were polished concrete, with the kind of finish that made them easy to hose down. As was the floor, which caused his rubber soles to squeak despite his best efforts. He found the stairs with his right foot and ascended slowly. Rounded the landing. Continued upward. The stench grew stronger with every step. The last time he'd been in a place like this, he was wearing a respirator mask. He would have killed for one now. The antiviral face mask covering his nose and mouth protected him from exposure to diseases and bodily fluids, but it didn't do a blasted thing for the smell.

Another steel door sealed the top of the staircase, only this one was flush with the ceiling. It was much older than anything else he'd encountered. The rivets were rusted or missing entirely in some spots. He pressed his cheek against the hatch and listened for anything on the other side, felt for subtle vibrations, then put his shoulder into it and raised it high enough to crawl out. He slowly lowered the lid and crouched against the wall. There was no sign of anyone around him.

He checked his Bluetooth. A single bar was all he needed. And probably all he got.

"I'm inside," Mason whispered. The sound echoed from a room he realized was much larger than he'd initially thought.

"Right on schedule," Gunnar said. "Any resistance?"

"Negative. At least so far."

"This is too easy, Mace."

"Don't jinx it. Maybe we've finally caught a break."

"You know that's not the case."

"A guy can dream, right?" He turned on his light and cupped the lens in his palm. "Are you in position?"

"Yeah. I've got to tell you, though. I'd feel a whole lot better about this if I had some sort of visual on the property. I can't even find a security system to hack into. This place is totally off the grid."

"Have you scanned the radio frequencies yet?"

"There's nothing on the cellular bands. I still need a few more minutes on the lower frequencies. Any sort of short-range handheld is going to utilize such a long wavelength that I'll practically leave be line of sight to intercept it."

"Don't get yourself killed trying."

"Certainly not foremost on today's agenda. Besides, I've got Alejandra watching my back." Gunnar lowered his voice. "You ever see a woman handle a grenade launcher? There's something incredibly sexy about it."

"I'm going silent now," Mason said. "Let me know the moment you have ears."

He started forward, still in a crouch, and swept his light from one side of the large room to the other. The ceiling had to be a good twenty-five feet high. Corrugated aluminum on a framework of rusted girders. Metal support posts flaking with rust. Pipes as thick as his thighs traversing the walls. There was an elevated platform to his left, the remains of the fallen staircase that had once serviced it on the ground beneath it. There was a door up there. The padlock on it looked new. The walls were covered with graffiti. No one had made any effort to paint over it or scrape up the oil stains covering the concrete floor. The only evidence that anyone had been in here recently were the sawhorses, wood scraps, and bags of cement surrounded by gray dust. The smell of death was stronger here, but the source was obviously somewhere else. And it looked like the only way to find it was by climbing the concrete stairs at the far end of the room, which led up to a platform that spanned the width of the building.

Mason started to piece together a mental map. He was in the loading dock. The bay doors were at his back, which meant that the main body of the slaughterhouse was directly ahead of him. When he reached the stairs, he switched off the light. The door was to his left. He figured it should open upon a large preparation room, where the product was readied for shipping.

He opened the heavy steel door as quietly as he could. The hinges creaked loudly enough to wake the dead, but it smelled like they were long past the point of caring. The horrific stench that rushed out to greet him was overwhelming. His first instinct was to duck back into the dock. It took everything he had to slip through the crack and into the room, where he promptly slid down the wall and into a crouch. He heard a buzzing sound from somewhere off to his right. One that he immediately recognized.

Flies.

He listened for any subtle sounds beneath the drone: footsteps, breathing, the click of a safety being disengaged. Anything that might betray the presence of someone waiting in the darkness.

"I have audio," Gunnar said. "The four hundred sixty-seven megahertz range. Three distinct voices. So far. No verbal identification. No indication of their locations. Are you getting this?"

Mason tapped the microphone twice in acknowledgment. He didn't want to make a sound. They'd agreed upon a system of two taps for yes and one for no to eliminate the possibility of an inadvertent answer in the affirmative.

"Be careful, Mace."

Another two taps and he risked turning on the light.

There was a long stainless-steel table to his left, discolored by oxidation and riddled with scratches. Directly ahead was a wall with a scraped Plexiglas insert, through which he could see the rusted blade of a massive saw jutting upward from another stainless-steel table. There were

enormous bucket sinks to his right. The floor utilized the same polished coating with textured particles for traction. It sloped downward
and away from him, toward a drain with a rusted grate. Everything was
marbled with crusted brown streaks.

He crawled underneath the table, through a maze of slender metal
legs, until he was able to see around the corner to his left and on the
opposite side of the floating wall to his right. There was a closet full of
broken wooden pallets and crates. A conveyor chute ran diagonally
overhead, presumably to the room with the locked door above the
loading bay. Another open doorway directly ahead of him revealed little
more than darkness. Maybe a table and chairs at the very farthest reaches
of the beam. To the right of the opening was another scored Plexiglas
insert, upon which someone had spray-painted a crude face looking back
out. The buzz of flies beckoned from his right, beyond the table with
the saw blades, past the heavy door of an industrial freezer, and through
a pair of swinging doors.

Mason drew in a deep breath. Blew it out slowly.

He crawled out from under the counter and darted diagonally to
his right. Passed the worktable. Grabbed the handle of the freezer door.
Pulled it open. Recoiled from the stench. Clogged drains in the middle
of the floor. Plastic wrap. Hair. Dead mice everywhere. Aluminum
peeling from the walls in sections, revealing the discolored Styrofoam
insulation. Hooks dangling from the ceiling. Clamped hoses where the
compressor had been mounted.

Clear.

He whirled, slipped back out. Faced the swinging doors. Circular
Plexiglas inserts. Flies buzzing beyond. The air seeping through the tattered rubber seal smelled worse than anything he'd encountered in his life.
He shined the beam through the porthole windows. Large, indistinct
shapes cast shifting shadows. He had a pretty good idea what they were
and would have been happy enough to leave the doors closed forever.

"Four voices now," Gunnar said. "Still no names. Two on the second
floor. At least one on the third. No idea where the fourth is. Probably
outside patrolling the perimeter."

Mason tapped his acknowledgment.

"Alejandra's moving into position within range of the building now.

The moment she fires that grenade launcher, whether she hits the target or not, we're out of here. The resulting chaos will only buy you so much time. If there are any survivors, they're going to see through our ruse pretty quickly, and then they'll be coming for you."

Mason wanted to tell Gunnar to get the hell out of there right now. The best he could muster was a double tap. While he was grateful for his old friend's help, he never should have allowed him to get this close. Coordinating their movements from miles away wasn't without risk, but the consequences were nothing compared to what these men would do to Gunnar if they caught him out here. Mason wasn't about to let anything happen to him, though. He'd bring the whole damn place down on their heads first.

He bulled through the swinging doors, low and fast, then rolled to his left. Waited for them to clap shut behind him. Directed the beam straight ahead and through a roiling black cloud of flies, which cast bulbous shadows across the carcasses hanging from hooks all around him. He lowered the light and swept it across the floor, below the bare feet of the victims. There was no one else in the room. Nothing but greasy blobs of decomposition, clumped beneath the suspended bodies and slinking down the slanted floor toward the industrial drains, beside which were the shovels used to unclog them and buckets overflowing with sludge. Four parallel rails crossed the ceiling, automated conveyors from which all of the chains dangled. But these weren't slabs of beef hanging from the hooks. They were human beings. Or at least that's what he thought they were. Or had been, anyway.

Now he understood what the blue-eyed man—this monster who called himself the Hoyl—meant by what he'd said to Alejandra.

There's just one problem we haven't solved. How do we dispose of all the bodies?

The final tumbler fell into place. The breadth and the scope of their plan was beyond anything he could ever have imagined. The culprits weren't merely greedy and self-serving; they were downright evil. These were men who thought themselves lords of the land and everyone around them little more than serfs.

No, worse.

These men thought of everyone else as livestock.

There was precious little left of the bodies hanging before him. They'd been absolved of every last bit of flesh. Only their skeletons remained, and it didn't appear as though it would be long before they disintegrated, too. The bones were eroding in black amoeba-shaped lesions that exposed the intricate matrices of calcium from which they were formed. The victims had been hooked through the holes in the bases of their skulls and the gaps between their ribs. Some had broken or missing teeth, most the color of yellow he attributed to unsanitary drinking water. Others had the kind of cheap dental work with metal crowns and tin fillings that hadn't been used stateside in his lifetime. These were more immigrants, more undocumented aliens like Alejandra, men and women whose lives had served no other purpose than to herald the impending arrival of hell on earth.

There's just one problem we haven't solved.

The bones were covered with a fine layer of pale, almost transparent fuzz from which tiny filaments grew. Some sort of fungal species or bacterial agent that was actively eating the remains. Like the bacteria that cleanup crews released into the ocean to consume the oil after a tanker spill, this species had been engineered to eliminate mankind's waste, only a waste of a different order.

How do we dispose of all the bodies?

It was a biological agent that consumed its host.

The most immediate and pressing problem that surfaced in the wake of any pandemic was how to handle the mass quantity of remains. They couldn't be left to rot in the streets. The bodies needed to be collected and incinerated, at great financial cost and at the expense of significant manpower. They threatened the health of the survivors and created conditions that allowed the virus to breed and mutate. To adapt and combat existing vaccines. They became the reservoirs of mankind's ultimate eradication and the final variable for which to account when designing a biological extinction-level event.

This was the Thorntons' contribution to the endgame. They'd provided the missing piece of a puzzle they'd started putting together on a lot full of dead pigs a century ago. Maybe even before that. This was about more than money, more than power.

It was about complete and utter world domination.

As he walked between the rows of deteriorating skeletons, passing the remains of human beings who had meant less than nothing to the men upstairs, to people like the Thorntons, he realized that the wheels were already in motion. This was the endgame of a plot that had been passed down through generations of evil men with the kind of patience it took not to realize their dreams in their lifetimes, but to sacrifice their life's work so that future generations would fulfill their fantasized destiny of becoming a master race.

"Do it," Mason whispered.

"What?"

"Do it now, Gunnar. Burn this awful place to the ground."

"What did you find?"

Mason stormed through the cooler and into the precooler, where the bodies hanging from the chains hadn't been up there nearly as long. He barely smelled the reek of decomposition or heard the buzzing of flies. He didn't look at the faces that appeared to rot before his very eyes as Victor's vile organism melted the fat beneath their skin or into the hollow sockets where their eyes had once been. He pretended not to hear the wet slapping sounds of flesh dropping to the ground.

His entire world had flipped upside down. People he'd trusted had looked him in the eyes and pretended to be just like him, while deep down they wanted nothing more than to watch him die. The job to which he'd devoted his life was little more than a puppet show performed on a stage where nothing mattered and no one watched. The men with the power had insulated themselves from the rest of the world. They merely sat by, biding their time until technology caught up with their imaginations. Not only were they going to decimate the global population, they were going to use the virus to corner the world's wealth in the process. There would be no power they didn't possess, no government they couldn't control.

Only those who could afford the cure for the pandemic soon to be released would survive. Or was the plan more insidious than that? Had they figured out a way to weed out certain elements? To choose the survivors based on their skills and jobs? Their bloodlines?

He was so angry, he was positively shaking. His vision throbbed. He wanted to lash out and destroy everything around him. He needed to be more than his wife's avenging angel. He was going to have to avenge his entire race.

A sudden shift in the air currents.

The squeak of a chain.

The body beside him moved.

A cold barrel pressed against the base of his skull.

"You so much as twitch and these wetbacks are wearing your brains," a deep voice said from directly behind him.

63

"What's going on in there, Mace?" Gunnar asked.

"Now slowly—slowly—raise both hands where I can see them." The man's voice was muffled. Tinny. Like he was wearing a respirator. "Don't think for a second I won't put a bullet through your head. I don't give a rat's ass who your old man is."

"You do realize these people will kill you, too," Mason said. "That is, if I don't first. And at this point, I'm kind of thinking I might."

"I'd laugh if I didn't think that by doing so I might accidentally pull the trigger of the gun that *I'm* holding to *your* head. You seem to have forgotten that little detail. Now let me see your hands."

"Talk to me, Mason," Gunnar said. "Should we accelerate our timetable?"

"No. I have everything under control."

"Everything under control?" the man said. "What world do you live in? The last thing you're going to see is a bullet exiting your skull between your eyes if you don't raise your goddamn hands!"

Mason held his arms out to his sides, his left hand open, fingers splayed. The Infinity was in his right, the barrel pointing up and away. The beam cast long shadows from the dead bodies, as though their souls were trying to depart their physical forms. He removed his index finger from the trigger and placed it on the side of the under-barrel light, where the man could see it.

"Just give the word," Gunnar said. "Alejandra can put a hole through the side of that building—"

"Like I said, everything's under control."

"Now drop the gun on the floor," the man said.

"It's a custom Infinity. I should set it down gently."

"I said drop the fucking gun!"

"I don't want to break it. Do you have any idea how much love goes into the manufacture of one of these things? I'm going to set it down gently. No sudden moves, right? I'm just going to lean over—"

"Drop it now or—"

Mason switched off the under-barrel light and ducked. The crack of gunfire above his head was deafening. He pivoted on his left foot. Came up hard with the pistol in his right fist. Struck the underside of the man's forearm. He barely heard the second shot over the ringing in his ears. The bullet went high and wide and careened off the ceiling with a spark. The man's pistol clattered to the floor.

"I heard gunfire. I'm making the call whether you like it—"

"Not yet, Gun—"

The man bulled into Mason's chest and lifted him from the ground. He collided with something soft and forgiving. Something that slopped cold sludge down beneath the collar of his jacket. It made a snapping sound as it gave way. He landed squarely on top of it, the full weight of his adversary on his chest. He sensed the blow coming in time to move his head to the side. The dead woman underneath him wasn't so lucky. Dampness spattered his cheek, but he was already rolling to the side. He switched the light back on and swung it toward—

Blunt impact to his wrist. The Infinity skittered away across the floor, spinning the light in circles as it went. He lunged for it, but the man grabbed him by the jacket and pulled him backward. He swatted away the man's arm and popped to his feet.

Gunnar was shouting in his ear, but he couldn't afford the distraction.

He reached for the Sigma under his other arm, but his attacker recognized what he was doing and charged him before he could draw it. He stepped to the right. Drove back into the man's body. Used his momentum to turn him around. Got in close, under his arms. Lifted and pushed—

With a snapping sound and a grunt, something pried the man from his grasp. Mason stumbled forward. Hit the ground. Rolled to the side. Grabbed his pistol. Swung it back in the opposite direction. The beam highlighted the man's twitching form and cast a long, swinging shadow across the wall.

"Answer me, Mace. That's it. I'm giving the order—"

"I'm fine, Gunnar. Like I said, everything's under control."

The man's body twirled from the chain, his feet dangling inches above the floor. He wore a glistening bib of blood. The hook had passed through the back of his neck and out the front at a severe angle. His arms hung limply at his sides. Only the fingers on his left hand continued to move.

Mason stepped closer and waited for the man's face to come around again, but it remained concealed by the spatter of blood he'd coughed out against the inside of the respirator mask.

"Under control? The others are converging on your position!"

The man's body jumped and blood burst from his shoulder. Right in front of Mason's face. He heard footsteps and the clapping sound of the swinging doors behind him and extinguished his light. Darted back into the maze of bodies. Bumped as many of them as he could. The chains squeaked as the bodies swung and spun, masking the sound of his movements. Unfortunately, the racket also prevented him from hearing his pursuer.

"I'm going silent," he whispered. "Stick to the plan. Don't fire the grenade launcher too soon. Give me as much time to find the Hoyl as you can."

Another shot rang out, but the bullet went well wide of him.

Mason stopped and stood perfectly still, listening to the squeaking and squealing slow and then finally stop. Assuming he hadn't lost his bearings, he was at the back of the precooler room with the cooler, where the bodies were further along in the process of decomposition, to his right.

The man hunting him was undoubtedly already moving into containment position to prevent him from advancing deeper into the building. He tried to remember everything he'd seen before he turned off his light. There were four rows of corpses, maybe a dozen per row, separated by five feet in all directions, which meant the room was roughly seventy feet deep and thirty feet wide. If he could pinpoint the man's location and get a clear shot, there was no chance he'd miss at such close range.

Unfortunately, his adversary knew this place better than Mason did. He knew the sounds, the layout. He also knew where the light switches were. If he turned them on, he'd expose Mason, but he'd reveal himself in the process. The whole confrontation would boil down to who could shoot the other first, and Mason liked his odds. It was a risk the other man didn't have to take, though, not when he could utilize the darkness and his familiarity with his surroundings to his advantage, which meant he would likely make the first move.

Mason was rewarded for his patience with the sound of soft footfalls approaching.

Slowly.

Cautiously.

The faint squeak of a chain.

The patter of fluid dripping to the floor.

Mason was behind the next-to-last body in the second row. One row to his right and he was in the cooler. Two rows to his left and he was cornered. The fact that his adversary wasn't filling the room with bullets suggested he was being herded toward a second man, who was already attempting to outflank him.

He decided to test the theory.

In one swift motion, he lunged right. Shoved the body beside him in the first row. Ducked back.

The man fired a single shot, which struck the body hard enough to knock it off the hook. The discharge from the barrel revealed him to be maybe thirty feet away and between the first and second rows.

Mason exploited the thunderous echo. He pushed the body in front of him, the one in the first row to his right, and the one behind him, then sprinted back into the corner behind the fourth row. The chains screeched for several seconds before twirling back into place.

He wasn't the only one who'd had that idea.

Bodies swung to his left, near where the first man had been when he fired. Presumably, he intended to use the distraction to move closer to where he'd last seen Mason, assuming he was going to make a break for the cooler rather than retreating deeper into the maze of corpses.

Mason concentrated and listened for any sound that would betray the location of the second man. He thought he heard a footstep diagonally to his left. And another diagonally to his right. The soft creak of a chain.

He inched forward until he was right up against the body in the corner. A naked male. Shorter and stockier than he was. Also hairier, apparently. He had an impressive gut, which—hopefully—would be big enough to serve his purposes.

"You have two in the room with you, Mace. Another coordinating their movements from the second floor. That accounts for all four, but I can't confirm there aren't more."

Mason tapped his confirmation.

It wouldn't be long before the men discovered his deception.

He slipped off his right glove and threw it across the room, between the two men.

Shots rang out from both directions at once and he marked his hunters' positions by the twin flares of discharge.

He pulled himself up onto the dead man's back, wrapped his legs around his midsection, and clung to him around the neck. The smell was nauseating. As was the feeling of the dead man's flesh shifting on his bones. The added weight minimized the squealing of the chain.

The echo of gunfire faded.

Mason pulled off his other glove with his teeth, quietly drew his Sigma with his left hand, and extended both of his arms so they crossed in front of the dead man's chin. Flexed his biceps against the victim's jaw to brace himself. Focused on where he'd seen the two simultaneous bursts of muzzle flare. Aligned the Infinity in his right hand with the man to his left. The Sigma in his left with the man to his right.

A loud cracking sound and he dropped half an inch. Maybe the hook was up to the task, but the dead man's bones weren't.

The footsteps immediately ceased.

It was now or never.

"Don't shoot!" he shouted.

The men fired at the exact same time.

Mason aimed at the flashes of discharge and pulled both triggers.

Bullets struck the dead man's gut. The force of the impact knocked Mason from his perch. He hit the ground a heartbeat before the corpse landed on top of him. Rolled out from underneath it. Rose to a crouch, with both pistols aimed into the room.

Listened.

Silence and darkness.

No sound. No movement.

Nothing but the thudding of his heartbeat.

Then a sound he didn't recognize. Not at first. A chuckling, gurgling sound.

He allowed himself to breathe.

It was the sound of fluid trickling into a floor drain.

Mason turned on the under-barrel light and swept it across the ground, below the suspended feet. He'd hit the man to his left with a lucky shot high to the forehead. His body was propped against the wall, a stream of blood rolling toward the drain between his boots. He wore a half-mask respirator. His eyes were blue, but not the shade Mason was looking for.

"Tap if you're alive," Gunnar said.

He tapped twice and walked toward the precooler.

"All communication on the channels I'm monitoring has ceased, which means I can no longer confirm the location of the fourth man."

Mason tuned Gunnar out and focused on tracking the man to his right.

The skeletal remains dangling from the chains cast shadows reminiscent of a forest in the dead of winter. There was a smear of blood on the floor. He followed it between the rows until it led him to a man lying facedown on the floor, dragging himself forward with his left hand and right elbow. Rich black arterial blood flowed from somewhere underneath him, only to be smudged by his exertions. Mason stepped over him and stood on his right wrist. He didn't have to grind his heel very hard to convince the man to drop his gun. He kicked it away into the darkness.

"Roll over," Mason said.

The man made a gasping sound and flopped over onto his back. Blood positively gushed from the inside of his right hip, near his groin, where the builet had clipped his femoral artery. He put his trembling hand over the wound, but it just vanished into the blood. His wide eyes above his respirator confirmed that he understood the nature of his injury and the gravity of his situation.

"The man with the blue eyes. The one who calls himself the Hoyl. Where is he?"

The man mumbled something incomprehensible through the respirator. Mason tore off the mask and revealed the rictus of pain on his face.

"Tell me where he is!"

He looked up and to his right and Mason had his answer.

This was where the Fischer bloodline ended.

Right here. Right now.

Mason turned his back on the dying man and headed deeper into the building.

"You guys ready to do this, Gunnar?"

"Everything's set."

"And we're still on schedule?"

"Close enough."

"Then let's torch this place."

He kicked open the swinging doors to the killing floor and went through with both guns raised.

64

The rail above Mason wound back to his right, past several industrial-size washbasins. There were maybe half a dozen corpses hanging from the chains. They were so recently deceased that it almost looked like they were sleeping. Their skin was waxy and blood dripped from their fingertips and toes. Their chins and upper chests were freckled with scarlet from coughing so violently. He had to get closer to see the black lesions where the microbes responsible for their decomposition were already eating through the tissue. Those whose eyes remained open demonstrated petechial hemorrhaging, an indication of asphyxiation. In conjunction with the blue lips and bloody sputum, there was no doubt they'd experienced some sort of acute respiratory crisis.

All these people had wanted was a shot at freedom, not to be subjected to a deadly virus and for every trace of their existence to be dissolved down a drain in this awful place, simply to prove the efficacy of Victor's awful decomposition-accelerating microbe.

On the other side of them was a wall made of bars, between which he could see an enormous oxidized metal structure with what looked like a dull guillotine suspended above the front end. The neck crush of the knocking pen. The pen itself was maybe six feet higher than the rest of the room. At the rear end was an iron door with a rusted chain and pulley system, which must have opened upon the cattle chute. That would make the recessed room beside it the bleeding pit, above which the conveyor rail system originated. The drains set into the floor were a full foot wide and the crusted line of discoloration on the bases of the surrounding walls indicated the blood had generally remained about four inches deep.

Mason passed through the inspection room and found two open doorways. One had an eight-inch concrete lip to contain the reservoir of blood, while the other opened upon a room that had no rails, but plenty of drains. He imagined men in knee-high rubber boots shoveling mounds of offal through the rusted hatch at the back, which looked like it would take a blowtorch to open. There was only one way to go from here.

He stepped over the lip and found a staircase at the end of a short corridor. The concrete steps were worn smooth and the cinder-block walls were covered with graffiti that demonstrated more creativity than anatomical knowledge. To his left, several doors opened onto exterior platforms overlooking the races and crowd pens. He paused at the bend, pressed his back against the wall, and listened.

If he were up there and had just heard his entire team die, he would take up a post at the top of the stairs and shoot down at anyone coming up.

He rolled around, popped up, and aimed his light at the top of the staircase.

Nothing.

Unless there was another way out he didn't know about, Mason had to believe the Hoyl was still up there somewhere. And he had a feeling his nemesis was looking forward to this confrontation every bit as much as he was.

But he still couldn't confirm that the Hoyl was the only one left.

"Any more radio traffic?" Mason whispered.

He waited.

No response.

He thought he'd lost the connection until he heard a faint crackle of static.

"Gunnar? Can you hear me?"

He tapped the mic to make sure he was transmitting. The blasted stairwell was probably interfering with his reception.

Mason turned off the light and crept upward slowly, silently, keeping close to the wall. He heard the soft whistle of the wind across the side of the building and the distant clanging of a broken roof vent. He paused again near the top and waited. Part of him was dying to check his watch; the other part simply didn't care. At five o'clock on the nose, Alejandra was going to use the gift Ramses had given him to blast this place into oblivion. Whether he killed the Hoyl or the Hoyl killed him, that monster would never leave this building alive. Mason had seen to that.

He dove from the top stair and slid across the floor on his side, clicking on his light as he went. The beam revealed a large room that had once served as office space. And maybe a locker room for the supervisory staff. Now it was something else entirely. The walls were lined with enormous silver vats. Stainless steel. Sparkling new. The kind with valves and hand wheels he associated with microbreweries. There were all sorts of digital readouts and access terminals. Temperature and pressure gauges. Clipboards hung beside them, whatever had once been clipped to them now gone. Only one still held a single scrap of yellow notebook paper, maybe a third of a page, torn diagonally.

There had to be more than twenty vats, he realized. Pipes lined the walls. There was a long table in the center of the room, which appeared to have been hurriedly cleared off. Broken glass glimmered from the surrounding floor.

Mason shined the light on the scrap of paper. Several handwritten lines had been crossed out. They appeared to be equations. No . . . chemical formulas. The one remaining looked like a jumble of numbers and letters. $[(CH_3)_2CHO]CH_3P(O)F + CCl_2FNO_2$. He mentally rehearsed it for later recall, in case it was important.

The room reeked of chemicals. It was a major improvement over the smell downstairs, though.

There were two doors off either side of the room beneath tangles of pipes. He could see a mattress on the floor through the first doorway to his left. A quick peek with the light revealed a refrigerated unit beside a locker freezer. Neither made a sound. Across the room to the right was a row of portable generators and tanks of fuel. All of them were silent and still. He thought about the kind of racket they would have made when they were on.

They'd been turned off before Mason arrived.

He looked at the hurriedly cleared table and the trashed room. The pages torn from the clipboards. Thought about the first attacker waiting for him in the cooler. Heard Gunnar's words.

This is too easy, Mace.

They'd known he was coming.

"Gunnar! Get out of there! Grab Alejandra and go! Now!"

Mason sprinted back toward the stairs. He'd been tricked into going as far into the building as he could go. The only exit he knew of for sure was on the opposite side of the slaughterhouse.

"Damn it, Gunnar! Acknowledge!"

He leaped from the top of the stairs. Hit the landing. Careened from the wall. His light swung wildly as he regained his balance. Rounded the landing. Stumbled down to the main floor.

"Acknowledge!"

The doorways flew past to his right. He hurdled the concrete lip. The Hoyl was going to burn this building like he had all the others. He'd lured Mason inside to take him out at the same time.

He burst into the inspection room, and suddenly there was a bright light shining directly into his eyes from across the chamber. He matched it with his own and squeezed the trig—

A muffled grunting sound.

High-pitched.

Female.

He eased the pressure off the trigger and advanced slowly, his aim affixed to the source.

"Identify yourself!" he shouted.

The grunts became squeals at the sound of his voice.

Frightened. Panicked.

Desperate.

They were coming from directly past and to the right of the light, which prevented him from seeing more than the vague outline of the upper portion of the knocking pen. There was no response other than what now sounded like someone crying into a pillow. The light remained static. No one could possibly hold it that still.

Mason moved to his right.

The beam didn't follow. It remained directed at the doorway from which he'd emerged. He risked directing his light away from the other one so he could better see into the surrounding darkness.

"Jesus," he gasped, and broke into a sprint. "Alejandra!"

65

Mason ran toward the metal ladder leading up to the floor of the knocking pen, where the operator would have stood with his captive-bolt gun, waiting for the next cow in line to stick its head through the neck crush. A flashlight was duct-taped to a chair in such a way as to momentarily blind him when he burst from the hallway. Behind it was a steel tube. Maybe a foot and a half long and shaped like a cannon, only the end facing away from the pen had a plunger rather than a fuse. The plunger had been drawn back five or six inches and attached to a cord that ran underneath the seat, and then in the opposite direction to where Alejandra held it between her bared teeth. The business end of the captive-bolt gun was nuzzled against her forehead.

The plunger cocked the weapon. If she released the cord from between her teeth, the bolt would more than stun her as it would a cow;

it would explode through her much thinner cranium and impale her frontal lobe.

Her throat rested on the bottom edge of the neck crush, with the upper, guillotinelike portion hovering mere inches inches above her spine. It had been designed to hold in place an animal weighing thousands of pounds. If it didn't break her neck when it fell, it would undoubtedly collapse her trachea and cut off the blood supply to her head. That is, if she was still able to maintain her grip on the cord with her teeth.

He couldn't see her body through the side of the pen. Not until he was halfway up the rungs.

She was kneeling on the floor with her arms behind her back, clinging to a rusted chain that ran up to a pulley, then down to the upper half of the crush. If she released the chain, the crush would fall. Tears streamed down her face, even from the milky eye on the scarred side. She was trembling so badly that he was amazed she'd been able to hold on to the cord at all. Her arms were pulled way too far backward and upward from sockets that hadn't been designed with that motion in mind.

She could let go of either at any moment.

Mason holstered his Sigma and approached the chair cautiously.

"It's okay." He tried to make his voice sound reassuring. "I'll get you out of this."

She whimpered and closed her eyes even tighter.

The bolt gun was the more immediate threat. It *would* kill her. No doubt about it. The problem was that any diminishment of the tension on the cord would cause the spring-loaded mechanism to jerk the cord from her teeth, strike the firing pin, and cause the .22 blank cartridge to propel the bolt half an inch through her brow.

"You're going to be all right. Don't worry."

Mason wasn't sure if he was saying it for her benefit or his own.

He pressed down on the metal tube with his right hand to hold it in place. It had been affixed to the seat of the chair with a single piece of duct tape, which had already begun to peel as a consequence of the downward force being applied to the plunger.

Alejandra whimpered as the pressure against her forehead increased.

Mason gripped the thin metal pole of the plunger with his left hand.

It was cold and greasy in his palm, which was roughly the same width as the distance between the plunger and its destination. He closed his fist around it, then turned and spoke to her as slowly and calmly as he could.

"We do this on the count of three. When I say three, you turn your head to the side and duck out of there. One."

She made a sobbing sound.

"Two."

He drew a deep breath and blew it out slowly.

"Three!"

In one swift motion, he jerked the captive-bolt gun upward and away from her forehead. The tape made a tearing sound. The plunger bit into the muscle on the pinkie side of his hand. The gap at the base of the tube lacerated the meat beside his thumb. The pressure was astounding, far greater than he'd expected. It was a miracle she'd been able to hold it for as long as she had.

Mason felt the warmth of his own blood in his palm, the pressure grinding his knuckles. He jerked his left hand away the second he was clear. The plunger made a snapping sound, then the resounding bang of the .22 blank. The bolt fired with enough force to nearly punch through the neck crush as it started to fall.

Alejandra barely ducked out from beneath it in time. The guillotine slammed down on her hair, halting her momentum and causing her to cry out.

He reached over the top, pulled the chain, and raised the crush just far enough for her to pull her hair free. Again, he was surprised by how much strength it would have required to hold it for so long.

The trap was ingenious. She could have been either shot in the head or decapitated. Likely both. Were it not for her almost superhuman desire to survive, the trap would surely have done just that, and right before his very eyes. But other than to demonstrate the Hoyl's cruelty, what possible purpose could it—?

It slowed him down.

The Hoyl had used it as a distraction to buy himself time to escape, but he couldn't have gotten far.

"Which way did he go?" Mason whispered.

Alejandra peeled the flashlight from the chair and directed the beam between two of the recent victims and onto the swinging doors that separated them from the maze of bodies.

"Where's Gunnar?"

"I do not—" She sputtered blood. She closed her hand over her mouth and shook her head. Had she been forced to hold that cord any longer, her teeth would probably have been ripped right out of her gums.

He tapped the microphone several times to make sure he heard the echo of an open line.

Nothing.

The connection had been severed.

Mason handed his Sigma to Alejandra, turned the Infinity's beam on the doors, and jumped down from the platform.

It was time to finish this.

He kicked the doors and stepped inside. One of the bodies at the edge of his light's reach was still swaying, ever so slightly. He passed through the human corridor. Stepped over the bodies on the floor. Rounded the corner and blew through the packaging room. His footsteps made a splashing sound. Some sort of chemical was leaking from the conveyor belt leading up to the office. He shouldered open the door to the loading dock. Swung his beam across the interior in one broad stroke.

The Hoyl could have been hiding in any number of places. Behind the ruins of the staircase or the heaps of construction supplies. Up on the ledge supporting the elevated office. Behind the piles of construction supplies. But Mason didn't see him as the hiding kind.

He was finally beginning to understand how the Hoyl worked.

He was the kind of monster who lured helpless victims into his lair and took perverse pleasure in torturing them. As his father had before him. And his, as well. It was all he knew. His life was the perpetuation of an illusion, the fulfillment of the sick destiny those who came before him had spent their entire lives imagining. Planning. Executing.

If the Hoyl had Gunnar, then he intended to use him as a shield to cover his escape or as a token to buy his freedom. And if he managed to escape, Gunnar was dead.

Mason led Alejandra down the stairs from the loading dock.

And stopped dead in his tracks.

The chemical smell was stronger in here. Unmistakable now that it was no longer competing with the stench of the corpses.

A sound. So soft, he'd almost missed it.

Fluid. Dripping from some unknown height. Like rain flowing over the lip of a gutter.

Mason recalled the fluid running down the conveyor on the other side of the wall.

He turned and raised his light toward the elevated platform. Ribbons of liquid spiraled down the support posts. Rivulets drained from the ledge. He lowered his light to the ground and a rainbow formed in the reflection on the fluid.

"No," Mason whispered.

He whirled, grabbed Alejandra by the wrist, and sprinted toward the hatch.

The sound of fluid splashing onto the concrete became louder. The entire supervisory office was probably rigged to explode. If it fell, it would bring the rest of the building down with it.

There was no handle on the hatch. Only a notch where a crowbar could be inserted to raise the front edge from the floor.

He caught a spark of light from the corner of his eye.

They weren't going to make it.

A whooshing sound behind him. The light grew brighter. Searing heat on his neck.

Mason dashed back across the room and underneath the suspended landing. Liquid fire rained down all around him. He grabbed a metal railing from the fallen staircase and hurried back to the hatch.

Suddenly, it was as bright as day. Acrid chemical smoke swirled around them. The air rushed past them to feed the insatiable flames.

He stabbed the leading edge of the rail down into the notch in the hatch.

A wall of flames rose at his back. A crashing sound as a section of the roof fell, throwing off a cloud of glowing cinders. A roiling cloud of smoke overtook them as Mason leveraged the hatch up as high as he could.

"Go!"

Alejandra crawled through the gap. Once she was inside, she turned around and braced the hatch on her shoulders. She was coughing so hard that she wouldn't be able to hold it for very long.

A deafening crash. A churning mass of embers enveloped him.

Mason took a step back and dove headfirst beneath the hatch.

The air turned to fire around him as he tumbled down into the earth.

PART VI

The individual is handicapped by coming face-to-face with a conspiracy so monstrous he cannot believe it exists. The American mind simply has not come to a realization of the evil which has been introduced into our midst. It rejects even the assumption that human creatures could espouse a philosophy which must ultimately destroy all that is good and decent.

—J. Edgar Hoover, *The Elks Magazine* (1956)

66

Mason tumbled down the stairs and barely caught himself before he spilled out into the open. He stayed low and against the wall, hoping Alejandra would follow his lead. They weren't even halfway down when a faint light washed across the landing below them and he heard the hum of an electric motor.

The tram.

He hurdled the stairs three at a time, then jumped to the landing. The moment his feet hit the ground, he rolled to the side and rose with his gun pointed toward the sound. He caught a glimpse of a dim light through the rear window of the tram before it abruptly went dark. Twin scarlet taillights bloomed underneath it.

They couldn't let it leave without them or it would be miles away by the time they reached the first surface access hatch. The Hoyl could disembark at any stop along the way and they'd never find him again. And if he had Gunnar . . .

This was Mason's only shot and he knew it.

The headlights burst from the front car and the tram started to roll.

He holstered his gun and sprinted toward the taillights. The rear of the tram was little more than one large rectangular window with a fifteen-degree slope. If anyone on board decided to look back through it, he'd be impossible to miss.

The tram rapidly gained speed.

Now or never.

He took three long strides and launched himself from his right foot.

His chest struck the Plexiglas window. He grabbed for the roof. Caught hold of a narrow rail. Squeezed it as hard as he could. Wedged the toes of his boots into the seam beneath the window.

Alejandra kept pace, but she wouldn't be able to do so much longer. The intonation of the motor climbed an octave and the whole train lurched forward.

Mason secured his grip with his right hand. Reached behind him with his left.

She lunged before he was ready. Hit the window. Her hands slid right off the rooftop.

One chance.

He grabbed for her with his left hand and caught her by the sleeve of her coat. Her hand tightened around his wrist as the tram accelerated. She flew out over the open air behind him. It was all he could do to hang on.

The walls of the tunnel rocketed past with a whooshing sound.

The strain on his shoulders was tremendous. He gritted his teeth. Squeezed his eyes shut. Prayed to hang on. The fingers on his right hand started to slip.

Alejandra reached for the tram and missed. She swung almost all the way to the wall and nearly took Mason with her. He shouted in agony. Pulled her toward him with every last ounce of strength he possessed.

She grabbed his waistband. Released his hand. He barely caught the rail on the roof with his left hand before she transferred the entirety of her weight to his back. He wasn't going to be able to hold on to the tram for very long.

The ferocious wind generated by the train's passage drowned out the whine of the engine.

Alejandra braced her feet on the window ledge. Wrapped one arm around Mason's waist. Reached for the roof with the other. Closed her trembling fingers around the thin rail. Pressed her body against the window beside him. Her long hair flared on the slipstream.

The dark mouth of a bypass tunnel appeared to their right with a sudden shift in airflow that nearly pried Mason from his perch. He hadn't even readjusted his grip before the other end whipped past.

Motion through the window. A diffuse glow. Distant.

The beam of a flashlight took form in the next car up, silhouetting the metal-post frames and chain-link walls of the cages inside. Mason detected the hint of movement through the windows between the cars. If whoever controlled the beam shined it straight back at them, he'd have them dead to rights.

Each of the four cars was self-contained and didn't allow passengers to move from one to the next like on a train, but with little more than empty cages in between, there'd be nothing to prevent the beam from reaching them. Or a fusillade of bullets, for that matter.

Alejandra recognized the danger and started to climb. She planted one foot in the middle of the glass, then the other, and the next thing Mason knew he was watching her shoes vanish over the crest, with the ceiling hurtling past above her.

The man directed his light from the third car diagonally into the fourth. The light splashed across the tunnel wall to Mason's left, then to his right.

No time to lose.

He braced one foot against the glass. Hauled himself up and over. The wind buffeted him in the face. Nearly swept him off. He pressed his palms to the flat roof. Pulled himself forward. The beam flashed across the wall below Alejandra, limning her silhouette to his left, then his heels behind him, and finally the wall to his right.

The arched ceiling whipped past mere feet above his back. An access chute announced itself overhead with a howl of wind.

They were heading north-northwest, with the station under downtown Greeley maybe thirteen miles away. The end of the line was seven miles farther, inside the new corporate headquarters of Global Allied Biotechnology and Pharmaceuticals on the secured AgrAmerica lot.

Another bypass tunnel flew past without warning. The shift in air currents caught Mason off guard and he slid backward. Barely caught the rail lining the top of the rear window with his toes. Hugged the roof. The other end of the bypass nearly dislodged him.

Alejandra slid down beside him. He could only imagine how much harder it was for her to hang on with as little as she weighed.

Assuming they were traveling at roughly thirty-five miles an hour, they would hit the station under Greeley in just over twenty minutes. The GABP complex twelve minutes later. They couldn't still be on the roof when the tram arrived, or they'd be clearly visible from all sides.

Mason scooted closer to Alejandra, whose hair concealed the majority of her face, until his lips touched her ear. Her eyes were closed and her nose was pressed flat to the metal. He had to shout to be heard.

"We can't be up here when the train stops! We'll be too easy to see!"

"You cannot be suggesting what I think you are!"

"Like any other vehicle, this thing will go through a standard deceleration progression as the transmission shifts down through the gears! The moment we feel it start to slow, we need to be ready to go!"

"We will be killed!"

"I felt three distinct gears when it was accelerating! We have to jump when we feel it shift down for the second time! If we wait any longer than that, we won't be able to put enough distance between us and whoever's waiting for the tram to arrive!"

"Just step off?"

"Bend your knees and tuck your head in your arms! Try to form a ball and roll to dispel your momentum! And stay clear of that rail!"

"We will still be going too fast!"

She was probably right, but now that he finally had the Hoyl in his sights, not even the laws of physics could stand in his way.

67

Mason tried not to think about Gunnar. The Hoyl could be doing horrible things to him right underneath them at this very moment. Or he could already be dead. Mason hoped his old friend had simply lost his signal and was searching in vain for them through the flaming ruins of the slaughterhouse, but his gut told him that wasn't the case. Gunnar was likely in the first car with the driver or in the third with whoever wielded the flashlight. With a minimum of two hostiles inside the tram and Lord only knew how many waiting for it at its final destination, every possible rescue scenario Mason ran through his head ended with Gunnar in a body bag.

He heard the change in the intonation of the engine a heartbeat before the wall fell away beside him. The tarps covering the building on the southeastern corner of the Greeley station snapped and flagged. The ornate facade of the building below the feed and grain store blew past. Then they were gone, falling rapidly into the darkness.

Mason knew where they were going now. Beyond all doubt.

His heartbeat was already racing. No matter how he envisioned disembarking from the train, he ended up broken and bleeding on the concrete. He had to start thinking beyond the moment of impact and start planning for what he was going to do once he stood up and brushed himself off. There were really only two options: He could backtrack to the access chute that would take him up to the surface outside of the perimeter or he could go forward and face whatever lay in wait for him. Force the confrontation. The element of surprise was just about the only thing he had going for him.

If he failed, the consequences would be catastrophic. He was now the only one standing in the way of the release of a global pandemic and a potential extinction-level event.

He cleared his mind as the walls blurred past. Focused on accepting the fact that one of his best friends was probably dead. Readied himself to potentially take the lives of his wife's brother and father. Reminded himself that he didn't currently have his badge, so the law was no longer on his side. There was only black and white. Right and wrong. And live or die, he would do so on the side of the right.

The motor lowered an octave. He felt the slight lurch as it stepped down a gear.

Mason turned and saw Alejandra's wide eyes staring at him through the scarlet glare. He nodded to her and pushed himself backward until his legs dangled over the open air. Continued to slide until his whole lower half was draped across the rear window. Farther still and he was able to snag the toes of his boots on the ledge.

The walls whipped past at an obscene rate of speed. A glance down at the ground nearly robbed him of his resolve.

Alejandra slid down beside him and closed her eyes.

Another soft jolt as the tram slowed again.

Mason looked over at Alejandra, tried for something resembling a reassuring smile, and let go.

He became weightless. A human projectile flying through the dark tunnel. He caught a flash of the taillights leaving him behind. Wrapped his head in his arms. His heels struck first. He skipped like a stone. Hit the ground hard. Took the brunt of the impact on his left shoulder. Bounced and rolled and finally caromed from the wall of the tunnel and skidded to a halt on his side.

A shadow knifed through his peripheral vision before the taillights faded altogether, sealing him in darkness. He felt like he'd been dragged across a cheese grater while being beaten with baseball bats. But he was thankful for the pain; it proved that he was still alive.

A moan from the darkness across from him confirmed that he wasn't the only one.

"Are you all right?" he whispered.

He waited. Alejandra didn't sound entirely certain when she finally replied.

"Yes."

A distant squeal from far to the north. Brakes. A quarter, maybe half a mile at the most.

Mason drew his Infinity and struggled to his feet.

"Can you walk?"

A shuffling, scraping sound.

"Yes," she said, again with a tone of uncertainty.

He followed the sound of her voice, stepped over the rail, and felt for her in the pitch-black tunnel. When he eventually found her hand, it was slick with blood. He pressed the butt of the Infinity into her palm and aligned her index finger with the switch on the under-barrel light.

"Head south from here. Go as far as you can before you turn on the light. You'll come to a ladder. Climb all the way up the chute. You'll find yourself in a small structure outside the perimeter fence." Mason removed his cell phone from the inside breast pocket of his jacket and closed it in her other hand. "Can you remember a number?"

"We should stay together. You will need my help."

"If I don't make it, someone else has to stop these people. You'll be the only one left who can do so. Now, tell me you can remember a phone number."

"Yes," she whispered, this time with more conviction.

Mason recited Ramses' cell phone number and made her repeat it back to him. He hoped to God his old friend had really been heading in their direction when he'd last spoken to him.

"Call Ramses and tell him the situation. He'll help you. I promise. Then find someplace safe to hide. If I don't call you on this phone in one hour, that means I'm not going to. Ramses will protect you until you can meet with my father, Senator J. R. Mason. Tell him everything. Outside of Gunnar and Ramses, he's the only other person on the planet I trust. Make sure he knows the FBI is compromised. He'll know what to do from there."

"Here." She made a rustling sound. "Take this."

Mason accepted the cold butt of his Sigma. It was like shaking hands with an old friend.

He made Alejandra repeat Ramses' number one final time. If he didn't survive this, he was counting on his old friend to finish it for him. Ramses might be a lot of things, but he was no coward. He would follow through, regardless of the consequences.

"Be careful," Mason whispered, and squeezed her hand in the darkness. "Remember. One hour. If I don't make that phone call, you get as far away from here as you can."

He released her hand and struck off toward his fate.

"When you find the man with the blue eyes, you must not hesitate." Her soft footsteps dissipated behind him. "This time make certain he is dead."

Mason jacked his clip, counted the bullets, and quietly slid it home again.

"There's nothing in this world I'd like more," he whispered, and advanced into the darkness.

68

Mason stayed low and against the wall. He knew he was getting close when he smelled fresh construction: sawdust, cement, and oil. The light started as a pinprick and grew progressively larger as he approached. He heard voices, but not clearly enough to make out the words. They sounded hollow thanks to the strange and distorted acoustics from the four-story courtyard beyond the dark tram, which sealed off the majority of the opening to the building, leaving little more than a horseshoe of light around it.

He had to believe the men inside the building thought he was either dead or miles away, but he couldn't afford to take anything for granted. They'd walked blindly into the trap at Steerman's and barely made it out alive. There was no way of knowing what horrors awaited him ahead.

The shadows faded by degree. It wasn't long before he could clearly see his own outline, not much longer still until he would become fully exposed. He ducked to his left and used the tram to conceal his final approach.

Mason paused and listened to the voices. They'd grown more distant even as he drew nearer. He made a break for the gap between the third and fourth cars. He could see just a hint of the open courtyard through the windows of the cars ahead of him.

No sign of movement.

He heard the footsteps. Farther away now. The voices were abruptly cut off by the sound of a closing door.

The lights snapped off with a resounding thud.

The resulting darkness was suffocating.

Mason waited several minutes, peeling apart the layers of silence, listening for anything to betray the presence of sentries inside the complex. He stayed low and sprinted toward the front of the train. Crouched beside the lead car. Listened to the echo of his footsteps fade into oblivion.

He mentally re-created the floor plan. Stairs diagonally across the courtyard to his right, leading up to the ground floor. To the left from there was a side entrance, alarmed from the outside. The main entrance was somewhere to the right of the landing, near where he'd last heard the voices.

The tram couldn't have arrived more than ten minutes before he had, but that was more than enough time to get Gunnar out of the building and into a car bound for any where in the world.

If they hadn't already killed him.

Mason sprinted out into the courtyard and veered toward the stairs.

The lights came on with an echoing boom, blinding him.

He shielded his eyes.

A slow clapping sound.

Clap.

Clap.

Clap.

"Bravo, Special Agent Mason." It was the voice that haunted his dreams. "Or should I say *former* Special Agent Mason."

A clattering sound. Metallic.

Mason turned toward the source of the voice and aimed his pistol at the silhouette emerging from behind a bank of spotlights, their blinding beams directed at the center of the circular courtyard. Right at him. There were three other sets. One to his left, another to his right, and a fourth at his back. He couldn't tell if anyone lurked in the shadows behind them.

A droplet of fluid struck the ground beside him with a wet slap.

"I was beginning to wonder if you weren't who we hoped you would be after all." His voice sounded mechanical due to the respirator he still wore over his mouth and nose. "I'm delighted to be proved right. Now put that gun away before someone gets hurt."

"I don't think so. That's kind of the whole reason I brought it."

Another droplet streaked across his peripheral vision.

"I wasn't referring to either of us."

There was a rattling, clanking sound as the Hoyl finally stepped out into the light. In his right hand, he held a long length of chain, which stretched up into the rafters. He wore a broad-brimmed bowler hat and a long-tailed black suit jacket over a silk vest and a black tie. Mason locked eyes with his adversary. Those blue eyes. They were the same ones he'd seen through the smoke and the flies in the quarry at the moment of his partner's death and in the reflection on his wife's sunglasses mere minutes before hers.

He sighted his Sigma right between them and tightened his finger on the trigger.

A droplet spattered the shoulder of his jacket with a soft *plat*.

"You really don't want to do that," the Hoyl said.

"I'm pretty sure I do. In fact, I've been looking forward to doing this for a long time."

The Hoyl shook the chain and droplets rained down all around them a heartbeat later.

"The problem would be that if you did, I'd let go of this chain," he said. "And while I'm confident in your abilities as a marksman, I question how well you can . . . catch."

He drew out the last word for effect.

Mason looked down at the ground, at the crimson droplets spattered on the concrete.

And then it hit him.

The Hoyl had beaten him again.

"That's right." The monster's eyes narrowed as he read Mason's expression. "Go ahead. Look up. I'll give you one glimpse for free."

Mason leaned back and looked way up toward the ceiling. The chain led at an angle from the Hoyl's hand to a pulley on the second level, and then to another one all the way up in the darkness, where even the blinding lights couldn't reach. And from it hung an inverted body, strung up by its heels.

Gunnar.

His arms dangled toward the ground. He slowly twirled one way, then back in the other. A droplet of blood materialized about halfway between them and seemed to take forever to hit the ground at Mason's feet.

When he looked up from the spatter of his old friend's blood, it was with sheer and unadulterated hatred in his eyes.

The Hoyl gave the chain a shake just to remind him of the consequences of doing what he was thinking.

"You're not going to be needing that gun." He nodded and Mason heard footsteps from his right. A small hand in a leather glove closed around the barrel. A woman's hand. She held on to it until he finally let go.

The Hoyl stepped forward, trailing the end of the chain behind him on the ground like a snake. He gave a slight bow and his hat rolled down his arm into his hand. His blond hair grew in tufts from his scarred scalp. He reseated his hat and accepted the pistol from the woman Mason recognized from his meeting with Paul. Ava Dietrich. The woman with the platinum hair and taut calves. Her face was devoid of expression.

"You can all come out," the Hoyl said. "He can't hurt you now."

Mason kept his eyes on the Hoyl as the others emerged from where they'd been hiding behind the trailers upon which the light assemblies had been mounted. A single set of footsteps behind him. Another set to his left. A third to his right, from the shadows where the woman had originally been. The men to either side still wore their security uniforms. He recognized them from the guard shack at the front gate of the Agr-America complex, just like the man he'd killed at Fairacre.

Dietrich retreated back into the shadows as two more figures emerged from behind the Hoyl and stepped into the light. Two men Mason would have recognized anywhere.

Victor strode forward with his head held high and a smirk on his face. It was the expression of a man who'd known from the start of the game that the outcome had never been in doubt.

Paul stayed a step behind his son. His expression was one of a sleepwalker awakening and finding himself in unfamiliar surroundings.

Mason looked from Paul to Victor, and finally directly at the Hoyl when he spoke.

"Make no mistake. I'm going to kill you. Each and every one of you."

"Perhaps one day," the Hoyl said, "but today is not that day."

69

"Quit playing with him and get this over with," Victor said.

The Hoyl stepped forward and shook the chain. More droplets of Gunnar's blood pattered on the ground. He looked down at Mason's Sigma in his hand, turned it over, and shook his head disapprovingly.

"A primitive weapon. Ugly and loud. Point and squeeze. *Bang!* Someone's dead. It's too easy. Your enemies are here one second, gone the next. They simply cease to exist."

"Maybe I'm missing something, but I was under the impression that was the whole point," Mason said.

"Have you used this archaic instrument recently?"

"My custom Sigma? Yeah. I used it to make several of your friends 'simply cease to exist.'"

"Friends? Friends are a liability, Special Agent Mason. I believe your current predicament proves as much. I have no doubt that had you elected to let Mr. Backstrom fall, you could have killed me and at least two of the others. Maybe all of us. Am I mistaken?"

Mason didn't reply. The Hoyl was trying to get inside his head, to keep him off balance, to prevent him from realizing that he still had a modicum of control over the situation. If his nemesis wanted him dead, he would have killed Mason the moment he hesitated to shoot. There was something the Hoyl needed from him, but for the life of him, he couldn't figure out what.

"What about the lovely Ms. Vigil? Pray tell. Even when you realized that the building was about to turn to flames around you, did you attempt to save her? Or was it already too late? Was it the sound of the blank firing that drew you to her bleeding corpse? Did you risk your own life in a futile attempt to save a woman you barely knew?"

Mason kept his expression studiously neutral. It might not have been much of one, but he'd gained a slight advantage.

"You're right," Mason said. "I didn't know her nearly as well as you did. I'll bet you think about her every time you look at that Freddy Krueger face of yours in the mirror."

The smile in the Hoyl's eyes never faltered.

"My only regret is that I didn't have the opportunity to spend her final moments with her."

"I'd be happy to give you the chance to see her again."

"You had that chance and you didn't take it. That particular threat rings hollow now."

"Don't think for a second that you're leaving here alive. You signed your death warrant when you murdered my wife."

"The lovely Mrs. Angela Thornton Mason? Did I kill her or was I merely the instrument of her demise? Like this gun." He waved Mason's Sigma in front of him as a reminder. "Do you blame the weapon for a person's death or the man who pulled the trigger? The gun exists for no other reason than to perform a single function. You point it at whomever you want to die and pull the trigger. It's quite a simplistic mechanism."

"So you're a victim in all of this? An innocent weapon that merely performed its designated function?"

The Hoyl held out the gun. The woman stepped into the light, took it from him, and aimed it first at Mason's chest, then at his face.

He kept his eyes locked on the Hoyl's the entire time.

"Unlike the gun pointed at your head, I am anything but a simplistic mechanism. I take great pride in what I do. And great pleasure. The gun derives no satisfaction from its task. It is little more than an extension of a killer's arm, while the Hoyl is death personified. In his various incarnations, he has crossbred pathogens, brought historical epidemics back from the dead, and created viruses more frightening than any God could design. He has engineered more vaccines than any pharmaceutical company, saved more lives than the Red Cross, and contributed more to mankind's understanding of disease than the CDC. He is the weapon wielded by men of prescience and the purveyor of their salvation. He is an avatar, the physical manifestation of a belief, and as such cannot be killed."

"I know all about your bloodline," Mason said. "You Fischers may have plagued the world for more than a century, but you're not immortal. I've seen proof of that with my own eyes."

"No individual is immortal, but the Hoyl is. He is the living embodiment of an ideology to which each of us has devoted his life."

"His lineage is one of inbred psychopaths who sell their services to men who'd exterminate their entire race to turn a profit."

"He's the only hope for saving mankind from itself."

"By murdering countless innocent people?"

"Consider them sacrifices for the greater good."

"And how much will the men 'wielding' you make from their 'sacrifices'?"

"Enough talk," Victor said. "Finish this."

"Perhaps you would care to do the honors, Mr. Thornton," the Hoyl said. "Or is getting your hands dirty not on today's agenda?"

"Don't forget that this is *my* agenda, Hoyl."

"Ah, yes. *Your* agenda. The one in which your enraged brother-in-law, the federal agent who's been stripped of his badge and blames his father-in-law for his wife's death, brings the venerable Mr. Thornton out here and murders him in cold blood . . ."

To Paul's credit, his face showed no indication of surprise. He was already lowering his head and closing his eyes when Dietrich swung Mason's Sigma toward him and pulled the trigger. A spray of blood and gray matter erupted from his temple. He toppled sideways and crumpled to the ground in a lifeless heap.

The Hoyl's eyes glittered with amusement. Mason suddenly realized why the woman was wearing gloves. He'd recently fired the pistol, which meant that not only had it discharged residue onto the back of his hand, his fingerprints were all over it.

"Congratulations, Victor. Your coup d'état went off without a hitch. You are now officially the president and chief executive officer of Global Allied Biotechnology and Pharmaceuticals. Huzzah."

Mason turned his fury on Victor.

"You orchestrated this whole thing? You had your own sister and father murdered? And for what? Money?"

"You don't understand, Jim. This is about more than money; it's about power. About taking my rightful place at the table." He flashed that smug, practiced smile. "The world is changing, whether you like it or not. And only those of us who are brave enough to embrace the vision of a new world order—"

"You're a monster, Victor. No . . . worse than that. You're stupid."

"Just shoot him and get it over with," Victor said.

"Don't you get it? Here's how this plays out: Your crazy brother-in-law shoots both you and your father before being gunned down by security. Or maybe he's merely wounded and his arrest is used to destroy the reputation of his father, the senator. Meanwhile, the men you've chosen to get in bed with—the same men who helped your great-grandfather breed the Spanish flu a century ago—will take complete control of your company and make billions—"

"And you call me stupid?"

"—off of the cure you've developed for a disease of your own design."

"I've already told you. This has *nothing* to do with money."

"That's not *entirely* true," the Hoyl said.

"Are you blind, Victor?" Mason said. "You're just a pawn. Did you ever really think you were in control, especially of someone like the Hoyl? Like the men for whom his bloodline has been creating pandemics for generations? You're nothing, Victor. In the big picture, you're less than nothing. They're using you, just like they did your great-grandfather. What did he get for his part of the pig farm? Forty-three million dollars? They made billions off a man they considered a stupid farmer. *Billions*, Victor. And now they've gone back to the trough again to find another stupid farmer—"

"I am not a stupid farmer! I am now one of the Thirteen—"

A deafening crack of gunfire.

Victor was still smirking when his head jerked violently to the side. The bullet lifted him from his feet and sent him sprawling. He hit the ground and slid through a wash of his own blood.

Dietrich lowered the smoldering barrel of Mason's Sigma and tucked it into the pocket of her leather jacket.

The Hoyl made a sweeping motion with his hand.

The blond woman took both Victor and Paul by a wrist and dragged them off into the darkness, the clicking of her heels echoing throughout the great room.

"So you have everything figured out, do you?" There was no mistaking the mirth in the Hoyl's eyes. "If that's the case, then why are you still alive?"

Twenty feet separated them. Mason could cover that distance in six running strides. Less than two seconds. The man to his left would get off a shot. As would the one behind him. The sudden movement might affect their reaction time and possibly their aim, but he had to plan on being hit at least once.

"A better question would be, why are you?"

He tensed to make the sprint. He'd tear the Hoyl apart with his bare hands, no matter how many times he was shot.

"Don't even think about it," the man behind him said.

Mason recognized the voice immediately. It lived in his subconscious. In his dreams.

Shoot him, Mason.

The ground dropped out from underneath him.

He closed his eyes.

Take the shot, damn it!

Mason took a deep breath and turned to face his former partner.

70

"You don't look happy to see me," Kane said. "I'd hoped that after all this time I'd at least get a smile."

"You betrayed us," Mason said. "You led us into a trap. People died, Kane. Good people."

"People die every day. Not all of them get a hero's burial."

"You sure as hell shouldn't have."

"Then you obviously don't understand the situation. There are more than seven billion people on this planet, and at the current rate of growth, we'll see eight billion in our lifetime. The next generation will see ten, maybe eleven. Now consider the fact that less than a century ago there were only two billion. Our resources are finite. We simply cannot sustain that many people for any length of time. And think about who's doing all the breeding. Uneducated and impoverished women in Africa are bringing nearly five children *each* into conditions unsuitable for more than insect life. These are children destined to starve to death or, if they're lucky, survive long enough to fight bloody wars over land rife with disease. These lesser-developed countries pose the greatest threat to our national security. They'll soon have no choice but to either expand or perish.

"Look at India. Its population will rival China's within the next fifteen years and its cities still have raw sewage running in the streets. What happens if its warlords organize the impoverished population and take up arms like the drug cartels did in Mexico? Indochina. Indonesia. Women in Chad and Mali and Niger are averaging—averaging—six to eight children each. They're driving down the quality of life with sheer numbers. Humanity is a virus that's breeding unchecked and within the coming decades will deplete all of our available natural resources. The Third World will drain its stores of fresh water within the next twenty years, and we, as a species, will exhaust our global supply in less than fifty. We'll run out of arable land before that. Our children's children will starve. Wars will erupt. Not wars of ideology, but wars for survival. And who will have the superior numbers? Diseases will mutate. Diseases we will neither be able to anticipate nor control, for which we may or may not be able to develop vaccines. We must cull the herd before we reach the point of global crisis."

"Don't forget all of the profit to be made from controlling those natural resources and producing those cures."

"There's no money in the cure, because it has *already* been distributed."

The Hoyl must have seen the surprise register on Mason's face.

"Oh yes," he said. "People have been receiving the inoculation for nearly a decade. In stages. Five doses in total, all of which are needed to develop an immunity. Think about the panics over the swine and avian flus. SARS. The media repeatedly worked everyone into a frenzy and had them clamoring for the vaccines. We could have injected people with anything we wanted, but instead, we gave them the promise of a future, whether they knew it or not. Well . . . some of them, anyway. We made the flu shots mandatory for all military and government personnel, all health-care workers and infrastructure support professionals. The people we will need to preserve peace and run the country, to staff our hospitals and educational systems. To maintain the continuity of our power and water supplies. Our leadership and morale. All of the necessities for a fully functional and advanced society. An enlightened society unburdened by its own cumbersome and unproductive numbers."

"A master race," Mason said.

"Think of it as you will."

"It's more than that," Kane said. "This is survival. Darwinian evolution for the twenty-first century. During the last fifty years, the U.S. population alone has risen seventy-two percent, roughly half of the world average, and yet the incidence of violent crime—we're talking murder, rape, robbery, assault—has increased by seven hundred percent. Seven hundred percent. That's ten times the rate of population growth. And this is America, Mason. The most civilized nation on the planet. A hundred years ago, we weren't discussing gangs or drugs or serial killers. We didn't have to worry about mass murder in our schools or the rising rate of illiteracy. Our country—and to an even greater degree, our world—has become a cesspool, and it will only get worse until we do something about it."

"And genocide's the answer? By your own logic, wouldn't that make someone who indiscriminately kills millions worse than all of the others?"

"Millions?" the Hoyl said. Mason could hear the smile in his voice. "Try *billions*."

"The Spanish flu was remarkably effective," Kane said, "but we couldn't control it. We weren't able to anticipate the virus mutating during the act of transmission, and especially not during the process of decomposition. We didn't foresee the challenges of disposing of the sheer number of remains. But we've learned a lot in the intervening years, during which technology advanced so rapidly that there were no longer limits to what we could engineer in labs. We created viruses capable of wiping out the entire planetary population a dozen times over, but it wasn't the scientific knowledge that proved most valuable. No, the most important thing we learned wasn't that we needed to create a more deadly disease or manufacture a better means of spreading it. We learned that mankind, by nature, is a selfish and stupid animal. Do you know what the ultimate key to the success of our agenda turned out to be?"

"Fear," Mason said.

"Exactly. Fear. If they're suitably afraid, people will line up for you to inject anything you want into their bloodstreams. They'll relinquish any freedoms. Submit to any rule. They'll welcome the military in their streets and Homeland Security into their homes. They'll pay any price, do whatever they're asked, allow themselves to be manipulated at every turn."

"And when people all around the world mysteriously start dropping dead," the Hoyl said, "we'll be their saviors. We'll offer them hope. The chance to survive. They'll do whatever we want. They will help usher in a golden age of humanity."

"You make it sound so noble," Mason said. "But you're buying into your own propaganda. You're not creating a master race; you're creating a race of slaves beholden to a select few. The few with all of the money and the power. A new world order ruled by madmen who would exterminate their entire species to corner the world's wealth, even if it means ruling over the ashes."

"Would you prefer society to continue its descent into oblivion? For the world to become a sewer? For laws to crumble and diseases to breed and wars to rage until the entire planet goes up in flames?"

"Sounds like that'd be right up your alley."

"You would turn your back on the opportunity to be a part of a new era of peace and prosperity? You would prefer our children fear for their lives in their schools, for them to be surrounded by drugs and the butchers who purvey them, to die in the streets like dogs?"

Mason opened his mouth, but nothing came out.

"Nothing smart to say to that?" Kane asked.

"Who gives you the right to determine who lives and who dies?" Mason said.

"When did the survival of our species become a negative outcome This is not a debate, Mason. This is going to happen. It's already happening. Humanity *will* survive and the world *will* endure."

Kane raised his pistol until the barrel pointed directly between Mason's eyes.

"You were my partner," Mason said. "More than that. You were my friend. I trusted you. Believed in you. Wanted to be like you. I mourned you. And how did you repay me? By having my wife killed. By taking the one thing from me that mattered."

"Angie's death was regrettable, but unavoidable. I loved her, too, you know. We were simply in a window of vulnerability and couldn't afford the exposure."

"You needed to perfect the decomposition aspect of the virus first."

"We were missing one key component. Victor's bacteria were dying off prematurely when exposed to oxygen. We needed a separate methanogenic bacterium that would produce the necessary anoxic environment for our bacteria to survive long enough to consume the remains of their host. And it had to be able to attach to the viral envelope without killing or altering the virus itself."

"That was what you were buying in the building by the old airport, wasn't it? That was the piece I couldn't make fit. You cut a deal for that one bacterium."

"And we had to know if it worked. I mean, what better way to test the methanogenic properties of a species than by turning it into the fuel for a bomb? Methane's only violently combustible over a narrow concentration range, so when you pulled open the plastic and flooded the tent with oxygen, it lowered the concentration of the methane gas to roughly ten percent, and *boom!*"

"You nearly killed your own man."

"Trapp was smart enough to survive. As were you. Not bad, considering neither of you were supposed to be there."

"You should have killed me right then and there and left Angie out of it."

"She was tenacious, Mason. She would have figured it out eventually. But you can't lay all of the blame at our feet. We wouldn't have even known she was digging around in our business if we hadn't had help from a . . . *friend.*"

"What do you mean, 'if we hadn't had help . . .'"

Mason's words trailed off.

Why are you doing all of this for me?

You're not the only one who has a personal stake in taking these guys down.

What's that supposed to mean?

Let's just say I don't take kindly to being manipulated.

"You mean he didn't tell you?" The Hoyl shook the chain and droplets of Gunnar's blood rained down on Mason. Struck his shoulders, his head. "Why, if one of my employers hadn't tasked Mr. Backstrom here with gaining leverage on the attorney general, he might never have discovered a certain federal prosecutor's indiscretions, which proved to be of significantly greater importance when he was captured on camera entering a rather unseemly motel with a fugitive with some rather *unmistakable* facial characteristics, whom I'd been *dying* to talk to for quite some time. Then along came an IRS investigator, who exposed a large chink in our armor. Her brother was more than eager to see her eliminated. After all, she would have shared his kingdom, such as it was. Her father was more reluctant, however, but everyone can be persuaded, especially when you have an ally like your friend Mr. Backstrom on your payroll. Granted, he didn't recognize the role he'd played until it was too late, but it wouldn't be unfair to say that your wife is now a pile of ash in a walnut box because of your friend up there."

"No," Mason whispered.

"In fact, we owe a great deal of thanks to Mr. Backstrom for the many contributions he's made along the way. Unfortunately, despite his demonstrable worth, we can't just let him go. He did turn on us when he discovered the extent to which we'd utilized his services. It is a shame, though. We could have used a mind like his. Maybe we can still scrape it up off the floor."

The Hoyl opened his hand. The coil of chain on the ground behind him unraveled and raced up toward the ceiling.

Gunnar plummeted from the darkness above.

71

Mason ran and dove for the chain before it slithered out of his reach. It pulled him up off the ground, but he managed to get a solid grip and regain his balance.

Gunnar had dropped a good fifteen feet. His body swung wildly.

The impact from that height would have shattered his arms and crushed his skull.

"All you have to do," the Hoyl whispered directly into Mason's ear, "is let go."

"I'm going to kill you!"

"All right. Here's your opportunity."

The Hoyl took the gun from Dietrich, walked about five feet away, and set it down on the floor. He returned to the blond woman's side and again faced Mason.

"Better make it count. This is the only chance you're going to get."

Mason had maybe three and a half feet of slack. Not enough to allow him to reach his Sigma, nor a fraction of what he needed to release the chain, grab his gun, and get back in time to catch it. Balancing Gunnar's weight was one thing, but raising him high enough to get the extra length he required was another thing entirely.

If he let go of the chain, Gunnar would die. No doubt about it. Assuming he wasn't dead already. If he didn't let go, he would surely be shot where he stood, and Gunnar would still end up falling to his death.

Regardless of which choice he made, Gunnar would die.

One of his oldest friends. The man who was indirectly responsible for his wife's murder.

Gunnar's life, literally, were in Mason's hands.

That was exactly what his adversaries wanted. To show him that the right choice wasn't always the easy one, that it was often a matter of choosing the lesser of two evils.

Mason looked at his Sigma.

Then at the Hoyl.

His gun.

The man who had killed his wife.

The Hoyl's eyes narrowed from the broad smile that formed beneath his mask. Mason recognized the expression.

Victory.

Not only did the Hoyl believe he'd won, he believed he'd broken Mason in the process. His only option was to release the chain and go for the gun. Even then, he'd be shot from three different directions before he pulled the trigger.

He looked down at the chain. Three and a half feet of slack. Forty-some inches. Not enough.

"I told you to take the shot," Kane said.

"Not as easy to make that decision as you thought, is it?" the Hoyl said. "Sometimes people have to die so that others can live."

Mason followed the chain upward to the first pulley, mounted to a metal armature on the second floor. Diagonally up into the pool of darkness that hid the ceiling, beneath which Gunnar hung by his ankles from the other end of the chain. Oblivious to the fact that he was about to plummet three stories and land squarely on his head. Were it not for the first pulley, Mason realized, he would have more than enough chain. Of course, he also wouldn't be able to hold his friend's weight with one hand. It would probably even pull him off his feet.

"I'll help you decide," the Hoyl said. "I'm going to count to three. And either you let go and take your chances or I'm going to have your former partner shoot you in the lower back. You'll die, if you're lucky, but you'll get to watch your friend die first."

"You should have killed me when you had the chance."

The Hoyl's eyes positively burned with blue flames.

"One."

Mason turned his whole body to better see the man to his right. Used the movement to discreetly wrap the chain around his right leg.

The security guard was little more than a silhouette standing in front of the bank of lights. He hadn't even drawn his gun.

Mason turned in the opposite direction and inconspicuously wound the chain around his left leg.

The second guard's posture suggested he thought his side had already won.

When Mason faced his nemesis again, the chain was tight around his right thigh and left calf. He pointed the toe of his left boot and twirled the chain around his ankle one final time.

"Two."

Mason leveled his gaze at the Hoyl.

"Look into my eyes," he said. "They're going to be the last thing you ever see."

"Thr—"

Mason released the chain and dove for the pistol. Grabbed it. The links bit into the flesh of his legs. The weight of Gunnar's inert form jerked him in reverse.

Voices shouting all around him.

A bullet ricocheted from the ground right in front of his face.

He flipped over. Slid along the floor on his back. Aimed at the second floor. Fired as fast as he could. His first shot sailed wide, but the second and third destroyed the pulley on the second floor.

The chain tightened and spun him around. Yanked him straight up into the air and suspended him upside down. He crossed his ankles and squeezed his knees. Grabbed the end with his left hand—

A blur of black across the light.

Impact against his chest.

The Hoyl wrapped his arm around Mason's back. He fired again, but the Hoyl's body had become entwined with his. Too close to get his gun between them. He grabbed hold of his adversary's legs and lifted.

They swung across the room and struck one of the banks of lights with a shower of sparks. Twirled back toward the center. Mere inches above the ground.

A sharp pain in his left flank. Searing.

The echo of a gunshot.

Mason cried out. Lost his grip on the Hoyl's legs. Struggled to grab them again before the Hoyl could get his feet on the ground and gain leverage, sending them spinning again.

He parted his knees as far as he could. Flexed at the hips. Got his thighs around the Hoyl's head. Squeezed.

A flash of light and debris struck them from seemingly everywhere at once. A thunderous crash. A bank of smoke and dust swallowed them. An explosion of some kind. His ears were still ringing when the chaos of gunfire erupted.

The cavalry had finally arrived.

Mason squeezed his knees together, compressing the Hoyl's head between his thighs. Worked his right arm free. Raised his pistol.

The Hoyl brought up his knee—hard—into the side of Mason's neck where it met his shoulder. An electric sensation shot all the way down to his left hand. The pain nearly caused him to lose his grip on the chain.

They swung across the room again, still spinning.

The Hoyl attempted the same maneuver again. Mason jerked his head away and took the brunt of the blow to the meat of his shoulder. Raised his Sigma toward the Hoyl's head.

Another explosion. A brilliant flash of light. A deafening boom.

Flames spread up the walls and along the balconies. The room was spinning so fast, it looked like the entire building was on fire.

The Hoyl caught Mason's wrist and twisted it backward. His shot screamed past the Hoyl's ear and into the smoke. Another sharp twist and Mason's grip went slack. His gun clattered to the ground.

The banks of lights extinguished with a sizzle and a thud.

Muzzle flare strobed all around him, leaving tracers across his vision as he spun.

The pain in his side was ferocious. He felt the warmth of blood running down his ribs and into his armpit. The Hoyl's fingers probed the wound. Penetrated the flesh. Worked their way inside him.

With a shout of agony, Mason twisted his hips and wrapped the chain around the Hoyl's neck. Grabbed the back of his suit jacket and spun him around. Tightened the chain.

The Hoyl removed his fingers from the wound and tried to alleviate the pressure on his throat.

Mason seized the opportunity and swung his right leg down. Freed his left ankle. Wrapped his left fist in the chain. Flipped heels over head. His feet missed the ground and he lost his balance. Barely managed to grab hold of the chain with his right hand. Pulled as hard as he could as they careened toward a fallen section of the outer wall.

Flames ascended the dividers between the cells, imbuing the smoke with a flickering orange glare. The fire roared and spread across the ceiling.

The Hoyl clawed at his own neck in an effort to get his fingers underneath the chain. It was wrapped so tightly that his inhumanly blue eyes bulged from beneath the lids. His scarred face was suffused with blood.

Mason's toes grazed the floor and he managed to find his feet.

The Hoyl wasn't quite tall enough. He thrashed and kicked, to no avail. The vessels in his eyes ruptured.

Mason tightened his grip and looked up into the roiling smoke. Gunnar twirled maybe forty feet above him, still not moving.

More gunshots. The crackle of flames. Someone shouted his name from what sounded like a million miles away.

Mason stared into the Hoyl's cold blue eyes and saw panic where victory had been only moments ago. The monster choked and sputtered in an effort to speak.

"The . . . new world order . . . is at hand."

Mason reached up and pulled the mask away from the Hoyl's face. It wasn't a standard respirator. It came away with a hissing sound. Thin hoses slithered out of his nose, a thicker one from his mouth. His eyes widened in sheer terror. The tube from his throat was the only thing keeping his airway from collapsing. The chain tightened his fingers against his muscles and spine the moment the tube cleared his tongue. His scarred skin took on a bluish cast.

"Mace!" he heard from a great distance.

The Hoyl had obviously gotten the worst of whatever trial form of the decomposition accelerant he'd injected Alejandra with. The carti-lage had shrunk back from his nose, leaving two teardrop-shaped holes. The curled bones were clearly visible inside. His lips were gone, as were entire sections of his gray gums. The exposed bones and teeth glistened with some sort of salve.

He gasped and clawed. Drew blood from his neck with his finger-nails.

Mason locked stares with the man who had killed his wife. Watched the light fade from his blue eyes.

"I told you this would be the last thing you'd ever see."

He released the chain and the Hoyl's body rose upward into the darkness.

72

Gunnar's body descended from the smoke until it reached a balancing point with the corpse of the Hoyl. A droplet of his blood struck the back of Mason's hand. Mercifully, it was still warm. Now that Gunner's body was lower, Mason could better see the laceration across his old friend's hairline, from which the majority of the blood originated. His left hand glistened with blood, presumably from a wound somewhere higher up his arm.

The flames grew taller. The smoke became darker, thicker. The heat intensified.

"Mace!" a voice shouted directly into his ear.

Someone grabbed him by the shoulders and pulled him backward. He looked away from Gunnar and was almost surprised to see a massive hole in the side of the building through the swirling dust and smoke.

Automatic gunfire crackled all around him. One of the security guards skidded across the floor on his back and came to rest near Mason's feet, the top of his head a craterous ruin.

"Damn it, Mace! Snap the fuck out of it! We aren't out of the woods yet!"

Mason turned and found himself staring into the face of a man he didn't immediately recognize. He was black with soot and bleeding from a cut along his jaw. His teeth and the whites of his eyes stood out in stark contrast.

"Ramses?"

"You didn't think I'd let you guys have all the fun without me, did you?"

He offered a cocky smile. An OTs-14 Groza Thunderstorm bullpup assault rifle hung across his chest. A finger of smoke twirled from the under-barrel grenade launcher.

"Where's Kane?" Mason asked. "Tell me you got him."

"Who?"

"My old partner. He's about a year late for his funeral."

There was no way in hell Mason was going to let him disappear again.

Two more people emerged from the smoke. He recognized Alejandra immediately, but it took a few seconds to identify the man in the black fatigues, especially with his face painted black. And without the cardigan and the tea service.

Seraph.

Asher Ben-Menachem, Johan Mahler's chief of security.

"I told you we'd be watching you," he said. "How many of them are there?"

"Five that I know of," Mason said. "Counting the Hoyl. But he's out of commission."

"Then we're still missing two." Seraph turned away, pressed his hand to his ear, and looked up at the main level as he spoke. A shadow appeared at the rail, followed by another. And then they were gone. "My men had both doors covered the entire time. No one got past them. They have to be in here somewhere."

There was only one other direction they could have gone.

Mason took off at a sprint.

"I know where they're heading!" he shouted back over his shoulder. "You guys get Gunnar down from there. I'm going after Kane!"

A red glow limned the circular mouth of the tunnel. He heard the whine of an electric engine. If he didn't stop Kane before he got the tram moving, he'd never be able to track him down again.

The tram had been designed so that either end could serve as the lead car, eliminating the need for it to turn around. It was already gaining momentum by the time he caught up with it. There was no need for discretion this time.

Mason raised his pistol and fired. The back window of what had been the lead car earlier shattered and cascaded to the ground. He ran as fast as he could and dove for the ledge. The broken glass cut his palms. His feet dragged on the concrete. Bounced from the rail.

He got his right elbow over the ledge, then his left. Hauled himself over the sill and fell to the ribbed aluminum floor. Struggled to his feet. Ran down the main aisle, between the rows of cages.

A red glow appeared through the windows ahead of him. Inside the next car in line. It focused into a dot on the glass. Then on his chest.

He threw himself to the ground.

Bullets shattered the window and filled the air all around him. He covered his head with his arms to fend off the rain of Plexiglas. Listened to the thumping and clanging sounds of bullets striking the metal hull and ricocheting from the aluminum posts of the cages. The window to his right shattered, admitting the howling wind.

The moment the shooting stopped, he leaped to his feet and started firing.

Muzzle flare lit up the blond woman in the third car, as though with the repeated flash of a camera. She hit the deck and vanished from sight. She'd come up firing as soon as she reloaded.

Mason wasn't about to let her get that chance.

He lowered his head and sprinted for the shattered windows between the cars. Lunged. Caught the ledge with his right foot. Pushed off over the nothingness. Plunged through the gap where the window had been. Got his left foot down. Shouted and hurled himself at the woman.

Dietrich slapped a fresh magazine into her assault rifle and looked up in time to take Mason's shoulder to her face. He brought the full weight of his body down on her. The Steyr clattered from her hand and slid out of her reach.

Mason palmed her forehead and ground the back of her head into the floor. Shifted his weight. Pinned her arms down with his knees. Aimed his Sigma right at her face. Turned away to shield his mouth and eyes from the blowback. Pulled the trigger.

Click.

Click-click-click.

He swore and reached into the inner pocket of his jacket for a new clip.

Dietrich bucked and screamed. Slipped out from beneath his knees. Freed her hands and shoved him squarely in the chest. Slid out from underneath him. Pushed herself up to all fours.

He couldn't let her get to her weapon.

Mason lashed out with his foot. Caught her under the chin. Snapped her head back.

The tram accelerated and the Steyr slid across the floor toward them. To his right. Her left.

He dove for it.

So did she.

His hand closed around the hot barrel. Burned.

Dietrich grabbed the strap. Jerked. Pulled it right out of his grasp.

He fumbled for a grip on anything. Anything at all. Caught the trigger guard as she yanked again. Felt the trigger against his knuckle—

Discharge exploded from the barrel. Flickered. Crackled. Spun the rifle away from him.

He watched as 5.56mm rounds sprayed in an arc across the floor. Strafing the wall. Ricocheting from the floor, the metal cages, the posts. Sparks flew. Tracked a course straight toward Dietrich. Raced up her arm. Tore through her chest. Her neck.

Thupp-thupp-thupp-thupp-thupp-thupp.

Her face disintegrated in the strobing light. Collapsed in upon itself. Hit the wall behind her as a mess of blood and bone.

The gas cylinder drove the piston on the empty chamber with a rapid snapping sound.

Mason swatted away the smoldering Steyr and rose to his feet. Felt warmth on his cheek. Wiped it away with his sleeve. Turned to face the two cars ahead of him.

A man stood silhouetted against the front windshield of the front car. Even from a distance, Mason could tell exactly who it was.

Kane.

Mason loaded his clip. Chambered the first round. Strode toward the next car in the series.

Two shots destroyed the front window of the third car. Spiderwebbed the rear window of the second, across the gap. A third destroyed what was left.

He climbed up onto the ledge. Braced himself against the tempestuous wind. Jumped across the coupling, through the hole where the window had been, onto the scattered shards.

Each car was maybe twenty feet long and was separated by two quarter-inch-thick Plexiglas windows and three feet of open air.

Mason was within forty feet of his old partner. His mentor.

His friend.

Their entire relationship had been built upon a lie. Right from the moment Kane had recruited him. Every word he'd said. Everything he'd taught him. All of it. Even when Mason learned that the man with the blue eyes had survived, he never for a moment suspected that his partner was still alive. He'd trusted Kane clear up until the moment he stood behind him with a gun to his head.

Kane had led them into a trap in Arizona and used the slaughter of their strike force to convince the world that he'd died with them. Had the plan been to kill Mason, too? Or had he needed a survivor to complete the illusion, to serve as a witness to his almost certain demise?

And that was what bothered Mason more than anything else. More than the lies. More than the betrayal. They'd stood face-to-face in the burning stone quarry on the Tohono O'odham Reservation. Kane with a gun to his head and the man with the blue eyes beside him. He'd told Mason to shoot the Hoyl. Had he done so, the threat would have been eliminated. Right then and there. There would have been no further experimentation with viruses. Their grand plan to kill billions would have crumbled. His partner's treachery would have come to light. And Angie would still be alive. So why had Kane shouted for him to do the one thing that would have foiled his endgame?

The answer was as simple as it was heartbreaking.

Because he'd known Mason couldn't do it.

Kane had exploited his only weakness in the field. His feelings for his partner. His willingness to take a bullet for him. He'd never doubted that Mason would engage the more immediate threat to him. He'd known Mason inside and out, while Mason hadn't known him at all. With one shot, he could have killed the Hoyl, saved the lives of his wife and countless others, and ended a plot that had been set into motion a century ago. One shot. Five and a half pounds of pressure on the trigger. Little more than a twitch. One single shot and he could have saved the world.

He would not hesitate again.

Two more shots shattered both panes of Plexiglas between them.

Mason climbed up onto the ledge. Felt the wind buffet his face, his shoulders. Tear through his hair. His flank was on fire from where the Hoyl's shot had grazed him, his waistband wet with blood, but he didn't care.

All that mattered now was Kane.

He bellowed in rage and anguish. Fired straight ahead into the first car to clear a path.

Kane ducked to the side, away from the front windshield and the headlights that silhouetted him.

Mason fired twice more and dove out over the coupling, hurtling over the blurred concrete. He realized his mistake when his former partner turned to face him with a smile on his face.

Kane hit the emergency stop and the brakes locked. Screamed. Sparks flew from the rail. Bounced from the walls like firecrackers. The tram slowed even as Mason fired like a projectile through the rear window. Hit the ground on his shoulder.

A bullet ricocheted beside his face. Another streaked past in his peripheral vision.

He slid straight down the aisle on his side. Raised his Sigma. Squeezed off a round. Another. Shot toward the front of the cab at Kane, who jumped over him and spun with his pistol in his hand. He aimed at Mason's head as Mason aimed at his.

Mason shot first.

The window shattered to Kane's right. He ducked into the cage to his left. Released a shot that passed so close to Mason's face, he could feel its heat.

He led Kane and pulled the trig—

Mason struck the base of the control panel, going twenty miles an hour faster than the car itself. Squarely against the back of his head. His flexed neck. His shoulder.

His shot sailed wide. His vision filled with stars. A fiery jolt of pain. Straight up his neck, into his skull. Down his arms, into his fingertips.

He fired blindly to prevent Kane from closing in on him for the kill shot. Glass flew everywhere. Sparks rained through the open windows.

The tram came to a sudden stop.

Mason fought the ringing in his ears and attuned his hearing to any sound that might betray Kane's location. Watched for the slightest hint of movement.

Held his breath.

Prepared for the impending attack.

73

Silence.

Glass tinkled to the concrete.

Mason sat up slowly.

Tasted blood in his mouth. In his sinuses.

Blue lightning fizzled and flared from the control panel on the wall.

His vision throbbed in time with the pounding in his head. The glare from the headlights cast his shadow across the aisle in front of him as he struggled to his feet. Shards of broken glass sparkled, crunched underfoot.

Acrid smoke settled over the vehicle, filtered through the windows.

He wiped blood from his right eye with his forearm. Dabbed at the stinging laceration in his eyebrow.

The cages around him were empty.

No shadows. No movement.

No Kane.

He walked back into the car in a shooter's stance, scrutinizing the aisle down the barrel of his Sigma.

There.

A faint reflection from the ceiling.

Mason stopped directly underneath it and looked up. Dark fluid. A high-velocity spatter.

He'd hit Kane when he fired up from the ground. High on his body, based on the trajectory of the spatter.

He looked down.

To his left. Nothing.

To his right. There.

Droplets on the floor. Leading through the open cage door and to a smear on the sill of the broken window.

Kane had climbed out into the tunnel.

He could be hiding in the darkness right now, his weapon aimed at the window, just waiting for a clear shot.

Mason went out the rear window instead. Crouched on the coupling.

Listened.

Craned his neck in an effort to see around the tram. No sign of his former partner. Peered around the opposite side.

Clear.

He stepped down carefully. Quietly. Followed his Sigma toward the front of the tram. Knelt at the very edge, where Kane wouldn't be able to see him through the headlights.

A distant scuffing sound.

Mason darted through the headlights. Pressed his back to the cracked windshield. Took a quick peek around the corner, toward the broken side window through which Kane had exited. Broken glass on the ground. No sign of—

Wait.

He walked toward a patch of concrete free of glass. Glanced up to his left. He could see the smear of blood Kane had left behind when he climbed over the ledge. He would have landed right where Mason stood, scattering the shards when he rose from the ground. But which way had he gone?

No sound from either direction.

Kane was a professional. His survival instincts were honed to a razor's edge. He'd managed to remain invisible for a whole year. He not only knew what he was doing, he'd been trained to anticipate what his pursuer would do. And he knew this tunnel. Either he'd taken up a defensible position or he was already in the process of enacting his exit strategy.

Mason couldn't let that happen, or he'd never find his former partner again.

He stayed low, his side against the tram, and studied the shards on the ground. Another patch had been disturbed to the right of the first. Hardly at all. Another farther to the right. A pair of footprints.

The headlights stared blankly into the tunnel. The twin beams diffused into a pale amber glow.

He walked slowly in that direction, outside the direct light. Surely Kane hadn't stuck around to kill him, or he'd likely be dead already.

Maybe he was more badly injured than Mason originally thought. If he'd decided to make a break for it, however, he'd already opened up a huge lead and it was growing larger by the second.

Time was of the essence.

Mason glanced down. Another droplet of blood. A teardrop shape with the tail pointing back toward the tram. It had struck the ground with forward momentum. Kane had definitely gone in this direction.

Five more steps and another droplet glistened in the headlights.

He took off at a sprint. Ran as far as he could, as fast as he could. A hundred feet. Two hundred. Three. He stopped and knelt on the ground against the wall. Breathed through his mouth to minimize the noise.

Listened.

The tram was a single point of light behind him. Ahead lay only darkness. He heard an almost imperceptible clanging sound. Then another. Another.

Mason started running again. He knew that sound. Knew exactly what it meant.

A trace current of cool, fresh air on his face.

He was too late.

Mason pushed himself harder than he ever had before. Felt for the movement of air, which was already beginning to stagnate and fade. He ran with his shoulder against the wall so there was no possible way he could miss the ladder—

A sudden blow to his upper arm. Like someone had struck him with a lead pipe. A dead sensation in his hand, followed by the onslaught of pins and needles.

He shoved the Sigma down the front of his pants, grabbed a rung, and started climbing. Ten feet. Twenty. The walls constricted around him. Thirty feet. He was nearly to the top before his hand decided to make itself useful again. He spun the wheel of the hatch. Shoved it open. Ducked back down.

No bullets sang past his head or ricocheted from the mouth of the chute.

He went up fast. Turned in a full circle with his pistol raised. Hauled himself out into the small, dark chamber. There was a sliver of light around the seam of the tiny door. He felt the crisp air on his bare skin. Turned the knob. Just far enough to disengage the latch. Scooted back. Kicked open the door. Threw himself backward.

Again, no shots.

He shoved the door through the accumulation of snow. The frigid wind cut right through him. It whipped the snowflakes up from the ground and hurled them at him.

Footprints led away from him to the south. Toward a line of trees that vanished back into the storm the moment he saw them. The wind was already beginning to erase the tracks.

Mason charged through the knee-deep snow, kicking up clouds as he went. Searing pain in his side. The bullet must have more than grazed him. The base of his skull throbbed from the impact with the control panel.

He tried to triangulate his location by his surroundings. He was somewhere between the AgrAmerica complex and the northern edge of Greeley. If there were access hatches every two miles, he was probably right about the four-mile mark. The highway was somewhere to his left. An eternity of grasslands, ranches, and marshlands stretched off to his right.

Droplets of blood stood out from the snow like neon beacons. Every ten feet or so. A soft tissue injury. Probably his shoulder, and the bullet had likely just grazed him.

Mason slowed when he neared the trees. Stopped twenty-five feet away. At this range, he couldn't possibly miss.

He watched the barren aspens and cottonwoods. Their naked branches glittered with ice, rattled on the breeze.

The tracks disappeared between two enormous cottonwood trunks, beyond which he could see only shadows and snow. Kane could be hiding behind either one of them, just waiting for his opportunity, or he could be heading in any number of directions toward a vehicle or cache of weapons he'd stashed for just this contingency.

Mason advanced slowly. Swept his sight line from left to right and back again. Tried to use the same footprints to maintain his balance.

The wind shifted directions with a scream and whipped his breath back over his left shoulder. Battered him with snowflakes. It was all he could do to keep his eyes open while he passed between the trunks.

No one lurking on either side.

Willow saplings and cattails formed a veritable maze leading through the snow. The majority had been flattened by the wind and buried under the accumulation, but sporadic sections still grew in chest-high clumps.

The tracks led straight through them, past them, and toward a smooth, uninterrupted sheet of white.

A dark shape materialized from the blowing snow at the very edge of sight. He barely caught a glimpse of the silhouette before the figure disappeared again.

Kane.

74

The cattails crunched beneath his weight. The thin ice underneath them popped and crackled. Mason used the footprints as a guide, and twenty feet later he stepped out into the open. The frozen lake was slick beneath the windswept snow. The ice was obviously strong enough to hold his former partner, but there was no way of knowing how long it would be able to support their combined weight.

Kane was maybe fifty feet away and heading in the opposite direction. His left arm hung awkwardly at his side. He held it high up near his shoulder with his right hand.

Mason aimed his pistol squarely between his mentor's shoulder blades.

"Kane!" he shouted.

The other man stood still for several seconds before finally turning around. The snow had begun to accumulate on his hair. He'd obviously lost a lot of blood. His face had paled and taken on a bluish cast. There'd been a time when Mason could read even his subtlest expression, but he'd never seen this one before.

He kept his Sigma leveled at center mass as he crept closer. He could see both of Kane's hands, but not his weapon.

The wind rose again and momentarily formed a screen of snow-flakes between them.

Mason wasn't surprised to see Kane hadn't tried to use the cover to make a break for it. He'd known exactly where he was going when he walked out onto the frozen lake. He was nothing if not a good soldier to the end.

A cracking sound, from the ice between them.

Mason continued to close the gap.

Kane lowered his hand from his injured shoulder. Opened his palms at his sides. Both were covered with blood.

"Why did you do it, Kane?"

He said nothing. Just stood there and watched Mason inch closer through the blowing snow.

"Talk to me, damn it! You owe me that much!"

"I've already said everything there is to say."

"All you've done is spew a lot of bullshit. Tell me why you led us into that stone quarry to be slaughtered. And don't give me any more of that ideological crap. We both know why you sold us out. How much were our lives worth? What was the price of your loyalty? How much did they pay you to turn traitor?" A twitch at the corner of Kane's mouth. "You deceived the people who depended upon you. Compromised the Bureau. Betrayed your country!"

"Everything I've done has been for my country!"

"How much, Kane? How much was your soul worth?"

"Money has nothing to do with this!" His shout echoed across the lake. "This is about survival. We're fighting a war, whether you choose to admit it or not. A war we're already losing. Our entire species is poised on the brink of extinction. We need to act decisively before it's too late."

"Any species that would eradicate its own population to survive has no business doing so."

"Tell me you don't see it, Mason. Our country is collapsing under its own weight. We have more than fifty million people on welfare. Eleven million illegals flooding our streets with violence and drugs. Two million criminals in prison and another five million on probation or parole. Thirty-three thousand gangs. A tenth of the population can't read. And that's America, the most civilized nation on the planet. The rest of the world is even worse. It's overrun by the impoverished and uneducated, by people who live like animals. Should we have to compete for food and water with these people who contribute nothing to society outside of their growing numbers? We cater to the lowest common denominator. We reward laziness and stupidity. These people aren't just a drain on the global economy, they're exhausting our natural resources at an astronomical rate."

"And killing them is the answer? Murdering billions of innocent people? All so you can control those natural resources? What gives you the right to determine who lives and who dies?"

"Maybe we were wrong about you from the start. You're nothing like your great-grandfather. Your grandfather. Your father. Men who had the strength to make the hard decisions. To do what needed to be done. You've let a lot of people down. Including me. I believed in you. I invested *everything I had* in you."

"This ends here, Kane."

"If you really believe that, then you deserve everything coming your way. I'm just a cog in the bigger machine. A machine that will continue to roll, with or without me. And there's nothing you can do to stop it."

"We'll see about that."

"I guess we will."

"Two fingers, Kane. You know the drill. Pull out your gun by the butt and toss it into the snow."

"You might not be able to see it now, Mason, but you will. I promise you. This is only the beginning."

"But it's definitely the end for you."

Kane smiled and turned his gaze to the west, toward the Rocky Mountains.

"Your weapon," Mason said. "Don't make me ask you again."

Kane made no indication that he'd even heard.

"Now!" Mason shouted. "Pull out your pistol and drop it in the snow!"

He moved even closer to his former partner. The ice made a rapid-fire series of popping and snapping sounds. He stood his ground.

When Kane finally spoke, it was in a voice so soft, Mason could barely hear it over the wind.

"You know Wild Bill Hickok's buried not too far from here."

"That's not how you want this to go down."

"Not even willing to give your old partner a sporting chance?"

"You and I both know I can put three bullets in you from this distance before you even raise your gun."

"Then why haven't you done so already?"

He lifted his shirt and showed Mason the butt of his .40-caliber Walther P99QA. The blood on the back of his hand smeared across his abdomen. He continued to stare off into space.

"Nice and slow, Kane."

"They say Wild Bill was the first person to kill a man in a quick-draw duel. Davis Tutt. Shot him straight through the heart."

"This isn't the Wild West anymore. Back then, the bad guys didn't hide behind their money."

"It never stopped being the Wild West," Kane said. "We just ran out of people like Wild Bill to stand up to the injustice. People gave up. Figured if they locked their doors and closed their eyes, the world would go back to the way it used to be when they opened them again."

He closed his right hand into a fist. One finger at a time. Pinkie to thumb. Opened it again. One finger at a time. Same order.

"It doesn't have to end like this, Kane."

"There was never any other way it could."

"You're wrong. We wouldn't be here if you hadn't killed my wife."

"We all have to come around on our own, Mason. Even you. And, believe me, you will. Sooner or later."

Kane faced him again. Tucked his shirt behind the butt of his pistol.

"It's not fair if you already have your gun in your hand," he said.

"You can't win."

"What are we now? Twenty feet apart? Not quite ten paces, but I'm sure it'll still work just fine."

"I've already beaten you. I spoiled your endgame."

"You think ours was the only game in town?" The wind threw a sheet of snow between them. "If you don't holster that gun, you'll have to

live with the fact that you cheated. You'll spend the rest of your life wondering if you would actually have been able to beat me fair and square."

Mason opened his jacket and lifted his shirt. Stared long and hard
at the man who had trained him. Tucked the Sigma under his waistband.

Kane smiled and inclined his face to the sky. Drew a deep breath.
Rolled his head in a circle, first one way, then the other. Lowered his
gaze. Looked his protégé dead in the eyes.

"You couldn't pull the trigger before. What makes you think you'll
be able to do so now?"

Mason heard voices shouting from a great distance before the wind
rose once more and drowned them out.

"Last time, I was worried I might inadvertently cause a friend's
death. This time, I'm kind of rooting for it."

He visualized exactly what he was going to do. Where he was going
to shoot.

Two bullets left. He hoped not to have to use them both.

Mason narrowed his eyes. Licked his lips.

Watched for Kane's tell. Anything to betray his inevitable move.

A twitch at the corner of his mouth.

He dipped his right shoulder and suddenly the world was a blur.

Mason drew his gun. Aimed. Fired.

One fluid motion.

A wash of crimson spattered the snow behind Kane. He jerked
backward. Half-turned. Stumbled. Toppled onto his side.

The report echoed across the plains.

Mason advanced with a two-handed grip on his pistol.

The ice snapped louder with every step.

Voices again. Far away.

He pushed them out of his mind. Focused only on Kane. As much
as he wanted to kill him, he wanted answers more. Then his former
partner would be free to die, but on Mason's terms, not his.

Kane started to laugh. It was a horrible sound.

He pushed himself up to a seated position with his left arm. Looked
at his ruined right. He'd been shot straight through the shoulder girdle.
As much as he was to Mason, that arm was dead to him.

"You want to try to take me in?" he shouted, again with that awful laugh. "Have you learned nothing?"

His Walther had fallen into the snow near his right foot. He glanced at it, then up at Mason.

"Don't even think about it."

Kane smiled. His lone functional hand moved in a blur.

Mason shot him in the left shoulder. Again. Only right through the joint this time. Knocked him flat on his back in the red slush.

The crack of gunfire rolled like thunder.

Mason continued forward, pointing his gun directly at Kane so he wouldn't be able to see the slide standing open from the empty chamber.

Kane's laughter was a repulsive, mocking sound. He rolled to his side. Worked his way up to his knees. Somehow managed to close his right hand around the grip of his pistol.

Voices. Closer now.

He struggled to his feet and faced Mason. Both arms hung limply at his sides. Blood dripped from his fingertips. From the barrel of his Walther.

"It's over," Mason said. "Drop your weapon."

"No, it's not. Like I said, this is only the beginning."

Kane pulled the trigger and vanished. Here one second, gone the next. He dropped straight down through the ice.

"No!"

Cracking and snapping from everywhere at once.

Mason felt it happening. The ice breaking apart. Separating. He couldn't let Kane get off that easily.

He lowered himself to all fours to distribute his weight more evenly. Crawled toward the hole in the ice as fast as he dared.

His name echoed from somewhere behind him. A woman's voice. Alejandra.

He brushed the snow aside so he could see the ice. It was opaque. Crusted with frost. Far thinner than he'd thought. Amazing that it had been able to bear their weight at all.

He swept faster. Lost the feeling in his hands. Watched cracks form and race through the ice.

A *thump* from below him. Ahead and to his right.

Mason scurried toward the source of the sound. Cleared the snow. There was a dark shape beneath the ice. Vague at first. It resolved into a human form and pressed its hand against the ice from the other side.

He clearly saw the outline of a head. Now closer.

Kane's eyes were open. His cheeks bulged with air. Blood eddied through the water. He smiled and small bubbles leaked from between his teeth. Then he opened his mouth. Bigger bubbles floated up against the ice, expanded, spread out. Trapped. He struggled, but only for a moment. His eyes lost focus. The current dragged him along the underside of the ice. His body slowly sank into the deep water and out of sight.

Mason rocked back on his haunches and bellowed up into the storm.

EPILOGUE

Some even believe we are part of a secret cabal working against the best interests of the United States, characterizing my family and me as "internationalists" and of conspiring with others around the world to build a more integrated global political and economic structure—one world, if you will. If that is the charge, I stand guilty, and I am proud of it.

—David Rockefeller, *Memoirs* (2002)

"Are you sure you're going to be all right?"

"Yeah, Dad. The bullet barely hit me. I won't be modeling swimsuits anytime soon, though."

"That's not what I meant."

Mason and his father sat on the front steps of what used to be his house. It still was, technically. At least until the title and deed were transferred, but the Realtor didn't need him for that. He'd just closed the door behind him for the last time. He hadn't wanted to go back in there. He'd made his peace with it and the life he'd lived within its walls when he left the first time, but he was grateful his father had practically forced him to do so at gunpoint. Sometimes he forgot that the senator understood what he was going through. It was hard to think of the mother he'd lost as the woman his father had loved. The elder Mason had found a way to come out on the other side a stronger man, so Mason figured it couldn't hurt to listen to him for a change. And despite all of their differences, he could think of a whole lot of fates worse than ending up like his old man.

"Does the pain go away?" Mason asked.

He couldn't remember the sun shining this brightly in a long time. The dog walkers and joggers in their skintight fluorescent spandex getups were out in force in the park across the street.

"No, son. It just becomes a different kind of pain. It's yours to keep. Part of what makes you who you are."

Mason nodded. He worried that if the pain faded, he would forget Angie. He didn't want to relinquish the pain.

Even though he had basically turned his old man's life upside down, his father had come back to Colorado to be at Mason's side. They'd gone through the house and cleared it out one room at a time. It was both good and bad that he and Angie seemed to have accumulated so little, and yet it was amazing how many memories were attached to every little thing. He kept the stuff that mattered most—the pictures, the sentimental trinkets, the notes and cards—but let everything else go. His father had made the arrangement for the rest to be carted away, and Mason had no idea where it all ended up, but he hoped Angie's belongings would find new life and make some young women who might not have been able to afford them happy. She would have wanted that.

Mason was glad his father did things like that without his having to ask. His old man made sure he pulled all of his pictures and maps off the wall in the guest room. Stood with him in the yard as he burned them all on the grill. He never asked what had happened at the AgrAmerica complex, and Mason never volunteered the details. Besides, as a senator, he had access to all of the documents and debriefings through formal channels. He probably already knew more than Mason did.

Sometimes he lost sight of the fact that J. R. Mason was a human being. Not just his father. Not just a senator. Not just the politician who one day might be the president of the United States. He'd been silent when all Mason needed was his physical presence, and had cheered him up when he sensed Mason needed him to. He'd handled Mason's not insignificant portion of the AgrAmerica inheritance without asking for more than a signature from time to time. He'd also helped Angie's mother unload her shares so she could distance herself from the nightmare that had claimed her entire family. And he'd even surprised Mason with a turkey club sandwich on Thanksgiving.

Maybe he'd never be the perfect father, but he was Mason's, for better or worse, and he'd been there when it mattered most. Even with prominent members of his party taking their lumps in the media for their various levels of investment in Global Allied Biotechnology and Pharmaceuticals and their incessant calls for public displays of support, even with the media hounding him personally for his involvement, he never laid it at Mason's feet. He just took the abuse on the chin with that patented smile on his face.

As far as the world knew, Paul Thornton, president of AgrAmerica, and his son, Victor, heir to the agricultural empire, had died in a fire inside their new corporate headquarters, along with three security guards, Paul's personal assistant, and an unidentified male believed to be an undocumented construction worker. No foul play was suspected, but the investigation turned up some improprieties that necessitated the seizure of some assets and computer files by a litany of three-letter agencies and put the final nail in Global Allied Biotechnology and Pharmaceutical's coffin. Mason made sure the contribution that had cost Angie her life received the proper recognition. The media was going to have a field day following up on all of the shelf companies housed in Commerce City. He looked forward to seeing just how many crooks they shook out of that tree.

He only hoped his relationship to the Thorntons and the subsequent destruction of their family name and company wouldn't taint his father's reputation. He'd worked way too hard and sacrificed way too much to put himself in this position, only to be undone by his son's actions.

To his credit, he'd never once mentioned it.

"Come back to Washington with me," he said. "Start fresh."

"This is my home, Dad."

His Town Car rolled to the curb, where it idled patiently.

"Your hearing still set for tomorrow?" he asked.

"I'm not sweating it."

"I could make a few calls on your behalf."

"No. Thanks, though. I'm fine with the outcome, whatever it may be."

His father clapped him on the knee and stood up. Set his empty beer bottle on the porch and shrugged into his overcoat.

"The offer stands."

"Thanks for being here for me."

His driver emerged and opened the back door for him.

He was nearly to the car, when he abruptly stopped and turned around.

"I'm proud of you, son."

He nodded to himself and climbed into the backseat. The driver closed the door, sealing him behind the tinted windows, and assumed his station at the wheel. With a wink of the sun from the chrome hood ornament, they were gone.

Mason stood on the sidewalk for a long time, staring at what remained of the life he'd never be able to lead again, before finally heading for his new Grand Cherokee.

It was all he could do not to look back.

NOVEMBER 27
Denver Division Field Office

Mason wore a bespoke suit to his hearing. He had no doubt the FBI would reinstate him, but nothing would ever be the same. It wasn't until he was sitting in a conference room across from the special legal counsel from the U.S. Attorney's Office, a representative from the Internal Affairs Division, another from the Department of Justice, SAC Christensen, and the associate deputy director of the FBI that he understood the degree to which things were about to change.

It was Trapp's complaint that had set into motion the sequence of events that led to Mason suspension. Since his former partner had been killed in a head-on collision, which left his incinerated body all but unidentifiable, before he was able to commit his account to record, the charges were dismissed. No one wanted a situation where it was Mason's word against a dead man's. Especially since the dead man was a highly decorated operative whose portrait now hung in the lobby beside those of the other fallen agents. Mason elected not to tell them just how far Trapp had actually fallen. Nor was it in his best interests to volunteer the information that someone had done a pretty good job of staging Trapp's death. That would only lead to conversations he wasn't ready to have. Not yet, anyway. Not until he had a better understanding of what had actually happened.

There were holes in Mason's story that even he couldn't fill.

And he had lived it.

Chief among them was the fact that the last two agents with whom he'd been partnered had served interests other than their country's. Not to mention the fact that they'd both gone out of their way to try to kill him, and a whole lot of other people. He didn't think he'd be able to find the answers he needed within an organization that had been compromised to such an extent, either.

Mason had his resignation speech all formulated and rehearsed, but when it came time to stand before the five people who held his future in their hands, he decided not to pull the trigger. Wild Bill Hickok had taken far more criminals off the streets as a lawman than as an outlaw. Justice was better served from within the constraints of the system, no matter how restrictive, especially given how easily the Bureau had been infiltrated, and how long ago that infiltration had begun.

He accepted his badge and his Glock with the appropriate contrition. Promised to meet all the conditions of his reinstatement—of which there were many—and again swore his allegiance to a flag that might not have flown as high as it once had, but one he would personally ensure did so once more.

Christensen collared him on his way out the door. The special agent in charge of the Denver Field Office guided him down the hallway to his office, closed the door, and sat in the chair behind his desk. He took off his glasses and rubbed his eyes.

"You going to tell me what's really going on?" He sighed and looked straight through Mason in that way he had. "I've been doing this far too long not to recognize when someone's blowing smoke up my ass."

"Not a lot to tell, Chris. Maybe someday."

"Make that someday sooner than later."

"I know you went to bat for me. I appreciate—"

"I didn't do anything for you. I went to bat for an agent with the potential to make a difference. If he can find a way of unscrewing his head from his sphincter, that is. Something's starting to stink around here and I could probably use some help sniffing it out."

"I suppose I could be talked into doing that, but I should probably point out that my nose isn't as sensitive as I once thought it was."

"Then be back here for assignment tomorrow morning. Oh eight hundred. Sharp. I expect bells, Mason."

Chris put his glasses back on and opened a file folder on his desk, as though he'd forgotten Mason was even there.

"Runway's down the hall, Giorgio."

"Thanks, Chris."

"You still here?"

Mason closed the door behind him with a smile on his face. It might not have been as fancy as his Sigma, but he had to admit it felt good to have his Glock back. And even better to have his shield, but it made him think. When it came right down to it, his badge was little more than a piece of pounded tin. The power it bestowed upon him was nothing compared to that wielded by the men who'd orchestrated the entire ordeal—the thirteen—who'd stripped him of it without the slightest effort. They'd infiltrated the Federal Bureau of Investigation and, in doing so, compromised the entire law-enforcement arm of the federal government. If he intended to root out that corruption, he was going to have to bend a few rules and he was going to need the help of a couple of friends accustomed to working in just that manner.

DECEMBER 1
Downtown Denver

"What's the password?"

"Don't be a dick, Ramses."

"Bzzzt. Try again."

Mason looked directly into the camera, batted his eyelashes, and gave him the finger.

"Just let me come up already."

"You got a warrant, Special Agent?"

"No, but I just dropped a small fortune on a Dartz Nagel Dakkar. Black. It'll take a while to get it here from Latvia, though. Thought you might appreciate the upgrade from the Hummer."

"Turns out 'I just bought you an armored SUV' *is* the password."

"I had a hunch it might be."

The doors whispered shut behind Mason and the cab started to rise. He leaned the dry-erase board he'd brought with him against the wall, which appeared to have been recently remodeled to exchange the mirrored surface for something a little more bulletproof. He was actually beginning to appreciate Ramses' vigilance; he was developing a healthy amount of it now himself.

Gunnar was waiting for him when the door opened. A big old grin on his face. He gestured toward his right foot with a flourish.

"Well? What do you think?"

"It's a foot, Gunnar. I have two of my own. You just can't see them because I'm wearing shoes. You know, like human beings do?"

"I got the cast off. Good as new."

"Not quite. The whole room smells like cheese you've been keeping in your armpit."

Gunnar's right ankle had been badly broken when he was strung upside down by the chain. An orthopedic surgeon had used two titanium posts to stabilize the bones in a procedure called a "rodding," which Ramses was never going to let him live down. The scar that ran from the crown of his head all the way through his hair, down his forehead, and over his left eye was a little more unsightly, but, Mason had to admit, it did give his face character. It kind of drew the focus to his blue eyes. Made him look a little dangerous. It probably would have made for a great story, had they not agreed never to speak of their experience to another living soul. At least not yet.

Not until they were ready to do something about it.

"How's that dump of yours coming along?" Gunnar asked.

"It's being gutted and remodeled as we speak. I think. Whenever I stop by, I seem to arrive right in the middle of break time. How about you? Find a place you like yet?"

Upon being discharged from the hospital, Gunnar had discovered that his list of clients had shrunk to a handful. His access to the secret network with the pretrading volatility index had been terminated. It took him all of about five minutes to hack back in, only to find that all user activity had ceased. He'd been ostracized from the business not for his involvement in bringing down a criminal enterprise, but for breaking the cardinal rule. He'd betrayed a client's trust.

Mason figured that was penance enough for his participation in the chain of events culminating in his wife's murder. They'd spent hours talking through it in the hospital with Gunnar's leg in traction and his face puckered with stitches. He knew his old friend never would have deliberately done anything to put his wife in harm's way and understood why he'd elected to attend her funeral via satellite. Mason had no doubt Angie would have felt the same.

"I'm taking my time," Gunnar said. "Believe it or not, I'm actually enjoying my current situation. For the time being, anyway."

"If there's one thing Ramses knows, it's how to entertain his guests."

"True, although I have to say I am a little disappointed. I expected a whole lot more Thunderdome than Neverland."

Mason rolled his eyes.

"Give me a hand with this whiteboard, would you?"

They carried it across the room through the maze of terrariums, which cast a brilliant bluish glow over the interior, while far to the west, the red sun set behind the snowcapped Rockies.

Getting the dry-erase board up the spiral staircase took some doing. The interior door from the waterfall room was already open. Ramses was sitting at his computer in the raised living room. He'd added components since Mason was last here, turning that entire corner of the room into what looked like the bridge of a starship.

They leaned the dry-erase board against the wall beside him.

Ramses was so lost in whatever he was doing that he didn't notice them. Alejandra did, though. Her face lit up and she bounded across the room in her bare feet to give Mason a hug. She'd grown comfortable enough around them that she no longer felt the need to hide her face. She seemed to wear her scars like a badge of honor, which was probably exactly what they were. It helped that she and Ramses had a little something going on between them. Probably nothing that would last, especially since she was preparing to head back home to Oaxaca.

Thanks to Ramses and some connections Mason would probably rather not know about, the land surrounding her village had been returned to the people and the cartel presence had vanished overnight. Mason's contribution had come in the form of establishing a supply and distribution channel between the agricultural co-op he financed for Alejandra and the entity once known as AgrAmerica—and almost as Global Allied Biotechnology and Pharmaceuticals. He also used what little clout he had at the FBI to help smooth things over for her with the

Mexican army. While they had no intention of welcoming her back with open arms, they certainly weren't going to turn her away, either.

For helping Mason rid himself of the AgrAmerica mess, his father's reward was getting stuck with the majority of the shares as the price plummeted. He never once griped, though, even as the company teetered on the brink of financial ruin and threatened to take him with it. He simply took the helm, changed the name to AGRInitiative, and started steering the ship back onto course. The things a father will do for his son.

"Saw your old man on the tube today," Ramses said. He didn't take his eyes off the bank of computer monitors. "He's really rocking that whole silver fox look."

"Tell me the media wasn't torching him again."

"Nah. Nothing like that. It was just a quick teaser for the five o'clock news. They're doing a feature on the most likely presidential candidates. You just might have to start watching the people you associate with. Can't have the most powerful man in the world's son hanging out with anyone of questionable moral character."

"Your morality doesn't concern me as much as your business interests."

"I was talking about Gunnar, Mace. Why do you always have to be such a prick?"

Mason looked over Ramses' shoulder at the setup. Each of the monitors displayed a different function: stock indices, global satellite positioning, different network feeds, and screens on which data and conversations scrolled past. He'd designed it to replicate the home page of the network Gunnar had once been able to access, the one hidden in the deep web that they'd taken to calling the Extranet.

"I've almost got this thing working like I want it," he said. "Another two minutes and this setup will be completely undetectable and untraceable."

"Where do you want me to hang this whiteboard?" Mason asked.

Ramses waved vaguely over his shoulder. Mason removed a painting from the wall and hung the dry-erase board in its stead. At the very top he wrote two words.

THE THIRTEEN.

Below them he drew the symbol Gunnar had used to access the Extranet: a cross with a diagonal line connecting the end of the right horizontal bar to the vertical line below it, then drew a half circle underneath it.

Off to the left, he wrote the words Thornton (Paul, Victor) and crossed them out. He drew an arrow from his in-laws to another name: Thomas Elliot Richter, the man who'd invested in the pig farm with Wesley Thornton and gone on to make billions. Beneath his name Mason wrote two others: the Hoyl (Fischer F1, F2, F3, and F4) and Spencer Kane. He drew an arrow from Richter's name to another on the right: R. J. Mueller, his partner in the penicillin coup. Mason wrote the number 1 above Richter's name.

Ramses turned and studied his work for several seconds before speaking.

"Once we open this box, there's no way to put the lid back on it. I can shut down this system right now and we can all just walk away."

He looked pointedly at Mason with an expression of genuine concern on his face. Ramses knew how much this investigation had already cost him, and how much he still had left to lose, but he couldn't walk away now. Kane's final words haunted him.

This is only the beginning.

"This is my fight," Mason said, "and I'm finishing it."

"Our fight," Gunnar said. "You're not the only one who's owed a little payback."

"Then where do we start?" Ramses asked.

"There are still inconsistencies I can't explain," Mason said. "Questions I can't answer."

"Like what?"

"The deal you tipped us off to. The one in the building out by the airport. It was an elaborate trap designed to incinerate all of the evidence inside, along with whoever broke the plastic seal. Our forensics guy, Todd Locker, called it a 'very sophisticated self-cleansing gas chamber,' which is a completely different MO than the Hoyl employed."

"You're suggesting he wasn't working alone," Gunnar said.

"I'm certain he wasn't working alone. Someone was obviously pulling his strings, the same someone whose bloodline has employed successive generations of Fischers to release their deadly diseases and capitalize on the cures for them. But I'm also starting to wonder if he wasn't also working in parallel. I keep coming back to something Kane said. 'You think ours was the only game in town?'"

"Don't tell me there's another psycho like the Hoyl out there," Ramses said.

"Locker said the dead men inside the trap had contractures, a specific autonomic response of the central nervous system to an external stimulus. At the time, I assumed the cause was biological, but what if I was wrong? None of the Hoyl's victims exhibited contractures."

"Then what could have caused them?"

"When I was inside Steerman's, before the whole place burned down, I found a room filled with enormous stainless-steel vats, like the kind breweries use. Massive tanks with pressure gauges and valves. The setup was completely separate from the rest of the slaughterhouse, and it almost looked like someone had been living in one of the adjacent rooms. Whoever it was obviously cleared out of there in a hurry, too. The only thing he left behind was a torn piece of paper with a partial chemical formula on it."

"You think they exposed the dead men in the building to this chemical and used the explosion to eradicate the evidence?" Gunnar asked.

"A nerve agent would certainly explain the contractures."

"Do you remember the formula?" Ramses asked.

Mason closed his eyes and tried to recall the letters written on the piece of torn paper.

"I need something to write with."

There was a pen on the desk beside Alejandra. She handed it to him and he wrote the formula on his palm. $[(CH_3)_2CHO]CH_3P(O)F + CCl_2FNO_2$. Held it out for the others to see.

Ramses grabbed him by the wrist and pulled his hand closer to the keyboard. He typed the first half of the formula into a search engine.

"That's not good," he said.

Mason stared at the results. It felt like the early had spun off its axis.

"What is it?" Alejandra asked.

"Sarin," Mason said. "Exposure to a few drops is fatal. Convulsions, paralysis, respiratory failure. An excruciating death within a matter of minutes. A single bucket could create a vapor cloud large enough to kill everyone in downtown Denver. And there had to have been at least twenty vats, each of which could have easily held a thousand gallons."

"What about the rest of the formula?" Gunnar asked.

Ramses opened another window and searched CCl_2FNO_2.

"*Dichloro(fluoro)nitromethane*," he said. "What the hell is that?"

"Move over," Gunnar said.

"Are you seriously kicking me off my own computer?"

"For once, would you just—?"

"Fine," Ramses said, and slid back from the console. "But I'm keeping the chair."

Gunnar sighed, knelt on the floor, and set to work. His fingers buzzed on the keyboard and lines of code scrolled past on the monitor in front of him. His brow furrowed and his lips moved as though he was speaking silently to himself. When he finally sat back on his haunches, the color had drained from his face.

"What is it?" Mason asked.

"Worst-case scenario," Gunnar said.

"What do you mean?"

"Imagine a chemical that not only ratchets up the effects of a volatile nerve agent, but also stabilizes it in the process. Makes it persist for indefinite periods of time in both liquid and gaseous states. Causes it to linger exponentially longer in the environment. That's what *dichloro(fluoro)nitromethane* does for sarin. The reaction of the two produces a single chemical with the formula $C_5H_8Cl_2F_2NO_3P$, which just happens to be the same formula as an experimental Soviet nerve agent known as A-234."

"There's no proof they were able to produce any of the so-called Novichok agents," Mason said. "They made their grand announcement during the Cold War, at the height of the KGB's disinformation campaigns."

"Whether they succeeded or not is irrelevant. Someone in that slaughterhouse was following their recipe, and if he managed to create a nerve agent that can do what the Russians claimed, we're dealing with an evolved version of sarin that's ten times as lethal and undetectable by conventional sensors."

"Jesus," Mason said. "And if those tanks were full, they have enough to wipe every major city in the world off the face of the map."

"Someone should probably make sure that doesn't happen," Ramses said. "What with us living in one of those major cities and all."

"You think?" Gunnar said.

"We have to do more than that," Mason said. "We narrowly averted one catastrophe, only to find another ready and waiting. These men will stop at nothing to get what they want. They're just going to keep coming and coming until either we stop them or they enact their genocidal agenda. We can't afford to let that happen, but with a hundred-year head start, it's only a matter of time before it does. Our only option is to go on the offensive. We have to find the Thirteen. And we have to destroy them."

ACKNOWLEDGMENTS

Publishing a novel requires a tremendous amount of luck, talent, and hard work; I'm lucky to have the most talented and hardest-working people in the business on my side. Alex Slater, literary agent extraordinaire, championed my manuscript from the beginning and made my dreams a reality. Pete Wolverton, my brilliant editor, challenged me every step of the way; this book is infinitely better for his tenacity and unerring vision. Jen Donovan not only kept this tram on the rails, she provided key insights and unlimited patience. Carol Edwards knocked the copyediting out of the park. The teams at both St. Martin's Press and Trident Media Group went above and beyond the call of duty on my behalf.

No less integral are the poor souls who don't get paid to deal with me: my wife, Danielle, who's always believed in me; my kids, whose support and understanding mean the world to me; my mom, who read all of my early work, and yet still encouraged me; and my dad, whom I wish, more than anything, could be here now.

Special thanks to: Andi Rawson and Kim Yerina, my invaluable beta readers and friends; Jeff Strand, as gifted a novelist as you'll find; Jennie Levesque, generous to a fault; Liza Fleissig; Don Koish, Shane Staley, and Paul Goblirsch; Leigh Haig; Matt Schwartz; Borderlands Boot Camp; Team TPMI; and to everyone else who's contributed to my success on a personal level: You know who you are and how much you mean to me.

I offer my eternal respect and thanks to David Bell, Steve Berry, Lee Child, Richard Chizmar, Douglas Clegg, John Connolly, Mark Greaney, Brian Keene, Jack Ketchum, Michael Koryta, Jonathan Maberry, Jim Marrs, Thomas F. Monteleone, David Morrell, Douglas Preston, Matthew Reilly, James Rollins, Michael Marshall Smith, A. J. Tata, Thomas Tessier, and F. Paul Wilson for the inspiration and kind words along the way.

My undying gratitude to all booksellers and librarians, who keep the torch of literacy burning.

And, most important, to all of you, my readers, without whom this book wouldn't exist.